GRIDLOCK

GRIDLOCK

A Scientific Thriller

By Alvin Ziegler

Discover more about GRIDLOCK at www.alvinziegler.com

Loma Vista Press

For my very patient wife, Ginny

"The Grid is expected to be the next World Wide Web."

—CERN, the Swiss research laboratory that pioneered both

"The effort to decipher the human genome . . . will be the scientific breakthrough of the century—perhaps of all time."

—President Bill Clinton, March 14, 2000

Acknowledgments

First and foremost, thanks to my wife for being a tireless champion of this book. She made the journey possible and thrilling. Writing instructor Margaret Lucke became my obi wan kenobi, lighting my way to discover Jude Wagner and the novel. I give special acknowledgment to my friend and technical guru, Josh Bernstein, who aside from fact-checking the story with me in a Peruvian cafe, toured me around Celera's gene laboratory in Alameda, California. Celera, of course, sequenced the human genome at a fraction of the cost of the U.S. government project. My chief scientific adviser was the extremely generous and knowledgeable Bridget Wells of Illumina who jumped right in as an expert consultant.

I'm hugely indebted to my gracious readers for flagging issues and offering ideas. They include: Jean and Ian Cartwright, Carole Taylor, Martha Jarocki, Writing Instructor, David Booth, Suzanne Stewart, Mark Solomon, Kent Marisa, Laurie Holmes, Sunil Maulik, Cynthia Baroumond, Sheri Bargman, Andrew Flessel, John Houghton, Tom Parker, Nick Booth, Kris Wilhelm, Anne Mahoney and Joanne Gomez. Apologies to those I left out. I received invaluable procedural advice from FBI Gang Unit Chief, George Q. Fong, FBI-trained hostage negotiator, Robin Burcell, Cyber Supervisor Jack Bennett—San Francisco Division, CERN Physicist, Simone Campana, author of *Police Procedure and Investigation*, Lee Lofland, SETI@home grid co-founder, Dan Werthimer, those very clever writers in NovelPro and helicopter pilot/yachtsman/private security company officer, Captain Richard Threfall. The *Gridlock* book video trailer was produced by the talented Nick Mead of Berkeley.

Facts

Biotechnology is transforming the world in unimaginable ways—promising to extend our children's lives by decades. Everyone has a stake. Doctors are diagnosing disease genetically using computers and the Internet.

The sea change in medicine began with the decoding of the human genome in 2003, but the genome remained locked because scientists understand less than one percent of it. Some liken the difference between decoding our DNA and interpreting it to the difference between identifying every part of the space shuttle and getting it to fly. Unmercifully, the sick and dying have been given a promise that science hasn't delivered—until now.

A lightning fast computer network called a grid is interpreting our DNA. It can solve virtually any question that can be calculated. Using grid technology, scientists—departing from the one-size-fits all approach to medicine—are creating custom drugs to treat diseases, such as cancer, that are as individual as a fingerprint. Like a giant tidal wave, the trend of personalized care is forcing countless businesses to rapidly modernize or be tossed aside in the wake of change.

This book was inspired by actual organizations, technologies, and science.

Prologue

Friday, October 28
Meyrin, Switzerland

Jűrgen rushed from his apartment at 9:05 a.m., tightening his watch strap. The Mercedes limousine waited at the curb. He climbed into the backseat clutching his briefcase. Leather upholstery squeaked under his long legs.

"Let’s go. I’m expected in twenty minutes," he said through the limo window.

The limo hummed through the foothills of the jagged Jura Mountains. He peered at the silver shimmer of Lake Geneva, surrounded by snow-capped peaks that extended to the Savoy Alps in France. Cloud mist swirled over the water, a fitting backdrop for Jűrgen's God complex. Through the Mylar glass, he glimpsed platinum-blonde hair beneath the driver’s cap.

Jűrgen looked through the limo partition. "Where’s Adrian?"

"Out sick."

This was no day for bumbling around in the twenty-six cantons of Switzerland.

"You do know the quickest way to CERN?"

Their eyes met in the rearview mirror. "Yes, Director Hansen."

At least the limo service had filled her in. He wanted everyone to know about CERN. No lab in the world matched it in the number of physicists it employed and the extent of its international presence. Twenty member countries ran it.

The car hugged mountain roads, passing schoolchildren playing tag at a bus stop. Jűrgen slid papers from his briefcase to occupy himself. Drumming his fingers, he studied notes and photos of attendees. He memorized the faces of executives of the medical community who'd flown from around the world to visit CERN. Their donations could do it, enable personalized diagnosis over the Internet, using a patient's DNA.

When the BlackBerry in his suit coat pocket vibrated, he scanned Tatiana's missive: *I'm wearing Escada perfume—soon that will be all I'm wearing.*

He checked the closeness of his shave. A petite redhead who traveled with silk handcuffs and a riding crop awaited him after his speech at CERN. Tatiana helped him unwind with sexual role-play. He text messaged a reply, giving her the address of their chateau. Tonight they would meet high in the Alps where he would star in her Russian seductress fantasy. He adjusted the knot on his tie. Jűrgen had picked up Tatiana at a Geneva club two weeks back. He didn't know yet how long he'd keep her—girlfriend shelf life ran five weeks tops.

Shrouded by tinted glass, he reclined against the headrest. Jűrgen envisioned Tatiana's lips working his chest while the limo cut along the highway, dropping in elevation—until the tires grumbled over rocks. The noise pulled him back to reality.

The driver had veered the limo off the highway.

"What are you doing?"

They'd turned onto a narrow side road. Giving way to clover and dirt, the lane settled into a partially paved cow trail.

He shouted through the divide. "Driver."

Without answering, the chauffeur pressed a button in the glove compartment.

Holding his BlackBerry, Jűrgen hit the three-digit Swiss code for emergencies. No cell signal. Communications were usually good here.

Looking through the rear window, his eye caught the lush Bernese Alpine Valley. "Where are you going?"

"There is construction, Sir," the chauffeur said sternly. "We're making a detour."

Jűrgen's hands went clammy. "A detour? Damn it."

Hunched at the wheel, the driver rolled up her sleeves. "We are close."

The limo halted at the edge of a lake.

A wave of nerves fluttered through his stomach.

The driver got out and whipped open Jűrgen's door. "Out."

Jűrgen gripped the edge of his seat. "Now hold it. What do you want?"

The hard-faced woman leveled a handgun at Jűrgen's forehead. "Whoa!" He raised his hands high.

The clearing had the calm of a cemetery. Jűrgen eased out of the back seat—his gaze trained on the woman. She had broad, competitive-swimmer shoulders. Caked on makeup covered her face, doing nothing to improve her masculine features.

She opened the limo trunk, revealing a coil of heavy gauge fishing line and a twenty-pound gym weight used for bench pressing.

"Remove the line," the woman ordered. "The weight, too."

Mouth stone dry, he lifted the weight. A buzz came from overhead. A twin-engine plane—a businessman on holiday, perhaps. If only Jűrgen could radio for help. His eyes swept over the wooded lake. Not a house within sight . . . who would come to his aid?

The plane noise passed. A breeze rustled crisp leaves over his feet.

"Tie the weight to your leg. Knot it tight."

Was this to keep him from running? He momentarily stumbled for words.

Cradling the weight against his chest, Jűrgen begged, "I've got money."

"Save your breath." The gun still trained on his head.

He bent and tied, tensing for his strike. "You're not going to stop the Grid."

Jerking into a standing position, he lunged, hurling the weight at the woman's head. She dodged. The weight struck her shoulder, knocking her down. The gun dropped from her hands.

Jűrgen leapt for the gun but the woman got to it first. She pointed the weapon and fired.

With a yowl, he went to his knees. He touched the burning wound on his shoulder, gasping at the blood oozing between his fingers. *Is this it? Will I die right here, at age 39?*

The woman got up.

"What is it you want?" Jűrgen's voice broke.

She lowered the gun. "Get the weight."

Blood snaked down his arm. He crawled over dirt and pebbles on his knees until he could pull the gym weight and fishing line close with one hand. With shaking hands, he bound the line around his ankle.

The woman pulled on her dusty cap and gestured for him to get up.

Jűrgen staggered to his feet, holding his shoulder. "Killing me or even Jude Wagner doesn't end the medical revolution. It only slows—"

He quit stalling when her expression darkened, and she motioned with the gun muzzle for him to step into the lake.

He hesitated then moved into the water. Waist deep, he stepped out of his loafers then ducked under the algae-covered surface, struggling underwater to untie the weight. The October sun had failed to warm the icy lake. With fingers going numb, he fumbled with the fishing line. He gasped at the surface again—and heard a blast.

In the first nanosecond he felt a sharp tap. No pain. But he could no longer fill his lungs with air. His carefree childhood reeled by in snapshots. Misspent teenage years vanished before him.

Another shot slammed into his forehead. Time stopped.

Ripples spread in symmetry above his sinking head.

One

Friday, October 28
San Francisco, CA

The dinged-up MX6 slotted into a perpendicular space along crammed Russian Hill. Lucky snag for Jude Wagner, just one block from home. Still getting a feel for his Mazda, Wagner noticed how snugly his broad shoulders fit in the bucket seat then climbed out. He snapped the door locks closed from his keychain. Seized in a drug raid, the Mazda bore the scars of its street-gang past—pelted with dents from its fenders to rear bumper. The perfect vehicle for parking on the street, thanks to his find at the FBI auction.

A foghorn groaned, bassy and long. Misty salt air whipped Wagner's tangled brown hair against his light forehead. Across the gulch, Coit Tower glowed, a beacon in the dark. Wagner navigated around a family of five on Hyde Street piling out of the local ice cream parlor. The store manager followed them out, flipping a closed sign on the glass door. The dad's scoop of ice cream hit the pavement and the kids shrieked with laughter.

Head throbbing from straight bourbon, Wagner realized he hadn't heard the infectious laughter of kids in years—a circumstance of his city living. Nostalgia came over him for his younger years in Kentucky. Without warning, his work routine had become his life pursuit at the expense of everything else.

A smile of pure amusement filled the mother's cheeks. It reminded him of his own mom and how she savored their last family sail.

At the entrance of his ground-floor flat, his foot touched an electric blue plastic bag. He picked up the bag containing his *New York Times*—a reminder that he'd fallen behind on world events amidst the confusion of the cyber hack. The FBI may have been running the investigation into Wagner's Stanford Grid computer breach, but it didn't alleviate matters. Just the opposite. Collaborating with the FBI ate up his time and ripped him away from his regular computer coding. For two weeks he showed up at the San Francisco bureau to fulfill his emergency duty, and it restricted him to only checking on his Stanford Bioengineering Department remotely.

He carried the newspaper through his front gate to the Mediterranean-styled three-story building. Under a trellis of ruby bougainvillea, he strode brick steps two at a time to his door. He shoved the key inside the Baldwin lock. It cranked too easily . . . no resistance. Slowly he pushed the door open. On the balls of his feet, he moved inside his narrow place. Ceiling spotlights in the hallway were on. Had he turned them off when he'd left that morning? Analyzing the vulnerability of his Grid made him forgetful. His gut tensed. Quieting his steps, he crossed into the living room.

The place had been ransacked. His bookcase had been emptied. His African carving, mystery paperbacks, San Francisco history books and rock concert ticket stubs blanketed the floor. Papers he'd stacked on the steamer-trunk coffee table were now strewn on the faux-oriental rug.

Odor of someone's cigarettes hung faintly in the air. Wagner's pulse quickened. *Could the intruder be here?* He listened for creaks in the floor. Nothing—only gusts lashed at the windows. Nerves on edge, he stepped to the kitchen. The cupboard drawers and doors were closed as he'd left them. Chips still sat on the counter. In the bedroom, though, his Chinese dresser doors were ajar. Shirts, suits and a high school wrestling trophy lay on the floor. In his mini-study, he checked his desktop computer. The shelf where his back-up hard drive sat gaped hollow and dark—the hard drive was missing. He cursed. His computer was locked to the desk, but the drive he backed up his data on wasn't. Someone could easily break into his backed up messages and get hold of highly sensitive information about the Stanford Grid.

Something scratched the floor, maybe hard-soled shoes. The noise sent a shiver down his spine. He braced himself. A door flung.

A man in a suit raced from the closet and outside the flat. Wagner gave chase through the hallway and barreled into the cold night. Wind buffeted off the bay.

The wide intruder bounded down the treacherous grade of the Filbert Street steps. Practiced at navigating the decline, Wagner clacked down the steps behind the lumbering figure. They raced past stucco apartment buildings and into North Beach.

Reaching the bottom of the hill, he pushed closer to his intruder. Wagner clipped by Washington Square Park. Just feet away, he lunged. Arms extended, he snagged the man's jacket. They crashed to the ground outside a neon-signed pizzeria. Concrete grated one side of Wagner's face. His skin burned.

The man grunted—gripping the hard drive beneath him. Wagner scrambled onto the man's back and planted a knee between his shoulder blades. He worked to control the man's thrashing arms.

"Call the police," a girl shouted from inside the pizzeria.

With heaving force, Wagner cranked the intruder's left arm behind him. A dark Chevrolet Blazer screeched to the curb.

The man twisted his arm, got on one knee and broke free of Wagner's control.

A karate punch darted toward Wagner's neck. Wagner blocked it on reflex with his forearm.

The hard drive dropped to the ground. Wagner reached and grasped it when he took a blow to his kidney.

The thud connected like a sack of flour falling from a top shelf. Wincing on his hands and knees, Wagner clutched the hard drive tight.

The man readied a swift soccer kick.

Wagner tightened his abdomen. Motion blurred. *Thwud!*

Gagging from the kick, Wagner curled knees to his chest. A high-pitched sound whined in his ears. Everything dimmed, even the neon lights glowing on Columbus Avenue.

Cars idled in traffic outside the crowded pizzeria on Columbus Avenue where Jude Wagner lay curled on the ground. The waiting Chevrolet Blazer had roared off as red and blue emergency lights beamed across retail buildings. A patrol car's P.A. chirped for traffic to move.

With his knees to his chest, Wagner had drifted to high school wrestling practice—a time when grappling was sport. A waft of cornmeal crust told him where he was as a sturdy voice hollered. "Wake up."

Wagner's eyes cracked open to three heads silhouetted against the night sky. Two cops and a bystander. The older officer with a bushy mustache stared stoically.

Cradling his wrenching gut, Wagner got up and stiffly handed over his billfold.

The bystander mumbled about a partial license plate and left the scene. Headlights from passing cars reflected on the younger cop's brass nameplate above his midnight blue shirt pocket. The name Flanagan showed as he studied Wagner's billfold.

Wagner wiped sidewalk dirt from the hard drive. "This guy was trained in hand-to-hand combat. Did you see the dark Blazer?"

"No. He was after that . . . computer part?"

"Yes." Wagner said, then cursed to himself. "I don't usually play tackle on Columbus Avenue."

The older officer's eyes narrowed.

Wagner shoved a hand in his pocket, reassured to feel his Grid access key.

The officer stroking his mustache came across Wagner's FBI Guest Pass. A biting wind rushed down the street. Wagner blinked dirt from his eyes, explaining that he worked at Stanford and was helping the FBI investigate a cyber hack.

The cop looked at Wagner again, considering his story and the blood droplets on his cheek.

"What? Don't I look like a workaholic?" Wagner remembered hearing that most on-duty cops resented the bureau altogether, that feds padded their arrest reports with busts made by beat cops.

While Flanagan scratched notes, Wagner got out his cell phone and dialed his FBI contact, Special Agent Nathalie Noiret, who was recently assigned to Stanford. Noiret said she'd come right over to his apartment.

He put his phone away to describe the would-be thief. After a ride up the hill in the squad car, Wagner clambered out the backseat—narrowly avoiding a lecture on the risks of vigilantism in North Beach. With his hard drive in hand, he went inside, and bolted his door lock. He started straightening loose papers as a way to cool down, then stopped. Agent Noiret needed to see this mess as he'd found it. The cost of losing Grid information was incalculable.

At his computer desk, he booted up to find his data files were intact. The pounding in his chest slowed, but only slightly. The back-up drive went into a locked drawer.

He went to the kitchen freezer and pulled out a bag of Birds Eye frozen corn for his throbbing cheek. He stared in the bathroom mirror at road burn texturing one side of his face. Next, he checked his bottom desk drawer. The lock was broken. His flash memory stick was gone. *Screw me.* His nerves rattled again. Documents pertaining to the Google deal were saved on it. Months of negotiations. This confidential deal, combined with Stanford's alliance with CERN, would destabilize mainstream medicine—the biggest industry in the world. Google would enable access to the Grid through their website. He thought about calling Niles. But with a plan to sail the next day, Wagner opted to tell him in person tomorrow.

Wagner warmed up leftover chicken, preparing for a draining night of fitful sleep. He removed his hot plate when a firm knock on his front door startled him.

Two

Friday, October 28
Meyrin, Switzerland

Alone on the second floor observation deck of the CERN laboratory, Hideo Onagi felt his heart thumping. Noise traveled easily in this all-white chamber, three hundred feet underground, beneath the Franco-Swiss border, beneath the sprawling buildings where thousands worked. It was where the famous Large Hadron Collider operated—the most expensive scientific experiment in history. The hum of high voltage electricity vibrated through the floors of the cavernous building. Hideo held the facility phone close. "What? Not even a message from him? Can't someone drive to Jűrgen's apartment and physically search for him?"

A moment passed when Hideo hung up the wall phone. His face flushed hot with frustration. Would he have to wing this entire presentation without his speech partner?

These strangers would render a pass-fail verdict on work that had consumed him for years. At the trial of his life, he was minus his expert witness. Rolling his sloped shoulders, he flipped through 3x5 note cards, reviewing his talking points. Returning the cards to his pocket, his finger brushed against something else there. He took out a photo. His daughter beamed in her fourth-grade school picture. Her gaze transfixed him, then he pushed the headshot back into his front trouser pocket.

Family turmoil and this fund-raising presentation for genomic medicine set off his ulcer. After months of jetting from city to city to find sponsors for the Grid, Hideo realized that work travel was ruining his marriage. His wife and daughter were his sun and moon and soon they could be gone. Once this ended, he'd fly to meet his estranged wife. Perspiration dampened his Polo shirt.

Below, maintenance staff worked on a ground level that opened into a tunnel. The vast space appeared like a subway platform from the future. But this wasn't built to transport any person or thing. Only light. The giant tube housed superconducting magnets—magnets which cooled particle beams, speeding them through a seventeen-mile subterranean circle. Running in opposite directions, the beams were guided to collide in an explosion that scientists used to study the fundamental particles of the universe.

The first few attendees were being led in by Jűrgen's assistant. They gawked at the girders and struts supporting the high ceilings. It all took decades to build. Just one problem: these were Jűrgen's contacts. His absence could wreck this chance for vital donations. Hideo walked downstairs to join the group. On the first floor, he nervously tapped his rubber-soled dress shoe while attendees looked about at the consoles connected by colored wires lining the walls.

Hideo had given up his private practice to join Stanford and change medical history. Delay of action on this genome project would mean hundreds of thousands of cancer sufferers would go on dying. But his area of expertise was molecular biology and chemistry—not physics. Jűrgen represented the CERN side of this partnership. As CERN's Life Science Director, Jűrgen said he'd handle the walking-tour part of this. Hideo used his cell phone to fire off an unusually direct text message. *Where are you?*

A dozen more consortium members arrived. They stared at him, huddled together like a mini United Nations. He couldn't hold off this meeting any longer. Sucking up embarrassment, Hideo introduced himself and gestured toward the huge bright blue metal pipe that lined the tunnel. "The amount of metal used in this pipe ring could build another Eiffel Tower. It's the most powerful collider in the world, operating at minus two hundred and seventy-one Centigrade—colder than deep space."

Gaining confidence, Hideo spoke up. "This nine-billion-dollar underground linear accelerator was designed to smash protons to analyze the questions of the big bang, cosmology—oh—and unified theory." Exotic instruments flashed on the wall.

A murmur rippled through the audience. The group was fidgety.

Hideo forced a smile. "Scientists wouldn't have gotten anywhere without an enormous computer to analyze all the data from these experiments. That's why I'm showing you this. CERN used a grid computer system to study results. That same grid computer is now helping Stanford medicine."

They started to chatter. One man rubbed his arms. Hideo was losing his audience.

A fat man said, "Like an electrical power grid?"

"Not exactly. Computer grids link thousands of computers to work as a single virtual super machine. Colliding particles produces vast amounts of data. Ultimately, this grid analyzes the equivalent of twenty-five million DVD's worth of information monthly. Stanford's Grid will answer anything that involves calculating, no matter how complex."

He paused to let the message sink in and was gratified to see he had eye contact.

A severe-faced woman dressed in black pointed at the flashing instruments. "So that's grid-based medicine?"

Hideo spread his hands broadly. "Partially. CERN's physicists built this grid to handle questions that no other computer system could handle before. Conveniently, the grid runs over the World Wide Web—which CERN also invented to analyze atom-smashing results."

A technician entered the room below and checked dials attached to electrical equipment.

Hideo raised his voice to speak over a new burring noise. "I'm proud to say that the computers here and the Grid computer at Stanford University are working as one through distributed processing."

Expressions were skeptical.

"Where is Jűrgen Hansen?" a bald man asked.

"Unfortunately, a personal emergency called him away," Hideo lied.

"Jűrgen has been talking to me about this for five months," the man said, "and you tell me he's not here? Isn't he the liaison between this lab and Stanford's."

"Yes, he maintains the pipes that link this Grid to Stanford. And thank you all for meeting with me at this glorified agricultural village. We've all heard our share of puffery about scientific breakthroughs."

The bald man shook his head. "So what does a linear accelerator have to do with healthcare? What's the scholarly revelation?"

Hideo's stomach churned. He needed to speed past Jűrgen's part. Attendees cared more about how their dollars could mine the genome, the ultimate human recipe book. The genome held four billion years of information on humanity. It was arguably the greatest discovery in scientific history.

"Listen, everyone. Traditional medicine is failing," Hideo finally said sternly. "It treats everyone who has cancer with a short list of drugs like we're all the same. In reality cancer is as individual as a fingerprint. It's time we matched individual treatment to individuals and that takes massive computer power. Let's go to Building Six. There I'll explain how Stanford is poised to conquer dozens of diseases."

With a flick of his CERN tour guide flag, he directed them. Mercifully, Hideo's attendees followed. He stole a look at his watch. Jűrgen was over an hour late. Good God. Could he be hung over from another night of carousing?

After an elevator ride to the ground level, they filed to Building Six. While the group exchanged hotel stories and restaurant recommendations, Hideo checked his phone. No messages.

Once in the conference attendees ate hors d'oeuvres until he motioned for everyone to get comfortable at the rosewood table. Bottles of Evian water and brochure packets were set on the table at precise intervals for each person. The orderly area reminded Hideo of his fastidious wife and their heart-wrenching probability of divorce. His daughter's face flashed before him. His thoughts drifted before he could resume his performance.

"In all my years of practice," Hideo finally said, "I've never seen a technology so perfectly poised to improve healthcare. But how? How will a partnership between CERN and Stanford do a thing for those suffering from illness?"

"Yes," a Persian man said holding his Evian.

"All disease has a hereditary basis and the genome is our roadmap to understanding it." Hideo fiddled with his wedding ring. "We're tapping that. The U.S. government sequenced the human genome in 2003, but that was just a start and that took two-point-seven billion dollars."

"Currently, side effects and misprescription kill over one hundred thousand people a year." Hideo took a deep breath. "That's unacceptable. As you'll find in your brochure, the Stanford Project works like this: a person would have his genome sequenced by an outlet which will soon appear in malls like a contact lens store. That analysis would cost the same as prescription lenses. When results come back to doctor and patient, the information can be accessed from a secured website on the Grid."

Several attendees nodded.

"What does genomic medicine do that traditional medicine can't?" the fat man asked.

"Personalized medicine is pie in the sky until we make it affordable," another man said.

Hideo expected this one. He stood tall to elongate his short stature. "Exactly. That's the point. We're democratizing medicine, making the costly part—research and diagnosis—much cheaper."

"How?" the same man interjected.

"First, genomic medicine allows us to use inexpensive information services versus costly clinical studies. Grids not only run over the Internet, which is virtually free, but they get power from volunteers' idle computers. In the packet you'll see how this grid at CERN relies on volunteers' computers."

Chatter interrupted him again.

"I see doubt. Believe me, with more funding great things will come. Isn't fighting cancer as worthy a mission as landing spacecraft on Mars? Why not invest a fraction of that to outsmart diseases like cancer, which claim fifteen hundred lives a day in America alone?"

Audience members turned to one another. Hideo scored a point. As the group opened brochures an elderly man on the far end raised his hand. "What specifically would our endowment funds accomplish?"

To Hideo's relief, eyes tracked him as he paced. "Your dollars will expand the system which runs like a worldwide database, bringing supercomputing power to desktops, virtually. It's replicating how researchers from 25 countries analyzed particle collisions here through a grid of institutions and universities around the world. And, yes, we'll need specially trained pharmacists to formulate the customized drugs. But at Stanford, we're already diagnosing volunteers' illnesses using their DNA.

Hideo elaborated until his mind strayed to his flight. There was barely enough time for him to get to the airport. After delivering his final plea for investment, he used the phone on the table to beckon an assistant. A young man in a tie, short sleeves and slim-fitting pants entered the room.

Glancing at the wall clock, Hideo said, "This fellow can tell you more about CERN."

Hideo checked his pocket to make sure that his plane ticket was there. "Excuse me, everyone, I must be leaving for a flight now. Thank you."

His pitch had to have won some new backers. But no word back from Jűrgen. Unbelievable. Fortunately, Hideo was quick on his feet. Any money raised today could help save countless lives. But, like it or not, mainstream medicine enjoyed an iron grip on the American public. Inevitably, the huge change that flowed from Stanford's Grid would provoke violent backlash.

Three

Friday, October 28
San Francisco, CA

After checking the peep-hole, Jude Wagner set down his chicken leg and unlatched the bolt. "You got here quickly."

Agent Nathalie Noiret strode in, visibly alarmed. "Like a fireman. You are all right, no?"

"I am. Some service I'm getting tonight. A thief, two cops and a federal agent with a sense of urgency."

"You are the center of attention," she said dryly.

He wished the media didn't advertise that he was the computer expert driving the human genome project. Wagner's computer code—a data mining algorithm which accelerated the medical computer network—had worked wonders, for sure. His breakthrough in the Grid project acted as a spark to accelerate personalized medicine, but the war against cancer had just begun.

She shook her head. "Your face. It looks awful."

"I'll take that as sympathy."

He was sore and sleep-deprived; she, the picture of poise and grace with French élan. Clad in a double-breasted coat and black turtle neck sweater, she carried a leather satchel which added to her rational perfectionist image. Exchange her sling back shoes for white bucks and the U.S. Navy would take her as one of their own.

He reflexively locked the door behind her. *Wired* magazines, auto insurance papers and Wells Fargo bank statements were still strewn on his living room floor. Part of him lay naked and exposed right there.

Agent Noiret moved into the living room, taking it in like it was a Jackson Pollack painting that needed interpreting.

"What did this perp—perpetrator—look like?"

"He was a walking oak tree with stubbled, blond hair. He looked paramilitary. A dark Chevrolet Blazer pulled up for him." Wagner worked to recall more for the special agent assigned to him. The trouble started two weeks back when his Stanford's Bioengineering Department Grid server was hacked. The intrusion easily qualified for the $100,000 threshold of damages to trigger a federal investigation. He and agent Nathalie Noiret now collaborated on investigating the breach. All they had so far were suspicious files on a computer server.

"Anything stolen?" she asked.

"Yeah. The thief got my memory stick which held confidential papers to the Stanford deal with Google."

"Why was that not under lock and key?"

"It was. You can see my snapped drawer lock where my computer is cabled to my desk. You'd think I was guarding nuclear missiles."

"It's fortunate for all of us you are not."

"Tell me about it." He was in no mood to be toyed with. Wagner had confided in agent Noiret that once Stanford partnered with Google, his project would have airtight security—then genomic medicine would take off.

She stepped around the papers, absorbing the scene. He could almost see her mathematics Ph.D. gears turning behind those intense, almond-shaped eyes. Maybe she was developing her theory; or maybe she was judging Wagner for his carelessness. He couldn't say. His bachelor quarters probably revealed something lacking in him.

Aside from his disheveled floor, Wagner's living room was sparingly decorated and self-contained. The only warmth came from a hand-me-down club chair in the corner. His starkly masculine furniture highlighted the 1920s crown moldings and Wagner's no-nonsense personality. The walls shone eggshell white—a fitting shade since the Stanford Program now rested on eggshells too.

"When will Stanford be connected to Google exactly?" she asked.

"November 7."

"That's ten days of vulnerability, no."

"Right. Ten days of sitting like a duck in a pond."

Blankly, she shook her head. Then she removed a small flashlight from her carrying case and walked outside. Without asking questions, he followed her into the dark. He pointed to where his car was parked. Alongside the passenger door, she crouched then nimbly dropped to her side on the ground to look under his vehicle. She moved the beam of light around its underside. "Your Mazda is worn like a used stunt car. No slap and track, though."

"That's something. I'm not being followed." They returned to his living room where he sat in his club chair.

She walked around his rug again, adjusting her worn satchel on her shoulder. "Tell me why your Stanford group severed its alliance with Johnston & Quib."

"The partnership no longer added up. If Google invests in us, we can keep diagnosis over the Grid cheap or free. A Pharma company Goliath like J&Q would change that. So we broke the deal with them two weeks ago. Besides, J&Q had a conflict of interest taking us on. They couldn't promote our personalized drugs without cannibalizing their traditional, big-bucks product lines."

"Okay. Did J&Q get its investment dollars returned?"

"Yes, but they're still panicking."

"You think?"

"I know. The "patent cliff" is dealing a body blow to multinationals like J&Q. These pharma companies earn more than half their money from blockbuster drugs. And drug patents are expiring left and right."

"So new alternatives threaten expensive, brand-name drugs," she said.

"Exactly. You don't have to rely on a giant company for drug discovery anymore. Small companies and even University settings are compounding—mixing custom drugs."

"So what's the impact, huh?"

"Big Pharma companies are going leaner through mergers, closing entire therapeutic lines. The most promising drugs are being designed for only a small sliver of patients."

He paused for dramatic effect and to see if she was fully listening. "Stanford is pushing medicine into the digital age. Curing people is binary now."

"I see," she said. "I hope you still have your access key."

He crossed his arms. "I do."

"At least something is safe." She said it like he had no cryptographic procedure in place. But he did. Without the authentication key the intruder had nothing. No one could access the Grid without the key and the owner's thumb print. The key, which Wagner carried with him everywhere, displayed a number that changed every thirty seconds—in sync with the Grid server—enabling Grid access.

She looked at him. "We need to view this apartment robbery like a break-in to a genomics lab." She pensively smoothed her hair. "First you had an electronic break-in and now a physical one.

He cracked his knuckles.

"We have the makings of a concerted attack to knock your Grid offline. Big money could be behind this."

The fine-boned, self-possessed agent was catching on. "If someone corrupts the medical Grid, the whole diagnostic solution would go up in smoke. It would take years to start over."

She had a quizzical expression.

He added, "A corrupted Grid would send the world a clear message: if a hacker could compromise the network and its privacy controls, it wouldn't be safe for the public to donate their idle computer power to it. Nor would they trust uploading their genome data to the Grid for analysis."

Wind bellowed through his metal-lined chimney. She looked as skeptical and focused on problem-solving as he was—two analytical peas in pod.

He wanted to get back to work on network protection. He'd made inroads on identifying malware that could penetrate Stanford's bioengineering servers, yet they hadn't installed the antivirus.

"What would happen if someone got hold of your algorithm?"

"Nothing. I've given it away on the 'Net already, making it open source. That's not a worry, but protecting the Grid from hackers is."

He gave Nathalie his hard drive in a baggie in case she could extract prints from it after isolating his own. Then he showed her the intruder's hiding place in his apartment.

She took her flashlight to his hallway closet, the only part of his hall that would not have been disturbed by foot traffic, and shined it low across the floor. The beam exposed dusty tread prints.

"Do you or any one you know wear hiking boots?"

"No, but that intruder was."

"Hmm." She pulled a plastic sheath from inside her satchel.

"What's that?"

"A gelatin lifter." She removed a sticky sheet of plastic from a foot-long pouch. Kneeling on the hallway closet floor, she carefully placed the lift over the boot mark to get a good impression. She let the gel lift set.

The silence became awkward while she worked. "How was your trip to Montreal?" he said.

"It was the usual family visit. A lot of food and debate about how life would change if Quebec seceded from Canada. No excitement, believe me."

"I'd take boredom over this."

"True. Put your Grid team on the alert." She spoke with unmistakable self-control. Or maybe it was her French Canadian accent which made her come off as ultra-systematic.

She gingerly slid the gel impression into its pouch and back into a separate divide of her satchel. "This could help us isolate a suspect."

"If we ever arrive at a suspect list," he said.

"Don't lose faith, not yet."

"Would you say that to an agnostic?"

Ultimately, her stopping by reinforced one belief: Stanford's bioengineering department needed the advanced security of a large organization. A rush of blood rose to Wagner's face and ears. He wished his team had already closed the partnership negotiations they started with Google.

Four

Saturday, October 29
Tokyo, Japan

The Ferris wheel rotated with its latest passengers on board. Dr. Hideo Onagi held his nine-year-old daughter's chilled shoulder and she clung to her vinyl seat. The ride paused again and the two-person car swung freely. From up here they had a mountaintop view of Rinkai Park and beyond, where city life crawled serenely. But the view did nothing for his marital predicament. His passive-aggressive wife steadily closed down lines of communication with him. His marriage was disintegrating and blowing away. Jűrgen's mysterious absence troubled him, but not as much as his wife. A looming divorce left him panic stricken.

The skyline didn't look the way it had when Hideo was growing up. More buildings towered as emblems to Japanese industry. The expanse framed five ports: Chiba, Kawasaki, Yokohama, Yokosuka, and on the west, Tokyo. The heavily-built landscape receded into gray. At midday, the autumn sun was breaking through a veil of Tokyo smog.

"Daddy look." Yomiko shouted, pointing at kids below chasing dancing kite strings.

"Clear day for Tokyo, isn't it, Yomiko?"

"It's beautiful, Daddy."

Coveting family time, Hideo once read manga comics to his daughter on weekends in Palo Alto, California. But those weekends had gone. His job jealously stole him away from his wife and Yomiko.

If he could rewind time, he would've struck a balance, listened to those who called him too dedicated for his own good. If only his Stanford Grid team didn't rely on him so much.

Right now, Hideo's wife, Asuka, was dining with her parents, probably strategizing about her permanent relocation back to Tokyo with their daughter. Asuka couldn't function outside of Japan. Like some endangered zoo animal, she had to ship back to her natural habitat or pine away. She had asked for a divorce, claiming she couldn't be Japanese anywhere else. That phrase haunted Hideo. He wondered if he was no longer himself. He couldn't remember the last time someone called him "the Little Bullet," the nickname that the Tokyo media had coined for him. But he couldn't foresee living in Japan again and abandoning his job. Fully Americanized, he drove a classic Mustang and, unbeknownst to his wife, shot pool and drank cosmopolitans after work. He'd even come to resent Japan's outdated patriarchal systems of hierarchy and its hidden xenophobia.

With a steel clank, the Ferris wheel lurched them higher. He rubbed his daughter's shoulders to warm them. Yomiko squinted into the wind. He knew how rarely he would see his daughter once Asuka moved her to Japan. This business trip was his opportunity to say goodbye to her for now, while Asuka reunited with her parents—parents whom, she insisted, they'd abandoned. How could he steer the Grid project when he couldn't keep his family afloat?

Shame.

Yomiko straightened her bangs while the Ferris wheel turned. He mumbled a poem he knew.

Time is eternity and eternity is time.
What is time and who am I?
Time moves on but I am out of time.
In between. Time moves. Time stands still.

"What are you saying, Daddy?"

"Nothing—look, Yomiko, that outline is Mount Fuji," his arm still around her shoulders.

His daughter pointed in another direction, at hazy spires. "And there's Disneyworld."

Precocious nine-year-old.

Windblown, they disembarked from the ride. Yomiko headed to a meal truck, pulling Hideo by the hand. They purchased bento box lunches and ice cream, then took a bench that overlooked Tokyo Bay. Yomiko ate her melting drumstick first. Hideo opened his box and savored a soy-dipped salmon roll. While his daughter watched the kids play with kites, he thought about how long he'd slogged away at the genomic medicine dream. His wife's words kept pushing from his subconscious. You're boiling the ocean, Hideo.

Sadly, this was the only way Asuka could express her frustration with his work.

But Hideo couldn't leave the Stanford Grid Project. Not after the holy grail of medicine was finally getting started—successfully evaluating diabetes test patients with a million times greater accuracy than a physician could. Stanford's massively distributed computer network analyzed molecular patterns like weather satellites that scanned the earth for climate changes. The Grid matched molecular information from tumors with exactly the right drug to suppress that tumor.

He had overcome the perception that genetic research tampered with nature and the ecosystem. Ten years ago Hideo had to wear moon-suits even for tasks done inside air-locked laboratories. Since then, attitudes had shifted as people came to better understand genetic science.

"Let's not leave, Daddy."

"I must—I have a conference in Palm Springs," Hideo said.

Yomiko scowled. "What kind of conference?"

"Computer medicine, *Neko*, for sick people."

She made an exaggerated frown. As she ate her lunch, he observed how her fresh, young face bore evidence of the refined beauty she would become. He wanted to preserve memories of her growing up, storing in his mind all that he would miss.

Yomiko leaped up. "Let's go." She tugged him by his cuff.

He dumped their paper lunch boxes and followed. "Where are we going?"

She turned. "You know, to our garden, without birds." She gave him a toothy smile of innocence, acknowledging his fear of birds. Chocolate ice cream streaked down her face.

He, too, wanted to relive their Tokyo memories from Yomiko's childhood. He followed her to their old nature sanctuary. The grounds appeared, clashing with the dense urban background of Tokyo. Nearing the garden, they looked at an entrance lined with a maze of shrubs that Hideo knew were Japanese boxwood.

"This way, Daddy." She pointed to the bonsai-filled menagerie. Inside the garden, they crept along pebble paths with red maples skirting lily-covered streams. An elderly garden visitor sat meditating upon sand and stones, surrounded by bamboo. "Daddy, I want to move back here."

He ignored that, aware that she may be moving back to Tokyo with her mother, but without him. "Select a rock, Yomiko."

"Okay—that one beside the red tree."

"Now, adopt it."

"How?"

"Name it. Remember it. And it's yours."

Yomiko threw her head back, closing her eyes. "I named it Chihiro, from the movie *Spirited Away*."

"Fine. We'll revisit old Chihiro one day. Say goodbye," he said softly.

She thought about it, focused on the rock and waved her arms. They meandered away from the garden, across vast yards of grass where families picnicked with wine bottle-sized Sapporo and Asahi beers. Strolling with her hand in his, Hideo rehearsed his Palm Springs speech. He removed an index card from his shirt pocket. But the dozens of birds that settled in a flock at their feet distracted him, along with the two vicious-looking dogs he saw sitting in the distance, behind cherry trees. His palms sweated.

"Yomiko, we must go."

"Daddy, I'll protect you from those black birds."

He squeezed her hand and put the note cards away. As they strolled toward the gift shop, her eyes suddenly grew large. She cried, "Daddy, watch out."

Hideo spun around to confront two white and tan dogs galloping toward him from the distance. A chill rushed up his spine to his head.

Fur raised on their necks. They rushed him.

Terror paralyzed his legs. The wolfish Akita Inu collided into his midsection. Hideo stumbled backward. A whoosh came out of him. His daughter screamed. The pair of predators snapped at him. He swung his arms, flecked with grass . . . anything to keep them from his daughter—the easier prey. One dog shredded Hideo's shirt sleeve.

Yomiko fled toward a tree.

Hideo anchored his heels into the grass to get up, but the growling animals pinned him down. Fetid breath and slobber spewed on him.

Yomiko stood—immobilized with dread. A picnicker ran up. He threw his arms around her to pull her to safety, but she kicked free.

While Hideo struggled to get up, he yelled at her. "Go!"

One berserk Akita closed its fangs on his forearm, sinking teeth into skin and bone.

The other animal bit Hideo's thigh. His extremities seared. He straight-armed a muzzle.

The dog's head snapped back, unaffected. Hideo's body was yanked like a flag in a gale. He gasped in agony.

More picnickers jumped to their feet to help.

"Daddy," Yomiko cried.

Kneeling, Hideo snagged one dog's ear and didn't let go. Furry tissue finally tore from its square head. Blood sprayed. The other animal sunk its jaws into his neck.

Hideo lost his grip.

Onlookers circled, but couldn't get close. Teeth gnashed into Hideo's throat like ice picks. Vertebrae crushed. A copper taste filled his mouth. Pain blazed through him in stop-action motion. Red, white and black strobed as Hideo's bladder released. Voices blurred. Wind sucked through his teeth. Finally, he dropped flat to the grass.

Yomiko fought for her breath. The dogs looked up as if they'd been called by a whistle. One after the other, they turned their heads. At once they tore off in the direction from where the sound came, leaving a crimson trail.

The canines sat on their haunches before a blonde-haired woman in a brown jumpsuit. She crouched behind cherry trees near the street where she fed her dogs a biscuit, then fastened their leashes. Her gold cross, dangling on her neck, glistened in the sun.

Yomiko scurried, then fell to her father's lifeless body, sobbing. She laid her hands on his head, but had to turn away. The brackish smell of blood made her nauseous.

The woman behind the trees was no longer in view. She must've driven off.

A siren sounded. With lights flashing, an ambulance sped onto the park knoll, swerving around parents who swept children out of the way. Two medics sprang from swinging double doors with a stretcher. They hurried to where Yomiko draped herself over her father. One medic examined puncture marks on the victim's throat. He put one hand on top of another and tried to resuscitate the gravely injured man. The other medic covered his nose with his forearm.

"There's no hope for this poor man."

The second medic knelt to comfort the blood-stained child. "What do you have?" he asked and pried two index cards from her shaking fist.

"They went over there," the girl shrieked, crying.

"Who did?"

"The dogs. A lady waited for them. She was here, but left."

The medic looked at the trees where she pointed but saw nothing. He read one of the note cards:

> "Algorithms like Jude Wagner's solve problems through computer instructions which greatly speed up the computational process of personalized medicine. How? Mathematically. Wagner's code mines key bits of data, digitally sorting molecular information of a patient's tumor. This generates a snapshot of one's illness. It's the first step to customized diagnosis."

The medic had no idea what he was reading, but it looked important. He returned the cards to the girl and eased the corpse onto the stretcher.

* * *

Scud looked out the double-paned airplane window, plotting how to stay ahead of the FBI curve. Bulbous clouds rolled by. This Tokyo job and Jűrgen's were almost too easy. Two major hurdles crossed. These hits rammed a baton through the gears of Stanford's Grid. That said, this would bring new urgency to the bureau's investigation. Fortunately, the FBI was under more pressure than ever these days, running in circles like hurricane chasers to manage cyber issues. Stanford already reeled from someone else's hack into its disruptive network. For once, Scud forgot about her history of being judged by others.

She discreetly peered at the human resource file, holding it close from the prying eyes of other passengers. The five-page job application showed great expertise in the man but erratic tendencies. Undoubtedly, that's why the company Scud worked for had turned him away. As a bounty hunter, he lived on the fringe, pulling whatever job came along to earn a buck. A fantastic find for cutting off Jude Wagner—the man who thinks he can play God with his Grid. Though eliminating Wagner was off the table while he sat in the lap of the FBI . . . just too close for comfort.

Niles Tully made a softer target. Killing him would still cleanse the world of another medical radical. Time to consider the next operation. Scud keyed in a text message to her bounty-hunter turned hit man: "Attach GPS trackers to the vehicles of Niles Tully and Roger Knowlan—usually parked at Stanford's Bioengineering Dept."

The next strike called for the utmost discretion. The FBI's suspect list for investigating the death of Stanford bioengineering academics had to cover acres, but these strikes needed to stay hidden. Most of all, Stanford deserved mayhem for playing high stakes roulette with private medicine and trillions of dollars—jeopardizing the jobs of millions. If Stanford's medical initiative took hold, repercussions would ripple from Wall Street to Main Street, knocking the whole social order out of whack. This so-called scientific advancement had to end. Scud would make sure of that.

Five

Saturday, October 29
San Francisco, CA

A foggy gray light streamed in too early to Jude Wagner's Russian Hill apartment. Fitting ambiguity for the dawn after an assault. He clicked off his clock radio and the annoying morning DJ while his mental computer warmed up.

In the bathroom, he looked over the bloody skin on the left side of his face in the mirror. He dabbed scrapes on his face with rubbing alcohol on toilet paper and recalled what the FBI boss had said: *The threat landscape has increased over the last five years.* The big man had a flair for highlighting the obvious.

He removed the T-shirt he slept in. Wagner's body had hardly changed from when he wrestled competitively in high school thirteen years ago. His resting stance resembled that of a grappler going into round one: legs shoulder-width apart, hands ready for action. According to his former coach, he had the quickness of a sled-dog; and summers he spent working construction jobs added muscle definition to his ropy arms. At the moment, he felt stiff just reaching for a shirt and putting his arms through the sleeves of his button-down. He checked his phone for messages. Nothing. Why hadn't Hideo returned his voicemail from last night about his break-in?

Wagner's foot caught his spindly carving of an African tribal man lying at the foot of his bed. On his haunches, he traced the brambly wood grain with his finger—a souvenir from his post-college trip to Africa. . . a departure that led him to medicine. He learned about the Kano village back in high school following his mother's death. After he'd holed up in his bedroom for weeks, he emerged to watch a Peace Corps video shown at his school. The grim school assembly about kids in Africa struck a chord with him. Finally, after his college graduation, he joined. The Corp assigned him to Kano, Africa. That year away changed his perception of the world forever.

Thunderstorms had rumbled when Wagner arrived in the African village of Kano. Sheets of water thudded onto the corrugated metal roof of the clinic in one of Nigeria's northern villages. June was Kano's rainy season. By week three of his eight-week volunteer stint, rain still poured. Wagner's clothes and his cot stank of sodden red earth and sweat.

The volunteer leaders called on Wagner for various tasks—none of which involved tech support. At first he resented being brought in under false pretenses. But since they didn't have access to running water, technology became secondary. So many kids were being transported to the medical clinic for treatment. He aided social workers by feeding and giving shots to children with meningitis, malaria and other diseases.

Luckily a pharmaceutical company, Maier, learned of the sickness that had become a meningitis epidemic and flew twenty-seven doctors to administer a new drug, Trovan. The village exhaled in collective relief when the American doctors arrived. Wagner returned to study computer science at Berkeley with a new appreciation for contemporary modern science.

Six months after coming home, Wagner received a short letter from his Kano social worker pen pal who was completing her law degree. The last three paragraphs hit him hard.

> Tragic news. I thought you should be updated on our Kano kids. Eleven of the thirty children we fed and looked after have died. I'm crushed. The remaining nineteen suffer, I hear, from acute arthritis and side effects from their Trovan therapy—remember Tina's bulging eyes?
>
> Incredibly, Maier may have known—the company's being sued by the Nigerian government, declaring the experiment was "an illegal trial of an unregistered drug," which violates Nigerian law.
>
> The International Declaration of Helsinki, which governs ethical medical research, reports the

drug was not only untested, it was administered without parental consent. And get this: ten of the twenty-seven doctors that Maier brought to Kano were paid African physicians, bribed away from their usual medical work in other parts of Nigeria. I hate to be the one to break this to you.

With sadness for Kano,
Juliette

Thank God Niles and Hideo had agreed to severing Stanford's partnership with the Pharma company, Johnston & Quib. J&Q would only milk the Grid for PR hype and profit. He forced himself to go to the field office again to analyze things. Outside he met a fog bank. The white mist hovered around apartment buildings, blurring the border between city and bay. Many hated this weather, but Wagner did his most focused coding on monochromatic days. Out on the bay, a foghorn sounded; the bark of sea lions strangely carried from the wharf. San Francisco appeared adrift at sea. Wagner could relate.

The ground rumbled and the noise of metal on metal screeched. A cable car rose over the crest of Hyde Street. It carried raucous tourists in sweatshirts and Bermuda shorts. Oblivious passengers hollered shrilly as the car, dinging its chipper arcade-like chime, plunged into the basin of Ghirardelli Square. He headed to his car. In the wind, Wagner took out his cell phone and rang the Central Police Station off Columbus Avenue. The police line beeped, recording the call. The line transferred from the front desk.

"Officer Flanagan."

"This is Jude Wagner. I'm calling about a police report to a robbery at my place last night."

"Which response was that?"

"An apartment break-in at 1168 Filbert Street and the—"

"Right, the street-fighter from Stanford. If you're calling about that dark Chevrolet Blazer's partial plate, nothing's come up."

"Really?"

"Hold on." The officer had covered the phone receiver to muffle his conversation.

Time was wasting. Restless and frustrated with police procedure, Wagner pressed END and reconsidered the missing Google files.

Stanford would have to spin the report like crazy if the guarded deal got out. He could see the headlines already: *search engine titan, Google, joins forces with Stanford University to extend the reach of genetic diagnosis, challenging standard healthcare practices.* Critics would seize that announcement.

In his Mazda, Wagner headed for the Berkeley Marina. He started to leave another message on Hideo's cell when he calculated it was just one-thirty a.m. there. He crossed the Bay Bridge with worries reeling in his head. As he had done a hundred times before, he turned into the Berkeley Marina parking lot to meet Niles. Although today wasn't typical. On top of everything, his sister was coming. He missed her, but hadn't even given any real thought to how he'd occupy her during her visit.

The marina was deserted on this blustery October day. None of the regular kids who lived on wind surfboards were hitting waves. Loose halyards flapped, dinging against masts. The constant settling of the land gnarled the asphalt parking lot with fissures. The only sign of a visitor was Niles's parked car.

Wagner had no desire to sail today. The mere idea of climbing aboard reminded him of what had happened on the water that humid summer afternoon on the family sailboat fifteen years ago. Down the dock, Wagner boarded the boat to find Niles doing sit-ups on the deck beside the boat as if he'd been waiting overnight.

Smelling of teak oil, Niles donned his wire-rim glasses and straightened his brown, slicked back hair. With aqua topsiders, he resembled a preppy, thirty-year-old version of Gordon Gecko from the 1980s movie *Wall Street*. If Wagner was the artist, Niles was the art dealer in their relationship: a spin doctor, a check-is-in-the-mail, we'll-sign-the contract-today Svengali. Though Niles seemed to have an extra chromosome for melodrama, Wagner counted on him to keep up on the day-to-day at Stanford.

Niles smirked. "Fancy this. I'm actually seeing phantom-Jude Wagner in the flesh. Your face is a mess."

Wagner touched his road rash from hitting the sidewalk. He knew he'd been scarce, working with the bureau. He'd missed their standing plan to sail on Saturdays. "Alright, alright."

Niles adjusted his glasses. "Did you notice, the boat is spotless?"

"Yeah, she's lookin' flash."

"And if the Grid makes us famous, I'll be saying that about a new fifty footer," Niles said in his Oxford English accent while the two climbed aboard. "I tested my new onboard stereo. It works. Eddie will love this when he gets back."

"That's something," Jude said, with one foot on the boat bench, stretching.

Niles's son, Edward, was on a see-as-much-as-you can whirlwind trip to England.

On Wednesday Niles would be flying to Switzerland to lock down the three-way partnership Stanford was finalizing with Google and CERN. The search engine company needed to resolve last minute Grid issues with CERN in Meyrin.

"I'm going to meet Edward while I'm over there. Don't get to see my bonnie lad as much as I'd like to."

Charlene, the egg donor in the relationship, raised Edward in an East Bay suburb, of San Francisco. "He's already turning thirteen. You should start a brood yourself one day."

"I might try a more conventional route than co-parenting with my lesbian friend."

"Thank God you've got all the answers. There is more to life than just cerebral challenges."

"I'm sure you're doing a fine job with Edward," Wagner said. "It's hard for me to even imagine starting a family."

"It's never exactly how you plan. No one's ever ready for kids, even when you find the right person to have them with. I don't see him enough. The word virtual is good when used for grid computing—bad when it applies to Dad. Charlene and I have sorted things, but life is definitely easier if you're straight."

Wagner looked away. "Don't be so sure."

"Right then, so what's her name?" Niles said.

Wagner chuckled. "There's no one."

Wagner was hard to read, but Niles had a way of seeing through his barriers. "No one but that FBI agent you mentioned."

"Forget I mentioned her."

"I will if you're not already under her spell."

"How did we get onto this?"

"It won't help matters if you fall for this government agent. In case you forgot, you like things uncomplicated. A woman with a French accent, a badge and a gun could be your demise. You're naive with shit like this."

"Is that a fact?"

"Yes. Come on, it'll take a toll on you . . . even if this agent does go for laconic men who deftly conceal their inner workings and put work before everything. The workhorse in you will try to make sense of her. You'll run yourself ragged analyzing it."

"Thanks for the advice. You're saving me a lot of trial and error. Why do I talk to you?"

"Good question. Why does a guy who's straight as an arrow like you have a best mate like me? One day, someone will give you grief for that."

"Yeah, well, we'll never fight over the same girl."

"I am the best wingman you'll ever know," Niles said. "Sounds like you got yourself in deep this time, though."

"Look, I won't be sailing today. Too much to do before getting my sister at the airport. She lands at five. And don't talk to me about the Zen effect a sail will have. I'm here to tell you my place was broken into last night. Some guy got my hard drive."

Niles squinted with dismay. "Your hard drive? Damn it, Jude."

"I got it back after I chased him to Columbus." Niles listened.

"But the Google papers are gone," Wagner said.

"No!"

Wagner could read Niles's mind with that judgmental glare. *The world is watching us with a magnifying glass: investors, doctors, patients, lawyers—and you lose files?*

If anything, though, Wagner was more personally committed to the success of this Project than Niles. Wagner's algorithm—his mathematical computer code—was embedded into the Grid.

Niles went on, "You've informed the FBI?"

"Yeah."

"What's their take on this?"

The mast jiggled in the wind. "We think it could be related to the prior hack. It's hard to say. The FBI feels that when they broke into our servers, the attackers could've been exploring our system structure as a setup for a real strike."

"Great."

"I know. The forensics guys are tracing the malware. I'm working on preventing intrusion. But the FBI has big limitations."

"Why? You said the bureau had Stanford on its watch list for hackers who might go after patient medical records sitting on servers."

"Yeah, but the gap quickly widened between the sophistication of its own cyber division and cyber criminals."

"I was afraid you'd say that." Niles gripped his crossed arms, looking reflectively over the marina toward the drab bay.

Wagner knew that millions of banks, particularly in small towns, were dangerously exposed to similar forms of cyber attack that often resulted in theft. But the need to protect patient information was even greater than the need to protect financial data such as credit card numbers. Credit cards could be changed whereas a medical record keeps a patient's blood type and disease history.

A bay breeze blew in their faces. Wagner tugged on his cap, blocking wind. "Hideo's unreachable right now in Tokyo."

Niles shook his head. "Let's hope he's whooping it up because he did a bang up job with his CERN fundraiser, winning over hearts. Either way, we've gotta find whoever nicked these papers—before they go public and hurt our deal. The rumor mill is always turning. Knowlan is going to lose it when he hears about this."

Roger Knowlan was Stanford University's bioengineering department's mercenary program director.

"He's beyond my control. Anyway, we have to assume someone knows about our Google deal if they took the papers." Wagner leaned on the wooden rail trim as a foghorn wailed from a distant ship.

Niles stretched his gangly legs. "If they didn't know before last night, they know now. It would help to pinpoint who would benefit most from ruining the Stanford Project."

"That's the conundrum. Who wouldn't benefit from slowing genomics? And how do you winnow down the healthcare industry?"

The boat rocked over small swells while tethered to the dock. Niles's cap blew off his head. Wagner caught it and handed it back to him.

Wagner went on. "And we can’t just look at physicians and drug manufacturers here. This thing could go higher up the food chain."

"Higher?" Niles tightened the clasp on his cap and put it on again.

"Sure. Genomic medicine is going to topple the apple cart for health insurance providers."

Niles held his hat. "Won't health insurers profit from predictive medicine? They’ll love knowing their customers’ susceptibilities to disease."

"Maybe in the long term. But this business depends on actuarials spreading risk. Patients could take advantage of insurance companies. The insured could use medical information from a genomic counselor and keep it from insurers. Healthy consumers would cut back on their policies while others would increase coverage . . . it could devastate providers who are banking on its customers not knowing their predispositions."

Niles looked perplexed. "So what do we do?"

"Whatever it takes, Niles. Deals can be broken, just like we did with J&Q. We have to see that Google connects to Stanford as planned and doesn’t get spooked. I've already started to change key user accounts and password settings."

Niles took a long breath through his teeth, looking out over the marina again. "I don't know what else I can do, so I'm going to sail, damn it." He winched the halyard, raising the sail. The sail flapped in the wind until Niles cranked the mainsheet. "I hope this FBI of yours does something meaningful."

"Tell me about it."

Niles gave him a weighty stare. "Jude, whoever thinks they’re going to bring us down, they’re not going to succeed at this. We can't let them."

"I know that," Wagner said. "They’d have to kill me first."

Niles's cell phone rang to an incongruous hip hop mix. "Sorry, no," Niles said. "I didn't find time to read the business section of the paper today. Why don't you just read it to me if it's that important."

Niles listened. The words on the other end of the line didn't take long to sink in. Niles's face turned chalk white . . . an even paler shade than his usual British pallor.

Evidently Hideo Onagi had suffered a tragic incident.

Six

Saturday, October 30
Emeryville, CA

Mark Ferguson's corporate office in Emeryville resembled a plush high-rise apartment, complete with a private sitting room, bar and bathroom. With Pharma revenues sagging for Johnston & Quib, it smacked of excess. The CEO stepped out of his office shower after his morning run and dressed. Dreading his next meeting about Stanford, he quickly rubbed molding cream into his thick gray hair and patted cologne on his square jaw.

He and his staff worked too many Saturdays. Times were simpler when medical insurance shouldered more of the payment for prescription drugs. Just five years ago reporters had swooned over him. Journalists praised him as the Michael Jordan of drug manufacturers for his unlikely rise from a Pennsylvania steel worker family to the tough-minded pill producer they depicted him as today.

How could they forget that he'd spearheaded J&Qs' blockbuster drugs which earned over two billion dollars a year?

Launching a blockbuster drug was arguably the highest stake game in business. It cost a billion dollars to bring one to market; yet, one-size-fits all treatment could lose out as personalized medicine rapidly claimed the altar of healthcare.

Ferguson thought he had remedied J&Q's problems by teaming up with Stanford's corps of scientists, the new darlings in genomic medicine. Then Stanford had the gall to walk. Operating by his own rules, Ferguson had downplayed the repercussions to principal partner, Olivier Ramsey. It didn't help matters that Ramsey was schlepping from New York to size up his J&Q investment.

Ferguson looked out his window, removed a pill container from his pocket and swallowed a Xanax with a glass of water. Emeryville looked small against San Francisco. Remove the strip malls and high rises and Emeryville's only merit was its proximity to the Bay Bridge, feeding commuters into downtown San Francisco.

His desk phone rang. Setting down his water, Ferguson picked up line two.

Heather, with her breathy voice, told him Mr. Ramsey from Pinsky Capital was here.

"Send him in," Ferguson said to the executive assistant extraordinaire, the only person he confided in about his illness.

Wearing laundered jeans, a button down shirt and Gucci slip-ons, Olivier Ramsey didn't merely walk into Ferguson's office as much as he suddenly materialized. Like a ghost, he glided in toting a carry-on suitcase, wolfing down the last of a croissant.

Under thick eyeglasses, a cheerless line for a mouth cut across his gaunt face. A veteran of multiple bear markets, Ramsey embodied Wall Street.

A sickening indigestion came to Ferguson at the sight of Ramsey. "Did your plane come in early?" Ferguson said, perfunctorily shaking Ramsey's hand.

"Mercifully. There was hardly any cabin space to breathe." Ramsey's speech lacked any note of inflection.

Ferguson made a comment about how Internet price wars killed the airlines.

"Commercial airlines, not the private jets you ride." Ramsey wheeled his luggage to an upright position. More than ever, the New Yorker looked like a high-level accountant. His thinning hairline was combed straight back. He took the chair across the desk from Ferguson and turned it so it squared off directly opposite him.

"How's your daughter?" Ferguson asked, prolonging the pretense of pleasantries. Having a daughter was the one thing they had in common outside J&Q. It wouldn't stave off the third-degree for long though.

"Well enough. As patriotic as ever."

"If only mine hadn't just hacked off her brown hair," Ferguson said. "The bellhop look must be in style."

"Must be. Short is how my daughter wears it." Ramsey turned off his BlackBerry, ending their preamble. Ramsey, who'd been J&Q's primary investor from the beginning, had flown in early for Monday's board meeting—the strategy session that would surely set off a political firestorm. Ramsey had banked on the teaming up of J&Q and Stanford University.

"How's the drugstore?" Ramsey finally asked in his brusque Manhattan manner.

"We're pushing timelines with the Huntington's drug. The breast cancer product is still a champ."

Ramsey said, "But we've got our share of side-effects to worry about."

Ferguson knew that Ramsey, being a major financial backer, read the side-effect reports almost as religiously as he did . . . and for good reason. The man had built his legendary financial reputation on pumping up Pharma companies' profits.

"How is J&Q coping with the fallout with Stanford?" Ramsey asked.

Ferguson coughed. "We're moving along with R&D." Ferguson never opened his mouth until his talking points were sealed like a can of tuna. But there was no avoiding the truth. The Stanford team, with its revolutionary computational biology, held the promise of ushering J&Q into the new age of science. Ferguson had persuaded Olivier Ramsey's investment firm to pump $60 million more into J&Q with the promise it would have first access to the revolutionary genomics network.

Ramsey's nostrils flared. "Those ungrateful academics. Can't they see how controversial online diagnosis is? Could they be any blinder to the complexities of gene scanning?"

"I don't know about that," Ferguson said. "They succeeded at keeping their dream of Internet diagnosis quiet while they drummed up donations."

"That's your fault for not spotting this. We just naively believed that the Grid Project would only be an incubator . . . all that we had riding on that is finished."

Ferguson looked away. "Perhaps." *Thank God Ramsey was scheduled to fly back to New York Monday afternoon.*

Stanford's Grid Project was emerging as Big Pharma's greatest competitive threat, and Ferguson had cheered it on. Pharmaceutical giants faced the same specter that newspapers did: modernize or die. J&Q's 20-year monopoly on brand-name drugs was drying up. Drug giants struggled to justify the huge expense of developing and marketing them. Personalized medicine had started undercutting mass commercialization.

Ramsey snapped his ballpoint pen open and closed. "I have more worrying information. I managed to see email exchanges between Wagner and Google. Google is up to something big. They won approval for a diagnostic service running over the Stanford Grid. It could change medicine."

"Good God," Ferguson said.

Ramsey watched Ferguson absorb the meaning of this. "That's right. Google is becoming the information gatekeeper to a universal healthcare alternative, and it's ganging up with Stanford to push customized drugs."

Ferguson coughed again. Independent pharmacies had started compounding drugs—a normal practice before mass production of medicine became commonplace. "How did you come onto this Google report?"

Ramsey squinted. "Does it really matter?"

"Yes it matters."

"There's a key to every lock, and my sources can source anything."

Ferguson rolled his eyes, "Don't say another word."

Ramsey turned the end of his pen in his teeth. His body language said he wanted blood. "Jude Wagner's algorithm makes Stanford cocky. That Wagner is as slippery as a rope. You know how vulnerable J&Q is to bad press? Our pants are down in front of the world. We should have your best and brightest on this."

"Right. We'll get on that right after the board meeting while you're flying home."

Ramsey sniffed. "Change of plans. I've postponed my flight."

Ferguson's heart sank.

"Don't look surprised," Ramsey said tapping his watch. "I'm obviously going to be in your hair the whole damn week. J&Q is skating on thin ice."

Ferguson reached into his drawer for a granola bar, his cigarette substitute. He opened it and took a bite, reflecting. He didn't need to tell Ramsey how right he was.

* * *

Hunched at his notebook computer in the J&Q conference room, Olivier Ramsey wanted to hang someone. He blew flecks of dandruff from his keyboard. Sweat accumulated under his collar from frustration. He couldn't believe he'd persuaded his boss, Nicolette Pinsky, to sink millions into J&Q. This could cost him his reputation and his job. Ramsey was too easily won over by the promise of the newly formed partnership that J&Q had with the Stanford Grid Project—now he had Google to worry about with its online computer presence.

Thinking about those arrogant scientists at Stanford made Ramsey see red. He needed ideas on how to stall the Grid—specifics that could go into action tomorrow.

Had he known Stanford was going to pull out, he never would've invested so much in J&Q. Ramsey's boss, Nicolette Pinsky didn't suffer fools gladly.

Wiping his mouth, he readjusted his laptop screen. He typed and got a late report that J&Q's stock had been downgraded by equity analysts.

Blood warmed in his ears. Flipping through the sequence of events that led up to his investment, he couldn't believe his stupidity. He thumb-clicked his BlackBerry, searching to see if news had surfaced publicly about this Google deal. He read:

> Since Stanford University's Grid team cut its ties with former partner Johnston & Quib Pharmaceuticals based in Emeryville, California, they have allegedly been shopping for a new dance partner. Industry analysts say that if Stanford teamed up with a search engine provider, the two

could pool medical information across thousands of databases to fight disease.

-Associated Press

It's all going to hell! Ramsey scratched his dry scalp. He'd invested a fortune. He knew full well what he was up against: the dawn of computational biology—a molecular economy that would be to Pharma what the Internet and computers were to the record, movie and publishing industry in 1990—a digital revolution of devastating proportions, with no turning back.

He couldn't let the Grid's medical diagnostics be given away without showing Stanford what he was made of. If this thing snowballed it could bring down the entire industry. Ferguson, that out-of-touch old man, couldn't be counted on. He'd lost his cold-blooded nerve, his knack for making cutthroat calls. Ramsey turned to what he typically did when ideas failed him: he removed himself from his surroundings, went to a secluded place, and roamed the Internet.

Checking in to his Claremont Hotel room, he fastened the brass chain on his door. Ironically, he turned to Google—the biggest threat to him right now—to kick off his plan of attack. He booted his notebook computer and typed COMPUTER HACKING into his browser bar. A long menu of listings came up that meant nothing to Ramsey. He needed help to navigate this and fast.

Ramsey picked up his phone and dialed Pinsky Capital in New York. "It's Olivier Ramsey, calling from California."

"Yeah." Chuck, the around-the-clock IT guy, was a man of few words.

"Got an odd request. I need help. It's for Nicolette Pinsky. I need to interview a top shelf computer virus hacker. It's all legit." He lied.

After what seemed like a long pause, Chuck answered, "Hold on. I'll ping a buddy."

Waiting for Chuck, Ramsey signed into the Pinsky online bank account where he managed millions. He saw that two hundred and ninety thousand dollars of that sat in a slush fund that he authorized. If absolutely necessary, Ramsey would borrow from that.

Seven

Saturday, October 30
Berkeley, CA

Blood steadily drained from Niles's face on board the *Tipsea* at the Berkeley Marina. He stared blankly at his cell phone after ending his call.

The sail quietly lufted in the wind. Wagner broke his silence after eavesdropping on one end of Niles's strained phone conversation. "What . . . what happened?"

With a halting gaze, Niles said, "That was Roger on the phone. Hideo Onagi died."

Wagner's stomach lurched. "What!"

"Roger is texting me a link to the article." Niles still had a white knuckle-grip on his phone when it vibrated. He clicked into the new text message. They looked at the screen together:

> **"Genomic Science Industry Leader Dies**
>
> Hideo Onagi, Ph.D., Program Chief of the global human genome research project at Stanford University, was attacked and killed by two Akita Inus while strolling with his daughter in Kasai Rinkai Park in Tokyo. The animals' owner has not been located for comment."

The loss jolted Wagner's senses. For several moments, he didn't move a muscle. They had both grown close to Hideo Onagi.

Niles's sallow complexion hinted that he could vomit. He opened a bottle of spring water from the ice chest and swigged from it as if it were medicinal. "Want some?"

"No. A freak dog attack in a Tokyo park?" Wagner said. "What else?"

Niles added, "Knowlan got the call from Weller." Thomas Weller was their Bioengineering Department Chair. "Weller's panicked. Says he wants to keep this out of the press as much as possible until we link with Google."

"In a world with six billion people," Wagner said, "a one-in-a-billion shot is going to occur six times a day."

Niles cleared his throat. "I'm numb. And we have this meeting. I already know who will end up filling in for Hideo." Hideo had solely arranged the logistics meeting with Google and CERN.

"You can do this," Wagner said. "And you will have to instill confidence in them."

"You mean while I'm jumping through hoops of fire like a trained terrier? I think not."

"Hey! We obviously have to reassure Google and CERN that we can function without Hideo. They can't see emergency lights going off in your eyes."

"Do you work at being slow and pedantic or does it just come naturally?" Niles asked.

"Said the vain and bombastic Brit."

Niles squinted. "Tell me this. How on God's earth do we protect the Grid with all that's going on?"

Wagner rubbed his bruised cheek as the knock-on effect of this reverberated. "I'll redo passwords and access management rights again, then go over system logs. I want to find another means of protection—in case we're forced to give up passwords. Meanwhile, take every precaution to be safe."

"This is doing my head in, thinking about him being ripped apart by dogs," Niles said. "All we want to do is treat people with the Grid."

"So much intellectual capital, gone." Wagner reconsidered the article about Hideo. "It sounds like the dogs' owner vanished. Akitas killed someone. I don't get why the owner didn't stick around to explain, you know, fill out a report with the Tokyo police. To leave the scene is like a hit and run."

While Niles stood dazed, Wagner called Nathalie and informed her of the dog attack of their Program Chief.

"Merde. How*?"*

"He was mauled by Akitas in Tokyo," Wagner said. "I don't want to read into this, but it's hard not to—"

"Never dismiss your intuition," she said. "Lock everything down, okay. Relay this to your team too. A cyber attack could devastate your Grid network, but now you do not even have a chief."

"Yes, but we can't shutter the project. We always knew our Grid would draw out adversaries. To retreat as if we didn't expect pushback would be the same as lying to ourselves. We'd be fools to quit or change strategy."

"What strategy is that?" she said.

"To plow ahead faster than every other lab, as fast as is humanly possible. Please check out the police report in Tokyo."

Wagner's phone vibrated. "I have to go, Nathalie."

Wagner clicked off. He checked his email.

"I'm afraid to ask," Niles groaned.

"It's from a manager at CERN."

Niles crossed his arms. "Just tell me they're pinging us with excitement about our Google proposal."

Wagner read his phone screen. "Not quite. He's asking if we've heard from Jűrgen Hansen. Apparently Jűrgen pulled a no show to his Stanford Grid presentation with Hideo on Friday. His girlfriend has reported him missing to the Meyrin police."

Eight

Saturday, October 29
Berkeley, CA

Hunched over his notebook computer, Cez@r mindlessly brushed bread flakes from his desk after lunch. As always, he was signed into the IRC chat application. The computer window remained open at all times in the top quarter of his PC's screen, keeping him logged in to the darknet chatroom.

IRC was like CB radio, but on the Internet: a set of chat room channels where programmers and hackers convened for online talk. It was free and easy to install software with a username and password.

A new virtual attendee's name popped up in the display window on Cez@r's PC. RAMSEY had joined the scrolling lines of dialogue.

Cez@r observed the usual suspects in the virtual room broadcast. Then he saw, "I'M TRYING TO REACH CEZ@AR." Cez@r returned his message. "What do U want?"

"I HAVE A JOB," appeared from RAMSEY.

"We all have jobs, man," Cez@r typed.

"I NEED A JOB DONE."

"U want a contractor?"

"YES."

"Hold on."

Cez@r sent an instant message invitation, using a private notification window. "This is far more secure. Go ahead." Cez@r typed.

"I NEED SOMEONE WHO CAN CRASH A GRID NETWORK," flashed in a small box under the name RAMSEY.

"U need a top shelf hacker. Which grid?"

"STANFORD'S GRID."

Stanford's Grid wasn't on anyone's radar until reporters covered its negotiations with a Pharma company. Now, tech bloggers were going wild about it, touting that Stanford was pushing the Internet to new capabilities.

"U want to stall that??" Cez@r typed, skeptically.

"CAN YOU?" appeared on Cez@r's display.

Cez@r thought it over. "Impossible," he sent via the instant message box.

"I'LL PAY TOP DOLLAR."

"First, U don't crash it. You'd have to bring down the millions of machines that contribute work units. Even then, there's no taking it offline, short of dropping a bomb."

"WHAT COULD YOU DO FOR ME?"

"U can compromise that Grid by uploading something harmful to it. Hurt its credibility."

"OK."

"Volunteers link up to the network and share their computer processing power," Cez@r typed.

"RIGHT."

"We could stall the Grid if we do it right. But there are no guarantees. Sometimes even great viruses only have very temporary effects. Grids are decentralized—self checking."

"CAN YOU EXPLAIN?"

Cez@r could do more than explain. He gained control over systems with the drive of a heroin junkie. Like a one man army, he covertly scoured private computer networks for security holes. Sneaking past computer firewalls sent a tingling ripple through his fingertips.

He typed. "It goes like this. On a grid, a single work unit can't be trusted—results are computed outside of the grid's control. The grid sends the same work unit to many machines, maybe thousands. Results are compared for accuracy. If the answers match, that answer is accepted by the grid and it goes onto the next problem. If the answers aren't in synch, then that work unit must be re-computed, slowing overall progress. What I can do is flood the grid with hits—job requests."

"WHAT DO YOU MEAN HITS?"

"It's a form of DDoS."

DDoS—distributed denial-of-service attack—was a high tech ambush. It occurred when a malicious computer operator took control of scores of computers and used them as "zombies" to visit one website simultaneously.

Cez@ar continued, "I instruct thousands of bots to upload erroneous information to the Stanford Grid. If successful, the accuracy checking resources in the Grid will get so tied up trying to validate results against other computers that the entire Grid service will freeze."

"THINK I GET IT."

"The good news is even if we don't do lasting damage to the Grid, we could create a lasting scare. It could cause volunteers to quit donating their computer processing time. Security is critical to grid systems."

"TELL ME. CAN YOU DO THIS?"

A rush of adrenaline coursed through Cez@r while he searched the 'Net. "Wait."

"WHY?"

More time passed. "I see some talk about Stanford looking to partner up with a search engine company."

"I HEARD IT'S GOOGLE. IS THAT A PROBLEM?"

"Wow, possibly. If Stanford connects to Google, their security will tighten considerably. You have a window of opportunity here before that."

Unlike a university, Google had red teams—undercover penetration testers assessing the security of an organization—working around the clock. "Hang on."

Cez@r came back again. "I couldn't get any more info on the rumor. I can do this, but I need upfront payment. $300,000—not much 4 the key to the kingdom." Cez@r made it known that he clearly understood the magnitude of Ramsey's task.

"250,000 TOTAL."

There was delay.

"If u wire a retainer for $125,000," Cez@r typed, "I'm in."

"HOW CAN I BE ASSURED YOU'LL DO THIS?"

"I'm confident Google and Stanford are not linked yet. And my online reputation is worth more than $250 K. Do u need time?"

"I WANT TO MEET YOU FIRST."

"No deal. U could b a cyber cop. This is as big a leap of faith 4 me as it is 4 u." Cez@r realized this person might want to do some sort of background check on him. Under other circumstances, anyone would research the person they were doing business with. But if hackers prized themselves on anything, it was anonymity.

"OKAY."

"Then, deposit the $125 K into my e-Gold bank account from an offshore account—not from the U.S. The other half is due when I tell you."

"CONSIDER IT DONE. HOW DO WE PROCEED?"

"I phone U with the e-Gold bank account number."

"OK, BUT WHAT'S YOUR EMAIL ADDRESS?"

"Don't try to contact me."

"AGAIN, HOW DO I KNOW YOU WON'T RUN WITH THE MONEY?"

"Because I want the other $125 K. To get that, I can't stiff u. I have to earn it."

"PROVE WHAT YOU CAN DO."

"Go to www.squawvalleyusa.com."

"IT'S UP. NOW WHAT?"

"Check that same website in exactly ten minutes and then come back to our chat."

Cez@ar felt aroused with anticipation, tapping at his computer. He froze the site. When this RAMSEY person refreshed his link to www.squawvalleyusa.com, the browser would only show a white page with the text message: "This Page cannot be displayed."

"ARE YOU THERE? THE WEBSITE WON'T PULL UP. IMPRESSIVE," appeared in the chat session.

"You believe I'm for real now?"

"YES."

"Send payment one tomorrow. Nothing happens 'till then."

"BUT YOU DON'T HAVE MY DETAILS."

Cez@r left the room. A little worry and wonder goads business negotiations, especially in hacking. Leave them hungry was Cez@r's motto. In the span of this online chat, he'd already started sleuthing what he needed to know about Stanford. He didn't bother trying to understand how his latest client, RAMSEY, got hold of him or what drove him. He couldn't even be sure he was a he from their computer talk. That was white collar crime: go undetected.

Cez@r had gone from hacking to botmastering, from the dark side to the darkest. Big dollars guided him. A job in corporate America was never an option. Why should he desk jockey for some no-imagination capitalist tool, when you could be a solo manipulator? Botmasters made millions—they were the global subculture which even transcended the hacker underground.

Cez@r now worked on RAMSEY's payroll, but he wasn't anyone's acolyte. He was way beyond anyone's control. Ideas for worming his way into that Stanford bioengineering department already started percolating.

Nine

Sunday, October 30
San Francisco, CA

Sunday morning sun washed through bay windows in the living room of Wagner's apartment. He'd given up his bedroom for twin sister, Kate, and rolled off the sofa just after eight. His five-foot eleven frame ached from a night of tossing on the couch with violent pictures of killer Akitas reeled in his head. He grabbed his phone off his coffee table and texted Jűrgen. It didn't make sense that the CERN liaison had deserted Hideo: "Earth to Jűrgen. MIA or OK?" Wagner wasn't going to hold his breath for an answer. Instead, he would see what Nathalie could do to look into Jűrgen's mysterious disappearance.

Wagner poked his head around his bedroom door to find Kate listlessly unpacking things she'd been too tired to deal with the night before. Tennis highlights played on his bedroom TV.

His sporty sister endured some turbulent life change over the last three years. Her divorce paralyzed her. She now refused to date, all because she couldn't get pregnant with her fertility-doctor spouse, the egocentric prick. She lived out a Romeo and Juliet drama, barring the epic romance. After their marriage had crashed-and-burned, she gave up on her dreams of motherhood and traded it for teaching, and teaching exclusively.

Kate pulled out her book on the Dali Lama and absently thumbed through it.

"Is everything all right?" Wagner asked.

She moved wearily. "Yeah. I just resent the flight time it takes to see my traveling bro'."

She'd nicknamed Jude the traveling bro after his jaunts to Africa and Alaska—even before he'd transplanted himself to San Francisco. The thousands of miles between them changed their relationship. They never talked it over, but they'd lost the casual spontaneity they once had.

"Like some coffee?" he said.

Kate stretched. "If it's not too high octane. Tell me, are you still shrugging off long-term romance or is there someone special I should know about?"

"I'm on dating hiatus."

She chuckled. "How can you go on hiatus if you didn't have anything lasting to begin with? The male brain never ceases to amaze me." Kate clicked off the TV and tossed the remote on the bed.

Wagner ignored what Kate was doing and made them coffee. Aware of it or not, she filled in for their absent mother, ribbing him for his fleeting relationships. At least she didn't tell him off directly for being overly guarded about forming close bonds.

He returned to the bedroom with two cups.

Kate took hers and set it down to cool. "You know, I drove through the old neighborhood the other day and caught a scent that reminded me of you."

"Bourbon or barbeque?"

Her naturally beautiful face lit up with a smile. "Neither. The smell of freshly cut grass. It took me back to your hay fever attacks, how you suffered mowing the lawn. That's one chore that's off your hands, huh?"

"Yeah. Clearing the driveway of snow is another."

Picture album snapshots flooded his mind from Louisville, Kentucky days: building forts with blankets and ropes in the front yard for summer sleepovers under shedding birch trees. Diving off the family sailboat in the rain, racing Kate to the shore. Stealing away from home in the station wagon at age fifteen to ice-sled down the country club golf course.

Like it or not, they were both prone to sentimental journeys. The smell of garlic fries or even a Nirvana song had Jude reliving moments from decades back. Kate unpacked two pairs of jeans. "You get such tunnel-vision with your work. Do you have *any* buddies outside of Stanford?"

Wagner sat on edge of his bed, sipping his coffee.

"That's what I predicted. Living alone leads to brooding. You could broaden your social horizons."

"I'll think about it."

"What would you do without me?"

"Drift off course, I suppose."

No one but Kate could relate to his personal mission. After their mother's death, Jude had retreated to his PC . . . glued to the blue glow of his monitor week after week. In the twilight of his bedroom, he explored how the virtual reality of computers could help save people. Undoubtedly, it was a strange calling. Teenage boys weren't driven by causes that pounded on them with the force of a vendetta.

"You think you'll ever come back to Louisville?"

"Maybe one day," he said doubtfully.

Awkward pause. "Okay. Then tell me more about your break-in." A subject they'd only started yesterday when he picked her up at the airport.

"There's nothing else to tell. It was an isolated incident." If only he could really believe that.

"There's more to it than that, isn't there?"

"Yeah, they snatched important papers to an agreement we're working on. News we tried to keep private could leak."

"What news? You're being cagey with your own damn sister. What happens if your partnership comes together?"

Wagner had a feeling Kate might pry this whole discussion out of him. She was wise that way.

"The deal would connect our Grid to Google and usher big changes."

"Big changes for medicine."

"By offering a healthcare alternative. Google would extend Stanford's reach to millions of users. It would really shake up status quo medicine. Google would bring easy access to the Grid through its search engine website."

"Really?"

"Yes, Google would offer users a free, virtual, personal diagnostic lab; a one-stop data site where health information—medical history, lab results, hospital records and decoded genomes—could be stored for doctors' access. You could elect to have your data anonymously pooled for researchers. Google also enables more volunteers to donate idle computer processing power, making the Grid more powerful and accessible than anyone's wildest dreams."

"You make me feel very mainstream."

"And those who are already fighting illness would be the early adopters," he said.

"I hope losing papers doesn't wreak serious havoc."

"We do too." He cracked his knuckles.

She winced. "Still a knuckle popper, huh?"

"Don’t tell me. It gives you a glimpse under the hood. Apart from a little neck strain, my acupuncturist says I'm fine."

She shrugged, which preempted a battle of wills.

In a split second, he considered how jaded he’d grown until this break in. Nothing in the local news—from apartment fires to convenience store hold-ups—fazed him. But this home invasion keyed him up. She must’ve sensed it.

She re-laced one of her K-Swiss tennis shoes. "I don’t know how you do it."

"What?"

"Do the work you do. This project of yours has sparked some fierce debates. It makes you so unpopular."

"Risk nothing, gain nothing. I must like the pressure of detractors."

"I guess you do. Call me predictable, but no amount of money or status would tempt me to trade teaching for what you do. I've got to admire it, though. Silicon Valley is brimming with geeks half as talented as you—most of them focused on earning their millions and retiring by forty-five. That’s just not what you're about."

He grinned. "Money is important too. That living room is begging for new furniture."

"And I could use a down payment for a new house," she said.

"Why not, if we hit a homerun with Google?" She grinned.

"See, I think about it," he said. "Still, my primary motivation isn’t to be care free, but to be useful."

"That's got a ring to it . . . like a page out of my Dali Lama book." They sipped their coffee.

"Do you think you would ever be doing this, giving so much of yourself to genomic medicine if you never went to Kano?" She admired him for his year spent with the Peace Corp in Africa after college.

"Probably not." Even now, visualizing that spot in Nigeria made Wagner's stomach knot all over again. Wagner took a fresh button down shirt from his drawer, changed into it and finished his coffee.

She knelt down to her suitcase on the floor. "Brought something to show you." She unzipped a pocket, removed a charm bracelet and shook it. The silver Egyptian bracelet jingle created the most evocative sound. It was his mother's. Its charms played like mad in the wind on the boat that day before she died.

"Did Dad give that to you?"

"Yeah." Kate looked at the bracelet again. To Jude, it was worthy of a family time capsule. Neither one of them spoke another word about it while she put the bracelet away, grabbed her curling iron from the dresser and moved to the bathroom to plug it in.

Wagner's cell phone rang. He guessed from seeing GOVERNMENT OFFICE on his caller ID it was Special Agent Nathalie Noiret. He picked up. "What are you doing now?"

"Catching up with my sister who just came into town yesterday."

"Oh. Could you, uh, break away?"

"Why?"

"I don't want to say on the phone. It is urgent. Please, come to the office right away—I will have another guest pass waiting for you downstairs with security." She clicked off.

That was just what he didn't want for the day. It ticked him off how little free time he had for his sister. Still, a ton of work waited at the bureau and Hideo's recent dog mauling wasn't helping him relax.

"Sorry," Wagner told Kate. "I need to shove off."

"Don't apologize. I wanted some alone time in San Francisco too. Just being here is a vacation from my dull, work-at-home roommate who never leaves our apartment. I also have course material to email to my teaching sub."

"Well, good. Because there's a security issue with our Grid network and the jam up is only getting worse."

* * *

Kate finished unpacking her things from her case as Jude ran out the door. A scarf, sweats and underwear went into dresser drawers that he'd emptied for her stay. She removed her biology book from her suitcase too. She compulsively turned to the text to plan a future lecture. Bone tired, she longed to tell Jude about her breast cancer, but she didn't dare drop this on him now. She wanted to make the most of this visit. Why ruin it on her first day? Besides, she was busy with privately researching her disease. She walked to the kitchen, reconsidering telling him.

No one but she, and possibly Niles, got Jude's contrasting nature: his wrestler physique, quick reflexes, and strong jaw only touched the surface. Underneath this thirty-one-year-old exterior ticked an analytical obsessive. That was Jude the Gemini, blessed or cursed with a mind that rarely shutdown. A tester of boundaries, he yearned to change the world and himself.

For now, she would hold off on telling him that she'd inherited the disease that killed their mother. In the bathroom, she swallowed her prescribed anti-estrogen pill, her first for the day. Although she recently read literature that questioned its efficacy. For the hell of it, she took a pro-biotic pill from her toiletry bag, and swallowed it too.

Kate bargained with herself on her biopsy results to keep her mental health. *Can't let the doctor's report run rampant and destroy hope,* she told herself. She'd gone from initial despair to research mode. Nothing was off limits.

J&Q was the leader in breast cancer treatment. She'd hear its CEO speak on cutting-edge drugs in San Jose this Wednesday. This was research she planned. Somehow, she had to quell the invisible march of this insidious disease.

Ten

Sunday, October 30
San Francisco, CA

Jude Wagner hopped off a cable car, antsy to hear what Nathalie had to say. He hoofed it the rest of the way to the bureau at 450 Golden Gate. Through the double doors he went, back into the largest federal office building west of the Mississippi River. Inexplicably, passing through a metal detector began to feel less strange—like even a normal way to start his day. On a gut level, he'd warmed up to his reliance on the FBI to help the Grid. Leaving the brushed-metal elevator, Wagner and his escort traveled along the linoleum corridor that ran nearly a football field long. Down the corridor wooden plaques on the doors read: LABORATORY SERVICES, FINGERPRINTING, NATIONAL SECURITY.

The escort saw Wagner off after they passed the cubicles and entered a door marked ELECTRONIC SURVEILLANCE. In her office area, Special Agent Nathalie Noiret worked quietly at her overly varnished government desk. She'd put her sable hair into a French bun which revealed more of her oval face and swan neck. Teaming up with this French-Canadian enigma was testing his focus. He took the empty desk facing opposite hers, garnering energy for more mental whiplash.

Her fitted blouse accentuated her toned shoulders and her lean, petite gymnast body. Every inch of her feminine. She'd removed her jacket and folded it neatly on her desk. Had her desk been stationed in the cubicle farm, more eyes would have been on her than just Jude Wagner's.

He saw a quote on a post-it note which Nathalie had obviously stuck to the wall beside her computer: "When sorrows come, they come not single spies, but in battalions. —Hamlet."

"Cheerful."

"I'm glad you are here," she said, sounding distracted. "I have made a disturbing discovery."

"You're determined to make Shakespeare prophetic."

"What? No." She rubbed her chin in earnest. "I was examining the Hideo Onagi incident, scrolling through new cases in Interpol when I saw a name which struck me as familiar: Jűrgen Hansen. Do you work with him?"

"Yes, he's our CERN liaison. What, what about Jűrgen?"

She pointed at her computer screen.

Wagner came around to her side and read the terse entry from the CAP—Crime Against Persons—report on her monitor. *Swiss Police ballistics have evidence that CERN's Life Science Program Director, Jűrgen Hansen, sustained fatal gunfire. The body and firearm were recovered from Lake Geneva. Weapon used: Glock C18. Serial Number 154400-11-25.*

Wagner took a step back, stunned. *Everything was coming apart.* His Swiss colleague, dead? Only a few weeks ago he'd met up with Jűrgen in Palo Alto. Onagi held his latest come-to-Jesus Grid strategy meeting then, followed by toasts to how their partnership with Google would enable the Stanford project to grow by thousands of databases. Wagner felt light headed.

The door to ELECTRONIC SURVEILLANCE opened. Nathalie took the opportunity to step away to the cooler.

A supervisory agent whom Nathalie spoke of passed through the work area and continued on to Information Services.

Nathalie returned with a cup of water for Wagner. After finishing it, he crushed the paper cup. Jűrgen's death had to sink in. Had someone killed Jűrgen because he headed up genomics at CERN?

He stared out the window of the thirteenth floor where cars and people passed below in usual ebb and flow and detachment from the surroundings.

She came up to him and put a comforting hand on his arm.

Back at her desk area, she read aloud. "A local hiker, or rather his bird hound, followed a trail to Lake Geneva where the body was found. The body was fully clothed.

Caught off guard, he recoiled. "What else?"

Authorities found fishing line tied around an ankle. His wallet was missing. They had to identify him with the Rolex watch that was still on his wrist. Local police contacted the watch maker. He, in turn, got the name of the owner by referencing the serial number that was inscribed on it.

"Hansen had been shot 'Mozambique' style: two shots to the target's chest, then a third bullet in the center of the head. This is the shooting technique used by all elite U.S. military units, the Navy SEALS, Army Delta Force, and CIA Black Ops."

Wagner's throat went dry picturing the lakeside menagerie with uniformed men and emergency vehicles. A pristine setting of mountains and clean air. The idyllic spot was probably known for its pure water until a dead body was dredged up there.

"I did not know what to make of this," she added. "But I, uh, am acquainted with the weapon. I fired it at Quantico's range."

Wagner listened, but remained closed to consolation.

"The C18 is not issued to civilians. It'll empty its mag between 1100 and 1300 rounds per minute. I found that out for myself during training. Shooting the weapon at full-auto felt like turning on a firehouse hose. It bucked in my grip, ejecting a brass stream of spent casings. It is quite a responsibility, a gun like this."

The agent continued, pulling up her chair at her alcove desk area. "Only the United States FBI had a C18 with that serial number."

Wagner sat motionless, still in disbelief, contemplating how Jűrgen's CERN partnership with the Stanford Grid project had led to homicide. Jűrgen reminded Wagner of himself: a wild card, but a risk taker and a key player. The project wouldn't be the same without him.

Nathalie's desk phone rang and she picked up. It was a callback from a message she'd left with Interpol, requesting that an English speaking person contact her from the police station serving Kasai Rinkai Park.

A genteel woman's voice came on the line. "I am sorry for the delay, Noiret-San, but I had . . . a . . . to verify your badge number. I do, uh, have a statement. The eye witness to this canine attack was the victim's daughter."

"Oh, really."

"Yes, this girl insisted that her father's death was deliberate."

"Was there any evidence to support that, that the attack might have been directed by the dog's owner with the intention to kill Dr. Onagi?"

"What the girl said has not been, uh, substantiated."

Nathalie thanked the police representative and hung up the phone slowly. She relayed the daughter's claim to Wagner.

"Speaking directly to Hideo's daughter might help," he said. "But even if we could track down where they are staying, Hideo's wife would never grant us permission to speak to her daughter about this."

"Time to shift our energy," Nathalie said. She worked at her computer when an incredulous look fell over her. "That's not possible."

"What?"

She lowered her voice, "That Glock. The one that was used in the shooting death of Jűrgen Hansen."

"What about it?" Wagner asked, sitting up to uncramp his lower back from his night spent on a sofa.

"It's registered to this office."

* * *

Cez@r flipped to *Yahoo Finance News,* diligently carrying out his homework on the Stanford Grid team. Turns out these Stanford scientists had ruffled more than a few feathers recently when they severed ties with that CEO, Mark Ferguson, and his monster-of-a-pharmaceutical-company Johnston & Quib. *Those corporate schmucks get what they deserve.*

Cez@r never felt more alive in his parent's garage in Berkeley, working for his mysterious client. Previously, he opposed the idea of freezing computer processes. A campaign such as that went against his grain as a hacker. But that's when his goal was to merely gain entry. He'd moved on to stopping systems. That's where the psychic reward was; that's what made history. If Cez@r succeeded at stalling the Stanford Grid, he would have a claim to fame—priceless respect in the bot universe. That's serious street cred. You could hold a city government hostage with the threat of electronic destruction. He started thinking big, really big. From the Stanford website he found a photograph of Stanford's Bioengineering Program Director, Roger Knowlan. This was a man with access to the Grid. He was a person to follow.

Eleven

Sunday, October 30
San Francisco, CA

It was only nine a.m. and Jude Wagner and Special Agent Nathalie Noiret were already confronted with a new crisis—one which extended to Switzerland. Stationed in Nathalie's semi-private alcove area, Wagner worked to make sense of what she'd just read to him about that federal firearm. "I don't understand. How could that Glock be registered to this office? Surely the FBI didn't do this."

"It would not make sense," she said. "Still, it needs to be determined through the internal FBI investigation that could be underway."

Wagner dragged his hand through his hair. "These internal guys should come to me about this. I can help. I'm the only real computer person here who knows the Stanford Grid." He couldn't stop obsessing over how losing Jűrgen, in addition to Hideo, would hinder the Grid's progress. Jűrgen was Stanford's point of contact, connecting the CERN network to the bioengineering Grid.

"No," she said. "You won't get pulled into the investigation in any serious capacity if that's what you want. Incidents of corruption, such as this, will be held in strict confidence, within the ranks."

He wasn't getting a clear take on anything except his own frustration. He kept switching back to Jűrgen's and Hideo's presentation for backers at CERN. It would've been Hideo's last big push for the Grid project.

Questions nagged at Wagner. "If Big Pharma's revenues are threatened, why would some rogue FBI agent be complicit in murder? Everything is unraveling and we're here just watching it."

"I can say this," she said. "It looks like we've got more than one saboteur to profile. Whoever they are, they operate globally. They could have made Onagi's death appear like an accidental dog attack. Either way, these are no amateurs."

"What about this FBI-registered gun, what can we do?"

"Not much."

"Why?" He refused to just blot this out.

"Nothing about this will be standard operating procedure. The FBI cannot investigate one of their own. This would go to the Inspection Division and the OPR—Office of Professional Review."

Wagner hated the possibility of wasting time. He'd read in a detective novel that a case that wasn't solved in the first forty-eight hours only had a fifty percent chance of being cleared. It didn't sound like fiction.

"What if I volunteered information to OPR directly? I obviously know things about Jűrgen that OPR wouldn't."

"Good luck, okay. You can try to talk to Hackman about it. He might respect your directness. That reminds me, he asked me to fetch you when you came in."

"Then what are we waiting for?"

"Nothing. Just don't expect miracles."

Wagner had heard a similar caveat two weeks ago that was handed down from Hackman himself: *The main job of the FBI is to increase situation awareness and disseminate critical information to decision makers. Don't look at us as the Federal Bureau of Network Security.*

Wagner didn't have a good feeling about Hackman, the SAC—Special Agent in Charge who only discussed major matters face to face. He was a dour authority figure. Nathalie told Wagner that agents were in awe of Hackman's formidable U.S. Government past and that he delegated most things, making middle-men disseminate orders to his assets.

Nathalie lowered her voice. "There's a story to Hackman you should know." He leaned closer.

She cleared her throat. "I will tell you when we're away from here."

"Okay," Wagner said, pleased to hear that she was opening up to him. She'd very much kept to herself initially. In two weeks of working together, all he'd really deduced about her was that her aptitude and experience in mathematics and quantitative reasoning had moved her up the bureau ladder, making her a liaison between Tactical Intelligence and Cyber Intrusion.

"Anything else?" Wagner said, wondering if she might divulge any other useful tidbit.

Nathalie shook her head and promptly showed him to Hackman's SAC office.

"Yes, come in," said the Special Agent in Charge.

Wagner stepped three feet inside the office and glanced around the drab room with his line of vision stopping at Hackman. The large man was ensconced behind a mid-century mahogany desk with a wide-screen computer monitor. What appeared to be a Brooks Brothers suit jacket drooped on a coat stand in the corner.

Massive metal filing cabinets and leather high-back chairs gave off a law office air. The touches of decor in the room came from a 1940s wall calendar with stylized pastel illustrations of cruise liners and two polished dingy oars. The old oars hung crossed on the wall behind the boss's desk, bearing the word *Titanic*. Something about those paddles got under Wagner's skin. Could corruption run up the ranks of the FBI? He dismissed the notion as a haphazard reaction.

A magazine sat on Hackman's director's desk which caught Wagner's eye. The glossy cover showed the image of a high ranking Catholic figure, maybe a bishop. The Special Agent in Charge was still looking at his computer screen, clicking his mouse and tugging on his sideburns when he slowly spoke, "Ye—e—e—s. What is it you want?" Access to Hackman's inner sanctum was not a privilege afforded to many. The special nature of Wagner's computer expertise at Stanford opened doors for him—literally.

"I'd like to discuss something with you regarding my colleague in Switzerland, Sir."

"Does this involve CERN?"

"Yes."

"You're referring to Jűrgen Hansen. I saw that on the CAP report."

"You know about the homicide at Lake Geneva, in Switzerland?" Wagner said.

Hackman let go of his mouse and finally directed his focus to Wagner. "Did you know him well?"

"Well enough." The words didn't come out quickly.

"I'm very sorry."

Nathalie described Hackman's hair as nearly nonexistent. It looked as if heated machinations from his brain had steamed off everything above. Those grey-blue eyes of his examined Wagner as if he suffered an serious case of attention deficit disorder. "So, you know that he was shot with an FBI gun."

"That's right. An FBI-registered service weapon was found on the scene at Lake Geneva. Did you learn about that from Agent Noiret?"

"Yes."

Hackman looked irritated. "I see. It was stolen, by the way, and I have no assets in Geneva."

Wagner felt foolish, annoyed with himself for bringing it up. It had to be a major concern for Hackman already.

"That's why I'm swamped." The SAC shifted his upper body and pointed at a book that resembled an oversized ledger. "These armory books are in a shambles. It'll be days before I find out if that Glock was properly released to begin with. And I've already got the OPR riding me about it."

"Since I knew him, I could give the OPR valuable information—"

"First off," Hackman said in monotone, "I realize the vic could have something to do with your Stanford Grid because CERN is your business partner."

"Yes."

"Practically, though, a hack into your Stanford Grid and a homicide in a different country are two very different incidents. I agree that a tie in is in the realm of possibility. But I also understand CERN has more than one controversial project going at any given time, so there's no telling what the motives were." Hackman pulled on his sideburn.

"You may not have the total picture of our Grid."

"Go ahead, tell me what I'm missing."

"Genomic medicine analyzes a person's health predictively, showing which drug treatments would be optimal for one gene-type, including custom drugs. Traditional medicine, on the other hand, is evidence-based."

"Yeah."

"So the old way depends heavily on expensive clinical trials and lab tests. Since Stanford's healthcare project is non-profit, we're saving billions of dollars on commercial advertising and even more on clinical studies."

"And that means?"

"That means certain executives would panic to see custom drugs selling at a fraction of their one-size-fits all blockbusters, drugs that earned more than $234 billion a year."

"Interesting. But our focus is still on the here and now. We can safely connect your apartment break-in to Stanford, for example. Agent Noiret briefed me on that. That's a no brainer. By the way, my sympathies to your team for Hideo Onagi's accident. I'm sure that's going to take a toll." Hackman coughed. "You *are* making progress on tweaking that malware defender program we gave you?"

"Yes," Wagner gave lip service, too distracted to concentrate.

"Remember. You're here to protect information, not investigate. I'll determine if we have a body count to factor relating to Stanford."

Hackman exhaled in a way that said this conversation was prolonged already. "Bureau resources are limited—we don't pretend we can safeguard proprietary networks like yours. But with so much medical data at risk, we are committed to updating your security strategy. That notwithstanding, we don't know where your threat is coming from. Do we?"

"No Sir. The forensic analysts are still dissecting and tracing the hack."

"So clearly just walling off your Department's perimeter is inadequate—a moat around the castle isn't going to cut it. This cyber incident is too malicious. I realize you have an eight-day wait before you're joined with Google security."

"That's right, assuming they sign our deal."

"We need to bust our asses and stay focused then."

Wagner nodded, knowing there was no proven approach to protecting information. Hackman tapped his computer mouse. "Computer security is worthless if it isn't tailored properly to the network, or so I'm told. We've got too many moving parts. You've probably assumed that because I wouldn't have given you a temporary desk and called you in here if we didn't need you. Can you make any sense of our anti-virus methodologies?"

"Yes."

The boss handed Wagner a new guest visitor pass. "This'll give you another two weeks of access. Unquestionably, the nature of your work puts you under fire from skeptics. We can't detoxify that. The fact is your team renewed public expectations for the Genome Project, so the real burden of keeping your Grid safe falls on your department at Stanford, not the FBI."

"Okay. Excuse me, Sir—about Jűrgen Hansen, the program director for CERN. I had a working relationship with CERN for a long time and—"

"That might be of value as the investigation progresses. We'll have a list of persons of interest and those details aren't your concern. Keep your head down, Wagner. Everyone else here has agent responsibilities with a caseload to manage. You may not have boundaries at Stanford, but you've got 'em here." Hackman cleared his throat. "And do me a favor. Resist any temptation to be a detective . . . or hero."

Wagner returned to his desk, agitated and restless with the SAC's business-as-usual demeanor when so much needed reverse engineering. Wagner would've loved to believe that the FBI was up to the task. But the cynic in him couldn't cope with leaving that alone. It all looked like rote business process to him . . . a far cry from a real solution.

* * *

Scud was making a part-time career of researching Stanford's Grid developments sitting in her SUV. She'd parked in the Berkeley hills in a small dirt parking lot at the trailhead to a scenic path known as the fire trail. There, with her notebook computer cozily resting on her lap, she blended in with college coeds who favored the great outdoors to the campus library for a place to study. She surfed away using her cell phone for an Internet connection.

A tickler alert she'd created on the Stanford Grid fed her breaking stories. To her amazement today, she not only received fresh corporate scuttlebutt on Stanford, but leaked emails from Jude Wagner's computer. According to his Stanford missives, the Grid team was pushing a major add on to its alliance with CERN. It involved none other but Google. *Google!?*

Scud let out an audible groan. She scrolled through more leaked messages. By the looks of things, Hideo Onagi was previously scheduled to fly to Geneva to close the partnership on November 2. With Hideo gone, who would fill in for him? Wagner was scrambling with the FBI. This only left two candidates, Roger Knowlan and Niles Tully. Scud texted her bounty hunter about this.

A helpful one sentence reply returned. "Since Knowlan and Tully work in the same office, I should be able to stick to these two like transparent glue."

Twelve

Monday, October 31
San Francisco, CA

Jude Wagner made his way back to Nathalie's alcove desk, stymied after his meeting with SAC Alexander Hackman. A voice in his head warned that doing anything half-cocked would surely backfire. His instincts and luck were pitted against FBI rules and regulation. A bile taste rose from his stomach. The idea of leaving these matters to others nauseated him, and blind trust amounted to deliberate negligence. He took a seat, pissed off with how the powers-that-be had told him to sit tight and stay in the background. He'd gladly comply if that would bring more data points to light. The pragmatic side of him couldn't buy it.

Nathalie gracefully strode off from her alcove area to Information Services. Wagner watched her as she turned the corner. Just then Supervisory Agent Warren Speer made his way over in his bland suit and red rep tie. Nathalie had told Wagner about this man whom they'd crossed in the hallways. Agent Speer headed up the Criminal Division and Organized Crime. Tall and cocky, Speer sniggered at Wagner. He had caught Wagner admiring Nathalie from behind.

"Here's our subject matter expert in action," Speer said.

Wagner barely looked up. He owned office furniture more animated than this company man and more refined too. Speer's receding chin oddly matched his deeply set eyes—his whole demeanor was distrustful.

"If you've got eyes for Agent Noiret," Speer said, "I'll save you energy. She's an emotional wreck from being ditched a month ago."

"Is that a fact?"

"Not much remains secret around here."

"I bet. It's like one happy family."

A rude grin crept across Speer's face. "You think you've got a Chinaman's chance with her?"

Wagner stood and laughed him off.

"I hear you're slicker than shit off a shovel," Speer said. "I look forward to seeing if you can add anything to our knowledge base of cyber corruption."

"Yeah, sure."

Speer smirked and turned.

Too busy to dwell on the supervisory agent's government-issued personality, Wagner started reviewing his network blueprint.

Nathalie returned to her desk. "What did Hackman say?"

"He ordered that I leave the investigation alone and steer clear of that side of things altogether," Wagner whispered.

"I thought so. We are working under his roof."

"Well, he's not my landlord and I don't respond well to gag orders."

"I can see that," she said impassively.

"Especially since I have a greater awareness of possible motives for this homicide than anyone else in the FBI. They can't deny that."

"No they can't and I am perplexed by how they are doing things."

"Good," he said.

She leaned closer. "I agree that there are circumstances when a person should circumvent authority. That is why we must work together, but discreetly. The unemployment rate is high enough without me adding to statistics."

It came as relief that Nathalie took a different view. He'd only had one round of questioning with the Cyber Supervisor and he summarily reminded Wagner that as a civilian he was privileged just receiving help with anti-virus preparedness from an FBI forensic examiner.

At the very least, Wagner was glad he'd been able to convince his interviewers that the Grid project was controversial—even threatening—to some. It's impact on healthcare had the potential to be seismic. The Stanford Grid could interpret a person's genome so precisely that a doctor could log onto Stanford's database and know exactly which drugs to avoid and which ones to recommend for a particular disease. This would profoundly reduce misprescriptions.

At Wagner's prompting, Nathalie called the American Embassy in Bern, Switzerland. She was transferred to the captain of Geneva police, Agent Fluhr.

Wagner sat across from her, listening intently.

After a short conversation, Nathalie set down her phone. "That is what I thought."

"What?"

"It will take time to get new information. Homicides committed outdoors versus indoors are a challenge to investigate. Neighbors can't be interviewed; rooms can't be examined for footprints or traces of DNA."

Hackman trudged toward them.

Wagner turned to his laptop computer.

Hackman gave Wagner a suspicious glare and continued plodding past the open door to Electronic Surveillance and toward the elevator.

"So, what next?" Wagner asked Nathalie.

"Hackman's gone to lunch, okay. In two minutes, follow me to the Crime Lab."

Nathalie led Wagner into the Crime Lab. The space, with ventilation ducts crisscrossing the ceiling, had various forensic analysis stations for technicians and lab assistants. Each station had its own work bench and instruments that were designated for handling evidence. In a few seconds Nathalie pressed Wagner's thumb and index finger into an ink pad, creating a copy of his own prints for comparison. "I want to see what prints I can find beside yours."

She pulled gloves from a drawer and put them on. She carefully removed his hard drive from its zip-locked bag. With him watching, she grabbed a spray bottle from the laboratory fingerprint kit and pumped it three times, covering the computer drive in ninhydrin. Her hands moved with finesse, like those of a surgeon.

She took a long lighter from the fingerprint kit and passed the flame an inch from the hard drive, allowing the heat to bring out any ridges in the ninhydrin. She picked up the black powder and dusted the hard drive with it.

Raising her brown sphinx eyes, she examined the metal casing of the drive for bifurcations using a magnifying glass and let him do the same.

"It’s a lot of dirt and grimy smudges. The surface texture of this porous metal is bad for prints also."

“So you've got nothing on this mystery man?" he asked.

She returned an adamant expression.

Wagner pictured his thug and vaguely recalled leather gloves poking from one of his pockets. Another dead end.

She handed him his hard drive.

Walking back to her desk, she turned, "You still don't have any clues who would want to break in?"

"I'm racking my brain for answers, believe me."

"On the subject of intruders," she said, "Hackman is giving me a new ticket on Cyber Intrusion, involving Internet terrorist chatter . . . something political is going on. He’s been talking behind closed doors. I can just see him in that office, pulling on what’s left of his sideburns. I am digging up more questions to run through with you after I speak with the analysts and forensic investigators again."

"Good. I’ll be on standby," he said.

"I have to say that the energy is strange in the office today. Tense for Monday."

"Why would that be?"

Nathalie folded her arms. "I noticed a lot of whispering this morning when file clerks and agents came in."

"Whispering?"

"There is talk about you. Speer is, how do you say—handicapping you." She stumbled with her pronunciation.

"What?"

"Speer bet Hackman was going to shut you out. He thinks this so-called threat to your Stanford Grid is nothing more than a resource hog."

Wagner wasn't shocked.

Nathalie added, "I wouldn't be too worried. Hackman must know how important this Grid is with your computer breakthrough in the news. And Speer jumps on these things like a housefly. I am sure that spotlight of attention on you—the outsider—is just too much for him."

Wagner had heard too many of those news reports himself: *His algorithm discovery promised to change medicine forever.* The few times he was mentioned on TV, he'd changed the channel; and he wasn't surprised to run into personality differences here, in this law enforcement world; and Speer, who was close to Wagner's age, had a smug entitlement. It presumably came with his supervisor title.

"Speer obviously sees himself as the office watchdog," Wagner said.

She nodded. "He's big on authority and can be a shit."

"I need a change of scenery."

She escorted him toward the elevator, through the hallway and past the library. He followed.

"Let's reconvene after lunch," she said.

"Join me. We could speculate over oysters," Wagner added, aware of their aphrodisiac effect. As the words came out of his mouth, he wondered if it came across as a come on.

"If a dinner of mollusks is what it takes to penetrate your shell, then yes."

"Calling me distant?"

"Didn't you tell me you've been an island half your life?"

"No. You're imagining it."

A probing look came over her that he couldn't interpret. Her bangs fell into her eyes, like birch leaves fanning finger lakes. She grinned. "Just don't try to read meaning into everything I say, okay?"

They walked toward the elevator, side-by-side, quietly carrying on their private conversation. Still, he couldn't decipher how she felt about their working together.

Speer turned from around the bookcase aisle, wide eyed. "Wagner, I told you. She's earning a salary here."

Wagner sighed.

"Lighten up, will you?" Nathalie told Speer, as he was moving toward them down the hallway.

"Hey, we all watch out for each other," Speer said.

"Especially me because I'm the lone female. Well, believe it or not, I can work without adult supervision."

Speer gave a phony laugh like a mule while Wagner walked ahead to the elevator and pressed the button. It would not help anyone's cause for Wagner to lose his temper here.

Outside the building he turned his attention to Jűrgen's murder. He had to take action. He weighed how Jűrgen's death could relate to the paramilitary intruder who'd paid him a visit Friday night. No one could say for sure that the two incidents were connected, but Wagner imagined they were.

He had to think carefully about the guy who broke into his place. But it would be futile to have someone dust for prints at his apartment—there were just too many surfaces where visitors could've left prints innocently, and Wagner was pretty confident he recalled seeing the intruder with gloves. Using his cell, he hit speed dial.

Quick to answer, Niles said he couldn't meet them for lunch today, but he offered Jude a lift home at the end of the day.

"Fine," Wagner said, gazing at the overcast sky.

"In the meantime, check out that restaurant I mentioned."

"Café Flore, on Market Street?"

"That's it." Niles hung up.

Wagner was putting his phone away when Nathalie tapped him on the shoulder from behind. She looked at him with a foolish grin. With so much darkness around him, Nathalie's fresh face lightened things up.

"Café Flore doesn't have oysters," she said, "but some colorful surprises will surely be there on Halloween."

"I'd be happy if it didn't live up to that. A boring and predictable diner would suit me just fine."

She rolled her eyes while he caught the eye of a cab driver.

Thirteen

Monday, October 31
San Francisco, CA

Wagner and Nathalie took a patio table at the bustling restaurant on Market Street that smelled of mac ‘n cheese. The customers in costume and drag gave the place a street-fair, circus vibe. Those not in costume wore tight denim and every variety of leather jacket. Wagner unbuttoned the second button on his open collar shirt. In his dark gabardine trousers and herringbone jacket he'd more than done his part to blend in with the feds, but here in the Castro District those who dressed conservative radically defied the norm.

Then it hit him; Niles’s recommendation of this spot was his practical joke. Café Flore was as gay a restaurant as they come. The long-windowed café looked to be a proud Castro Street landmark. Leave it to San Francisco to have a progressive lesbian and gay neighborhood right next door to conservative Nob Hill. Nob Hill still maintained gentlemen's and ladies’ clubs as sacred.

Wagner grinned.

"What’s so funny?" Nathalie asked in her bolero jacket with epaulets, ready to go on war assignment like a devoted news correspondent. "Is it the fact that I’m practically the only woman here? If that’s it, I don’t mind."

"We just stand out, I think."

"Really, on Halloween?"

The place had an informal, European café feel. They had found a seat at the busiest time of day.

A waiter in need of a shave took their orders.

Wagner decided he'd put off talk about Jűrgen for later.

“You must think our office is dysfunctional," she said. "You can see why I don't partake in the after work drink on Friday."

"It’s not the most personable crowd."

"Apart from me, no?"

"Yes, apart from you."

He felt a tinge of powerlessness at the unspoken boundaries of their work relationship. But suddenly she no longer kept him at professional arm’s distance. It was good to be away from the bureau office . . . a place with the warmth of a mental institution. He felt himself battling to get to know her personally while they looked after Stanford's cyber security. "How did you come into this line of work?"

She cleared her throat. "You won't believe it. It started when I was age fourteen." That was only a year before Wagner's mother died and when his world had changed. "It's when I found my adoption papers," she said. "At that point, I felt that my whole life history was a lie. But it nudged me into action. It forced me to ask questions about myself, sort of led me into this profession." Her burgundy lips formed her consonants with the light precision of a pianist. Her French accent had a power of its own.

She continued, "After finding my adoption agency, I visited City Hall. The Office of Vital Records," she said with irritation, mocking its importance. "Anyway, I searched for my biological parents, but I was having a hard time. No one would help. But I couldn’t quit, you-know. I had to find my true identity. I sifted through records and learned that I was born in the U.S. and my mother lived in Quebec. I called her, although she refused to see me. She couldn’t tell me where my father lived. I still have not located him."

She seemed to know what he was thinking. "Don’t be sorry," she said. "All that shaped who I am today. One always goes back to one's roots. That discovery motivated me. Since my birth mother and I were born in the U.S., I was able to go to college in New York, at Columbia and live in the lower forty-eight."

"And you still go back to Canada?"

"Yes, to unplug. Now, tell me more about your inventive algorithm. Your *cause célèbre*."

"The algorithm has really opened up the bottleneck. It's making analysis much, much faster. The new science makes popular medicine appear obsolete—like sixteenth-century blood-letting through leeches."

She said, "You're so driven about this. Whatever got you started?"

Between bites of his *croque monsieur*, Wagner described how he and Niles had met at Berkeley, doing a job that isolated them: working at the Search for Extra-Terrestrial Intelligence project—SETI. At the time, SETI@home was the largest grid in the world, connecting five million computers. The computers scanned information that was received from the world's largest telescope in Arecibo, Puerto Rico, scouring for light patterns or signals that might point to life in space.

The problem was that the SETI computers were bottlenecked by the sheer volume of data hitting the telescope. Wagner set out to develop a solution. Eleven months later, he had designed an algorithm that mathematically uncorked the SETI grid, letting data flow.

She bit into her shiitake mushroom-cashew burger again. "But you're no longer searching for ET, is that not so? And neither is Niles, the friend you told me you went to school with?"

"Right."

"*Je me souviens*. I remember. It's the motto on the Quebec license plate." She gave an angelic smile.

"Yes. Niles is my impetuous Grid partner. Stanford hired both of us from Berkeley, where we used the Grid to search outer space. We're doing the same work we did at SETI, only searching through data at the molecular level."

"So, where does healthcare come in?" she asked.

Wagner's thoughts wandered to Hideo for some reason. "The medical world faces the same data-sifting dilemma that SETI did."

Nathalie sipped Calistoga, a glint of excitement in her eyes. "But with computer processing speeds practically doubling every year, getting ahead of disease is just a function of time."

"Time and incredibly complex analysis, which is all dawning now." Wagner was pleased to have her ear.

She nodded, energized. "It's quite avant-garde."

"The Grid wouldn't address day-to-day emergencies like broken arms, cuts, burns, or baby deliveries," Or homicides, either, he thought, remembering Jűrgen with a shudder.

"But it would be the ultimate diagnostic and treatment tool for long-term problems like heart disease, stroke, cancer, and more."

"And rivals might want to protect their scientific territory, no?"

"I think so. As far as turf wars go, this was primed to go nuclear."

"So who loses the most money from this breakthrough?"

"Big Pharma and insurance companies for starters. But this is revolutionary. It'll impact doctor's offices across the whole United States."

That mathematical mind of hers wouldn't let their conversation rest. The Grid's potential appeared to be crystallizing for her; she tapped her chin with her index finger.

Another question struck her about Stanford's genomic medicine therapy. "I think it's going to take lawsuits to compel drug companies to modernize," she said. "People will have to sue insurers to get personalized drug therapy paid for."

"Maybe so, but individualized treatment is fast becoming the standard rather than the exception."

Wagner heard a plate smash in the kitchen. He saw a waiter apologizing to someone.

As they finished their sandwiches, he was heartened to have such an avid listener. It helped with all that weighed on Stanford's Bioengineering Department. She looked as ready to get back to work on this as he was. When they got up to leave, he caught the peek of her cleavage showing between buttons. Blinders could've come in handy. Then again, all his senses needed to work double duty on this excursion into obscure territory.

* * *

Still planted in his computer chair in the Berkeley garage, Cez@r drafted a plan for his new malware program. Armed with nothing but his PC, he put his talents to work—certain that he could stall the Stanford Grid. He'd come light-years from his hacking days of digital-freedom fighting . . . humiliating authority. Crippling the Grid would put his stamp on the all-holy Internet. It would blow away those who just exposed corporate arrogance and governmental complacency. He didn't give a shit if his ends justified his means. If he ever got pinched, he had his defense memorized: *penetration testing does everyone a favor. When a bank claimed their systems were foolproof, one solid attack proved their incompetence. Society needs such teachers—it cleanses the world of hubris. Guys like me improve things, forcing better technology, adding value to society. What some call jail breaking I call making information open source so more can better understand how things work.*

Truthfully, Cez@r no longer cared about this hacker credo crap. He'd moved on from outsmarting barriers to private networks to threatening to blow up things, like freezing vital institutional websites. Cez@r's hobby started when he became a licensed radio operator. The airwaves put him onto the binary universe. He taught himself until he broke into the U.S. Defense Information Systems Agency. That's when the tall, lean, uncouth, twenty-three-year-old Cez@r, plugging away in his garage, took control of several systems for over thirty days. He'd even downloaded propriety software which ran their networking equipment.

His parents, with their patronizing smiles, stereotyped him as an outcast sitting at home. According to them, Cez@r's computer was pure escapism, a tree house for a misfit. They took their son for having Asperger's syndrome. They got it all wrong, and how would they be any wiser with his money hidden in an offshore account. Silicon chips were the pulsing neurons of modern man, and young Cez@r, armed with the skill-set of a super criminal, could command them like killer locusts. Each computer intrusion job grew bigger and riskier . . . an opiate to creative nonconformists like Cez@r and his keyboard class. Racing ahead of the law was the chase; overcoming boundaries, the challenge.

Fourteen

Monday, October 31
San Francisco Bureau

Reeking of fast food hamburgers, the cab back to the office didn't miss a bump or rut in the weary city streets of San Francisco. In the backseat, Nathalie's dark eyes still sparkled with curiosity and mesmerizing focus. She glanced at him, then out her half open window.

Wagner said, "I'll fill in the other blanks to the Grid if you give me Alexander Hackman's story."

Nathalie grinned, buzzed her window up and lowered her voice. "Hackman was the intelligence czar who ran the National Reconnaissance Office in Chantilly, Virginia for years and years. He spearheaded the reconnaissance satellites program and made the National Reconnaissance Office vital to the armed forces. He masterminded the "eye in the sky." Eventually, he was demoted to SAC in San Francisco. I heard it's because he handled professional misunderstandings as if they were personal attacks."

The taxi hit a pothole that rocked the car and jostled them. Nathalie strapped on her seatbelt and continued, "Just, uh, watch your step around him and respect our protocol."

Wagner thought about his prickly talk with Hackman.

"I heard something else," she said. "The field office is under professional review."

"And that means?"

Nathalie couldn't keep this one quiet about her boss either. "Hackman received written censure, of some sort, for noncompliance. I heard he mismanaged an FBI subcontractor organization. It is likely DeltaCorp."

"DeltaCorp?" Wagner had heard the name DeltaCorp mentioned but didn't know specifics. He primarily associated private security companies with the military. The Department of Defense had spent some sixty billion dollars on PSCs since the United States invaded Afghanistan. Big wartime business. "So what does this mean for your office if he did mismanage DeltaCorp Security?"

"Office of Professional Review—OPR—could put in oversight mechanisms. The way things go round here, we may never hear our dirty details."

He didn't know what an oversight mechanism was or what bureau contractors might do, but he decided not to delve into FBI process all at once.

"I'll be looking into a threat. It could have something to do with your Stanford University."

"What kind of threat?"

"I don't know yet," she said. "Hackman is preoccupied with justifying his delegation of duties and he left me in the dark. There could be suspects we never expect."

"Okay," he said reluctantly.

She twirled a strand of her lustrous hair back in place after it came loose from her French bun. "I do see how improving medicine became your *raison d'être*, but I am curious how this squares with the FDA?"

"The FDA doesn't impose the same clinical regulations on such precise diagnosis. The whole predictive drug discovery process of genomic medicine bears a much lighter burden for proving its safety."

Nathalie's cell phone vibrated. She looked at a message. "It's an email from the Swiss attaché. Meyrin police are pulling photos from a limo security camera."

They couldn't actually see the driver who transported Jűrgen Hansen to CERN. He or she had taped over the lens. But while the lens was being masked, one image was captured. Enlarged, the photo showed an inscription on a pen which the driver carried in his jacket pocket.

Nathalie looked at her phone. "The captain says there are minute markings on the pen shaft."

Wagner listened intently. "What else?"

"The captain says, 'It was an onerous task. The heavily used pen caused the matte plastic surface of the gold embossing to fade. The first two words are illegible. For the last, we have, -OMP-NY.'"

“The last word is obviously COMPANY," he said.

"That makes for one baby step," she said, getting out of the taxi. She put her hand on his arm. "Not to worry. Working as partners, we will make twice as many baby steps."

"Is that what we are, partners?" He wondered what she implied by that exactly.

* * *

At the foot of the federal building, Wagner waited impatiently for Niles's lift home. He'd made frantic progress studying the latest anti-virus strategies for defending against attackers. Through the afternoon, he dug into the bureau's machine-learning program that could detect unauthorized executable code. The program was becoming familiar to him. It contained a computer agent that could be distributed across a grid network to contain malicious software.

Considering who might be a suspect, he glanced back at his temporary place of work: copper-colored window frames ran in geometric tracks across a monolithic slab above a sidewalk smelling of stale beer. The generic entrance could've used something inspiring . . . maybe some engraved quotations or sculpture of Justice with her scales. Clocking in here was a strange detour from Stanford, and he wouldn't be able to relax into his planned dinner with Kate with Jűrgen on his mind.

Wagner wondered how much of this high-pressure city existence had he brought on himself—quite a bit, to be fair. He refused to join his father's family engineering business, and when his college acceptance came, he packed up his Honda Civic for Berkeley, California. Wagner recalled his father's reaction with bristling clarity. 'Jude, you're on your own with this *Huck Finn* escape from responsibility.' Dad had always been the family’s anchor who made the rules. Jude's mom, the sail. Jude longed to become his own captain.

Wagner took to Berkeley like bamboo does to a dousing of Miracle Grow. He rooted himself in computer studies. His idea for how he'd fight cancer crystallized in a biology lecture with what his alluring Columbian instructor said.

> *The genome holds four billion years of information on humanity. Sequencing it was supposed to help cure disease. But when scientists decoded the genome, they merely replaced a biological puzzle with a computer one. One person every minute still dies from cancer in America because scientists understand less than three percent of it.*

He woke up from the Latina-teacher-student-role-play fantasy as her lecture became her soapbox. Wagner wondered what it would take to unlock the power of the genome? Whatever it was, on some cellular level, he vowed to do just that.

Science needed obsessive computer types such as Jude to crack the code to diseases like the one that shortened his youth. Every signpost resolved into a meaningful life picture. The kaleidoscopic confusion of his mother's death vanished.

Big changes had happened since that lecture. Wagner turned to the stopped traffic where a double bus spouted exhaust. A car horn blared—typical commuter road rage. His watch showed 5:45 p.m. White clouds overhead scudded along, adding to a fog bank in the west. A few yards away, a stray seagull pecked at a flapping pigeon in the street. The wind shifted and a foul smell blew by. Wagner weighed how tough it would be for anyone to piece together who had killed Jűrgen in a remote area of Switzerland. Only scant photographic evidence had turned up.

Far more questions swirled than even hazy answers. Jűrgen had boasted by email about his new wild-child girlfriend called Tatiana. Maybe Tatiana knew something, but she'd already told the cops her story. Ultimately, whoever was pulling strings to both Wagner's break-in and Jűrgen's death in Switzerland would have to be highly motivated, organized and threatened by the Grid project—especially if Hideo's death wasn't an accident.

Niles's racing green BMW emerged from the line of stop-and-go commuter traffic and swung to the curb. The beat of techno music blared from his car. Wagner slid into the passenger seat.

Niles flicked the last of his cigarette out the window. "I don't know why San Francisco doesn't have a congestion charge like they do in London." He wended back into the rush hour snarl. "What's the urgent news you have to download?" Niles turned down his stereo. "Any leads on that break-in at your apartment?"

Wagner scratched his head. "Let's get out of this traffic. Take a longer route. Kate's at my place, probably reading. I want to talk in private."

Niles huffed, continuing their course.

Wagner gazed out the passenger-side window. A helmeted mother pedaled a bicycle alongside them. A child rode in a framed pack on her back. She cranked away, taking them up California Street.

Wagner said, "Very bad news. Jűrgen is dead. Homicide."

Niles swerved, nearly crashing into the cyclist.

"Look out!" Wagner shouted.

The bicycle woman jerked away. As Niles corrected back to his lane, she flipped him the finger.

"Murdered?" Niles turned to Wagner.

"Yes, pull over and park somewhere."

Niles turned off the stereo. "Why?"

"I can't talk to you while you're driving."

Niles drove a few more blocks until he found parking on the tip top of Nob Hill. They climbed out into a biting wind between Grace Cathedral and the Masonic Center, edifices vying for attention. Wagner kept walking the exclusive hilltop street without sensing any spiritual brotherhood for his fellow man.

In the "Wild West" days, the top of Nob Hill was home to the four railroad barons of the Central Pacific Rail Line—C.P. Huntington, Leland Stanford, Mark Hopkins, and Charles Crocker, the Big Four. All of those mansions were gone, but Nob Hill still represented power and wealth.

Tonight, with gray, brooding skies and the icy San Francisco wind at Wagner's back, the surroundings resembled a location from Hitchcock's *Vertigo*.

The force of wind pressed their trousers to their legs. "Go on. Tell me what happened," Niles said.

"Jűrgen was shot and found in Lake Geneva." Wagner started relaying what little he'd learned.

Niles adjusted his wire-rim glasses. "Any idea who did it?"

"All I know is that his killer used an FBI automatic."

"FBI?"

"Yes, if you can believe that."

"I can't. This is damned serious. Should we notify San Francisco police?"

Wagner dragged his hand through his hair. "It wouldn't help. Police jurisdiction keeps them from touching a crime committed overseas. And my break-in would never make it to police homicide squad's radar."

"So, what next?" Niles couldn't contain himself.

"I'm working on a plan, but agent Noiret has to drive this."

"I hope her tight body, which she undoubtedly has, isn't driving you. What about her boss?"

Equally as irritated, Wagner explained how the FBI honcho had shut him down. "A big part of this investigation is being handled by what's called the Office of Professional Review."

"Okay. Couldn't *you* go to this Review Office? Tell them what you know about Jűrgen?"

"I wouldn't even get the chance to have them laugh in my face. This is strictly internal. The bureau boss is tougher than a two-dollar steak."

"Well, while you're sussing this out quietly with the agent, you should remember that you don't have infinite CPU power in that head of yours. The stress alone from this thing might kill us. Maybe these events are signs to cool off. Discretion is the greatest part of valor."

"Hang on. Do you doubt what we're doing? If we believe we're sunk, we're history or so you've told me. What happened to your laws of attraction talk?"

Niles looked worked up. "Get on with it. We're talking about murder and robbery at your place. No one's looking out for us!"

"Then find us body guards. I'm not stopping you."

"I looked into that," Niles said. "They're called security specialists these days and for protection against getting a bullet in your head they charge $2500 a day."

"Okay then. Now we're back to formulating theories. We're up against big schemes. We need to anticipate the next brazen thing." Niles tugged on his wire glasses frame.

Wagner ruminated, well aware that more controversy would stir up once news outlets picked up that Stanford had signed a deal with Google. Surely, the press would report how this big alliance threatened traditional Pharma. The mood for medical revolution was palpable. The cost of healthcare kept rising in the U.S. as the quality of treatment kept slipping. "I'm working as closely as I can with this agent Noiret. Will you tell Knowlan about Jűrgen?"

"Why me?" Niles asked.

"It would be helpful."

Niles gritted his teeth. "And two days ago, I thought we were making stunning progress with the Google deal."

"We still have to focus energy on that," Wagner said.

"Did you check out my restaurant recommendation?" Niles asked, switching gears.

"Yeah, you got me."

A knowing grin crept across Niles's face.

Wagner walked toward the Mark Hopkins Hotel. Niles followed, tearing a wrapper from a breath mint. It felt odd that Jűrgen would never see the CERN-Stanford-Google partnership do its part to fight cancer. The wind had their suit pants flapping. "Jude. Keep it quick. It's freezing."

Wagner walked ahead.

Like Wagner, Niles took a moment to mourn over Jűrgen. Visibility had diminished into a cloudy wall. In their few minutes of reflection the hill had become alien. A few steps farther and California Street plummeted east into downtown. Wagner stopped at the crest, and Niles joined him at him at his side. Two taxis skimmed past them in a yellow hurry, tilting off the steep grade. Wagner could only make out the outlines of the high rises below, hugging the waterfront like city ambassadors standing at attention to dazzle arriving tourists. Buried beneath the Transamerica Pyramid and other nearby buildings were the scraps of tall ships from 160 years ago. The forty-niners who had rushed to California to find gold in the Sierra foothills, left everything behind—even their ships. The ships' graveyards became the Financial District.

Wagner related to the journey. He'd also left home, burning bridges when he moved from Kentucky. But he wasn't chasing gold or the gambling, crime, and prostitution, which had thrived in the Barbary Coast. He just wanted to fight cancer. Or was he also caught up in the rush of success? He wondered what Nathalie would say and wanted to know her better outside of a work context. That was new for a man who habitually walled out non-Stanford people.

"I'm turning to ice," Niles said. They went to Niles's car.

Niles drove Wagner to his flat where he knew Kate would be waiting. "You know, Jude, if our killer is onto our Google deal, I wonder what else he's onto?"

"That's exactly what I'm thinking. Anyone dead set on interfering with the Grid could be surveying things to gather information . . . and plan another assault." Wagner opened the passenger door, intent on getting a break on this situation and finding the assailants before anyone else got hurt.

Fifteen

Monday, October 31
Piedmont, CA

The iron driveway gate at Mark Ferguson's primary residence on Sea View Avenue shuttered and retracted. Grumbling to himself, the CEO drove through the entrance and up the slate-paved circular drive to his Piedmont estate.

A posh enclave entirely surrounded by Oakland, Piedmont existed as a city within a city. Some likened Piedmont to the Vatican inside Rome. Unlike Rome, though, Oakland had one of the highest murder rates in the country.

Even in Piedmont, Ferguson's faux French manor house made a statement—or would have, if the eight-foot-high adobe wall and oak trees surrounding the property hadn't kept it from public view. A chef and housekeeper occupied a wing that looked like a second large house; it hid a pool and patio with a palatial valley view.

Lori had designed the security system for the estate. The perimeter walls had square security lights at twenty-foot intervals, and a camera was mounted above the front doors and back. The system had other features, so elaborate that Ferguson wasn't sure how they all worked.

Parking his Bentley near the front door, he saw his daughter's white SUV roll up the driveway behind him. She hopped out and hugged him. Her usual dress looked out of place on the opulent, conifer-covered grounds. With shortly cropped brunette hair, she wore black jeans, boots and a waist length brown jacket. The only color about her showed through her passion for her work.

"When did you get back from your trip?" he asked.

"Just a few hours ago."

He opened the iron-banded oak door and Lori followed him in. She unzipped her jacket and removed it. In the foyer, Zeus came to her side, wagging his tail. She kissed the Rottweiler's head and turned to her father. "Daddy, you don't look so hot. I'll make homemade pizza for you tonight."

"Your old Dad's not feeling like himself."

They talked about his condition.

"No work today?" she asked.

"I'm just home between meetings—as much as I would have loved to call in sick today and take a break from J&Q. I envy your time off."

"The CEO has to call in when he's sick?"

"Even CEOs have responsibilities, darling. The meetings never end. Can't leave people in the lurch."

"If you're going to take it easy, make it count and rest. I'd like to hear about your week, but that's not going to take your mind off things, is it?"

"You're quick," he said, fully aware he was off to do more work at home as he always did no matter how he felt. He was relieved that she didn't ask anymore about his work pressures. He felt bad enough that his daughter worried about him. With no other family, they had to stick together. Lori's mother, a longtime alcoholic, had deserted the house years ago. This daughter of his spoiled him, insisting on choosing his groceries to ensure he ate low-cholesterol foods . . . as if the Pharma CEO couldn't manage that.

"You don't even want half a sandwich?" she asked.

The question alone made him queasy. "No thanks, doll."

"If I can't spoil you, I'm going to walk Zeus," she said.

"Good. Wear him out." Earlier this morning Ferguson had tried to take the Rottweiler his daughter had given him for a walk, but he trudged back up the mansion driveway after just five minutes. He felt dizzy and heard things. Lately, voices in his head came and went. He took them as an omen that the company could soon collapse. He wondered if his fears had any real basis. Huntington's disease did bring on neurotic tendencies.

He made a fist and gently tapped his daughter's firm shoulder. "I'll be in my study."

"Remember, I'm around if you need me."

He went to his study, his private haven. It met his blended needs of a home office space, entertainment center and exercise studio. There he beat on the speed bag that hung from the ceiling in the corner. A dedicated boxer in college, he delivered snappy punches with rolling wrist action. His energy drained rapidly. But he forced himself to continue, refusing to let his peak condition decline without a fight.

I've still got the Midas touch, he chanted. Years ago he was known for fattening bottom lines by producing billion-dollar drugs that involved minimal risk and produced maximum returns. He'd confided in his daughter a month ago that the stock he intended to leave her might plummet. His eyes welled, the first time in twenty years.

Ferguson had started J&Q himself. The company had soared as a drug treatment superstar until side-effects came in from its cholesterol control product, Flostin.

He pummeled the speed bag, imagining every strike was connecting with Jude Wagner's nose. Genomic medicine would shorten the era of blockbuster drugs. Drug manufacturers needed to rapidly reposition themselves or face shattering losses. Just when Ferguson thought he'd secured J&Q's future with the Stanford relationship, Wagner had pulled the rug from underneath him.

With a grunt, he pulled off the gloves and flung them across the room with all his might. That release of tension cleared cobwebs from his mind. He put that clarity to work, analyzing his next move in this boxing ring called life.

* * *

At the J&Q office conference room, Olivier Ramsey checked a voicemail message that Heather Styles had taken down for him. The message didn't leave a name or anything meaningful—it simply said, *Olivier Ramsey, call*, then gave the number. He had a hunch who had phoned. Though he didn't know how Cez@r had found him at J&Q. Ramsey stuffed his pen in his shirt pocket, raced out of the building for privacy, dialed and heard a recorded message:

"The e-Gold account number is 1127671021, include your corresponding bank name and account number. The name you are sending it to is Liberio Russo, the amount is $125,000. First payment must be received within 24 hours at www.e-gold.com. You will get updates."

Acting on this, Ramsey went online to check on the Pinsky Capital slush fund. There was enough in that New York account to cover his first payment and most of the next.

Sixteen

Monday, October 31
San Francisco, CA

Of the fifty-two weeks in a year, Kate's visit couldn’t have come at a less opportune time. But there was no way to fix it and, admittedly, Jude Wagner needed a breather. Head in a daze, he had committed to make tonight his uninterrupted dinner with her. In his bedroom he pulled on his only trendy dress shirt which had 1970's flair, determined to enjoy this evening out.

While Kate readied herself in the bathroom, a news alert vibrated on Wagner's phone. Headlines stated the first international genomic medicine convention was being held in Saudi Arabia. The photo on his cell phone screen showed spotlights flooding against a stately façade of some hotel building with formally-dressed individuals pushing past a semicircle of demonstrators. The protestors stood between the attendees and a doorman in tails.

Hideo Onagi had cautioned Wagner to expect a backlash from the media attention the Grid had received. The last few days surely testified to that. Wagner thought about how simpler life was when he quietly studied theoretical computing at University of California at Berkeley. According to the news story, organizations such as Stanford’s biotechnology department represented Dr. Frankenstein’s monster to the religious right. Protestors waved placards bearing slogans such as: Heathen Pigs, Go to Hell, Don’t Play with DNA, Those Who Play God are Damned.

Wagner's thoughts wandered. Whatever trace of inner calm he had fluttered off. Kate came out to his living room, a sheer silk scarf draped elegantly around her neck.

He tucked his phone away.

After she rubbed her underarm uncomfortably, she did a little modeling spin to show off her lilac dress with the v-cut back. Her loosely-curled blonde hair fell on her tanned shoulder blades. Standing 5’ 8", she was statuesque, with a high forehead, intense green eyes and total self-assuredness.

"You’re the mirror image of Mom," Wagner said.

Kate showed a little smile. "I decided to dress up."

"I see that."

She stood tall. "You only live once. Anyway, you ready? It's not nice to leave a lady waiting."

"One drink first. We're early." He quickly made them margaritas with extra lime slices and handed her one with a cocktail napkin.

She sipped before asking, "Do you remember Mom saying, you can do whatever you set your mind to? Dad insisted the world was our marble—that we etch ourselves into it but Mom said we're the stone. The world chisels character into us, sculpting a masterwork. Don’t be afraid of change."

"Mom was fearless. What prompted that?"

Kate twisted her cocktail napkin. "You inherited her gutsiness. I got other things."

He couldn't argue. From birth, Kate proved to be the cautious one. It was Jude who surprised the family when his computer hacking sent him to Juvenile Hall. His Mom's death when he was fifteen only made him even more stubbornly independent.

After his mother’s death, Jude barricaded himself in his bedroom, delving deeper into medical websites. Virtual reality had become his refuge. There was no talking him out of it. Only an obsessed sixteen-year-old boy could love his computer the way B.B. King loved his guitar, and Jude’s PC was his Lucille.

Kate sipped her drink while looking out his window.

Jude's thoughts drifted to his mother . . . it happened on the *Buttercup* sailboat, one balmy afternoon on Kentucky Lake. Dad lectured about Kentucky Lake being a manmade thing that backs up the Tennessee River for 184 miles. "It won't kill you to learn about energy in this day and age of global warming," he said, wearing baggy khakis, which typified his weekday, mechanical engineer look.

Mom admired the luft curve of the sail and sang part of *Madam Butterfly*. Ever the overdressed opera singer, Mom's Egyptian silver bracelets jingled in the wind. She'd replaced her dreams of singing at the Met to raise kids. Her voice broke.

It was hard to hear. She wasn't the captivating, radiant blonde performer she used to be. Her hair, wrapped in a scarf, had thinned from chemotherapy.

Jude dropped anchor for lunch. With Cicadas *cra-a-acking,* he dove into the water in his Quicksilver trunks and did his long underwater swim stunt. He swam around the boat then snuck a breath of air under the bow before submerging again. He waited for Kate to fling the life preserver.

But he'd run out of air and had surfaced. Kate hadn't slung the donut. Treading water, Jude saw that Mom had gone flat on the deck. Dad had started CPR on her. Back in the boat, Jude gripped his Mom's left hand as though that prevented her from slipping away.

Finally, she coughed. Dad stroked her wet head, saying. "You're light-headed from the medicine."

Dad and Jude worked to get them home quickly but the wind disappeared and the boat motor stalled. Cicadas got louder. Their rattling language came as some strange rejoice. She died that night in hospice—what was left of her blonde hair splayed on the pillow. Her breast cancer had spread irreversibly. She'd asked for one day of sailing for fresh air. After burying her, Kate and Jude realized they were no longer kids.

Jude's subconscious trapped that outing in time like an exposure of light on film or a binary bit in a computer sector. Swelling water still surrounded his dreams. Minute muscles in his jaw twitched.

"You look, sort of . . . under strain," Kate said, drawing him from his reverie. "What's going on at Stanford?"

"What's going on? Everything and nothing. I think it'd be easier to build a nuclear deterrent system than keep this project on track."

"I admire your passion but would you really trust the genomic approach over mainstream medicine if you really had to choose?"

"There's no question I would. We're doing years of research in days. Even if a certain cancer isn't hereditary, it's still gene based. Only a small number of mutations to the genome can cause cancer." His gaze intensified. "And our Grid is about a thousand times more powerful than the computer which beat world chess champion Garry Kasparov in 1997."

"Deep Blue."

"That's right," he said. "Did you know that even when you type one hundred words a minute on your PC, valuable processing power goes wasted? The most valuable world resource—more vital than the burning property of oil—is computers that sit unused on our desks."

She made a dour expression. "I love that you're a visionary, but there's a downside too."

"Yeah?"

"Too much forward thinking can prevent you from just living in the moment. Speaking of which, if I don't get some gnocchi or clam linguine in me soon I'll cook something here myself."

"Ha."

"I knew that would motivate you to leave."

They breezily strolled out his place as if neither of them had a care in the world.

Seventeen

Monday, October 31
San Francisco, CA

Kate nodded off to bed right after the two of them had come back from dinner. Unlike her, Jude Wagner couldn't sleep, not with Jűrgen's and Hideo's deaths still so vivid. His watch hands pointed to ten. Still enough time for a drink.

Pulling on moccasins and his suede jacket, he softly left his apartment and stepped into the night for his neighborhood haunt. He trudged down shop-lined, leafy Hyde Street where the lampposts were forged from another era.

He heard high heels tapping in the misty dark. He looked over his shoulder. An eye-catching young woman strutted under a streetlight in the same direction behind him. Her feminine gait reminded him of Nathalie. The curves of Nathalie's body, even the taper of her waist was etched in his brain.

Adults in costumes sauntered by, hollering at each other—the aftermath of Halloween partying. On the corner, an Asian woman wearing dishwashing gloves paid no attention to them while she rummaged for aluminum cans in a waste can. A cable car pulled along its tracks outside of the Hyde Out bar. As the name suggested, losing people could've been the house special. Wagner was okay with that tonight.

Inside, a burnished dark wood bar curved from the front door to a metal restroom sign. Regulars drank solo, slouched at the counter, wearing an aroma of hops. The brass tap pumps dripped. Don Henley*'s*

Hotel California warbled from the 1950's jukebox as he took a stool. The bartender took his order for a Sierra Nevada. Stomach acid gnawed inside him. Just when the Stanford project was gaining momentum, the Grid looked as fragile as a newborn child. There were no guarantees in this life.

He looked at his hands. His cuticles looked rough and torn. Picking at them was a nervous habit. Kate had warned of such compulsive behavior representing a cognitive disconnect between mind and body. Kate's Eastern philosophy was never far behind her, though her psychoanalysis didn't sound far-fetched.

Downing his beer, he noticed the same intriguing young woman he saw outside take the stool next to him. Clad in a V-neck sweater with cleavage, she gave him a lazy-eyed stare. She went to the bathroom and returned without her sweater, wearing a semi-transparent white tank top shirt. Her strawberry-blonde hair framed her young face like a page out of *Cosmopolitan Magazine*.

He took it all in, eyeing her guardedly. The Irish barkeeper refilled his stein. The regular customers at the sticky bar appeared to be extras hired for atmosphere.

"How was your day of work?" Wagner asked the young woman beside him, starting the dance. He didn't mind a little sexual distraction.

"Highly forgettable. I'm so thirsty, I could drink mouthwash."

He introduced himself.

The glamorous stranger mumbled, "Heather." She looked him up and down. "So, what's up? You look frazzled."

"Do I?"

"You from the south?" A reference to his drawl.

"Kentucky." He pulled on his amber draft, looking around the bar.

"That's open space country with bluegrass. The only wide open space I ever see is when I visit my Dad in Virginia." Her whisky voice aroused him. He watched her reapply lip gloss, dotting her mouth, when a clunking noise made her jump. She went on with what she was doing after finding the source behind the bar: a relic of an ice maker.

"What do you do?" she asked.

"Science research."

"We're going to need a translator."

"Basically, it's computer work," he told her.

"At least you're not trying to cure cancer."

He chuckled.

"Are you laughing at me?"

"No. Actually fighting cancer is part of what I do."

"Well, that's more than most of us can say. Is that why you look so wound up?"

"Maybe. It could all go down the tubes."

She had a quizzical expression.

"Don't ask," he said. "There's just been a series of unexpected disasters." He wasn't going to say more. Not to a perfect stranger.

"Bad times. Life is random and hard."

That resonated. Two weeks ago he had a driving confidence in the Stanford project. Now he had to remind himself of what the Grid could do. A part of him wanted to tell her how grids were running the world. . . working in the background to manage everything from airline reservations to the mapping of the earth's surface and global warming, then he reconsidered. "Life isn't easy, but talking about it doesn't change a thing." Part of him wondered if this fantastic-looking strawberry blonde could be up to something. With such cat eyes and runway-model good looks, she didn't need makeup and certainly didn't need to vie for a man's attention. But some degree of paranoia had to be acting on him.

"Life's an uphill climb with Mount Whitney waiting on top." She smacked her shiny lips at the last sip of her beer. She signaled to the bartender for another and leaned close to Wagner.

He felt the warmth of her breath. Under other circumstances, he'd take her up on her offer. She must've thought she had him, flipping her hair, "Say, I once read that computers are going to help people live longer with a new medicine. Do you believe that?"

"I don't want to bore you." He couldn't allow his fantasies with her to become reality. Not tonight.

"I have a high tolerance for boredom with the right beer and guy." She took his wrist. "Show me your hand."

Wagner stretched his fingers, opening his palm.

Judging by her hands, she must've been close to thirty, same age as him.

She traced the line that ran up from his wrist toward his index finger. "Whoa."

"What?" he said.

"Your lifeline splits. Some big event is happening for you. I wonder what that could be?"

"Why don't you tell me," he said.

She held his palm closer. "It looks like you're on some mission. Is that right?"

He didn't feel like being quizzed but he wanted her. An even bigger part of him wanted his hot and cold, hard-to-read FBI contact, Special Agent Nathalie Noiret.

They finished another round while bar girl dreamily went on. "You have the life line of a . . . a truth seeker. Your path is going to be a quest, like something from Greek mythology, but you hold a lot of it inside."

He looked up at her. "I get the feeling you've done this before."

"Excuse me. I have to visit the ladies' room again. Promise me you won't leave."

"Okay," he said.

With controlled slowness, she slid her legs off her stool and went to the bathroom.

She exited the women's room and went to the jukebox. She quickly glanced to see if Wagner was still sitting at the bar. Appearing satisfied with that, she fed the glass and chrome machine then tapped her selection. As U2 began to jangle, her phone rang. She stepped away from the juke box and answered it. She spoke loudly over the music. Watching her over enunciate her words, Wagner tried to read her lips. It appeared that she said, "I'll pick her up at one-thirty. Goodbye."

After she hung up her phone, she quickly returned to her seat. "I have to go. Wanna walk me to my car?"

Wagner did not trust himself with her and told her he needed to head straight home.

She signed her credit card bill. The bartender took his merchant copy.

She slung her purse over her shoulder. "You sure you don't wanna come?"

"Positive."

She took a pen from the bar counter and wrote her number on a cocktail napkin. "Call me sometime."

His mind reverted to work again as he took the napkin. He started to leave on his own.

With hands on her sides, she blocked his passage through the door.

He pushed by, ignoring her.

"Wait . . . when's your birthday?"

"June 11," he said.

Her eyes lighted as if she'd discovered something diabolical. "Sign of the twin. That's a masculine, air sign. Ruled by Mercury. Romantically, we're a classic fit, and I really would like to hear more about your cancer work."

"Maybe next time." He waved and checked her out from behind as she went, weaving down the street.

Heading home, Wagner visualized how Heather's slid her legs across that leather bar stool. Why did he have to be so finely attuned to the pull of the opposite sex? He passed shadowy Victorian buildings with burlesque facades and maintained a steady pace. Good fortune or bad, he had to live with the sign of the Gemini and whatever ills that brought to light.

Eighteen

Monday, October 31
San Francisco, CA

The soft but rapid knock on Jude Wagner's door came just before midnight, minutes after his return from the Hyde Out. He drew a chef's knife from the kitchen butcher block and peered through his peephole. Unlocking the top bolt, he cracked open his door with his blade in hand.

"Easy. It's me!" Niles said, smelling of breath mints. Niles looked as if he'd dressed in the dark. His wool dress trousers, with their sharp crease, contrasted his down jacket with a hood.

Wagner lowered the knife. "Why can't you pick up the phone like a normal person?"

"Are you going to let me in or just stand there like a homicidal security guard?"

Wagner opened the door wide enough for Niles to enter, closed it behind him and locked it. Niles marched in, carrying a manila folder. "Kate's sleeping. What d'you want?"

"Just lose the damn knife."

Wagner lowered it and walked to his kitchen with Niles following.

"You have any open wine?"

Wagner pointed at his counter and set the knife down. "What on earth is going on?"

Niles tipped red wine into a water glass, drank half of it, put the glass back on the counter top, then handed Jude the folder. "Read the three letters on top. I only handled the pages from the edges."

Wagner took the folder. "What?"

"It's been weeks since I went through our Crank File and I just came across something."

"Weeks? It's your job to track that."

"So, I fell behind with the bumph. Get on with it. At least I thought to bring the file with me to my new door-manned safe house."

"Where?"

"The Huntington Hotel. I checked in to be on the safe side."

Wagner looked over the three letters of feedback to the Stanford project. One typed page read: "You've seen what we can do to abortion clinics you God-forsaken heathen. If you and your Grid continue to tamper with DNA, you will pay."

Another said, "1 Corinthians 6:19: 'Or do you not know that your body is a temple of the Holy Spirit within you, whom you have from God? You are not your own.'"

The others had the same tone of religious contempt. "Each of these arrived within the last month," Niles added, "shortly before the murders. As you can see, they're anonymous."

"Whoa, these are something. Well spotted. I'll get these to Nathalie." Wagner then pulled a plastic baggie from his kitchen drawer and carefully put the letters inside.

Niles sighed, still distraught. "We have to think about religious groups, who would most want to suppress scientific interpretation, as if we didn't have enough haters. Do we know anything?"

"Whoever is directing this is probably hiring experienced men. It's likely they are in their twenties or thirties."

"Why?" Niles asked.

"Nathalie says that's the baseline for hitmen. The one who broke into my place could've been thirty."

"I'm gonna piss myself." Niles had paced from the club chair in the living room back to the kitchen.

"We've got religious conservatives coming out of the woodwork. We can't dismiss their opposition to Stanford bioengineering."

"I'm not dismissing anything. Do not forget we also have dozens of industry leaders in Pharma who want our hides. We have to gather dots before we can connect them."

"Still—"

"What?"

"Some anonymous person has threatened that if we don't drop what we're doing at Stanford, they're going to make us pay. What do they want—for us to hand in our resignation?"

"Maybe."

Niles shook his head. "Bloody hell. I'd oblige them if I weren't leaving town already. At least I'll be removing myself from circulation here." Soon he would be off to Switzerland.

"Unfortunately, it appears we are no safer away from San Francisco. You have to be vigilant every minute."

Niles groaned. "For the first time in my life I think fame of any kind is highly overrated." He hastily buttoned up his down jacket and let himself out.

* * *

Cez@r readied himself for another late work night. He shut off the shower at his parents' house just as a revelation struck him. He had to put a back-up attack into effect. The computer virus he had planned on releasing could be cleaned, blocking the intended damage. That just wouldn't do. He considered corrupting the data itself. If he could access the Grid server, he could implant a program he'd used before. The program could rejigger numbers and letters in databases, automatically tabbing through form fields inside records. He'd read a Stanford professor's academic paper about the how the Grid worked and was confident his program was compatible.

And what if he could control the electricity that flowed from one of the three Stanford substations to the Grid's data center? Then he could shut down the Grid at will—it would be the perfect failsafe if Stanford security removed his virus. This could be his magnum opus. A Grid can't function on back-up generators alone.

Feeling refreshed, he dressed in a hurry to get back to his college desk in the garage. Hijacking part of the power grid was an idea he'd toyed with off and on; although he didn't have the capability. Before he'd finished his cup of coffee, he stumbled on an obscure chat room on the darknet—an area of the Internet where activities can't be traced to a computer. In a room called cypher café, likeminded cyber terrorists flaunted practical tips for cracking into operational control systems to critical infrastructure. Within ninety minutes, these cyber strangers took such a shine to Cez@r that one boasted he had working code.

A tingling sensation flowed over Cez@r's body. This guy just might pull this off. Cez@r hunted the 'Net for more information about the Stanford campus. Trying a dozen different keyword combinations, he found what he was looking for: a public document to Stanford's electrical substations. This white paper from construction contractors detailed how the newly-designed substation transformers operated on the latest technology of microprocessor-based relays. The find was almost too good to be true. Cez@r sent this link over to his new darknet buddy.

The buddy wrote back, "Jackpot. This'll b fun. I'll do this for just five hundred. Get me access to this Grid's administrator's computer terminal. From there—I can screw with the power source, reset the electrical breaker limit and flip the Grid off and on like a kitchen light switch. There is a fire hazard to this."

Cez@r didn't mind. Not only did this feel like child's play, but it also guaranteed his hacker payday. He started evaluating how he could make a special visit to the Stanford lab to search the place for a Grid access key.

Nineteen

Tuesday, November 1
San Francisco, CA

Temperatures had swung from brisk to warm, another schizophrenic fall day in San Francisco. Wagner waited for Nathalie at her alcove, considering his progress on anti-virus code. Reality was setting in, even more than Jude had realized. Even that flirtatious stranger, Heather, must've picked up on his nerves. The last four days had been unreal—not what he or anyone could've anticipated.

Nathalie walked in clutching an accordion file folder, wearing a knee-length, black skirt with a long-sleeved, scoop-necked blouse. She acknowledged him with a little nod. She set down her file on her desk and pulled up her swivel chair. "You look exhausted."

"I am."

She quickly tidied papers on her desk. "I've been analyzing these horrible events. We could see if Hackman might offer his opinion—"

"I'd rather do this on our own."

"Why? Because it was an FBI-registered Glock that killed Jűrgen?" A line furrowed in her delicate brow . . . perfectly unselfconscious. "Collusion is a possibility. Just don't make reckless assumptions."

"I'm simply trying to find a connection," he said.

"Follow the evidence. You cannot uncover something new if you know what it is you intend to find. That is Meno's paradox."

"Maybe forcing conclusions is better than no conclusions at all." Wagner removed the baggie from his pocket that contained the three threat letters, then carefully took one of the pages from plastic and held it to the desk lamp at Nathalie's alcove. A subtle outline of a watermark showed.

"What do you have there?" Nathalie asked, leaning closer.

Wagner explained how the letters sat unopened in the Crank File that Niles had neglected. He handed them to her.

"Wait here," she said with purpose.

* * *

Nathalie couldn't have sidetracked the workflow in the Crime Lab if she had tried. She eased by a senior technician in the Lab who argued with a younger one over protocol for handling evidence.

"Anyone mind if I use the light table?" she asked.

The older lab staffer fluttered his hand in the air, not wanting to be disturbed.

She flipped on the light table and adjusted a large magnifying glass affixed to a pivot, hoping to get a good view of the watermark. When she put the page on the clear glass surface, the high-wattage bulbs underneath illuminated the subtle demarcation. It read UNITED BISHOPS ASSOCIATION.

Noiret was surprised to find anything. What was the UNITED BISHOPS ASSOCIATION? The name meant nothing to her. She looked over her shoulder. The lab was empty now.

She carefully inspected the two other letters which showed the same mark. She found no fingerprints, so she carefully tucked the watermarked sheets into the baggie before returning to her desk.

* * *

At her alcove area, Nathalie briefed him. "There is something. All this correspondence has a watermark with the words, "UNITED BISHOPS ASSOCIATION."

Wagner flashed to the religious protestor news story, thinking about their slogans. "Now we have our religious adversaries to sift through. But which religious zealots? What faction would commit murder? And why would they draw attention to their deeds so carelessly by using paper with a watermark like this?"

"Any scrap of new information is good," Nathalie added. "But the serial number to the handgun which killed Jűrgen doesn't help. Hackman has no record of it being issued out."

"But when a crime occurs," he said, "it always leaves a trace, right?"

She gave an affirming nod. With it came a sly look that reinforced her willingness to work in cahoots with him. She then sat before her computer and clicked to the FBI agent manifest. It had been months since an agent had worked in Switzerland, although she managed to pull up a list of FBI agents who were guarding embassies, consulates and select dignitaries. She took down names before further conjecture about motive.

Losing Jűrgen's help at CERN would have a disruptive effect on medicine. Rubbing his neck, Wagner considered their next move . . . the religious threat letters piled more worry on top of everything. Wagner circled back to Nathalie's desk. "Another thing that annoys me is that I have an impression Hackman doesn't hear me out."

"I'm not surprised," Nathalie said, glued to her computer screen. "You are polar opposites. Your work depends on the Internet for good and from his standpoint, the Internet is the favored weapon of the modern terrorist. Computational biology is not an easy concept for him to warm up to. And you cannot expect agents here to like you when they don't yet understand you."

Wagner saw a text message on his phone. Roger Knowlan reported that Hideo's office had been broken into and the lab at Stanford had been vandalized. Even though Hideo was dead, this came as yet another insulting blow. "I can't believe this."

"What now?"

Wagner explained what had happened while thinking about possible suspects again.

His mind reverted to Stanford's break-up with J&Q.

"This situation is spiraling," she said.

"I have to go to Hideo's office and check the lab."

"You're going to Stanford now?"

"Yes, I have to see this myself. The text from our Program Director says the computers have been busted up." Wagner patted his pants pocket, checking for his car keys.

"For an outsider, you certainly push protocols."

"I should remember my part in the play, right?" he said.

"What? No. Just keep your head screwed on."

"Got it. I'll try not to go too far off script."

She appeared mildly concerned. *"Mieux vaut plier que rompre.* It's better to adapt and survive."

"Look. Don't try to stop me," he said.

"All right, then I am going with you. OPR is going to keep Hackman busy today anyway."

She was proving her unpredictability again.

"What do you mean the OPR is going to keep him busy?" he asked.

"I'll tell you on the way. Anyway, if I go with you, I can cover for us if anyone questions what you are doing."

"You sure about this?" he said.

She picked up her sweater off her chair, and knotted it over her shoulders decisively. "I'm ahead on my work now. See you at the elevator."

He didn't ask again and just started walking.

Nathalie showed up at the elevator carrying a boxy, nylon bag over her shoulder.

Presumably, she had borrowed it from the lab. "What's that?"

"A fingerprint kit." She tightened the shoulder strap. "You said there was vandalism so I'm coming equipped. I may be in Intelligence Analysis, but I still know how they do things in the Crime Section. Besides, it troubles me to imagine that you, personally, could be on the firing line for meddling."

He didn't say it, but he was glad that she would be riding along.

Twenty

Tuesday, November 1
San Francisco, CA

Without speaking, Wagner and Nathalie walked through the parking garage to his Mazda. He caught himself liking the sound of their footfalls echoing in unison on the slick concrete. Nathalie's company was calming, but her closeness was distracting. Bad sign. A routine walk with her like this shouldn't ignite a rush of excitement.

Before opening his car door, he peered through his back window. He didn't see anyone hiding in the back crouched on the floor, so he opened up. Slinging his coat on the backseat, Wagner caught a whiff of Nathalie's French lavender fragrance. He turned the key in the ignition without delay. As the motor hummed, he collected his addled thoughts and drove out the garage. "Let's go over how much has happened in this short span of time. I'm assuming these homicides are tied to my unwelcome visitor."

"Thoughtfully planned homicides indicate that the perp is educated and intelligent," she said. "I doubt that, uh, this is the work of one suspect. The mastermind probably lives in the Bay Area."

"Why?"

"They are organized. The hostiles would be well acquainted with Stanford and likely be in its vicinity. Also, they would eliminate victims as far from home as possible to throw suspicion . . . law enforcement screens for motive, means and opportunity. Do you know of anyone who might feel wronged? Be out for revenge?"

"Maybe someone from J&Q," he said. "Our Stanford team's sudden pull out of that partnership could've driven someone to desperate measures, but I doubt—"

"We need to work with vigilance to make a list and cross off every potential suspect until we are left with one. There's no easy way to do it. You truly believe the motive to upset the Stanford Grid?"

"Yes."

"Then it is business-motivated and we have terrorists," she said, "professional hit men and women who will defy serial profiles."

At a red light, Wagner cracked his knuckles. "What about those boots on the guy who broke into my place?"

"He was wearing Danner boots. A military style. Size eleven. I know the brand. Anyone could buy those boots, you-know. The lab showed it's a new shoe, so we can forget matching tread wear to suspects."

"Oh." He flipped the air conditioning on high.

"Jude. Do not look at these as dead ends, but as doors we're closing in a hallway with too many passageways."

"I'll try." Wagner had an itchy feeling between his shoulder blades, driving down the freeway south to Onagi's Stanford laboratory. "At least we're moving through the madhouse."

Nathalie's phone vibrated. "It's a text from an analyst I am friendly with. There is office talk about that FBI-registered handgun that killed Jűrgen Hansen."

Wagner's gaze shifted. "And?"

"The rumor is the field division armory book shows the weapon was swiped from an FBI SUV lockbox two months ago. At that time, the incident was attributed to a gang theft. But the OPR is questioning that. New evidence has come from bullets found in Hansen's body. My friend says, 'Whatever they found, it means heavy interrogation of Hackman.'"

"Whoa. I wonder if Hackman was involved in some cover up?"

She turned. "Maybe. I want to know who you think at Stanford would be next on this perp's agenda?"

"I'd say our Program Director, Roger Knowlan or maybe Niles. They're both picking up Hideo Onagi's duties."

She gave him a cockeyed look that didn’t clarify matters. "But it's your algorithm that made the Grid what it is."

He wasn’t sure how to take that, but it felt good to hear her concern.

"It’s true, but what would taking me out do? Great chunks of my code are in the public domain already. Computer algorithms are a mishmash of public property just like the Internet is."

"No. I think any one of you could be the next victim."

"Okay, but what can I do? Get a handgun and carry it with me at all times?"

"Sorry. San Francisco does not issue permits for carrying a concealed weapon."

"Then why doesn't your office put body guards on us around the clock?"

"I tried. Hackman denied my request as being unjustified. The only physical harm done happened out of this country. He is under close review at the moment, remember."

"Okay. But frankly, Nat, that doesn't mean a lot to me."

"Why is that?"

"I have a sickening feeling that Hackman is not the only one who is being closely watched."

Twenty-One

Tuesday, November 1
Stanford, CA

Wound up tight as a spring, Wagner cruised his Mazda through the vast Stanford campus with Nathalie at his side. The meticulously planned village of squat Spanish Mediterranean archways, pillars and quads created a sheltered escape for ambitious academics.

Nathalie turned. "Even before I received that text from Morris, I heard office gossip to the Hackman investigation."

"Concerning the OPR?" he said.

"Yes, the talk is that he's slipping up since he's nearing the barn, whatever that means."

Wagner smiled. "It means Hackman's cutting corners because he's approaching retirement. Not being fully accountable."

"Oh, really?" she said. "Maybe he'll get sacked before we have a confrontation with him."

"Yeah, right."

"Then he'll have more time to go to church."

"Is that joke?" Wagner asked.

"Not really. All of floor thirteen knows he is a seriously pious man. But it is not something he talks about. He becomes, how do you say—*cagey* when someone asks about his denomination."

Wagner mulled that. He rolled his Mazda up to the chemistry complex, a cluster of three-story buildings. There he saw Roger Knowlan's new Jaguar with PIONEER on the license plate, then parked beside Hideo Onagi's empty parking spot. Seeing his late colleague's name on that space made Wagner's insides clench. An image of Onagi streamed to mind—how he insisted on going double or nothing when he lost at pool and bought that round of drinks as an enticement. There would be no more marathon Sake dinners with Hideo.

Wagner nosed into a spot, stopped the engine. "Can you wait here for a moment while I scout the situation?"

"What? You go inside while I burn alive out here? No. I can't get used to these temperature swings. I'm coming."

He apologized, removed the keys from his ignition and led the way.

Stepping into the stiflingly hot car park, he spotted a hummingbird buzzing from a flowerbed. Hideo shied from birds. It flew forward, backward, then hovered in place. A brilliant red marked the bird's head. In a nano-second, it flitted skyward. Maybe the humming bird had sensed the sting of death in the air. Through the breezeway and doorway, they entered the Research Institute. The administration office was empty except for a security camera which hung on the wall behind the front desk facing the glass entrance.

Shelly, the Australian lab tech, rounded the corner lugging a box of files. She set the box down and hugged him. "He was a dear man," she said with a catch in her voice.

"We're going to support each other," Wagner said. He introduced Nathalie as an FBI Agent while a familiar sight caught Wagner's eye from behind the front desk: a giant mounted graphic with dozens of black-and-white striped lines. It was Craig Venter's sequenced human genome breakthrough from 2003.

The picture hung there every day at Stanford for years, and Wagner never really looked at the genome blow-up until now. The squiggly pairs of lines morphed from a blueprint for bioinformatics to a diagram for mayhem.

"I've got something to show you," Shelly said with a lilt, gently leading them away from the wall and toward Hideo's office, a private room one door down from the lab.

Wagner wasn't surprised to see the lab door crisscrossed with crime tape, but he didn't feel entirely prepared for it either.

"Have you been in his office?" Nathalie asked.

"Yes, but I didn't touch anything. I called the police straight away. They left two hours ago."

Nathalie looked around the office with Wagner. "Do you know if a print team dusted this room?"

"They haven't. The police said two men would come to get fingerprints, but so far nothing. I was told to keep out of the lab, where the vandalism occurred."

"So, Roger is here?" Wagner asked.

Before she could reply, Roger Knowlan turned the corner and entered the office.

Nothing was visibly out of order. Hideo's computer monitor was still intact on the steel desk. The chassis on his tower appeared untouched. The shelves with books behind his desk and even the ergonomic chair looked undisturbed. Shelly left for the front desk again.

"You think Shelly will be all right?" Wagner asked.

"Once she gets over the shock. Onagi's family is in Tokyo, by the way."

Wagner nodded with acknowledgment.

"Wait until you poke your head into the lab." Knowlan said, after his stare had drifted to a framed photo on the desk of Hideo hugging his daughter. He looked up to make eye contact. "Does anyone at the FBI know about this?"

"They do now," Wagner said. "Nathalie, this is Roger Knowlan. He's our Department Director."

"How do you do?" she said.

"Not great, thank you." Knowlan tugged at his sport coat.

Wagner looked at Knowlan. "FBI Special Agent Nathalie Noiret has offered to assess the office. I'm glad you called."

Nathalie took a quick look at the window. "No forced entry here. Does anything appear missing to you in Mr. Onagi's office?"

Knowlan shook his head, clearly anxious to ask Wagner something. "Niles may be the best quality assurance tester in Silicon Valley, but can he close the deal with Google by himself? The people at CERN had a rapport with Hideo. They trusted him."

Nathalie folded her arms.

"They'll have to trust Niles now," Wagner said. It dumbfounded him that Hideo had remained close friends with Knowlan through all of the heated debates about commercializing the Grid, though they had both wanted to see the project work miracles. Knowlan glanced around the office, obviously lost in thought. Wearing a finely tailored blazer over a button down shirt without a tie, Knowlan looked down toward his polished shoe boots. His attention to men's fashion appeared as a shot at compensating for his small-boned frame and moody social awkwardness.

Knowlan, acting withdrawn, sat on the corner of Hideo's desk.

Wagner heard the front desk phone ring. Shelly shouted down the hallway, "It's Niles on the line. I told him you were both here."

Wagner asked her to transfer the call to Hideo's office.

After three beeps, Wagner put the call on speaker phone. Knowlan paced.

"Niles, it's Jude and Roger here." Wagner positioned the phone so Niles could hear them clearly.

Niles's voice carried into the room. "What the devil is going on—people are dying."

"No kidding," Knowlan shouted back. His raw nerves in full display.

"Did you find out anything more about these vandals?" Niles said.

Knowlan huffed. "You're getting ahead of us."

"I do have some news," Wagner said. "We spoke with Tokyo police. Hideo's dog attack may not have been accidental."

Knowlan whipped around, giving Wagner steady eye contact for the first time since he'd arrived. "How do they know that?"

"His daughter," Wagner said, "the only material witness, told police that someone commanded the dogs to attack him."

"Bloody hell. What do we do with that?" Niles voice overmodulated on the speakerphone.

Knowlan rubbed his forehead.

"No traceable abrasions, contusions or fibers," Nathalie said. "It's a clever way of making an attack look unplanned. And how do you prove that an animal's owner premeditated homicide when all he's got to do is whisper *attack*."

"I can't believe this," Knowlan interrupted, wide-eyed. "We've faced enough scientific obstacles without this."

Knowlan said. "I need air. So long, Niles. I'll be out front, Jude." Knowlan left the room.

Niles's voice crackled back on. "I feel like we're all walking around with targets painted on our backs."

"I know," Wagner said. "Nathalie did find something on that threat letter. There was a watermark with the words, United Bishops Association."

"What the hell?" Niles sounded more baffled than exasperated.

"We know how religious fundamentalists feel about genomic medicine."

The future they had worked so hard for had finally arrived, but with the crash landing of a meteorite.

"But what about me?" Niles asked. "Jűrgen was murdered at CERN and I'll be filling in for Hideo, meeting with CERN executives in Switzerland. Can the bureau do anything for my security?"

"It's not my call," Wagner said.

"I suppose Jűrgen didn't officially work for Stanford and Onagi's dog mauling could still have been an accident."

"Right. And as much as I'd like to be head of a covert operation to solve this I'm not. I actually thought since you'll be with CERN people *you* could ask questions, peck around."

"Fine. Heave me onto the train tracks."

Wagner resisted the bait to go into this further. "We'll compare details after your trip."

"Is that our action plan from the bureau, magnum P.I?"

"Look, Niles. I know what you want. I can't go back to the head of San Francisco FBI and press him about an FBI-registered weapon. No chance."

"Fine."

Wagner hung up the phone then walked outside to meet Knowlan under the breezeway.

"Jude," Knowlan said. "I wonder how worried we should be for ourselves? I can't just drop the ball on this cancer validation testing."

"We all need to be on guard. I can't assure you we're safe when these heinous things happened overseas. And if I knew anything definite about who is sabotaging us, I wouldn’t be standing here talking with you. I can only say one thing with certainty."

"Please, enlighten me." Knowlan said.

"The crime pattern suggests that this isn't personal—it's more like a war than a duel."

"Because."

"Because we know who Hideo and Jűrgen were. They had no real enemies."

Knowlan touched the beard stubble around his mouth. "It bothers me even more to imagine these two as nothing more than faceless targets on a map."

Jude Wagner had not planned on playing mediator between the FBI and his Stanford Program Director, Roger Knowlan, the moment he arrived to the Lab. All he cared about was seeing the vandalism.

Knowlan said through his teeth, "You should know this much. Weller—the Department Chair—is bringing in private investigators. Says the FBI is just wasting our time."

Nathalie approached before the Program Director could get another word out. She held her bag unflinching. "Am I interrupting?"

"No." Wagner glared at Knowlan. He was in no mood for fielding criticism about the FBI.

"Agent Noiret," Knowlan asked. "I have a question."

"Yes."

"As an FBI Agent, could you question the CEO of Johnston & Quib?"

"Unfortunately no," she said.

"I cannot just interrogate CEOs. Not without extremely good cause."

Wagner had to get a look at the lab next door. He gestured for them all to move on. Knowlan put his assertiveness on hold as they angled to the doorway covered with the yellow police tape.

"Technically, I shouldn’t go in here," Nathalie told Wagner.

"I trust you won’t write yourself up."

"You are too much." Nathalie gave in and peeled away the three strips of tape and entered the room.

Wagner watched with Knowlan from the doorway.

Nathalie's way was blocked by chairs and books that had been flipped. A desk lamp was broken on the floor. White glass crunched beneath her feet. She stepped carefully. Wagner could see her weighing the situation.

"*Mon Dieu*," she said. "Looks like a hate crime."

"Why?" Wagner said.

"On the whiteboard there's a quote written in bright purple marker."

"Can you read what it says?" Wagner said. "I can't see it from here."

"Those who play god will be sacrificed," she said.

A chill crept over Wagner, pondering it. He recalled the protesters' placards again on the Internet news report.

Knowlan interrupted. "So, they ransacked some of the computers here, but not Hideo's lab workstation?" Knowlan said. "What do you make of that?"

"Maybe they wanted to do damage but also find his Grid access key and use it here. They had no idea that you and I were the only ones carrying a key."

Knowlan looked at Wagner. "What do you propose I do with my key?"

"Hang on to it. There's no safer place."

Knowlan silently fidgeted, obviously wanting another answer. Shelly the lab technician came by and hovered at the door.

Knowlan moped off to his office.

"Why do you think Hideo's computer wasn't destroyed?" Nathalie asked.

Wagner leaned in. "I can only imagine they thought the Grid access key was saved on it."

"Makes sense." Nathalie went ahead to dust the keyboard for prints. She first removed a pair of latex gloves from her fingerprint kit, blew air into them, one at a time, and pulled them on."

She worked for over thirty minutes. "Looks like they wore gloves," she said.

Wagner still looked on from the doorway, clear of the scene.

She wiped clean the black print powder off the tops of the keys. Had they left the powder, she would've had some explaining to do to the police fingerprint crew.

Wagner leaned around to look at the computer on the bench. "Nathalie, can you sit at the computer and boot it up?"

She followed his keystroke instructions then hit ENTER. "You put me into the history buffer. Well done. The last set of operations performed at this computer are coming on the screen. I'm scrolling through them in reverse chronological order."

With the printers broken, she saved the screens to a flash drive Wagner gave her from Shelly's top desk drawer.

"I'm done." Nathalie removed her gloves and zipped the little drive into a pouch. "I'll print these keystrokes for you at the office."

They all moved toward the building entrance. Roger followed them with his cell phone in hand.

"If you find anything, call," Knowlan said. "Hopefully these are just religious freaks and they have nothing to do with what happened to Onagi and Jűrgen." Wagner agreed that was possible while Nathalie took her kit to the car.

Wagner asked Shelly, "How can we access the video log from the security camera in the lobby?"

"The police have already checked that," she said. "The video monitor power was turned off for three hours in the middle of the night, then flipped on again."

“Hmm.”

"I’d say Godspeed with solving this," she said, "but I’ll go with good luck instead."

Wagner walked to the car.

"Wait," Shelly called. She ran to catch up with him. "Take this." She handed a blue paper crane to Wagner. "This was Hideo’s. He gave it to me and I want you to have it."

"Thanks." Wagner took it, aware of Hideo’s habit of giving origami cranes to colleagues. *Ori means fold,* he would say. *We’ll make magic through folding proteins.*

Wagner looked at the crane, remembering something else Hideo once said: *We are both dreamers. Without us, the Grid will go nowhere and the ruling elite will squash the revolution.*

Wagner reflected how there may be fewer revolutionaries on the field, but those surviving this just became more determined.

Twenty-Two

Tuesday, November 1
Piedmont, CA

At the wet bar in his multi-use home study in Piedmont, Mark Ferguson mixed a weak, quarter-filled glass of scotch and soda, well aware it would take more than whisky to alleviate the pressure that weighed on him. His talk at the San Jose Chamber of Commerce in a few hours had to make a big impact. He swilled a sip from his favorite reclining chair, taking in the view of the surrounding hills beyond his estate wall.

Doctors had advised him years ago that he had a fifty percent risk of contracting Huntington's disease since his steelworker father had died from it. Five years after a gene for HD was found, a blood test had confirmed that Ferguson suffered from the deadly disease.

No cures for the disease existed yet, so he'd started developing one himself. He now awaited results on preliminary testing of a new drug.

Before he could settle in, the phone rang.

Ferguson swigged deeply from his scotch before going to his desk and lifting the receiver.

"Ferguson, you schmuck," the male caller said. "Where the hell are you?"

Ferguson began to speak when Ramsey shouted, "Forget-about-it. Get in this office and start explaining where we are with damage control. Be prepared to grovel."

Ramsey's end went dead.

Ferguson grievously resented having to jump whenever Ramsey rang, but Ramsey's firm had that huge stake in J&Q, and Ferguson was still owning up to his coordinating J&Q's failed partnership with the Stanford Grid. Aching, he took a foil-sealed tablet from his pocket, unwrapped it and swallowed it.

While driving to his office, Ferguson rang his physician. "I'm calling to check on results from my latest visit."

"I'm sorry, Mr. Ferguson. You and I need to go over our findings in my office."

"Dr. Metcalf, I'm the type of person who can't wait. Please just tell me what you've got."

"This isn't something that—."

"Isn't it my right to know now?"

"Okay. Unfortunately your Huntington's disease has advanced."

Ferguson stared at the road ahead.

The doctor continued, "Mr. Ferguson, are you there?"

"How long do I have?"

"Impossible to say—six months to a year, maybe less."

Ferguson hung up with thoughts swirling. He'd be dead sooner than he expected.

On the quiet executive-level floor of Johnston & Quib in Emeryville, Olivier Ramsey passed Ferguson who was stepping out of his private office.

"I'll be right back," Ferguson told him.

"You better not be avoiding me. Nicolette wants to do a call," Ramsey said. Nicolette Pinsky was Ramsey's boss in New York.

Ferguson shook his head. "I'm getting coffee for us. Meet me in the small war room where the good speaker system is. And your attitude isn't helping."

Crisis management tested the fiber of all CEOs. Ferguson dreaded the public announcement that Stanford officially joined forces with Google. Then he'd have to face another tirade from investors—a fiery defeat in the waiting. He had half a mind to call the corporate security company, DeltaCorp., he was a board member of to order body guard protection in the event that some hysterical investor came charging into his office.

Minutes later Ferguson carried two mugs of coffee and a granola bar into the war room. Ramsey sat at the head of the polished mahogany conference table, as if he, not Ferguson, were CEO of J&Q. Ramsey's bleached white shirt glared like a spotlight in the windowed room, and his gaze didn't budge from his laptop screen in front of him. Ferguson was accustomed to not getting eye contact from Ramsey. The financier suffered from prosopagnosia, or face blindness. Ramsey relied on clothing, gait and voice to identify people. Ferguson considered it ironic that he never forgot a face and Ramsey never remembered one.

Ferguson handed Ramsey a mug, pulled out one of the leather-seated chairs and sat down. "It's Kona, brought it in myself," he said, resting his own mug on the table.

Ramsey shook his head as he slowly read the motivational quote that was plastered on his mug: A FAILURE IS A MAN WHO HAS BLUNDERED, BUT IS NOT ABLE TO CASH IN ON THE EXPERIENCE. ELBERT HUBBARD.

"Ironic quote, Mark. Should've kept this mug for yourself."

Ferguson took a tablet with a sip of coffee, still reeling from his doctor's report: *You're dying, Mark.* Ferguson didn't track what Ramsey had said last.

Ramsey's gaunt face darkened. "How has Stanford gone from bringing us into the age of digitized records to becoming a competitive threat?"

"We didn't see it coming."

"It's not we, plural and royal, it's you, singular and moronic. I hope you have your shrink on speed dial because after this pow-wow you'll need to increase the strength of those prescription pills you've been taking."

"It's just indigestion. I'm perfectly fine."

"Don't deflect, Ferguson. Neither of us is perfectly fine."

Ferguson took a big bite out of his granola bar. He put on a calm façade whenever his illness cropped up—it had become his most coveted secret as a CEO.

"How did this Google deal happen so quickly?" Ramsey said sharply.

Ferguson crossed his arms. Monogrammed cuffs underscored his presidential rank. "I'm sure Jude Wagner had a hand in this. Who could've predicted they were going to become the Mother Teresa of genomic medicine?"

Ramsey ignored the posturing. "Stanford's alliance with Google will crush stockholder confidence. It'll extend Stanford's Grid to databases everywhere."

"But we can transform J&Q and still be a drug provider." Ferguson was only placating Ramsey now.

"But it will take years to adapt J&Q's one-size-fits all business model and workforce. You think that will sooth investors? On Wall Street, perception is reality, reality is perception."

"But it is possible." Ferguson set down his granola bar.

"Did you give up red meat?" Ramsey shook his head. "The Grid is going to decimate J&Q. Read my lips: genetic scanning is going mainstream. That should galvanize you. And any dime store Pharma company can manufacture base chemical compounds. All of those Blockbusters J&Q has spent billions on with research for patents would be junk. Even if we could pull a rabbit out of the hat and make this Internet-based treatment profitable, we'd only get pennies on the dollar."

"Proof still depends on Stanford's execution." Ferguson admitted to himself that

Google would be a powerful stimulus for personalized medicine, web-enabling an index of the genome and private-sector databases. Though Stanford's name would appear on the Grid's public-medicine home page, Google would be the search-engine intermediary, the invisible middle-ware, transferring the patient's genetic data to scientists.

Ramsey was right. Linked with Google, Stanford's Grid would be unstoppable—at least in the near term. Ferguson should have moved J&Q toward personalized medicine sooner, and now he felt wretched. Fighting his illness had put him off his game.

Ramsey's face turned purple. "God damn you, Ferguson. You must've known something. I'm losing millions with your stock. J&Q has gone from being a partner with Stanford to being their pawn. The wealthiest industry in human history is about to get sucker punched and you've walked us right into those brass knuckles."

Ferguson cleared his throat. "You did hear that the Stanford/CERN liaison, Program Director Jűrgen Hansen, died in Switzerland."

Ramsey's eyes glimmered. "Really? That's a pity."

"It's awful to say, but it could be fortuitous," Ferguson said.

"It could slow 'em down." Ramsey's voice calmed. "But their plan to offer online diagnosis, genomically, will be disasterous if I'm still holding your goddamned stock then."

Ferguson shook his head.

Ramsey added, "And Jude Wagner's algorithm makes it all that more efficient. The Grid could make thousands of Pharma employees redundant."

"This medical revolution will leave waste in its wake," Ferguson conceded. "To quote my daughter, no one's safe these days."

Ramsey tried to meet eyes with Ferguson while maintaining his distance.

"Thankfully," Ferguson added, "Lori is no longer calling herself a bored little crab in a bucket. She's in the private security business." The CEO continued to stall, elaborating on her training and how good it was for his daughter's self-esteem.

Ramsey poured himself a glass of water. "You're walking a tightrope here, Ferguson. You promised your board and Pinsky Capital that partnering with Stanford would put us in the genomic game. But I reread the corporate agreement last night. Nothing bound them from backing out. How did you overlook that?"

Ferguson's in-house legal counsel would hear about this.

Ramsey removed his glasses to rub his deep-set eyes. They showed fatigue—which Ferguson was glad to see: the invincible banker had vulnerability beyond his impaired vision.

The conference room phone rang. Ramsey clicked the receiver button to answer.

"Olivier Ramsey."

"It's Pinsky." The gravelly female voice crackled over the speaker phone from New York.

Ramsey grimaced at Ferguson and hit MUTE. "Time for a reality check."

Ferguson finished pouring himself a glass of water. He hated this. With Ramsey hovering like a pit bull and barking at him about how dire the state of affairs had become, Ferguson was feeling like a gnawed bone.

Ramsey unmuted the speaker. "Hello, Nicolette. I'm here with Mark Ferguson."

"Mr. Ferguson. It's Nicolette Pinsky," the woman said.

Ferguson had never met Nicolette, but the acerbic voice captured the gritty image which preceded her. Ramsey's boss sounded like a hard-faced tyrant.

She didn't wait for a response. "We are not going to sit around idly watching our investment go down the tubes. Ramsey says Stanford's new partnership moves the goal posts, threatening quarterly returns. What are you doing to stop this?"

Ramsey had once told him that Pinsky had fired a new banker who was expecting twins because she got tired of hearing how happy fatherhood would make him.

Ferguson spoke into the squawk box: "I take responsibility for what happened."

Pinsky rasped, "That doesn't change where we are and we're not the Make a Wish Foundation. That's what we'll become if we let this online system diagnose the world's diseases using their genomes. Let's be honest, Mr. Ferguson. Your Board will hand your ass to you on a platter when they hear about Google."

"That's right," Ramsey said, wiping his glasses with his shirt.

Interesting, Ferguson thought. He'd never conceived that Olivier Ramsey feared anything until now. "I've got things moving," Ferguson bluffed.

"That's not what Olivier tells me," the New York voice pushed. "This Google deal fucks us like we begged for it. We need to go on the offensive to keep Wall Street and the public from believing J&Q's business model is outdated."

"I say we create a scare," Ramsey added.

"There's an idea," Pinsky said.

Ferguson laid his hands flat on the table. "A scare?"

"We're beyond polemics, Mr. Ferguson," she said. "Go on, Ramsey."

Ferguson downed his glass of water in one motion.

"We've been goddamn hopeless at stopping this," Ramsey said. Then he looked up brightly. "I do have a short term solution."

"What?" the Pinsky voice said.

"The best way to kill a supplier is to dry up demand."

"Get to the point, Olivier."

"The Grid survives on public trust—belief that it's secure to download the software to a personal computer."

"Go on."

"Suppose we leak the threat of a Grid virus," Ramsey said. "It'd create fear, compromise public trust in the Grid program."

"You're on to something," Pinsky said. "Nobody would volunteer his or her PC if they knew it exposed them to a computer virus."

"It could tarnish the Stanford Grid's image and discourage Grid volunteers for months. In fact, why just leak a rumor that there's a virus?" Ramsey said.

Pinsky said, sounding upbeat, "Right. Why not actually release it on the Grid?" She laughed herself into a smoker's cough. "Fight technology with technology."

"Oh god," Ferguson said softly. "You're confusing mass disruption with mass destruction."

"All's fair in love and business," Pinsky said.

Ferguson stood up, wringing his hands in disbelief.

Pinsky ordered over the speaker phone, "Ramsey, this is on you—it's your responsibility to make it happen. Find a virus writer, assess the cost, and tell us when things will fly—or crash, in this case. And cover your ass, Olivier."

Ramsey said, "I've made headway on this already. You'd be surprised."

The gravelly voice went on. "Good. And no one wants this much knowledge dropped in their lap. Who can deal with knowing what diseases their genes carry and when they're going to die?"

"You hear that?" Ramsey said to Ferguson.

Pinsky continued, "Imagine us all walking around knowing we're prone to anal cancer like Farrah Fawcett, or whatever disease?"

"But wait," Ferguson said. "Knowing our risks is a good thing." If only Huntington's disease were curable. Maybe he could have taken preventive measures. Now, it would even be a miracle if custom drugs could help.

"Mr. Ferguson, I wish it were that simple," Pinsky said. "Even your children aren't safe, Ramsey. Excuse the example."

"Mine?" Ramsey turned, accidentally knocking over his mug, spilling his coffee. Ramsey grabbed napkins, wiping up the coffee to Pinsky's voice.

"Suppose someone draws a genetic correlation to that face-blindness disease you have. One day when your kid gets pregnant she'll be slapped with the percentage chance that the baby will inherit your disorder. Too much knowledge is a burden."

Ramsey balled up wet paper towels, seething.

Ferguson couldn't help grinning.

Ramsey turned a dagger look at him.

Pinsky grumbled again. "Do whatever it takes to stop these hacks and their Grid.

P.S., don't worry about what the SEC or any other papacy will forgive, we're doing this to help people." The phone line suddenly clicked off.

Ferguson broke the deadening silence by rolling back his chair. "You'll have to excuse me. My doctor had a cancelled appointment which I'm going to take."

Twenty-Three

Tuesday, November 1
Highway 280, North of Woodside, CA

The Mazda engine thrummed effortlessly at seventy MPH, proving it had more to it than just bruised fenders. Wagner and Nathalie sped north in silence along Highway 280, heading toward their San Francisco office. He pondered the meaning of the threat they had found on Hideo's white board.

When two Harley Davidson motorcycles blasted by them, Wagner and Nathalie jumped in their seats. They chuckled at their jitters. Nathalie buzzed her car window halfway down. Fresh air had a calming effect on his nerves. Wagner let up some on the gas pedal.

The Junipero Serra Freeway took them through miles of green hills and along Crystal Springs reservoir, the government-protected watershed formed from a natural rift created by the San Andreas Fault. Wagner thought about how much water was piped to Crystal Springs from Yosemite National Park. Millions of people depended on that water, but few gave it a moment's notice. It ran through a grid of pipes . . . another vitally useful grid.

Wagner turned to Nathalie. "About this religious connection, I saw a news story about a genomics conference in Saudi Arabia where crazed demonstrators held placards saying things like, "*Heathen Scientists, Go to hell.*"

Nathalie worked her mini-computer's keys. "I'm checking for other contexts where quotes like that appear, including that one on Hideo Onagi's white board."

Wagner glanced over at Nathalie, scrolling through websites.

"Listen to this," she said. "According to this BBC story, two staunch Catholic groups—the United Bishops Association and a group called Human Life Forever—cite these verses when they are demonstrating against genetic biology and stem cell research." Nathalie sighed. "Maybe the religious conservatives are lumping you and your genomic research in with abortionists."

"United Bishops Association?"

"It's possible."

Wagner reconsidered leads, from Jűrgen being shot with an FBI service pistol in Switzerland to dogs attacking Hideo in Tokyo and the hate mail. How'd it all connect with the United Bishops Association?

The bureau boss posed a separate question. Hackman seemed to have it in for Wagner. But was Wagner just suspicious of Hackman because he was a religious man? Just because a very small group in the religious right vehemently opposed gene-based science—it didn't mean Hackman did also.

Nathalie's phone vibrated. She checked a text from the Swiss police captain. "Jude, they enlarged that photo again."

"What photo?"

"The one taken from Jűrgen's limo. The driver's pen. Under magnification, they got the letters DEL-A---- ---UR- -Y preceding COMPANY."

"Okay, now we have something to focus on," he said.

She didn't move a muscle. "Yes. We can definitely work with this. We have to, for everyone's sake at Stanford."

* * *

Wagner and Nathalie traveled the freeway off-ramp that led into downtown San Francisco. Wagner fidgeted in his seat with restless energy. He felt as if he was scaling a glacier, kicking at footholds for leverage. "I wonder what motive the Bishops Association could have for shutting down a medical Grid," he said. "I guess it could be the threat of genomic medicine going mainstream because it's predictive and deterministic. But that doesn't seem motive enough for murder."

"It's all speculative without forensic evidence. And drug manufacturers might want to see Hideo and Jűrgen fall and slow down the Grid," she said. "But we still need individual suspects. Suspects with the means and opportunity to actually pull off that dog attack in Tokyo after taking aim at Jűrgen in Switzerland the day before. I will say we have at least two, tightly coordinated attackers, possibly frenzied activists."

Wagner went silent. As they rolled into the federal building's garage, they passed a blue Cadillac exiting.

"It's Hackman," Nathalie said.

Wagner noticed a fish symbol on the back of Hackman's car bumper, stuck there like an advertisement.

An impulse came to Wagner. He cranked a U-turn at the bottom of the garage ramp and trailed Hackman out onto Van Ness Avenue.

"Why are you turning?"

"We're following him. I want to know more about Hackman. As long as the Stanford Grid is lined up in cross hairs, no one is above suspicion."

"What? How far do you intend to follow him?" Nathalie asked, sounding fearful of Hackman's invective.

"I don't know yet."

"You distrust everyone. Tell me, is your life always this out of control?"

"If I did, would you believe me?"

She shook her head. "If we get burned, you'll regret doing this. I know you are desperate to pin responsibility for these homicides on someone. But it is a mistake to force inferences from facts. It's not a computer problem."

"Okay, you told me," Wagner mutterd. He crossed Market Street anyway, following the boss's Cadillac onto the 101 freeway. "Hackman seems like an odd bird. I wonder if the stress of this review is getting to him?"

She adjusted her air vent. "He will certainly have to answer for how much he outsources."

"What do you mean?" said Wagner.

"He's very dependent on private security. Put it this way, DeltaCorp has its hands full with contract work to Hackman. I think we are its largest client."

"I get the feeling we're scratching the surface to something big."

"Yes. That's it," she exclaimed. "---UR--Y, on the pen. It stands for SECURITY. SECURITY COMPANY. And DEL-A---- must be DeltaCorp."

"Okay, that's strange. You said they are subcontractors to your San Francisco field office." Wagner sounded unsure, watching the blue Cadillac.

"They are. And if our suspect is with DeltaCorp, he or she is trained to kill."

Wagner glanced over at her, scrutinized her momentarily then refocused on the freeway.

"You said your intruder seemed to know what he was doing, no? Describe him."

"He had short hair and the body of a lumberjack. He was driven off in a dark SUV, a Chevrolet Blazer." Wagner changed lanes and sped up.

"All I can say is that sounds like DeltaCorp." Nathalie typed at her mini- computer. A barely audible sound of confusion came from her.

"What?" The Cadillac changed lanes. Wagner kept an even pace with it.

"You will be very surprised to hear who is on DeltaCorp's Board," she said.

"Who?"

"Mark Ferguson."

Wagner turned to her. "Hold on." He refocused on the freeway.

"Here is a press release from two years ago. '*Atlanta—DeltaCorp Security Company announced today that Mark Ferguson, CEO of Johnston & Quib, joins its Board of Directors.*'"

Wagner dialed down the air conditioning so it was quieter. "Could it be possible that Ferguson and Hackman know one another?"

"Hackman easily could have met Mark Ferguson at one of DeltaCorp's securityconferences."

The connection was making Wagner's head spin.

Wagner now trailed three car lengths behind Hackman's deep blue Cadillac.

"Be careful," she said. "Don't let him see you."

"I'm being as careful as I can be without losing him."

"So your intruder wasn't alone. Maybe this has something to do with the DeltaCorp staff who are working in our office."

"Who is DeltaCorp again?"

Nathalie said, "They're subcontractors backing up field operations while Hackman is reorganizing the San Francisco field office. He would prefer not to call on outside resources like yourself. Our SAC keeps it pretty confidential, but he's worked with DeltaCorp for a long time through this upgrade."

She went on to explain that DeltaCorp had operated in the shadows for years. Doing defense work for the Department of Defense was its forte. Private military companies were the government's end run around Congressional oversight. They weren't beholden to codes of conduct that US soldiers had to respect. They were called on to break the rules, sidestep the Geneva Convention.

"Quite a cottage industry," Wagner said. "But how does that relate to San Francisco?"

"It doesn't directly. However, a DeltaCorp connection fits with the limo photo. They could've accessed the pistol from that lockbox and . . ."

"And what?"

Nathalie's accent sounded stronger. "Four days ago there was a Crisis Meeting held at the office. DeltaCorp employees had operated as rogue agents."

"We need to match that shoeprint with a DeltaCorp employee," he said.

"There are a lot of DeltaCorp employees, even if I could get a bead on their activities in San Francisco. And with many of them owning that same kind of shoe, we'd need to get every short-haired stocky male wearing size eleven to volunteer his impression for a match."

He shook his head, annoyed. They passed a sign for San Francisco Airport.

"You are just going to keep driving aren't you? No matter how far he goes."

"Yes. Could there be a photo roster of DeltaCorp employees?"

"Extremely unlikely. Could you ID the intruder from a photo?" she asked.

"Probably."

"I'll do what I can to find a photo catalogue." She adjusted her seatbelt across her chest. "Remember, Hackman is paying DeltaCorp's bills in this city. He is the one who calls the shots. I have told you a lot."

"Yeah, and I'm counting on you to confide in me." Wagner concentrated on trailing Hackman's Cadillac from the 101 junction onto Highway 280 south. He was hot on the boss's trail. Wagner had a visceral sense that they were getting somewhere. Only he wasn't sure if his gut call to shadow the FBI's SAC would result in some sort of fallout that would hurt them.

Twenty-Four

Tuesday, November 1
Highway 280, Woodside, CA

It wasn't in Wagner's character to hang back when circumstances failed to line up as they should. For better or for worse, he had to know more about Alexander Hackman. Going back in the direction from where they came, Wagner drove several car lengths behind Hackman, through a jockeying line of traffic. Some thirty minutes south of San Francisco, the Cadillac turned off at the Woodside exit, heading into rural suburbia.

Wagner knew Woodside. He blew off stress running its pristine nature paths when he worked at Stanford. Like Niles's sailboat, Woodside was a private oasis from civilization for Wagner.

He and Nathalie followed the boss off the freeway, careful not to get too close behind. Wagner allowed two cars to come between them, then he trailed up the hill until the narrow two-lane road turned to gravel. He passed a woman on horseback, then Wagner turned to the side of the road for fear of being spotted. The Mazda idled beside a low wood slat fence that marked the boundary of an estate with a terracotta- roofed house and a stable.

He saw Hackman's Cadillac climb King's Mountain, out of sight. Wagner watched from afar. After a moment, Hackman's car appeared again, winding up the serpentine country road.

"Why is he in Woodside?" Wagner said.

Nathalie looked overhead at the circling birds of prey. "Nothing is here but horses and hawks."

"And miles of park trails," Wagner added. "And rich people."

"Them too."

More livestock than residents populated Woodside. Its ranch-style homes belonged on the cover of Sunset Magazine. A sharp contrast to the nouveau riche mansions in the surrounding area.

"Look," Nathalie pointed. "He's stopping."

Hackman had reached the summit of the hill. They watched him park the Cadillac in a patch of dirt behind several other cars, including nine or ten Volkswagen Beetles. Wagner saw a small house nearby and a portable building of the kind found at construction sites. From the foot of the hill, they watched Hackman work his way out of his car and mosey into the portable.

Wagner shut off the ignition. He and Nathalie unfastened their seatbelts and got out. A woman on horseback came up from behind their car then pulled on reins when she reached the driver's side. "What do you think?" The horse forced her to do a tight circle.

She pulled on the reins to regain control. "Secret society?" the woman said as her face darkened to a grimace. The horsewoman wore a wide brim straw hat that coordinated with her honey-colored mare. She fixed her sights on the nearby hilltop.

"Ma'am. What's happening up there?" Nathalie said. "I'm law enforcement – just looking things over."

This triggered an emotional button in the woman. "The old man who lived there for sixty years died. His children just sold the entire sixteen acres to a church group called Holy Blood. They found a zoning loophole to build a church. I think they're a cult."

"Really," Wagner said.

"Some parish member bought the land and twelve Volkswagen bugs, one for each deacon." She removed the sun hat, revealing a short tower of gray hair piled on top of her head and used the hat to fan herself.

Nathalie sneezed, probably from the pollen and dry ranch dust in the air.

Warming to the subject, the horse woman continued, "Old nature-lovin' guy's rolling over in his grave. Most of Woodside is fuming, but we're hog-tied."

"When did this start?"

Her mouth tightened. "The church just broke ground for their building. Ninety-five hundred square feet. Can you imagine such a thing up here? They're already conducting mass in the portable. I'd sooner see down-and-out high school kids put in a marijuana crop than have this abomination." She removed a water bottle from a saddle pack, sipped on it and glared at the hilltop again. "My husband heads our homeowners association. He drives up there once a week and gives 'em hell, but so far zippo—no progress. I wish someone could stop this damned monstrosity."

"Thanks for the info," Wagner said. "You've been a help."

"Well at least someone is keeping an eye on things, for what it's worth." The woman nudged the reins and the horse trotted off.

"I'm going to go up there," he told Nathalie. "Do you want to come?"

"This time I don't mind sitting in the car like a poodle. I'll stay and be lookout, no."

He handed her the keys and gingerly picked his way up the incline, moving as quietly as possible. He covered over a hundred yards curving up the hill when he heard voices. Chants or song—he wasn't sure which—came from inside the portable building. He spotted a window in the rear wall, but it was too high to let him look inside.

Scanning the area for an object to stand on, he located a construction sawhorse. He lugged it to the portable and set it parallel to the wall. Putting one foot on it, then another, he grabbed hold of the window frame, clasping onto the aluminum to steady himself.

A horse whinnied from afar.

He peered inside. From behind the congregation, he saw three dozen stiffly postured people, seated presumably for a church service. Several wore heavy brown robes, though Hackman was still dressed in his understated plaid business suit, squeezed into a chair at the front. One of the cloaked men faced the group. He lifted a baby over his head as others bowed their heads solemnly, then lowered it into a font filled with water. It appeared to be a baptism, which the leader performed entirely in Latin.

Three cloth banners hung proudly on the wall: one had an image of Jesus and Mary. The second said, *Last true pope: Pope Pius XII.* The third banner featured a symbol Wagner didn't recognize: two crossed skeleton keys over a parasol handle that was topped with a cross.

Hackman turned his head, glancing toward the window, directly at Wagner. For a millisecond, Wagner froze. His mouth gummy.

He heard a car engine pass behind him. It must've been a late arrival to the service. The driver barked, "Reporter."

Wagner lost his footing on the sawhorse. Scrabbling, he toppled, banging his forearms into the portable wall trying to catch his balance. The voice from inside had gone quiet. This collision must have carried. Did he bring the service to a halt?

Wagner scurried to his feet. As he sneaked around the corner of the portable, he saw the man who had just arrived. The portable door banged open. Glancing back, Wagner saw a robed man nearly collide into the late arrival. Now both of them charged his way. Apparently something as innocuous as a baptism was not meant to be seen by an outsider.

Wagner blazed down the curving path.

But they were taking a straight short cut down the hill, past the winding driveway.

They knew their way around. Wagner was shaken by how quickly they gained on him down the embankment. If these religious men got closer, he'd take a swing at one.

Wagner slipped on loose gravel and fell with a short skid. Dust blew into his lungs, his back slick with sweat. Hacking, he looked back again and he saw the man and hooded figure approaching where the two trails met. No one else from the portable had come out.

Wagner scrambled over loose rocks. He got back on his feet.

Suddenly, from behind, the first man caught up. He grabbed the back of Wagner's shirt, throwing him off balance.

Wagner tripped flat on his knees and elbows again. Scraping in dust, he concentrated on his Mazda down the hill.

Yet the robed man who was taller had caught up. He yanked Wagner's pant leg with an iron clasp.

Wagner kicked his captor's bony fingers, drawing a grunt from the recess of the hood. Jude twisted round to see the man bent over him. His eyes bored onto Wagner's. Gasping, Wagner knocked the hand repeatedly with the sole of his capped-toe shoe. Finally, the man's grip loosened.

Wagner had wrestled himself away. He jumped to his feet and sprinted to his Mazda. Nathalie had jumped into the driver's seat.

Wide-eyed, Nathalie leaned to open the passenger side door.

Wagner clambered in, his shirt and pants stained with dirt. He grabbed the door handle. Before he could hit the door lock, his driver's side car door flung open.

She turned the engine over with a vroom of gas.

The robed man grabbed Wagner's arm and yanked it.

Wagner's arm muscles flexed. His brain synapses fired wildly. He leaned away, fighting to release himself and close the door. But the tall man had already made his move. He'd pulled Wagner halfway out—a fire of hatred burned in his eyes.

The other man stood on the opposite side of the car banging his fists on the windows to intimidate the driver. His fists and palms showed white and pink on the glass. He jerked Nathalie's locked door handle.

Wagner heard frantic rattling. The car rocked from side to side. While he fought to free himself, Nathalie revved the engine.

The robed man pulled hard, trying to yank Wagner from his passenger seat. "You've got questions to answer."

Wagner had one foot in the Mazda and one hand firmly gripping the door handle. But he was being pulled by his wrist. The strenuous force drew Wagner's muscles, testing the tolerance of his ligaments.

"Get away," Nathalie exclaimed.

Fists thundered against the car. Nathalie clasped Wagner's left arm, adding to the tug of war. In one of his frantic heaves, the tall man lost his footing and slipped to one knee beside the car; though he still held onto Wagner's wrist.

Nathalie reached for her gun. Wagner seized the moment. Freeing his left arm from Nathalie, he grabbed the man's wrist. In a single motion, Wagner rolled his right hand away from the man's fingers and pulled it loose.

The man fell away.

Before he could come again, Wagner pulled his leg in the car, reached, snagged the door handle and swung it closed. Nathalie leveled her Glock on the attacker on her side. He stopped his pounding.

Wagner flipped the door locks.

Nathalie brought the car to life with another vroom of gas. Wheels spun in place, scattering dirt and dust at the enraged faces. The men shielded their eyes and lowered their heads. The rubber took hold. The car lurched into motion and revved away.

As the Mazda sped downhill, leaving the angry men behind, Wagner's chest heaved. His shoulder joints throbbed. Nathalie drove, aghast. "I should've pulled my weapon sooner. I hesitated with Hackman in the vicinity."

She pointed his Mazda away from bucolic Woodside and back to busy San Francisco.

Wagner gasped audibly from his sprint down the hill as his car sped onto Highway 280, leaving Woodside. He twisted in his seat to look behind them.

"What on earth happened back there?" she said.

"It faintly resembled a Catholic service, but in a very old style."

"What do you mean by old style?"

"In Latin. They had a banner with two keys beneath an umbrella topped by a cross."

"That sounds unusual," she said. "How typical is it to hold Mass on Tuesday afternoon?"

"You tell me. Aren't you Catholic? It looked like a baptism."

"Wait," she said. "It is All Saint's Day."

He turned. "Do you have a pad of paper?"

"A little one in my purse."

He shifted in his seat to pull her mini-pad and pen from her purse. He quickly sketched the religious banner he saw.

A quizzical expression came over her.

He grabbed her mini-computer.

She gave him her password. He searched the Catholic banner. "That symbol. It's Sedevacantism."

"Sedevacantism?" she said. "Let me guess. It is a demonic cult that practices ritual human sacrifice."

"Not exactly. But be careful what you wish for. Apparently the Sedevacantists are a minority Catholic group."

"I was right."

He continued, "They've adopted the position that the papal office has been vacant since the death of Pope Pius XII in 1958, and the five subsequent popes are illegitimate.

The word Sedevacantism is actually two Latin words combined, which mean *the Chair is vacant*, referring to the chair of Peter."

"This is too much. Is there anything else?"

He read from her screen. "Evidently, they've got branches all over the world, even in Tokyo and Geneva."

"Interesting. I've never heard of them," she said.

"They have about 100,000 members in the United States. Sedevacantivists zealously guard their privacy."

"Obviously."

"Says here Sedevacantists claim the church is defined by its unity, holiness and apostolicity. The refusal of all Popes since Pope Paul VI to wear the papal tiara is most objectionable to Sedevacantists who deem it a papal requirement." Wagner stopped and turned to her.

"Okay," she said, "could this Sedevacantivist church in some way be tied to Hideo and Jűrgens' deaths? And would this church have anything to do with DeltaCorp? One doesn't have to relate to the other, but the religious nuts hate you for your genomics work. And from what I can tell, Hackman does too."

"Right, this is odd, but it doesn't implicate Hackman in murder."

"No," she added, "but it could tie in with why Hackman wanted to monitor you so closely."

Could Hackman have a hand in these murders? It seemed highly unlikely that a respected member of the Justice Department could've fallen so far, but Wagner's other suspects were just as improbable. Who would believe that anyone from the medical community would be knocking off the competition? Unanswered questions piled up.

Nathalie said, "You could have chosen an easier person to investigate. It would be nice to keep my job."

She had her eye on going up the FBI ladder, and he probably wasn't doing anything to help her in that respect. "Wait a minute," she said. "I remember seeing correspondence in the office with the name United Bishops Association."

"Really?"

"Yes, but I can't place where," she said. "Could you be imagining it?"

"Possibly. The name sounds very familiar to me now."

Wagner's phone rang. Seeing Kate's name in LED, he flipped it open. "Hey Kate."

"Jude, when are you going to be home?" There was vulnerability in her voice he hadn't heard in years.

"What's wrong?"

"Nothing's wrong," she said defensively. "I was just wondering."

"I'll be there soon." He hung up.

Nathalie turned toward Wagner, overhearing one side of the conversation.

"We'll concentrate on these quotes later," she said.

Wagner absently nodded. She kept her eye on the highway.

They drove in silence until they arrived at the federal building where she got out and he took the wheel. As he pulled away from 450 Golden Gate, he checked his rearview mirror and caught her watching him drive away. He had really let his guard down about how vulnerable he felt about his Grid project. Hopefully that choice would not be one he'd live to regret.

Twenty-Five

Tuesday, November 1
San Francisco, CA

Wagner closed his front door, leaving behind the unnerving trip to Woodside with that pair of enraged parishioners. His paperbacks and magazines were straightened in his bookcase and the coffee maker and grinder had been tidied. He was pleased, and even felt a twinge of guilt, to see that Kate had cleaned his apartment and returned it to its original minimalist state. Taking in the mundane normalcy of his living room was like stepping through the looking glass after what he'd encountered with those religious men only two hours ago. But the serenity of home vanished as a sobbing sound came from his bedroom. He went in.

She lay on his bed, her head sunk in his pillow. "What is it?"

"Nothing, really."

A yellowish medicine vial sat on his dresser. He picked it up. "What's this?"

"Medicine. Jude, I expected it would be just another mammogram, but it wasn't. I have breast cancer. That's why I came, to tell you in person. That and to clear my head miles from my roommate. I'm on a two week medical leave from the University."

Her laptop was plugged in. What looked like student papers sat beside it. As always, teaching assignments appeared to have followed Kate. The screensaver displayed DNA in swirling multicolored double helix strands on a black background. Everywhere he turned something reminded him of his work and the promise of what the Grid should accomplish. The computer rested beside a book on the Dali Lama and her charging cell phone.

"Breast cancer? How serious is it?"

"I have a cyst like a little walnut under my arm. My doctor says I show clear signs of metastatic breast cancer. The biopsy indicates I'm stage three."

Jude went stiff. "That's deadly serious."

"I know. I've started on the hormones twice a day, and I'm waiting to hear." Kate's cheeks went red. She pulled her knees to her chest.

"Goddamned cancer," Wagner exclaimed. "I'll get you some water."

Jude returned with a filled glass and a bag of Gummi bears from the kitchen.

"Ah, Gummi bears."

She took the bag and grabbed a small handful.

She continued, "Anyway, the doctor advised me not to go on this trip, but I insisted." Kate rubbed her eyes, switching the subject. "You know how we used to sneak into Dad's den . . . play Mom's recordings. I miss that. How we listened like she was here. My best memories were those years."

If he wasn't careful, she'd have them both in tears. "When skateboards and those disasters movies, *Jaws* and the *Towering Inferno*, were too cool for school and teenagers weren't texting and driving."

"And the airlines gave you honey-roasted nuts and didn't charge for luggage."

"What's your prognosis?" he said.

"Hard to say. It could be spreading to my auxiliary lymph glands. If that's the case then the cancer is systemic."

"What are your options, surgery? Chemo?"

Kate nodded vacantly. "My doctor is calling back tomorrow with more information from the tests." Her face flushed with anxiety. "You're taking this well."

Wagner paced the length of his room then glanced outside. Finally, he said, "Kate— I'm in shock." He worked to keep his emotions in check. He thought about holding her, but he wasn't even prepared to do that. As he searched for something to say, he stared again at the animated screen saver—the DNA image that once inspired him. The twisted pairs signified wondrous possibilities, magical threads for creating life, but he couldn't help but see the double helix as Kate might: a hereditary death sentence.

He dropped into the winged-back chair in the corner of his bedroom. "Why didn't you tell me you had a bad mammogram?"

"I didn't want to admit this was happening, not even to myself." She pointed at a printout she'd brought about a new drug. "It's something that Johnston & Quib will be putting on the market."

"Johnston & Quib?"

"I know—it's the company you had that falling out with."

"That's right and there's a reason."

"This is about me, okay. It's not business. And don't talk to me about side effects. There's a downside to everything."

"We'll talk about that later." He was too busy wrestling with how cancer had preyed on his family to get into it with her about J&Q.

Her expression turned more detached. "Apparently breast cancer is a much more aggressive disease in younger women."

"What else did your doctor say?"

"He said radiation and chemo might stop cancer from getting into my bones. Once that happens, it goes to the lungs, liver, skin and brain."

Jude cleared his throat. "Breast cancer is many different cancers rolled into one. No traditional doctor will see the complexity of your illness. But if we run your genome on the Grid, we'll not only get a molecular view of you, but also a customized prescription.

We're already giving a diabetes control group custom compounds. The results are phenomenal. And after going through this with Mom, we know your doctors only have a short list of treatment options. I've got someone for you to see."

Kate covered her mouth, overwhelmed.

"Just hear me out. Breast cancer is profoundly complicated. You need exactly the right therapy for your tumor type. You inherited your cancer from Mom, so we have to look at you on a gene level and not treat you like a million others. Your disease is just as gene-based as your response to drugs will be. Breast cancer is the most common form of cancer in women but treating their tumors as the same is deadly."

"And I would be your first breast cancer test run on your vast computer network?" The questioning tone in her voice made his suggestion sound speculative and radical.

"Yes. Look at it this way, it's an alternative to some oncologist nuking you to kingdom come. If your breast cells are dividing out of control, you need an individualized protein inhibitor drug to stop it—tailored to you."

"I'll try to keep an open mind."

"Inheritability doesn't have to translate to inevitability."

"That's a good line."

"It's true," he said. "Think of your cancer as a tennis ball. Now, imagine throwing a tennis ball into the sea. No one could predict where that ball will land. But what if you could factor in every dynamic—tides, current, wind, rain, the weight, shape and buoyancy of that ball—everything affecting its path. Then you could pinpoint where the ball would beach to within an inch."

Her eyes fixed on him as he picked the cuticle of his thumb in his chair. "Now, consider your situation. Your doctor diagnosed you with Stage III breast cancer. And surgery, radiation, chemotherapy and immunotherapy—they all have side effects. But suppose beforehand you learned you could be treated with the same degree of precision that was used in tracking that tennis ball, stopping cancer in its tracks, greatly reducing the chance of side effects and freeing you from unnecessary procedures."

She smiled. "Gotta admit, you certainly can do one hell of a sales job. But all of this online medicine is just emerging."

"Yes and no, Kate. We already have a lot of databases working seamlessly with pooled patient information."

"What would be the first step for me at Stanford then?"

"Your tissue sample would go into a DNA sequencer, a machine that looks a bit like a high tech microwave oven—marvelous inventions."

"Go on," said Kate.

"Your DNA would be decoded and then uploaded to the Grid website where your genome would be interpreted. That website would scrub your information of personal identifiers so it could be statistically pooled. Your doctor would then enter your full medical history and query your issue. The system puts more medical knowledge in a user's hands than an entire hospital could. Is this too much right now?"

"No, I want to hear this."

Wagner seized this opening to finish. He explained how the Grid would compare her genomic data against millions of other online medical records, isolating tissue samples from patients with other markers to that disease. Ultimately, the system would analyze Kate's reactions to drugs molecularly and generate a customized prescription to treat her disease.

"It all sounds slick." A hint of hope welled in her eyes. "You're making me feel better."

He gave his argument a rest, knowing she needed to rationalize everything just as he did. She'd weigh the pros and the cons of the information her brother had presented in private, then draw a conclusion that she would commit to and act on. He watched her chew on another Gummi bear, twisting the cellophane packaging. He knew she rewarded her best students with the candies. She read the back label aloud, "'Gummi bears were invented in the 1920s, but the history of gelatin traced back to the Egyptian pharaohs.'" Maybe eating the Pharaoh food would channel the immortality of Egyptian gods. Their culture survived for 5,000 years."

"Now *you're* going to have to stop telling me to get real," he said. "Seriously, what can I do for you while you're here? Do you want to get a second doctor's opinion? I could try to take a little time off."

She shook her head. "That's why I held off on telling you about this. I want you to work as normal. During the day, I'll research this. I'm going to make full use of having a substitute teacher."

After going back and forth with him over it, he acquiesced. He'd lost all enthusiasm for work but dealt with it and made an evening trip back to the bureau. Stanford needed him. If he let up now, the Grid wouldn't be the only thing imperiled.

Twenty-Six

Tuesday, November 1
San Francisco, CA

Jude Wagner felt hollowness in the quiet of the bureau's coffee room. With it being six-thirty p.m., this was the first time he'd been in the field office without Nathalie supervising his activities. Something of priority had called her away from the office early today. He had no idea what and relied on a security person to accompany him to the floor. Unsettling thoughts about loss ticked away. Niles and Knowlan had volleyed so many telephone calls at Wagner while he drove to the bureau, he'd reached his stress limit fielding their concerns. Finally, Wagner muted the ringer on his cell to escape the endless phone loop of distress calls. Kate's chances for survival were on the rapid decline—processing the situation wrung him out, though he refused to let this to hijack his concentration.

He found instant oatmeal in the cabinet, poured some in a bowl, added boiling water and stirred. He actively forced himself to stop dwelling on Kate. It was time to follow up on what Nathalie had started researching on Sedevacantism.

Taking his healthy snack to his alcove area, he found two pages left on his desk with computer commands from Hideo's office. Nathalie had printed out what she'd saved at the Stanford lab for Jude to look over. He wanted to take this home with him, so he tucked it into his pocket. Also, a Post-it note was stuck to his visitor's chair.

Tried reaching you. Call me. —Nathalie

Getting a simple message from her instantly buoyed his spirits. Whatever she had to say, he wanted to hear it right away. He picked up the phone. After two rings, she answered and recognized his voice. "Come to my place." She gave him her address.

"I can be there in, say, ninety minutes. I have loose ends to tie up."

"Okay, fine." Her end clicked off.

He ate his oatmeal in a hurry and spent half an hour catching up on antivirus coding updates the analysts had emailed Wagner. They'd made serious progress on tagging malware. Completing those messages, he searched the 'Net on Sedevacantivism.

Sedevacantivists cited that the first Pope John XXIII was convicted of sins and was deposed. Vatican II then violated tenets of the One True Church. This supported the case that John and his successors were interlopers without papal authority.

This might have meant more to Wagner in a college sociology class on religious subcultures. Here it didn't strike him as revelatory, though he copied the info to his suspect file nonetheless.

Then he opened an email from FBI analyst, agent Morris—now this was someone who spoke Wagner's language. Morris had unearthed quite a discovery: he concluded that the Grid's single greatest vulnerability existed with its computer donors. The Grid, of course, was sending and receiving work instructions from donors as a means of breaking down big, biological problems across many machines. Morris wrote, "If a hacker could pose as a Grid volunteer, he could infiltrate the network and compromise it using corrupted instructions that went back to the Grid for processing."

Thankfully, Morris worked up a partial solution to Wagner's existing antivirus software. Conditioned to encountering obstacles without clear fixes, Wagner was thrilled to get an attachment to Morris's email.

Wagner clicked open the attachment. He saw some very clever code indeed. It allowed Wagner to tag computer instructions which the Grid sent to its computer volunteers. This could help him track and isolate infected instructions. Now, if a set of computers were sending bad results, all Wagner needed to do was identify the computer source and then use Morris's tags as an identifier to filter them from the Grid server. Wagner spent the next twenty-five minutes analyzing how this would work in practice.

After this, he left behind what he was doing, got back into the Mazda and drove to Noe Valley. It felt strangely satisfying, except his rushing over to her place didn't entirely make sense. He had taken a shine to her, yes, but why pin hopes on their hooking up? He needed that like a heart attack. Their separate worlds wouldn't normally intersect with her being a career agent. Once this threat at Stanford quieted, she and her San Francisco bureau would plod on to bigger things. Nothing more. His emotions took him for a ride. A loneliness had set in from Kate's situation, and the idea of working with Nathalie softened the blow. These hours he was spending with her drew him into her universe. He'd have to tread carefully or risk seeing something romantic forming that just wasn't there.

Added to that, sleeping with Nathalie would only muddy the waters while he defended the Grid. The pressure alone should've hindered his interest in seeing her, but it hadn't. Wagner rolled by the Castro Theater. Its Spanish colonial design was brightly lit. Various walks of life mingled outside restaurants. The festive atmosphere clashed with Wagner's unsettled frame of mind.

He motored up the hill and angled his tires into the curb at Diamond and 24th. She opened the door. With thumbs on the top of white denim pants, she nodded for him to come in. The sight of her dressed down put him off balance. She appeared considerably softer, as if she had two personas: one for field office duties, the other on reserve for civilian life. Evidently, she switched between them with the ease of superman.

A mischievous smile came to her as she leaned against the door. "I'm glad you got my note."

Moving to her living room, he took in her sheer silver camisole. It revealed the curve of her breasts.

She picked up two wide-mouth glasses of red wine from the coffee table and offered him one. Hers was half empty. "You have some catching up to do," she said in a celebratory tone. Her lips formed in the shape of a kiss at the end of that sentence. He wanted to see her in a professional light but had a hard time not imagining her olive-skinned body naked. Her French accent turned simple phrases into come-ons. It tested his man-pledge of self restraint. Kryptonite had been thrown in his path. The slippery slope had him bracing for his fall.

Wagner accepted the glass of wine and sipped. "So what's going on?"

She picked up a piece of hardware that resembled a garage door opener in size. "Before I forget, take this. It's an audio jammer. It knocks out recording devices in a thirty-foot radius. Keep it at home, you-know, in case someone gets in again and plants a bug."

Wagner thanked her. He tucked the jammer in his jacket pocket, then sat on her red leather sofa. Her chic furnishings showed her sense for retro design, her creative side. Under the glass coffee table sat a 1960's-style shag throw rug that ideally matched the corner fig tree with floor lighting and the Eames lounge chair with ottoman.

"I hope your news is good," he said.

She sat beside him. "It is, but I can see something is bothering you."

"I must be pretty transparent. My sister has breast cancer."

"*Mon dieu.* That's awful. How advanced is it?"

"Very."

"Really? Jude, is there any way I can help?"

"Only if you have favors to call in with a higher power."

"And she's your only sibling. Health surprises are so hard," she added.

"I agree. I'm going to do what I can using the Grid."

"Really?"

"Truthfully, it's a stab in the dark, but it's all I've got."

Wagner sipped his wine. "You had something to tell me?"

"It's not all that critical."

"I drove over here, didn't I? Go ahead. I need the distraction," he said.

"You've probably guessed what I am going to say." She finished her wine.

"I'm not telepathic."

"Things would be easier if you were," she said.

He wondered why women wanted men to understand what they had in mind without speaking. "You've teased me long enough."

"I have?"

"Nathalie."

"Okay, okay. I think I am getting a promotion."

He wondered if his disappointment showed.

"How'd you hear that?"

"Speer told me." She sat down beside him.

"Speer? That needle-neck automaton? He's about as sharp as a mashed potato."

"I understand how you feel, but listen."

"Wait. Did you have a boyfriend who dumped you hard a month ago?"

"Did Speer say that about me?"

“Yes."

Nathalie rolled her eyes. "It's not true. He's playing inside your head. Just hear what I have to say. After you dropped me off at the office today, I was going over everything that had happened with those religious guards chasing you and those Bible quotes in Hideo's lab, when I bumped into Speer. He said that if I joined him for a glass of bubbly down the street, he'd enlighten me about some company news that would put a skip in my step. You know how he calls the bureau the company?"

"No, I don't." Wagner rubbed his brow and put his glass down.

"Anyway, I told him I didn't have the time, but he pushed and pushed for *a tête-à-tête*."

"What?"

"You-know, a private moment."

"So you went?"

"I did, with reservation. We went to the Redwood Room in the Clift Hotel where he tried to kiss me."

"No." Wagner rubbed end-of-day stubble on his chin.

"I didn't let him. I know you don't like him. If you don't mind my directness, I think you take too much personally, okay?"

"Everything's personal and everything's political, especially in your field office."

Her gaze wandered away from him. "To be honest, I forgot all about his little move after what he told me. Apparently Hackman's slated me for a transfer to the Los Angeles unit where they are short on resources in Cyber."

Wagner shifted in his sofa seat. He didn't want her moving away—no matter how separate their worlds were. But that was quintessential Nathalie—exceedingly independent.

He took her glass from her hand and set it down on the coffee table beside his. He leaned over and placed his hand on the crook of her jaw beneath her ear. It had the slope of a desert dune. She touched his fingers that stroked her face.

She whispered, "What are you doing?"

"Looking at you."

Her lips curled at the corners.

Before she had a chance to pull his hand off her face, he wrapped his arms around her small waist. Desire pounded . . . building for days. Her large brown irises stared at him.

He put his lips to hers. The smell of her filled him. But her lips didn't reciprocate.

This could end with a swift slap.

Then her lips opened.

Suppressed feelings surged like a warm gust. Her open mouth followed his. They fell into her sofa cushions then rolled to the carpet. Her camisole came undone. With little movements, he pulled it over her head and slender arms. She tossed it on the floor. Her leg swept languidly across his.

He lifted her in his arms. Legs straddling his torso, he marched to her bedroom.

Holding her with one arm, he yanked the bedspread down. He set her on the bed as if she were fine china. Lying motionless on her back, she watched him. On hands and knees, he stalked her.

He kissed the instep of her foot, then flicked the top button on her pants and steadily removed them. After he had kissed his way up her calf and thigh, she writhed, then groaned.

They became passionate arabesques. Sexual energy hypnotically mounted from a slow and tender staccato of tongues to a savage tango of their entire bodies. Twenty minutes or an hour later—Wagner couldn't say how long it all had lasted—he collapsed at her side. The cathartic release misted them in sweat.

She let out a giggle. "My legs feel like they're floating. By the way, you don't smell anything like an agent."

He chuckled. "I suppose that's good. What does an agent smell like?"

"Ambition and nerves. You-know, that American *Mennen* deodorant and coffee. Our job draws that type."

"What do I smell like, besides sex?"

She traced his Adam's apple with her pointy nose, then rolled her head back and locked eyes with him. "Youth."

"Ha."

She rested her head in her hand. "Men or boys I dated at Goddard in Columbia—they had your scent. Their heads were still their own. They weren't molded for anyone else's purpose. The rat race hasn't spoiled your beliefs yet either.

He didn't answer. The rumblings of his mind receded into background noise. He didn't want to think about her relocating or anything outside of her bedroom.

Their relationship was moving in reverse. From coldly rational to spontaneously emotional. A less than ideal prescription for crime-solving partners. He touched her half-open lips with the tip of his finger.

Her breathing slowed. They lazily gazed at one another, savoring the silence. She stretched. "This doesn't make any sense does it?"

"It makes perfect sense," he said, "we're drawn to each other."

Using two fingers, she gently wiped sweat off his forehead. "And I am leaving San Francisco."

"Yeah, right when we get together," he said.

"Exactly. Hackman would frown on this. At least it could be more than six months before this transfer is processed and probably longer before I leave for LA." With his hand in hers, she tightened her interlocked fingers. Then she climbed on top of his naked belly, traced his lips with her finger and kissed his face from above. "But we still might get a pious lecture from him about the mortal sin of premarital sex."

"Well then, maybe we should stop what we're doing, just for him."

She looked at him sharply.

"I hope Speer wasn't just smooth-talking you to warm you up."

"You mean to get me naked and in bed?"

"Yes, lucky for him it failed."

"What do you mean, failed?" She spread her arms, proudly showing her naked, symmetrical breasts. "It worked, but for you. Not him."

"He's lucky he didn't try to push it farther with you."

"Why, would you fight him for me?"

Wagner held a fist. "There's a possessive side of me."

Nathalie looked away, then back at him, irritated. "We still have to be careful. We have a killer out there we have to stop. And I don't want this—what we are doing—to throw us off."

"I agree," he said.

"Nothing in life is easy, right?"

"You've gotta go to the mat for every little thing. Take me for instance. I'm judged for being from Louisville. I can see it in their eyes—Californians think I'm a hick with horseshoes and manure in my blood but what do they know?"

She dropped her chin in her hand. "You sort of have a romantic side to you. Do you realize that?"

"Maybe. I've been called a dreamer."

"I hope it doesn't scare you to hear this," she said, "but there is a lot of life to live away from a desk and a PC. To figure out yourself completely is an entirely different investigation."

"I'll consider this talk a warning before I make another sudden move," he said.

Twenty-Seven

Tuesday, November 1
San Francisco, CA

Shortly after eight p.m. Alexander Hackman plodded heavily along the bureau building's wood corridor with his lower lip protruding into a frown. The FBI SAC had had dinner and returned to his office late to deal with Jude Wagner for overstepping his boundaries. Fortunately, the professional review officers were no longer roaming the hallways. At last Hackman had the freedom he needed to tend to Jude Wagner. He could revoke Wagner's visitor pass, but it was preferable to see what the Stanford man was up to first.

Hackman passed the night agent's desk, unmanned computers in empty cubicles and eight-foot-tall bookcases. To the head of the FBI field office in San Francisco, those stacks of leather bound volumes represented a more reliable and true source of information than anything in electronic form. They would have been donated years ago had he not ordered that they stay put. His cynicism of computer specialists ran contrary to the expectations of a FBI bureau chief. Cyber intrusion had become increasingly central to federal law enforcement. The Justice Department, especially since the Patriot Act had become law, coveted its computer network. But not Hackman.

He suspected that his staff whispered, "Luddite," behind his back, but his misgivings about computers came from experience. A web-enabled bureau translated into increased exposure to outsiders. Anyone with the sophistication to break the bureau's network security had access.

Once in his corner office, Hackman glowered through his window at the lifeless avenue below. An ambulance siren whined nearby. Streetlights shot yellow cones on the pavement; otherwise, this section of Civic Center was cloaked in black. Lumps of humanity hunkered in stairway corners or building entrances. Hackman hated passing their sleeping bags on those occasional nights he returned to the bureau. The stench of urine and excrement rose through grates from a long outdated sewer system. Even underground gas lines were dilapidated and desperately in need of repair by the city's public utility. San Francisco had long suffered budget deficits. The last ten years would've been easier if he hadn't been reassigned from Houston. Of fifty-six field offices, he probably would have felt more at home anywhere but in liberal San Francisco. The one redeeming quality that this wayward town had was its bay views.

The only other occupants of the federal building at this hour, besides the night agent, were security guards pulling graveyard on the ground level. Hackman threw off his overcoat and parked his two hundred and fifty pounds in his burgundy chair. Clearing his desk of a backlog of file folders, he made space around a stack of newspapers clippings, memoranda and stapled agent reports—he preferred to have most items printed.

The FM jazz station that droned by day from a radio on his credenza remained off and so did most lights outside of Hackman's office.

Hackman maintained distance from staff, but he wasn't oblivious to his agents, subcontractors or visitors; he knew their habits, down to the year of car they drove. When Hackman had exited the freeway at Woodside Road, he'd recognized Wagner's red car in his rearview mirror. The boss could see that someone else was with him but couldn't make out the face. Since then his Church people had informed him that Wagner was accompanied by a brunette. It could've been Noiret, but then it could've been any woman.

When Wagner was bird-dogging him, Hackman wanted to see just how far the computer techie would press his luck. After the skirmish at the church service, Hackman had jammed on the gas pedal in a hurry to reach his office. Now it was time to find out why this Grid computer expert was on him.

He opened his locked file cabinet. With his thick index finger, he poked through folders stuffed with reports that special agents had written. Shaking his head, he read the non-FBI personnel file he'd started on Wagner. Pages of information fell under the category of special skills, including his work at Stanford and theoretical computer study at Berkeley. Hackman refreshed his knowledge of the impetuous young man . . . he had some ambition if he thought he could improve medicine. He and his Stanford Grid colleagues were tampering with things they shouldn't. Maybe Wagner was oblivious to what he'd started with his mathematical formula.

He thought about the immense access that Wagner had to the FBI computer system, and then reached a decision. With a few mouse clicks, he activated a tap on Wagner's personal cell phone. But there was no telling how long that would triangulate his movements by GPS. Wagner could trash his phone after that situation in Woodside.

But why was Wagner following him? He couldn't be sure. Hackman phoned Supervisor Speer. Warren Speer's dedication to his work and all of its rules bordered on obsession, but it earned him Hackman's trust. Hackman heard the phone receiver knock off the cradle on the fourth ring.

"It's Hackman."

A groggy voice answered with a yawn. "Yes, Sir. What happened?"

"I need you to track our subject matter expert, Jude Wagner."

"Can I get the details about this in the morning?"

"No. It's a priority. You got it? Follow him."

"Yes, track Wagner."

"And very discreetly."

"Understood. What should I be looking for?"

"Just forward to me what you find—in your usual folder. Don't leave a computer trail."

* * *

Propped up in his queen-sized bed at The Claremont Hotel in

Berkeley, Olivier Ramsey endured an early evening phone call with his boss, Nicolette Pinsky.

Pinsky said, "I couldn't sleep. I've been trying to reach you for hours."

"What is it?" Ramsey asked.

"Stanford's Grid program chief Hideo Onagi had been killed in Tokyo by a fluke dog attack."

"Oh. That's, ugh . . . truly something." Ramsey felt a tinge of pity for Stanford, but a larger part of him felt relief. His personal stock ticked up.

"What have I missed over there?" gravel voice asked.

"I have a virus writer working frantically. He sounds quite confident in his abilities."

"Is that all?" she said.

"I'm working on more inside information."

"Anything to stem this sell off that's bleeding us to death. Enough said, I'm going to bed." Pinsky's end hung up.

Feeling anxious, Ramsey washed his face. He opened a can of assorted nuts from his mini-bar and ate them in bed, pondering matters. Stanford would be in a frenzy to reorganize with their program director absent. This scored points for Pinsky Capital, but he'd never use those words. Ramsey feared the Grid could go on without Hideo Onagi. Ramsey had reassured Pinsky that he had matters under control. If only he could convince himself of that. He had built his reputation on bringing equity investors to big Pharma. So much was riding on the survival of traditional drug companies.

Ramsey's BlackBerry vibrated. It was an email sent from @@@:

"If I get Grid access, my program should jumble their database entries, firewalls permitting. Backup strikes r all set. A leak says the Grid will be connected to Google on November 7. It's time.

-Cez@r."

Ramsey bit his lip. He looked at his phone again and the very email he just read disappeared. He got up and opened his drapes. Cez@r, the hacker, sounded a little out of control. The Bay Bridge shone under yellow lights. The city, surrounded by bridges, seemed to protect its own with its moats. Using his BlackBerry again, he called Ferguson. No answer.

Normally a headline junky, Ramsey picked up his hotel-delivered newspaper. A story in the back stated that the Stanford Grid team was *carving out a new niche in medicine with computational biology while swimming against a sea of detractors*.

And they're about to sink miserably to the ocean floor, Ramsey thought. He slapped down the newspaper. Before long everyone will bear witness to just how hackable Grid computers are.

Twenty-Eight

Tuesday, November 1
Berkeley, CA

While she'd killed seven people in her career on missions across the globe, she'd never done an operation on American soil until tonight. The blonde woman weighed the situation from behind the wheel of her SUV. This job broke new ground. She refastened a clip in her wig. If she were following usual procedure, she'd have no knowledge about her target, except name and appearance. The psychology was to separate emotion from the job. Emotion cluttered a calculated hit. Briefings on all matters were succinct. Although on this task she'd briefed herself on this Stanford prick.

The blonde, whom colleagues called Scud, quietly closed the door to her vehicle, zippered her jumpsuit to shield herself from the cold bay air and pulled a hood over her head to help conceal her face. She had waited outside the Berkeley Marina to watch park security drive by. She had to hurry. Security would circle by again in thirty minutes.

Under a crescent moon, Scud moved through the Marina parking lot to the gated dock. Hunching over on the wooden plank deck, she shone a miniature silver maglite to see what type of lock she needed to pick and open the dock door. She was in luck. A cylinder lock, just as she'd hoped.

She had been trained by the world's elite, a covert U.S. government fighting squad. One of America's largest corporations retained her on a renewable contract as an overseas operative. They even gave her the

Russian missile moniker, Scud, for her tactical savvy. Although this assignment didn't come from a superior or the usual chain of command—the DOD, the Pentagon and the President of the United States. Quite the opposite. This job was personal. This time she'd call her own shots, without relying on others' instructions about how to complete the task.

Lastly, profit wasn't the only lure. She had a burning wish for retribution against the Grid. J&Q stock had the volatility of an atom bomb. No PR team in the world could help J&Q's poor CEO. Even a money-grubbing parasite like Olivier Ramsey should see that the company was beyond media spin. Impairing the Grid would salvage everything. It would prove herself to that one person who never noticed her.

Scud set her tote bag down, readjusted a rubber band around her hair so she could see clearly and put on thin black gloves. Then, after making sure she was alone, Scud removed a long steel shank and a flathead screwdriver from a zipper pouch. She controlled the beam of the maglite, mindful of it not reflecting moonlight.

Adjusting the beam, she inserted the screwdriver in the keyhole and turned it clockwise. The cylinder lock had a moveable bolt extending from door to metal frame.

Her screwdriver served as a tension wrench to expose the pins. She inserted the pick into the keyhole and lifted the pairs of pins to their fullest height, two by two. She agilely pushed the pins until she heard the bolt retract and click, unlocking the gate.

To the sound of lapping water, she walked along the docks, panning the flashlight beam across each berth, searching boats until the name *Tipsea* glimmered in gold across a stern. Stepping on board, she unzipped her small bag and removed her standard plastic explosive—just gasoline, oil and Styrofoam, wired for detonating with a timer switch to a battery-operated clock. In her bedroom, she'd simply melted Styrofoam, cooled it, mixed oil, then mixed gasoline. Once her concoction got to 88 degrees Fahrenheit, she molded it. Like Dynamite it was inelegant, primitive even. But it was ideal for that very reason. The more people who could readily make this, the more suspects police would have to interrogate. And unlike Dynamite, this explosive left no purchase trail.

The *Tipsea* offered a pleasant surprise too. Muddling around in the dark hull, she smelled petrol. She shined her light on the aft storage box, opened the latch and found a stowed gasoline can. This told her the boat was gas-powered, not diesel. Gas engines were cheaper, more efficient, and far less costly to maintain than their diesel counterparts, but they were also more flammable. Once satisfied with her handiwork on board the *Tipsea*, Scud closed her briefcase and tiptoed away. She drove straight home. There she reassessed her stock portfolio and the sensation the media would make of the accident.

Twenty-Nine

Early Wednesday, November 2
San Francisco, CA

The Russian Hill flat sweltered with dry heat. Unable to sleep, Kate Wagner flicked on Jude's bedside table light at 12:30 a.m. Cancer haunted her. While he camped on the living room sofa, she propped herself upright on his bed with doubled over pillows. Concerned for Kate, Jude had cranked the thermostat dial to sauna temperatures, then crashed on the couch. Unable to find the thermostat, she opened his heavy wooden bedroom window to admit a cool breeze. Framed photos on the wall distracted her for a moment—pictures Jude had taken from a trip he'd taken to see glaciers calving in Alaska. The Wagner family of four had certainly scattered.

Kate felt envy for those like her mother who had religious faith . . . a grounding belief in God. If only she had inherited her mother's beliefs instead of her breast cancer. Spirituality, for Kate, only amounted to a dabbling in Buddhism. It didn't render comfort in salvation through the hereafter . . . as much as she would like to be shepherded to quiet waters while walking through the valley of the shadow of death. Kate had always been her own rod and staff anyway. This illness wasn't her first life test.

She snatched the TV remote from inside his Chinese dresser. After dabbing her sweaty forehead, she climbed back into his sleigh bed. She flipped TV channels, then settled on late-night news. An in-depth story featured Johnston & Quib. She sat up abruptly to look at the man being interviewed. She knew the face, that hard jaw and those piercing eyes. The businessman in a suit resembled an older Daniel Craig, the blond Bond. Wait—that's Mark Ferguson, the CEO. The same man she'd hear speak later today at the San Jose Chamber of Commerce. Obviously a man of great influence. He had a strikingly masculine face under thick gray hair.

She pressed VOLUME UP on the TV remote.

The reporter with the blow-dried hair opened with, "Mr. Ferguson, you've said the sale of drugs over the Internet compromises intellectual property rights, hurting inventors and entrepreneurs."

"I have."

"The Grid's getting a groundswell of praise and condemnation. What do you think of Stanford's Bioengineering Project?"

Ferguson's cracked-blue eyes narrowed. "Genomic research is exciting, that's why Johnson & Quib supported Stanford's Grid initiative. But frankly, the way it's being given away undermines private enterprise."

"Please elaborate."

Ferguson leaned into the news camera lens. "Many popular, branded blockbuster drugs are reaching the end of their patent-protected lives. When patents expire, manufacturers will lose thirty to forty percent market share as generic alternatives come out. Also, we are facing patent infringement from Canadian companies, who are making copies of patented drugs. We've seen how musicians and movie makers are being bankrupted by the rampant Internet pirating of music and film. We're at that same threshold moment today with genomics that we were at with the Internet in 1980. The same phenomenon is undermining legitimate drugs."

The reporter cut in, "Okay, but doesn't Stanford's Grid have the right to give people what's theirs—knowledge of their body chemistry?"

Kate smiled, considering Jude's pivotal role in the Stanford Grid.

Ferguson continued, "Private citizens don't know what to do with their mapped genome any more than I know how to build a sport utility vehicle."

Ferguson wiped his mouth. "And this Grid is an attack on intellectual property in the name of medical therapy. It's nonsense.

How will a no-fee network replace private research? Such free science deters investors, undermines capitalism and is dangerous. Even Bill Gates implied that free software developers were communists. You'll see, first this, then drug patents will go on the chopping block—just wait."

The interviewer looked down at his notes, grasping for control. Ferguson continued, "We're being seduced by the Grid and its gene-based diagnosis. It's haphazard. This is why the pharmaceutical industry exists, so drugs are researched and manufactured according to standardized practices."

Kate half-dismissed this industry ranting. He wasn't the first to argue against the Grid. Yet she didn't expect Ferguson—the drug company leader—to rail against it on CNN.

Ferguson added, "Where's our American heritage of discovery going? Internet-driven research, global outsourcing. It's all polluting our way of life."

Ferguson was riling himself up so much that his face had turned a rosy shade. He practically spat to get his words out.

"Keep a watchful eye on Stanford's public Grid," Ferguson continued. "Computers speak to each other, and many databases can communicate, and more are coming together all the time. Soon, some search engine company will offer a source of universal knowledge. That borders on absolute power. Will this power be used for good, to cure? I'm skeptical."

The interviewer finished, "They once called him Golden Throat—whenever Mark Ferguson spoke, investors opened checkbooks."

I bet, she thought. Still, he was an industry leader on breast cancer treatment. Kate clicked off the tube and turned over to rest.

Only a few short hours of sleep and she awoke to the ticking of Jude's alarm clock. *Insomnia.* She slammed a pillow against the wall at three-fifteen. Pictures of disease stalking her body, destroying her white blood cells, rolled through her mind: textbook images, virulent slide samples. Teaching Biology made her condition far too familiar.

Feeling nauseous, she fanned herself so she wouldn't vomit. It didn't help matters that clothing in Jude's room held the faint aroma of bourbon. Completely awake now, she fished through medical publications Jude had stacked beside his bed. It staggered the imagination that one of every eight women in the world developed breast cancer. The good part was that reading one article on genomics had her sleeping until dawn.

Waking with a start around nine in the morning, she hopped into olive slacks and pulled on a fine-gauge crew-neck sweater. She'd take a rental car to San Jose and absorb everything she could about what Johnston & Quib was doing with breast cancer therapy. She needed to keep active and find who or what therapy might rescue her. Intelligence had got her to where she was today. If anyone could outsmart this malady she could.

Then she stopped in her tracks. Was she getting ahead of herself with excitement over hearing Mark Ferguson speak in person? She turned to Jude's full-length bedroom mirror to size up the person who'd been diagnosed with cancer. Bloodshot eyes gazed back at her with faint age lines creased in the corners. Her blonde hair and tired face resembled her Mother's, especially after she'd lost weight. She removed her mother's favorite bracelet again and jingled it. Family life for the Wagners had dissolved rapidly after their mother died. Their dad, Benjamin, taped photos of her on the fridge then sunk himself into his engineering business. The bracelet went back into her suitcase.

She stubbornly refused to give any appearance of being on death's doorstep. She brushed her hair and applied makeup with a shaking hand. The apartment was empty. Jude had probably left for work already. After pulling on tennis shoes, she located her car rental key. The apartment door snapped shut behind her as she breezed outside to the parked car.

Thirty

Wednesday, November 2
San Jose, CA

Ninety minutes south of San Francisco, Kate motored on the freeway through sprawling Silicon Valley. The traffic knotted her shoulders, then the stress extended to her neck as she exited to San Jose's wide streets. She drove by streams of newly minted, contemporary block-styled buildings before coming up to the West Santa Clara address she was looking for. Like the other commercial constructions in the megatropolis, this complex resembled a post office, circa year 2000, an organization which, like herself, faced the danger of extinction. She nosed the rental car into a space behind the white four-story corporate building housing the Chamber of Commerce.

Out of the car, she shook out her arms before heading into the conference center. She basked in the warm San Jose sun beaming on her forehead. It did nothing for cancer, but even in her short walk, she enjoyed knowing that ultraviolet light was germicidal.

With all the chairs taken in the conference room, Kate stood like a sentry by the door.

The front row appeared to be occupied by reporters. Photographers stood on one side of the chairs with the large glass windows at their back. Mark Ferguson seemed to run things with the charge of a monarch in front of eighty plus attendees. Those who held paper cups, deferentially timed their sips of coffee between talking points. Could this distinguished Pharma CEO hold answers to her predicament . . . be her cavalry for rescue?

Thirty minutes later, Mr. Ferguson clung to the podium, capping off his spiel with passion. "We are in for a devastating defeat in the global drug trade. The world is copying products without bearing the expense of R&D. Copying intellectual property is economic terrorism, pure and simple. Sure, corporate America can save money by farming jobs out to India. And we do. But this is slippery too. The drugs that Johnston & Quib brings to market will not be surpassed. Integrity must save the day. This year and every year."

Applause followed the close of his talk and the room emptied. She wanted a private moment with Ferguson and didn't dare approach the podium to speak until the place had cleared out. For the first time in her adult life, she realized there was no obligation more pressing than this: no place she needed to go next, no lecture to plan, papers to grade or teacher-student appointments to consider. None of the professional duties that mattered before she became terminally ill mattered now. The only appointment in life now was with herself, to find a cure. Every other duty, from Kentucky to California, came second, to this captain of industry, Mark Ferguson.

But would he speak to her, knowing she was Wagner's sister, knowing her allegiances?

The CEO looked weaker than the Mark Ferguson she saw on TV. He had a pocket square that elegantly matched his exquisitely tailored suit, but the overhead light emphasized the way his skin hung around his mouth and jaws, diffusing the gruff image she had formed of him. She stood back while he finished a final chat. As the CEO grabbed his folder, she stepped up to him.

"Mr. Ferguson, I'm Kate Wagner. You may have heard of my brother, Jude Wagner, with Stanford."

"Oh yes." He folded his coat over his arm. It fanned musk aftershave her way. "I hope you took notes here to pass along to him."

She wondered if that was going to be the end of their conversation.

"There's a resemblance between you," he said flatly. "I hope that doesn't hinder you."

She half chuckled. "That was one thought-provoking talk. That's coming from one who lectures on science five days a week."

"Thank you for indulging me in the histrionics."

"Theatrics, I'd say. I wonder if I could trouble you with specifics around the delivery of your newest drugs."

His eyebrows raised. "Because?"

"Oh, I'm sorry. My brother hasn't put me up to this. I'm here for my own health interests."

"Which are?"

"Besides my being a college biology professor, I'm seriously ill. I'm hoping you can point me in the right direction, in terms of understanding my treatment options."

"I'm sorry to hear that." He blinked three times, each time slower than the last, as if his toy soldier batteries had rundown. He was contemplating something. "I'm sympathetic to your plight. A dear friend of mine also suffers from a terminal illness. When I say there's promise for drugs that are coming out, I'm hoping it will help him and, of course, so many others."

She suspected that someone could be he. "Tell me, truthfully, besides yours are there any other breast cancer drugs on the market I should look into?"

He elaborated on basic breast cancer treatment options for the most common of cases. She moved right alongside him, sharing the elevator ride down. By the time they reached the ground level, she'd described her form of tumor.

"I'm no oncologist, but our new drug, Remedacil, has relieved symptoms better than any similar therapy. In some cases, it's put cancer into remission. It depends on the stage and type of cancer."

"Of course." Kate remained optimistic. Even another thirty minutes with this man could be invaluable. Spontaneously, she asked if he cared to join her for lunch.

He considered it. "I barely have an hour. But I know a dinner place that now serves a quick lunch. Follow me."

He waited for her out in front of the restaurant while she parked. Bella Mia comprised two floors with two indoor dining rooms and a patio. A small sign on the wall at the front door advertised jazz nights. The main room had white tablecloth dining.

They chose the less formal area with antique sconces on walls over green Victorian wallpaper. With the restaurant half-empty, they took a quiet corner table in the front, overlooking the street.

They got their pasta orders in straight away. Organizing questions in her head, she couldn't believe she had Mark Ferguson one-on-one.

He smiled politely at her. "You've heard my thoughts on Stanford's work, I'm sure. I was obviously a big supporter. I still believe that Grid-based genomic testing is ground-breaking but it shouldn't be free. In fact, it's still premature. No offense to your brother but talk of his world Grid being a panacea is science fiction."

"Perhaps," she said skeptically. His gaze turned slightly curious.

"But as Jude says, the genomic era is here."

"Your brother is quite the cancer crusader," he said drily. "But without our backing I'm afraid the path he's on is fraught with complications."

"How so?"

"Stanford's genomic science is still in research mode—it was going to be nothing but R&D for us. They made strides with their diabetes tests, that's all." Ferguson put his elbow on the table. "In business, we have a way of telling ourselves that things are ready for prime time before they really are. After the sequencing of the human genome, scientists reported that soon they'd be tweaking our DNA, remedying our flawed chromosomes—curing heart disease and Alzheimer's. It hasn't happened. They said gene therapy would be like taking an antibiotic—simple and certain. And we're still waiting."

"True," she said. "It'll be a long time before we eliminate diseases altogether with the genome. But we've started and it's a leap for human medicine." He scratched his nose, visibly disinterested in a debate.

She surprised herself by arguing Jude's point, defending the new science. Another rare moment where she felt as one with her twin. Their conversation was interrupted by a family leaving with a crying baby. When the front door closed, the place returned to quiet. The waiter set down their plates of pasta.

"You're forgetting the whole privacy issue," he said, blowing on his pasta.

"What about privacy? Security has gone way beyond that of the ATM business or so I've read." Kate tried her food.

"Your brother's Grid brings genome sequencing to the masses. That's dangerous business."

"Why?" She took her first bite.

"You can't let the public decode their own genetic data. That's lunacy. Genetic information needs protecting, safeguarding. If not, crackpot freelancers will spring up, promising to tell you whether or not you'll have a heart attack before you turn fifty."

"But maybe genomic data should be protected by the patient *and* physician," Kate said. "Corruption can happen on either side. Who's to say a medical insurer couldn't buy off doctor records for business advantage? Jude's team is simply speeding up disease discovery. I'm afraid you just don't like the way they're going about it with that Google partnership."

"So, you know about that?" Ferguson said, starting his dish.

Kate realized that she was talking too much. "Nothing specific. I did hear something about George Clooney becoming a celebrity sponsor. Imagine that."

He gave a steely stare. "The Google deal is simply a spinoff from something called

Google Compute . . . another tech bandwagon for Silicon Valley cognoscenti. Your brother's work has caused a premature frenzy."

"It could be timely for me. I just might be his first guinea pig," she said, surprised at her own words.

"Seriously?" He lowered his fork.

"I'm cynical, being a scientist myself, but the Grid is moving along. I'd still like to consider your new breast cancer drug."

"Good for you."

She felt stabbing join pain in her knees and tolerated it. "I'm, I'm glad to know about it. Would that be used in conjunction with chemotherapy?"

"Yes," he said.

"But you say it's not labeled as a cure?"

Ferguson smiled a bit arrogantly. "It's effective therapy when added to a traditional regimen." Ferguson asked what else she knew about the Stanford project.

Kate wasn't expecting to be fielding his questions. He was moving in all different directions at once.

They talked for another fifteen minutes when she handed him a business card. "I would like to keep in touch. For now, Stanford is treating me." She said it on the spot despite her need for more information.

Taking his last forkful, Ferguson said with unexpected warmth in his voice, "Update me." The CEO finished his last bite of ravioli, announced he had to be on his way and left.

On her way out the door, Kate considered something Jude once said: "An algorithm is like a recipe—a logical set of instructions like a recipe you'd use to bake a cake. That's a static algorithm. Mine is adaptive. It learns from every failed search it runs and keeps trying until it finds the result."

Kate's neck muscles tightened while she mulled her treatment options: Jude's Grid or drugs from the leading breast cancer drug supplier like Johnston & Quib? As long as she was already taking a hormone prescription, it would be foolish to rule out either one. She resolved to hedge her bets. She'd continue to explore both traditional medicine and whatever Stanford could do. The resolution quieted her mind—relief she desperately needed. Either way, though, nobody guaranteed she would get any better.

Thirty-One

Wednesday, November 2
Berkeley, CA

Earlier that day Jude Wagner felt tire vibrations through his steering wheel. The narrow road to the Berkeley Marina skirted the heavily traveled freeway from Alameda County to San Francisco. Road construction caused fine dirt to blow across the windshield. He'd done this route for years although it drove its roughest today, calling for both hands on the wheel. He jimmied his coffee cup into the car's plastic cup holder.

He'd be hanging out with Kate if the cancer presentation in San Jose didn't take precedent. "The salt air will do you some good," she told him with a grin. "Besides, Niles's boat is a private escape for you."

She had a point, and their last sail of the year would be brisk. Ultimately, Wagner gave in. It would be easier to get Niles's buy-in on treating Kate with the Grid without her onboard anyway. Most of all, Wagner would need Roger Knowlan's blessing and help. Clearly Wagner also needed to regroup to get a firm handle on what he was recommending.

Wagner arrived later than he'd promised. Could he be too late for Kate also? It was still uncertain how far her condition had deteriorated. He must not see his sister's diagnosis as a replay of their mother's death. If Mom had lived another fifteen years, genomic medicine could have identified her susceptibility to breast cancer tumors before onset. It could've granted her many years of life. Wagner shrugged off his morbid reminiscence. Wagner wished Kate didn't think he was sugarcoating reality. Nothing else rivaled the Grid. His eyes twitched from fatigue. He took more coffee, but the pseudo-therapeutic properties of caffeine had its limitations. It slightly reversed the effects of that red wine he had the night before, but it didn't change the facts. Wagner couldn't tow all of these lines alone. He needed help, even if the best he could get would be Niles's advice.

Wagner swallowed the last of the coffee, crushed the cup and cranked up the volume to the comedy opera, *Le Nozze di Figaro,* on his car stereo. He didn't get a word of Italian, but the ethereal melody soothed his mind.

Art heals, his mother loved to say.

If only, he thought.

Niles had insisted that they put sails to the wind no later than 8:45 a.m. so he would have time to pack before his evening flight. It was 9:30 when Wagner pulled the Mazda into the parking lot. By now the cover would be off. The halyard would be hooked to the sail and ready for hoisting.

Niles opened the security gate on the dock to let him in. "Punctuality is a hallmark of good character."

"Screw good character." Wagner stepped aboard the boat. Sure enough, she looked rigged and ready.

Niles shrugged. "Nice attitude." He'd assumed the role of project taskmaster with Wagner immersed in antivirus work. Though Niles was too nervous to go near the Stanford campus and too stir crazy to prepare for his trip to Switzerland sitting in his hotel room.

"Hey, I brought CDs to break in the new on-board stereo. That swagger rock stuff you like: Johnny Cash, Chris Isaac, Roy Orbison, Tom Petty. We have to keep our chins up." Niles waved the CDs, doubled a rubber band around them and went below to stow them in the galley.

Wagner unfastened a weathered tie for push-off and warmed up the outboard motor.

"Is something else wrong?" Niles asked, coming to the deck.

"I'll tell you once we're moving," Wagner said.

Niles took the motor handle and pointed the little twenty-four-foot Cal cruiser out of the marina. "In the meantime, I've got a confession.

Knowlan received a little buzz from your own personal J. Edgar Hoover."

"From Hackman?"

"Not exactly from Hackman. But from his footman, a Special Agent Warren Speer who rang on his behalf. Knowlan told me that Speer did some probing on you, crosschecking what security precautions we were taking on campus. Knowlan said he accidently let it out that Weller was hiring a private investigator."

"Did he really?" Wagner didn't hide his agitation.

"Yeah, agent Speer went ape shit. Said Hackman expected you to keep Stanford in line behind their FBI directive."

"Ugh, Wagner said, "like I have the Department Chair under my thumb. We cannot let these bureaucratic bastards bully us. We're the ones with the project on the line."

"That's true." Niles killed the motor and took the tiller.

Wagner stowed a sail cover under the seat bench.

"I say we go toward Treasure Island today, Sherlock," Niles said.

"Give it a rest." Wagner released a blue bumper from the sailboat railing, and yanked it up.

"Why are Americans so uptight, huh? Everyone has a moniker they loathe. You know Bruce Springsteen hates being called *the Boss*, but he copes." Niles hummed, finishing with, "You were born to run."

"You know, buddy, if I'm on the run, that makes two of us. You're just as connected with the Grid as I am. Whoever is pulling strings here has scribbled both our names on a knock-off list."

"Some piece of work you are."

Wagner fished through the cooler and lifted out his bottle of tequila.

Niles halfheartedly looked over at Wagner. "I stored that to celebrate how we *were* going to be more famous than Darwin."

"Hey, this Google deal is happening." Wagner unscrewed the bottle top, poured a shot into two plastic cups and handed one to Niles who set his aside for later. Wagner took a gulp before setting his cup down and hoisting the jib. Sails burst open with a loud flap. The wind changed, pitching the boat into sideways motion. Wagner pulled in the main. The boat leaned and they adjusted to the high side of the deck.

"And away we go," Niles cried. He slapped sunscreen on his face and put the tube in his nylon bag.

"Listen up," Wagner said. "Bad news."

"We've had plenty of bad news, great computer laureate, why not surprise me with something good?"

"My sister Kate has breast cancer."

Niles went wide-eyed. "Oh, God. Never a break in the shit storm."

Wind picked up. Wagner stifled his emotions for a second, let out the sail. "We have to be able to help her."

"You're not suggesting using the Grid, are you? I don't want to sound uncaring but we don't have the breast cancer databases lined up to—"

"I'll find the database we need," Wagner said flatly.

"I don't know how. The entire Pharma community is treating us like we're a couple of Dr. Kervorkians on the loose."

Wagner reiterated for Niles all the steps they'd planned for the first test case. He argued that taking Kate on as a patient didn't blaze new paths and that Stanford was ready. All the wheels were in motion. They'd sequence the test patient's genome and compare it against one of the largest database partners, NCBI—National Cancer Biotechnology Information. Then they would match the diseased patient's results against similar gene types that had responded favorably to targeted drug therapies. With those results, they could produce the most precise therapy possible through Insilico—molecular modeling that was performed only by computers.

They braced themselves against a cold breeze while the *Tipsea* rode up a white cap, dipped then rose again.

"If only NCBI was online," Wagner said.

The National Center for Biotechnology Information database was only in test mode.

They were up and running for diabetes sourcing, but not for breast cancer.

The wind died down.

Wagner knew obtaining such a database would be exceedingly difficult; he'd need a key code and an invisibility cloak to avoid getting caught accessing Pfizer or Johnston & Quib's cancer catalogue databases. In time, things would be very different. Stanford would have NCBI online and pooled information from hospitals and researchers. But two years could go by before that.

"There's gotta be a way," Wagner said.

"I want to help, but that tequila is going to your head if you think you can just say *open sesame.* Shazam. And then you're into a private repository. Seriously. You would tell me if you had some FBI, mission-impossible angle cooked up?" Niles asked. "I might tell you, if it didn't needlessly implicate you."

"Oh, relief," Niles said.

Wagner and Niles adjusted their seat positions under a swinging boom. "Without the clinical data," Niles said, "I just don't see how."

"Niles, let me think." The bow kicked up, throwing little splashes of water.

"You have to talk to Knowlan."

"I will, but—."

"—You're not sure if he'll go for it."

"I'd rather call Alfonso."

Alfonso was a friend of Wagner's and Niles's from Berkeley days who now toiled in Johnston & Quib's Information Technology Department. Part of his day-to-day life revolved around managing J&Q's medical databases. In college, he was known for throwing parties so lavish that students had likened them to Mardi Gras.

"Maybe he can help," Niles said flatly. "But I'd get on with it before he's falling down drunk, paralytic."

Wagner looked at the shimmering horizon, gazing into the sublime force of the water, the unwavering rise and fall of the water line. Bay winds billowed across their faces. Flowing water hissed alongside them. Niles broke their quiet sway. "What about that watermark on that threat letter left for me? The United Bishops Association marking begs the question: what about religious backlash?"

"Absolutely. I haven't ruled out that some Catholic extremist group could be out there committing homicide."

"Abortion clinics have been targets. Anything is possible," Niles said louder. "But I'm grasping at straws."

"I refuse to be intimidated, though."

Niles downed a small plastic glass of tequila. "I just want to get on this plane to Switzerland, get Google and CERN synched up, finish our testing, and move on with our vision."

"Will you see your son?" Wagner said, knocking back more.

"Yes," Niles said, operating the tiller. "I'm depending on that little scallywag to take my mind off things. We're going to hit my favorite restaurant in London and go to the movies."

Wagner fidgeted with the boat winch. A fog plume hid the Golden Gate Bridge's tower tips over the port side as he and Niles bantered and sailed. The majestic Marin Headlands appeared to be painted behind the bridge's north tower, with Angel Island dabbed in on the right. Two dozen pelicans made formation ahead.

Their prehistoric necks and beaks stretched as they flapped their way south from San Francisco to bluer skies. Out of nowhere Wagner said, "I'm going to call that Roger Knowlan. Negotiating with him is masochistic, but I'm going to try. Kate could be ideal for a test run."

"Won't hurt. I'd appeal to his ego." Niles said, wiping spray from his forehead. Wagner prepared himself for a frustrating conversation and pulled out his phone.

"Roger, it's Jude."

"Yes."

"I need help with something serious," Wagner said.

"We have a lot to do with Hideo's absence, you realize that."

The sail fluttered as the wind changed directions. Niles pulled the tiller, changing the sailboat's direction.

"Right. I hope we can . . . work things out. My sister was just diagnosed with breast cancer."

"Breast cancer? Oh boy that is shit news! I'm really sorry to hear that. My sympathy to you both."

"I'd appreciate your hearing me out. I'm wondering . . . well, if we could use her as an initial test run for validation?"

The boat rocked, tumbling an empty plastic glass across the deck. Wagner picked it up.

"Hmm," Knowlan said. "We'd be getting ahead of ourselves. Don't get me wrong. I do want to help. What do you propose without genetic data to reference against?"

"I'm working on a scheme for getting more data."

"You're getting us access to a DNA repository?"

"I'm certainly going to try."

"Where is Kate, by the way?"

"She's staying with me. I would like for her to see you. Before you turn me down, consider this. If we can treat her with any degree of success, sponsors will come to us.

I'm not saying we'll have the world on a string, Roger. One statistic won't change medicine, but why not use this to put free medicine to work?"

It was hard to make it out over the phone, but Wagner detected a cough on Knowlan's side that sounded like a coming compromise.

Wagner added, "I know you've felt like the Grid team has been unwavering on a not-for-profit drug program."

"Jude, you've made your case. And with the University waiving copyright protection, I don't think we'll get a red cent from privatizing this, not anytime soon. So, I agree. Part of something is better than part of nothing."

Wagner's spirits lifted wildly.

The *Tipsea* came about sharply, tacking and tilting at thirty degrees to the breeze.

Wagner and Niles moved to sit on the opposite side of the boat. Niles released the jib and sheeted it on the new side.

Knowlan continued, "And I trust if I say no, you'll team up on me with Niles again. It is pushing things, but we need to move beyond testing diabetes."

"So what is it?" Wagner asked.

"Have Kate call me. She'll have my full attention down here."

"Thank you," Wagner said eagerly.

"Don't get used to favors. When can she come?"

"She happens to be heading to San Jose today around lunch time."

"Have her come to the lab after she's done."

The instant Wagner hung up, Niles shouted, "Did he just say yes?"

"I can't believe it myself."

"Congratulations."

"Hold on." Wagner called Kate to relay the amazing news.

"What?" she asked.

"Roger Knowlan at Stanford agreed to evaluate you. He'd collect information he would need from you to proceed with genomic cancer treatment."

"So, what would he do exactly?"

"He'd take a tissue sample and sequence a targeted part of your genome. He'd need to do that to get things started," he said.

"You might be surprised to hear me say this."

"You'll do it?" Wagner said.

"Yes. I'll save my closed mindedness for another debate."

Wagner detected a smile in her voice. "This is a very good thing we're doing, Kate.

Stanford is only twenty-five minutes north of San Jose. Can you get there this afternoon?"

"Yes. I'm already down here," she said.

"You are? Okay, then. I'll text you the address for your initial consultation."

"She's giving it a try!" Wagner said eagerly as he hung up, half paralyzed over what had just transpired in back-to-back calls.

Niles gave Wagner control of the tiller.

"How about some music," Niles said as if he were giving the go-ahead to the Macy's Thanksgiving Day Parade to do its march along Central Park. He hobbled down the ladder, disappearing into the cabin. A gust sprayed the deck with seawater.

Niles returned to the deck holding the railing and waving a CD in hand. "I spent six hundred dollars on this stereo and it doesn't play." He frisbeed the CD across the bow and into white caps.

"Let me look at that stereo," Wagner said. "Maybe something was knocked loose."

"I'm telling you, it's a piece of rubbish—kaput."

Wagner stepped below, then kneeled over cushions to get a close look at the metal-fronted Pioneer stereo. It resembled the one in his previous car. It was one item of consumer electronics he'd fiddled with. He could see that a custom cabinet had been built for it. The wood bore a close match to the rest of the boat but wasn't perfect. Still, the cabinet framed the receiver nicely. Wagner was able to gently remove the thin wood panel that was fastened to the boat wall inside with plastic clips. Clear tape held red and blue wires in place behind the components. Wagner followed the clear tape, looking deeper into the dark cabinet. He found another set of black wires. They didn't at all appear in keeping with the sailboat's design. They were also taped down, but he could not see where they connected.

As Wagner inspected the electronics, he verified that the black wires behind the receiver did not connect to the stereo but ran behind another cabinet that didn't house a speaker. As he rummaged through the shadowy cabinet with the wires, he traced them to a small box resembling a clock. The box was nestled behind a rain poncho.

A bead of sweat dripped from his forehead. He leaned out of the cabinet, found a flashlight and came back to the side wall opening. Wagner pulled the poncho, shining the flashlight. Something he did made the stereo power light flicker. Something was activated. He uncovered what appeared to be a tight red bundle of flares—when realization struck.

"Niles, jump." Wagner shouted. He bolted to the hatchway and scrambled up the cabin steps to the deck.

"What?" Niles asked.

"Bomb!" Wagner dove into the bay.

A *kaboom* blasted overhead. Flames and smoke shot skyward. Fiberglass shards spattered. Wagner landed sideways in undulating swells. Smoldering teak, plastic and canvas rained down. Embers sizzled as they hit water around him.

Wagner tumbled underwater in slow motion. His ears rang. Soot-filled water surrounded him. Air. He needed air. He crawled through cold water. He paddled his arms and legs. Through the deep, he worked toward the swaying surface. Boat debris and kelp grazed his face. One of Wagner's sailing nightmares had returned, but this time it was stark reality.

Thirty-Two

Wednesday, November 2
Berkeley Marina, CA

After kicking off his shoes, Wagner trod water on a surface sprinkled with pieces of charred boat. Salt water stung the corners of his eyes. He wiped his irritated lids and blinked. The explosion had littered the water as far as he could see. Where was Niles?

"Niles!"

No answer. Seconds passed.

Wagner breathed through his mouth, avoiding the nauseating sulfuric odor in the air. Swells yawed. He swayed to and fro beneath clouds sweeping over the bay. He watched the *Tipsea's* mast angle and then surrender to the swaying bay, leaving nothing but scattered deck cushions and teak slivers. A shiver of fear ran through Wagner. With the salt water in his eyes, swells and wood remnants all around, he didn't see Niles. Had he gone down with the *Tipsea*? Using his fingers, Wagner cleared his eyes again above the rising water. He cupped one hand to his mouth and hollered Niles's name repeatedly.

"Jude." Niles's voice came from behind.

He spotted Niles moving his arm from side to side in the air. Wagner exhaled in relief and shouted, "You okay?"

"I'm sore." Niles appeared to be treading water well enough.

Ponderously, Wagner swam breaststroke to a floating seat cushion. Once he slung his arms over it, the waterlogged cushion sank with most everything else.

"Good try," Niles yelled, doing a weary crawl to within talking distance of Wagner.

They kicked toward long pieces of floating wood and hung onto to them carefully so they would not go under too.

Niles gasped, "Wonder how long we can tread water before freezing to death."

"Don't know, but if this wood sinks, I'm gonna try floating on my back." Niles groaned. "Got a gash on my arm."

"You bleeding?"

Niles raised his arm to the water level to look at it. "It's not a big cut, but blood's oozing."

"I hope this salt water stops that." Wagner said.

"I won't bleed to death. Not from this anyway."

"That's not my worry."

Niles shot Wagner a glare while he adjusted his arm grip on the wood. "My worry is attracting sharks," Jude said.

Niles's eyes widened. He squirmed, pressing his hand to his arm to stop the bleeding.

"Try not to kick," Wagner said. "Sharks seldom come in this far, but outside the Golden Gate there are great whites. They hunt for seals. Especially on overcast days."

"Shit, Jude—shut up or I'll swim over and do it for you myself."

"Quiet. Did you hear that?"

A buzzing motor noise knifed the air in the distance.

They turned their heads north. "Yes," Niles said, "something's coming."

Wagner saw a rugged fishing boat skipping and smacking on whitecaps. Neck-deep in water, Wagner and Niles waved broadly at the three men dressed alike. Wagner then realized it wasn't a fishing boat that was approaching but the Coast Guard. The engine noise grew louder. Such commotion never sounded sweeter.

"Let's not talk a lot to the Coast Guard," Wagner said.

"Alright, then." Niles fixed on the nearing vessel.

The silvery Coast Guard motor boat slowed as it approached. She could've been forty-seven feet. The coxswain cut the motor while petty officers flung life jackets to Wagner and Niles. The heavily dressed seamen, in glowing orange jackets and black wool beanie hats, helped them up a chrome drop ladder against buffeting wind. Shivering, Wagner and Niles crossed their arms.

The crew, quick on their feet, flung thick towels for them to dry off as best they could. One officer directed the sailboat survivors to the fiberglass seats on the deck where he opened a First Aid kit then bandaged Niles's arm. The crewman also handed out hot-water bottles to warm them.

Still shaking, Wagner checked himself over to find tenderness on the back of his head. Something flying from the boat must've struck him. "Do you see any splinters?" An officer checked the back of Wagner's head. "No, I don't see anything."

Wagner rubbed his head again and stood up to survey the *Tipsea's* remains. The Cal 24's hull started submerging. To Wagner, the sight resembled a plastic model going under in a bathtub when the nearby officer firmly grabbed him by the arm to pull him down. Another crew member slung a small buoy. It landed a few feet from where the *Tipsea* hull was disappearing, marking the spot for any future investigation.

The coxswain took the helm again. Being the first petty officer, he announced, "Getting underway" over the loudspeakers and with a tilt of the wrist, he hit the throttle.

Wagner and Niles hunkered down in their deck seats. The powerful boat knocked over the swells, wind on their faces. Wagner wanted to ask the Coast Guard if they had spotted any bomb fragments, wires, batteries or plastics when they whisked them into the boat, but he chose not to involve them. Besides, almost no one could make sense of this crime scene. Most of the evidence had probably already sunk to the bay floor.

One of the Coast Guard crew members asked Niles if he knew why his sailboat exploded. Niles shrugged. "I sort of hoped you could tell us something."

Nothing registered on the officer's face. "Our primary responsibility is to get you two to shore and see that our salvage guys remove any wreckage."

The Coast Guard handed them dry shirts, which Wagner and Niles rapidly changed into. Pale and nursing the cut on his arm, Niles was less communicative than the leather-faced Coast Guard officer. Niles's hair sprang in every direction. Seeing his pal beaten up by the blast reminded Wagner of what a loyal ally he had been. They had beaten tough odds in the past, but today's mishap could've been fatal.

"Can you believe I have a flight at seven tonight?" Niles groaned.

"You feel well enough to fly?"

"No, but I've gotta see Edward. It's a red eye. I'll sleep through it. Besides, I'm the Grid's lone emissary."

"You'll have to get checked out first. We need you coherent for Thursday's meeting with CERN. I want a piece of whoever did this," Wagner said.

They had to see things through the operation stage to guarantee that Stanford actually connected with Google.

The Coast Guard edged up to the dock. The captain shut down the motor and his crew escorted Wagner and Niles off the vessel, down the plank and to a grassy clearing at the Berkeley Marina. A waiting ambulance pulled closer and parked alongside the clearing. Wagner barely stifled his frustration when the crew asked for their IDs and said they'd be ticketed for not wearing flotation devices. After showing their wet identification to a crewman, the officer instructed them to wait on a bench for the medical response team.

Wet and cold, Wagner rubbed salt water stickiness from his eyes. The EMTs came out of their vehicle carrying boxes and started right in on examining Wagner and Niles.

On bent knee, a young male paramedic took Wagner's blood pressure and heart rate.

The older one treating Niles was a talker. "Sounds like that sailboat motor of yours was overdue for an overhaul."

Without question, the explosion had nothing to do with a worn-out motor. "You own a boat?" Niles asked his medic.

"No," he said.

"Then let's hold up on speculating. That motor still had good life in it."

The paramedics continued working. Wagner knew how lucky they'd been. Had he not spotted that explosive deep inside the cabinet, and had they not jumped overboard in that instant, pieces of them would have washed to shore to be hauled off in body bags to the county morgue. Someone or some group had taken out Jűrgen and Hideo, and now they wanted Niles. Wagner believed this was an attempt to carry out what the threat letter had warned. Someone was hell bent on ending the Grid. Instead of saving lives, Wagner's algorithm was cutting down its founders. Maybe it was foolhardy to go on. They lacked anything substantial to go on and Wagner felt they were more vulnerable to a personal attack than ever. But a determination had hardened inside him. He had to see this project through to completion.

"Are you almost done?" Niles asked his EMT.

An ambulance worker advised Wagner and Niles to ride with them to the ER. They insisted they could drive just fine. Finally, the paramedics had Wagner and Niles each sign a waiver attesting that they refused a ride to the hospital.

The emergency team then packed their supplies and took off without them. The Coast Guard's first petty officer returned with paper on a clipboard and a pen. He fired procedural questions to complete his write up of an incident report.

Wagner stood up. "What next?"

"We're done," the officer said. "Berkeley's law enforcement takes it from here. If there's cause for an investigation, they'll handle it. Though our experience is that these things are usually chemical related or are insurance scams."

"Yeah, right," Wagner said, dismissing the insult as the officer's walky-talky chirped with talk about how the sailboat's remains would be a simple cleanup. What Wagner got from this explosion didn't quite match up with what the Coast Guard crew construed.

A Berkeley police cruiser pulled up. A brown Crown Vic trailed right behind. "Uh-oh. Now what?" Niles said.

Two cops stepped out of a cruiser, and Speer hopped out of his car. He threw a glance Wagner's way.

"Not Speer," Wagner said impatiently.

"You know one of them?" Niles asked, coming to his feet.

"Unfortunately I do. That's agent Speer, the man who thrives on tyrant-bullshit games."

"Stay calm," Niles said.

Special Agent Speer had his badge pinned to his jacket. The brigade of three wore shiny aviator sunglasses as they marched toward Wagner.

"Look who it is," Speer started with a gloating expression on his face. "The divining rod for disaster."

Wagner threw Speer a mocking salute.

"Nice, Wagner. Just what I'd expect from a Grid geek."

"What do you want?" Wagner asked.

"You're stuck on making things bad for yourself, aren't you?" Speer said.

Wagner took an aggressive step toward Speer.

Niles said, "Hey now. Let's all just get through this and move on."

Wagner didn't want Niles to give in to Speer, so he took the lead. "How'd you find out about this?"

"I'll answer that, then you answer my questions. I'm here because I know something exploded and because our bureau visitor here happens to show up in the middle of things again. What happened?"

"I wish we could say." Wagner touched his sore head again. "The Coast Guard suggested it could've been chemical related."

"Was that a gas or diesel-powered motor you owned?"

Niles rolled his shoulder with a grimace. "The sailboat was mine and it was gas."

Speer removed his aviators. "Then the motor could have just overheated somehow and exploded. How old was it?"

"Maybe five years," Niles said.

The officer beside Speer scratched notes on his pad.

Wagner crossed his arms. "That's it then. The boat spontaneously combusted. And here we are chatting away like old friends."

"Look, dumbass," Speer said. "Did you see anyone suspicious when you set out?"

"No."

"Chilly day for a pleasure cruise, don't you think."

"It is, especially without a wetsuit." Wagner wondered if Hackman somehow had Speer keeping an eye on him. It could all be part of his connecting Wagner to two dead men.

"You have insurance on this former sailboat, Mr. Tully?"

"Just basic homeowner's."

Speer handed Niles his business card, then asked that he send him a copy. After Niles answered more questions to describe the Cal 24' and its approximate value, Wagner said, "Look, Speer, we're ice cold, can't we reschedule this?"

"I'll release you when I'm ready. What's your personal theory about the cause of this?"

Wagner sighed. "My theory is that we've trespassed across some invisible boundary with our Stanford Grid Project and now we're paying for it."

"An invisible boundary? You really believe that?"

"Yes. And if I think of anything else I'll call. Maybe I'll even send you an Instant Message on AOL if that's what you use in the middle of the night when you're trolling for a date. If you'll excuse us, we'd like to go home."

"You can avoid explaining things, but soon Hackman'll want answers—and not your fast-talking filler. Now give these officers a report so we don't go back reporting that you took the fifth on some basic questioning."

One officer got a thermos from the cruiser, poured himself something hot into a styrofoam cup, finished the cup and then rejoined the group. After a few more minutes of questioning where Wagner gave stock answers to the cops and Speer, Niles complained about ringing in his ears. "I could have permanent tinnitus."

The cop asking the questions looked at Speer, then turned back to Wagner and said, "That's all we need."

"Wait. Now for a bigger question," Speer said. "When was the last time you had contact with your late CERN colleague, Jűrgen Hansen?"

Wagner paused before responding. He wasn't certain. "It's been months unless you're talking about email."

"How often did you email him?"

Annoyed, Wagner said, "I'm on an email distribution that goes to the Stanford Grid Project team. Messages would come to me almost daily."

Speer scratched his jaw. "You must have something more substantive than that."

Wagner raised his hand to signal, *stop*. "Look, I'm aware that Hansen was a homicide victim. Believe me, it's a much bigger concern to those who knew him than it is to you. I'm trying to parse for myself who's behind it."

Niles rubbed his ear with his finger. "Jude, are your ears ringing?"

"Yes."

"I'm almost done here," Speer said turning to Niles. "How about you?"

"What?" Niles asked.

"When was the last time *you* had contact with Jűrgen Hansen? Forget that. Can you imagine any threat he or your Hideo Onagi would've posed to anyone?"

"No," Wagner and Niles said in unison. "Can we do this some other time?" Wagner said. "I feel underdressed. Besides, I thought all of this was on Agent Noiret."

Speer looked them over, arms crossed. "She's not the only one tasked with this now. Anyway, looks like we'll have to do this later. In the meantime, you two should watch your backs." Speer half-waved the air to say that he was done with them for now.

The officers dismissed them. Speer tipped his sunglasses to give them a parting stare-down reprimand. They got in their cruiser and left.

"Well, that was a hell of a lot of fun. We should do it again soon," Niles said.

Wagner rested his hands on his sore ribs with an arm that throbbed. He hobbled along. As they reached their cars, a young man approached them wearing a blue blazer over a tan sweater, pressed khakis and Timberland shoes. With a slim body, drooping eyes and a rosy nose of an alcoholic, this reporter reminded Wagner of a Carrion bird.

"Jude Wagner, right? The Grid guy? Mike Finlaw with the *Chronicle*."

"And Niles Tully," Niles interjected.

"What do you need, Mike?" Wagner said.

"Just a few questions."

"I didn't know your newspaper was still around. I thought it had shrunk to nothing." Niles quipped.

"Readers like the smaller format."

Wagner couldn't wait to leave. He went to his Mazda. Niles clicked open his doors. The reporter followed Wagner. Niles and Wagner got inside their cars.

"Can you tell me about the explosion." The reporter snapped his ballpoint pen, out and in.

"No," Wagner said.

"Do you think this was accidental or foul—"

"Come on. Why would someone go after us?" Wagner said, turning away from the guy.

"It's your friend's boat, isn't it?" the reporter asked.

"Yes."

"Maybe someone has it in for him." The reporter glanced at Niles. "You're both part of the Stanford Grid Project, right?"

Wagner didn't have the patience to go through the story again. He kept his back turned to the reporter. "It was a motor malfunction, alright. No further comment." Niles started his engine and revved it.

In his car, Wagner pulled his cell phone out of his pocket and looked at its blank screen. The phone was damp but after removing the battery and inserting it again, the screen surprisingly lit up. He checked messages while Finlaw tapped on Wagner's window. There was one from Roger Knowlan. Wagner started up the Mazda and drove out of the Marina as a couple of TV news vans were driving in.

Wagner listened to Knowlan's message while driving. "Kate's here with me. She wants me to pass along that she'll be staying late at the lab, watching me work my magic. Anyway, a lanky FBI Special Agent named Speer dropped by, asking me a lot of questions about Hansen and Onagi. Head's up for you. He may be from your office, but I wouldn't be surprised if he ran you down for the same interrogation.

Wagner said under his breath, *Too late Knowlan, but not to worry. You can do me another favor and help remedy my sister's disease. If you cooperate with me, the enemy might just go down.*

Thirty-Three

Wednesday, November 2
Stanford, CA

In the women's room at Stanford's Department of Medicine, Kate Wagner noticed blood in her urine—a typical breast cancer symptom. She had excruciating joint pain in her knees and ankles. Limping from the bathroom, she caught a hint of cigarette odor. Probably no one else noticed. Her sense of smell had become so acute, even the faintest scents overwhelmed her. She made her way down the long hallway. Oddly enough, that luncheon with Mark Ferguson left doubts in her mind about trusting her life to traditional medicine.

With a shiver of anticipation and a notepad in hand, Kate caught the attention of a male aide in a lab coat and tortoise-shell glasses.

"Got an appointment?" The aide asked.

"Yes, with Roger Knowlan in the Cancer and Bioengineering Departments."

The aide scrupulously checked the photo ID of her driver's license and asked her to come with him to his admin desk where he called Roger Knowlan. "He's waiting for you, but visitors must wear badges." The impersonal aide made out a guest pass sticker.

Kate followed the young man down the fluorescent-lighted hallway, growing more anxious with every step.

How ironic, she thought: she practically lived in a classroom firing questions at students about biology, and now she had become the guinea pig.

Standing in a sky blue lab coat with arms crossed, Knowlan said, "Kate Wagner. You're right on time."

He had tightly wound brown-gray hair that topped his studious, disciplined face.

With curious eyes, Roger Knowlan smiled and clasped her hand. "I understand you teach Biology in Lexington. You won't be a stranger to what we're doing here—not entirely."

Leading the way, his ponderous speech and soft hands made him appear more at home in academia than anywhere else. She imagined him to be a social hermit; though his V-neck sweater over a French blue shirt and Italian blue jeans reached for something trendier. The middle-aged MD could've been dressed by the style editors of *Esquire Magazine*.

"How are you faring?" he asked.

"Not great. Sort of feel as if fate has sunk me down a rabbit hole. My mother died from breast cancer."

"I see. Your treatment will be nothing like hers by the way. We'll split the problem of analyzing your proteome into millions of smaller problems, ripping them at twelve hundred teraflops per second. That's twelve hundred trillion calculations per second."

"Jude told me something about this. He also said you were preparing for cancer candidates such as myself."

"That's right. But we didn't always see eye-to-eye on the Grid."

"Why not?"

"Making the Grid project free to the public seemed too aggressive at first. But I'm a convert. J&Q would've sat on this for years before they could integrate genomics into their product line. Your brother and Dr. Onagi made me see the light, Professor Wagner."

"I go by Kate."

"Call me Roger. And we're getting the backing now to exceed our wildest dreams." He patted her shoulder. "Your brother devised quite a unique algorithm."

"He's not as unique as you might think."

"Why do you say that?"

"We're twins, you know. I tell him he takes after me—not the other way around." She pulled a smile out of him. "You do look alike." He escorted her down the hall and opened a large door to reveal an enormous workspace. He made a sweeping gesture like he was welcoming her to Oz. Before entering, he pulled two pairs of booties from his lab coat pocket and handed a pair to her. They snapped the paper shoes over their own shoes.

From what she could tell, the department used state-of-the-art equipment. The sterile room had been divided into half: one part dedicated to two long benches with computer workstations, while the other half was reserved for the laboratory work of computational biology, outfitted with four upright freezers which probably held blood samples. The place, with its brushed cement floor and high-tech instruments, looked singularly efficient. Kate had half-envisioned a laboratory with pedal-operated, stainless steel sinks, like the ones she'd worked with in graduate school.

He swept around her to a laptop. He radiated a mischievous look of excitement, a passion to test the Grid's capabilities. Briefly, she saw a Silicon Valley entrepreneur in him. That scientific curiosity had her feeling like a lab rat preparing for vivisection. "What will happen with my tissue sample?"

"Soup to nuts, you're looking at three stages. Today, we decode your genome using the sequencer. Tomorrow, we run your genome on our worldwide Grid computer to analyze your disease molecularly against a database of similar patients. Lastly, we treat you. I'll go more into treatment later. Can you feel your lump?"

"Yes."

"Then I can do a fine needle biopsy. It's an outpatient procedure."

"Here?"

"Right where we're sitting. With that sample, I can sequence your genome and analyze your tumor type."

She showed him the lump on the upper area of her breast near her underarm. He felt the region, marked it with a felt pen and removed a new long needle from a plastic pouch.

She bit her lip.

"It's intimidating, but try to relax."

"As a college biology professor, I usually feel right at home at a University, especially in a science building. But here I am a bundle of nerves."

"That's normal. This is about your body chemistry. You told me earlier that you're excited about Mark Ferguson's new drugs. What J&Q is doing without us is inexact— plain and simple. They lack the precision that can only be realized through genomics. I'm not saying Ferguson's not smooth. The man can make a sow's ear into a silk purse, and he's quite the social magnet at fund raisers."

Kate momentarily lapsed to the lunch she had with the CEO. "I'd like to know more about what happens with my tissue sample." She noticed she was fiddling with her watch and set her hand at her side. He had a self-satisfied way about him that irritated her. Then she wondered why she cared. She'd put up with a hell of a lot more if she knew he'd successfully treat her disease.

He stuck her with the fine needle.

"Ow."

Using both hands he slowly drew back the syringe to collect the tissue sample. Next, Knowlan fastidiously trashed the needle part of the syringe and scrawled the date and her name on the remaining plastic vial. He showed it to her. "What we have in this little container unlocks the door to detecting your cancer. Shall we?" Adjusting his lab coat, he directed her to the back of the room beside the tall refrigerators. She looked around again, considering the unfamiliar analytical equipment. The DNA sequencer machine was nothing like she'd imagined it to be. It sat on a work bench and resembled a miniature commercial printer. Totally unassuming, it was only three feet wide and two feet high. The names *Illumina MySeq* gleamed across the machine's front panel beside a mini-led computer display.

He continued, "Sequencers like this once cost half a million dollars, but this only ran us fifty grand—it'll do the priceless task of decoding your genome."

"There's a sound byte for a commercial." Coping with nerves, Kate said whatever came to mind.

Knowlan transferred her tissue sample into tubes. Kate lost track of time while Knowlan prepped her DNA, enriching the sample to target the genes specific to breast cancer. An hour later, he inserted drops of the prepared sample into the DNA genetic analyzer cartridge and he sealed the door.

It appeared deceptively easy—like changing a printer toner cartridge. From the machine's touch screen, Knowlan selected TARGETED SEQUENCING, PAIRED END, 150 BASE PAIRS SELECTION, then he pushed GO.

He directed Kate to his tablet computer.

Knowlan tapped the screen to show Kate a video presentation that replicated what was happening. A row of lights glided from left to right across the display. With a faint whir, the lights picked up speed. The whir became a faint vibrating sound.

He narrated the process with the pride of a teenager launching a homemade model rocket. "The machine sequences millions of unique clusters. It reads each nucleic base so the DNA can be decoded. The clusters are excited by a laser emitting a color that identifies each unique base G, A T C. The machine records the reflection—like a photograph, capturing detailed measurements. This photographic process takes two hours. We collect the digital data of your DNA fragments and run those shapes through the computer to analyze and convert them into binary logic that generates your personal genome."

Pent up energy spun through Kate's nerves and veins. "And this helps identify my mutation somehow?"

"It gets us started with microscopic photography. But we won't be mapping your entire genome."

"Why?" she said.

"Because we've already narrowed down one hundred regions of the genome that are predictors for cancer. Only two genes—"

"BRACA ONE and BRACA TWO cause hereditary breast cancer," she added.

"Exactly. The test will reveal just how aggressive your tumor is. That's the easy part. The tough part is interpreting your genome against databases and analyzing it using the Grid. The Grid analyzes your biomarkers and directs us to which targeted drug therapy will inhibit your cancer. Hopefully, we'll stop the spread of your tumor entirely."

"What next?"

"Have you ever done genetic counseling before?"

"Never." Kate crossed her arms defensively.

"This will go into your sequencing profile. It'll only take a few minutes. You said your mother had breast cancer. Was she diagnosed before the age of fifty?"

"She was fifty-one. You should know that I've had bleeding from my urinary tract and joint pain."

Knowlan frowned sympathetically. He queried her for fifteen minutes, then set down his completed genetic counseling questionnaire. He went back to the sequencer and pressed SUBMIT to complete her genomic DNA.

"How long will this sequencing process take in total?"

"Ordinarily, two days, but since we're zeroing in on breast cancer alone, we'll have it in five hours. And once we pinpoint your cancer condition we may not even need to create a custom drug for you. But . . ."

"But what?"

"Your brother still has to provide us with a database—one that's robust. Let's hope he gets hold of it."

"What do you mean?" Kate braced herself, expecting to be doused with more details."

"Data is always the lynchpin."

"I thought you had what you needed?"

"Not entirely. However, if Jude obtains what he says he will, that database could list drugs that worked for similar cancer patients fitting your profile. This includes drugs that never went to market. We would simply isolate their drug response and duplicate those drugs. If necessary, we could even custom-tailor a drug for you using a compounding pharmacy. And the Grid has reduced the time required to make an exact diagnosis. But we need that database soon."

Evidently, Jude had kept a very important feature of this process to himself to avoid worrying her.

Thirty-Four

Wednesday, November 2
San Francisco, CA

Outside his apartment, Wagner fished out his keys from his pocket. The shirt which the Coast Guard had given him clung tight around his chest. His pants rode higher now, exposing discolored socks. He braced himself for the explanation he would have to give Kate if she came to the door.

He was saved the worry. No one was home. He rummaged through his fridge, refueled and went to his bedroom where he saw Kate had folded his clothes, and tucked her suitcase in the corner. He quickly showered, changed into clean clothes and checked email. Nothing. His bruises flared up. He heard hollering and car horns honking on the street. Maybe another wedding party moving up Hyde Street on a cable car. He tuned out the noise, considering if he had put Kate in jeopardy by letting her stay in his apartment.

He texted Roger Knowlan to warn him about the suspicious accident on Niles's boat. The light on his answering machine blinked on the kitchen counter. He cycled through messages from news offices, hitting delete until he came to Kate's voice. "Hey you, Roger Knowlan and I are working away at the lab. Good progress. About this critical database we need. You do have a solid plan, right?"

"You have no new messages," the machine droned.

At least Kate and Roger Knowlan were hitting it off in the bioengineering department. Wagner could only see one way to move ahead—although this alone wasn't a total remedy. Picking up the phone, he consulted his list of contacts and tapped in a phone number to one of the cyber analysts at the bureau. "Morris, it's Jude Wagner from Stanford. I'm going to email you the latest code I've written for defending virus attacks on our Grid network. Could you penetration test it?"

"Yeah. And not only that. I've prioritized a list of things that'll keep you busy."

"A list of what?"

"Speaking statistically, I've highlighted which computer attacks you would have the toughest time stopping, even with our electronic surveillance backing you up."

* * *

Ramsey swung the door shut to the J&Q conference room—his makeshift office. Motion-sensor lights flicked on. Looking out the floor-to-ceiling city view, he saw the skyline of San Francisco in setting sunlight. He had heard that the hotel where he was staying practically sat directly on top of the Hayward fault line. Life was absurdly capricious and so were these high-rises he was looking at. Uncertainty never festered inside him more, especially the possibility of earthquakes in California. He disliked traveling to San Francisco, fearing the ground here could start shaking without warning. A segment of that damn Bay Bridge had collapsed during the last major quake. It would take twenty-four years to replace the eastern span. Great—a shiny monument to man’s frailty.

He wondered if the J&Q building sat on landfill. With a press of a button, Ramsey shut the drapes. Olivier Ramsey longed for an inside look at how the Grid was developing. He itched to get details on its vulnerabilities in security, but a well known Pharma investor couldn’t very easily traipse through the halls of Stanford’s Bioengineering Department, making inquiries himself. These days everyone was vigilant about corporate snooping. Taking a conference room chair, he snagged the phone across the long table and tapped a five-digit extension. The call went to the one executive assistant who had the job of looking after Ramsey's administrative needs when he was in town. "Heather."

"Yes."

"It's Olivier. Please come by the conference room."

"Yes, Sir."

Ferguson had told Ramsey that twenty-something-year-old Heather had already worn many hats: won the Miss Virginia Pageant, worked as a reporter for *The Alexandria Times,* and then landed a job with Johnston & Quib. Ramsey had another scheme in mind for the former beauty queen who was known around J&Q for being the can-do EA who never said no.

Hearing a rap on his door, Ramsey welcomed her in.

She softly closed the door behind her. "My guess is you'd like an update." She whispered, "On Jude Wagner."

She had a curvaceous figure and breathy carnality.

Ramsey straightened his tie. "Yes. Why don't you sit down." He hoped she had come with good info, although she appeared reticent, tensely gripping her notepad.

Ramsey's rapport with her deepened each time he came to this J&Q office. No man who worked on the top floor missed Heather Styles or her bouncy strawberry-blonde hair. Her body would make spending big money easy. She more than fulfilled his fantasies of an executive assistant. He adopted her as his EA whenever he visited Johnston & Quib.

He was pleased by how readily she had agreed to his previous request. He knew she'd been instructed to cater to his business needs. Still, befriending the competition was more than he could have hoped from an admin. Thankfully, he had a talent for pushing other people's boundaries. If Cez@r failed, Ramsey still might get something from Heather, picking up breadcrumbs of information along the way.

"What did you find out from Jude Wagner, and how did you go about it?"

"Like you suggested, I watched his apartment at night and did what I could." She took a nervous breath. "I followed him by foot Monday night and managed to get a seat next to him at a place called the Hyde Out."

"And?"

She fidgeted sheepishly. "He started to tell me something significant but cut himself short."

Ramsey tsked. "Damn it, Heather. Did he mention *anything* about a deal Stanford did?"

"I'm afraid not. He was under a lot of stress. It threw me off." Ramsey dropped his pen on a notepad.

She apologized. "I thought I'd have more luck."

He swallowed his frustration with his femme fatale. At least she managed to deposit the money for him in the Cayman Island account.

"I'm still fuzzy about what Jude Wagner has to do with J&Q now," she said.

Ramsey mulled things over. "Forget it. I have another idea."

"For obtaining inside information?"

"Yes, but leaving Wagner out of it. We can't have him getting onto you."

She pushed her curled strawberry-blonde hair over one ear.

"I'll need you to work this into your schedule right away. Same as before, you must conceal your affiliation with Johnston & Quib for what I'm asking of you."

That shouldn't be too difficult, he thought. *She's built for tempting a man away from work.*

"And what is that you need now?"

"Weren't you a reporter for a time?"

"Yes." She listened closely.

"Then you've chased down a story or two?" He pulled his glasses snug to his head.

"For two years."

"Suppose you call on your experience and do one last story assignment. But this time you'll only pose as a reporter."

She looked puzzled. "You've lost me."

He touched his slicked-back hair. "Hear this out. See if you can arrange an interview with Stanford's Grid program director, Roger Knowlan." Ramsey jotted a phone number, tore the sheet off of a company letterhead pad and put it into her delicate hand.

"Get to him ASAP. Find out what you can on Grid security and what the Stanford Grid team is doing with Google."

"And you're guaranteeing me that Ferguson will give me an end-of-year bonus?"

"Yes. If he doesn't, I'll give you a ten thousand dollar Christmas gift myself."

"Just one meeting, right?" she asked.

"Yes. Just concoct some cover story, and leave my name and Johnston & Quib's out of it," Ramsey said.

"I can probably swing that, Sir. Can you tell me why all of this needs to remain such a secret?" She asserted herself more boldly than he had expected.

"Yes and no. What I can tell you is that a divisive competitor is about to wage an attack on your company."

"What kind of attack?"

"Don't worry about that. Just know that there's a very big competitive threat which could make our future dim. We need whatever information is out there."

"I see," she said.

"Good. With your background as a reporter, I have confidence in you." After another minute of conversation on the matter, Ramsey shut it down.

Heather turned toward the door. Ramsey followed her sway. Even he was amazed over his power of persuasion. Briefly, he considered what it meant to lure this malleable employee into corporate espionage—implicating her in a plan to hobble Stanford's ingenious health project. Then he quickly justified his actions in his mind. Heather was hungry for advancement; this would boost her career.

Besides, collecting information was the currency of his craft. He couldn't be without it. Being on the periphery of this situation was tying his hands, hastening the demise of Johnston & Quib. J&Q's stock value relied too heavily on Ferguson's next two big-money drugs. If either one of those failed, it could spell ruin. At least Ramsey had Pinsky to rely on as his co-conspirator in defending J&Q. He punched in his boss's phone number to update her on his latest scheme.

* * *

Cez@r pulled microwaved Chinese egg rolls from his oven, dribbled red sauce on them. Chewing, he considered how his code was becoming a work of art.

He licked sweet-and-sour sauce from his fingers, then hit ENTER on his laptop to test his work. The code ran without error. *God yes.* Minimally, this program could alter results on the Stanford Grid locally. His final attack will have far reaching effects. Cez@r had a three-pronged strategy. First cripple the Grid, then control its power, then annihilate it. His first ploy should disrupt their precious results, the second should cripple their usual flow of power and the third would hurt the entire global network. This would also instill fear in the minds of every volunteer and patient. Ultimately, this hit would silence those who doubted if he was worthy of his nickname.

Thirty-Five

Thursday, November 3
Geneva, Switzerland

In a double-breasted suit and Ferragamo shoes, Niles Tully was loaded down for travel. He lugged a notebook computer under his arm with the sling while pulling a carry-on bag into the train station. He once read that this efficient European railway structure— containing its own police station, supermarket and underground car park—handled over two-hundred and thirty train arrivals and departures a day. Geneva clearly took pride in its transportation system. Swiss planners situated the Gare de Cornavin station right in the city center. The antique brick building conveyed a timeless architectural elegance. A sidewalk covering with skylights lined the entrance under an old world clock and flag. To him, it all looked like sweet victory after settling the terms of partnership with CERN and Google in Switzerland. Next stop, London.

Niles clacked up a ramp of steps inside the terminal smelling of cigarettes and baked bread. Pausing, he waited out a pain which throbbed in his shoulder—a not-so-trivial reminder of the *Tipsea* ordeal. In the glass-ceilinged arrival hall, he straightened the sling. At least the Google deal was safely on track. The departure board showed he would make it to London as planned. Major relief. It had been weeks since he'd seen Edward's bright grin; weeks since Niles heard Edward go on about the mechanics of cars, boats and planes—a trait he inherited from his gadget-loving Dad. Charlene, Edward's mother, was bringing him to a gastro-pub. It was logistical hell to co-parent a kid like this, but Niles and Charlene were pulling it off with rendezvous and telephone calls. Both gay, they had a partnership through Edward only, their angel.

Up ahead a sign in French, German and English read CONCOURSE PASSENGER BOARDING AREA.

There the agent punched Niles's ticket and handed it back. He'd crossed the Channel by underground train often to attend Grid meetings with CERN, but the TGV never got old—light years away from the Tube he once commuted on. We lost the Jaguar to the Yanks, he thought, but Europeans still get some things right.

Niles rang Wagner. "Finally good news, console cowboy."

"Niles."

"CERN is over-the-moon about our Google deal. They'd already replaced Jűrgen and have confidence we'll recover from this Hideo nightmare. They love how we're going to be downloadable from the Google toolbar. The Google product guy walked us through a toolbar mock up. We met from 9:00 a.m. through lunch. I'm still paranoid, though. Am I waking you?"

"What do you think? It's 5:30 in the morning."

"Sorry." Niles added how good it would be to meet up with his son for dinner at the Notting Grill.

The announcement system blasted, "*Der Zug wird in drei Minuten abweichen* ..." English followed. "*The train's leaving in three minutes.*"

"Have a safe trip."

Jude sounded downcast, still in a tailspin from all of these events. Niles realized he'd forgotten to ask about Kate's condition. "We'll talk more about Kate soon," Niles said. Clicking off, he hurried to the train, nearly colliding with a young couple schlepping backpacks. Holding hands, they could've been honeymooning on a shoestring. The beaming pair stepped aside for Niles to pass. He envied their freedom, though he should have been content as long as sailboats were out of his sight. Niles thumb-typed a quick text message to Roger Knowlan to relay that the Stanford Grid team had sealed the huge agreement with Google to advance the high-tech healthcare project. Niles wished he could've given Jűrgen and Hideo the news.

* * *

Across the TGV platform, a former bounty hunter with determined eyes watched Niles through Steiner 7x50mm police binoculars. A lifelong traveler, the man had acquired a working knowledge of train operations. It came in handy when you were on the move, tracking someone, from plane to train and probably automobile. Although the usual privileges he enjoyed as a recovery agent—entering a private property without a warrant and taking a fugitive without reading them their Miranda rights— didn't apply overseas. Regardless, ninety percent of the time he got his man, and tracking skips was no simple task.

The hunter eased closer to his subject. Some twenty feet away, he held a railway map. Fortunately, the acoustics in this station amplified the spoken word. Within earshot of Tully's telephone chat, the hunter managed to pick up that the target would be meeting a woman and someone named Edward at a Notting Grill. That was sufficient. Today's job was purely illegal, but a priceless opportunity to prove his skills, especially after Scud's recent attempt had failed on the bay. The hunter wanted his boss's job: Scud worked SWAT operations in places like Afghanistan. She identified and neutralized terrorist threats globally as part of Homeland Defense.

While taking a six-foot-four man from the busy streets of London required skill, he had confidence he could elude the usual eyes and ears. They would never see him. And after a restful flight back home, he'd be fifty thousand dollars greener. On top of that, Scud said that cutting Niles Tully down would better the world—that gave him a sense of duty which also added allure.

* * *

Olivier Ramsey pushed his laptop away. At the conference room table he pondered Jude Wagner, the writer of the data mining algorithm, the one bastard capable of dashing his plan for a virus attack. Ramsey grabbed the phone and punched in Ferguson's extension. "Tell me what you know about Jude Wagner."

"Why?"

"We cannot let Stanford's Grid get too far in front with Google. Wagner's a vital player. There's a Wall Street saying, *beware of geeks with formulas*."

"I don't know what that means. I can tell you I just had lunch with his sister."

"Really?"

"Yeah, his twin, Kate Wagner, is in town visiting. Strangely enough, she sat in on a talk of mine, then we had lunch. Wagner has to be preoccupied with worry about her," Ferguson said.

"Worry?"

"She has breast cancer. She'll be the Grid's first cancer lab animal."

"How unfortunate," Ramsey said blandly, turning the idea over in his head before hanging up.

Thirty-Six

Thursday, November 3
Geneva to London

The TGV glided along from Geneva to London while Niles tested the movement of his arm. Sitting alone in his train aisle, Niles considered how crazed Jude must be managing the recent deaths and his sister's diagnosis. Niles put his arm back in its sling and recalled the last work dinner he had with Hideo Onagi. The specter of his dog mauling made Niles tense. To dispel the bad energy, Niles pulled out a book from his suitcase and read *Steve Jobs, The Greatest Second Act* to the breezy purr of the train. He peeked from his book through the dark window to see the streets of Geneva fall away behind the train.

European trains served as Niles's private office on wheels: a more work-conducive environment for him than any other. Some ninety minutes later, the PA clicked on. "This is Conductor du Bord. The driver has informed me we're now traveling at our maximum speed of 210 kilometers per hour."

Niles worked on his notebook computer. He'd dozed off before he looked about to find a heavy set man sitting on the aisle opposite him. The aloof passenger with short yellow hair had the rectangular head of a Viking. He didn't even appear to be breathing. A trench coat lay folded at his side. Niles glanced over again. The man sat idly in a zipper-neck sweater with plain brown trousers and hiking boots. His dull-eyed stare into space gave Niles a cold feeling.

Niles touched his hair repeatedly, pressed an ALT KEY combination on his notebook to activate a password-protected screensaver, and turned his Word application to black.

Holding his sore shoulder, he took his computer and lumbered to the cafeteria carriage. Nearly empty of passengers, the dining car had tables covered in white linen, and it smelled of pot roast and onions. The train crossed a bumpy patch of track. Niles took a seat to steady himself. His nerves finally settled down after snacking on cheese and crackers there. He fixated on getting to his stop at King's Cross when the man appeared, sitting diagonal from Niles at the same table. Something threatening radiated from this passenger's stolid manner. The stranger's small glassy eyes bored into him. Niles couldn't shrug off his neurotic suspicions about this man possibly being an assassin.

Bloody hell. I have to lose this guy before I get to King's Cross. Niles attempted to talk himself down from a state of panic. The train light overhead strobed in his eyes, adding to his fatigue. He stared at the carpet and looked up again. The man wasn't going anywhere. Niles felt exposed waiting alone. At last, he got to his feet. If only the TGV train security could do something. But Niles had no specific complaint to work with.

Dizzily, he checked the bandage on his arm, moved cars again and searched for a bathroom. As some of his light-headedness passed, he noticed his mouth had gone dry.

Niles looked back.

The man was following, his trench coat slung over his arm. It was a thin cover for what appeared to be brass knuckles made of black metal. No, those weren't brass knuckles. It was a knuckle blaster stun gun. Niles had seen the type advertised as protection for runners.

Niles's balance became unsteady. In the chaos, all of his and Jude's altruistic visions of helping society turned frivolous. Any reasonable person would think they had a death wish carrying on like this. Niles sped to the train lavatory and snapped the thin partition door shut. Locked inside, he waited. Before long someone banged on the lavatory door, asking if everything was all right.

"Yes," he shouted. He forced down three paper cups of water in the confined space to calm his nervous system.

The train slowed. It must have been coming to the station. He felt boxed inside the bathroom while the train ground to a halt. Twitchy as ever, he wanted to make a quick escape.

He resolved to push people aside if need be to exit the TGV quickly and dash to a taxi. He speedily maneuvered out the collapsing lavatory partition door, dashed into his original train carriage, grabbed his small suitcase from where he first sat and stood impatiently by an exit door. He had to remain level-headed. A voice inside him said, "See, Jude. We should've dropped this entire thing when we first saw a hint of danger."

Niles looked out the passenger car window. A throng of passengers waited to board.

He wondered where his stalker was now. The exit whistle blew. He ran off the train. Looking over his shoulder, he spied men, woman and families leaving the TGV, trundling luggage. The station crackled with tourist activity. Safety in numbers, he thought. As relief washed over him, he got a grip of himself.

He considered going to the TGV station police. But he was torn. He was in no mood to seek out an underground security office where he'd have to plea for protection. The police would be of no help without a substantial threat anyhow. They'd probably hand him a business card and tell him to ring if he saw anything more unusual.

He made his way to the taxi rank instead. Dragging his luggage, he walked upstairs to the main level and out the doors to locate a black cab.

Glancing around for a taxi, he questioned how he was going to meet Edward and not imperil him. He knew he looked haggard, like a condemned man who'd escaped a runaway train. He wanted to call Edward's mother, Charlene, to cancel, but she'd insist on knowing where he was and call back repeatedly. Aware that his phone could be used as a tracking device, he shut it off and removed its battery. He still couldn't avoid the arrangement that was set in motion to meet his son for dinner and have him spend the night at the hotel; and he certainly couldn't leave his son waiting. Maybe he'd simply imagined everything after all. He nervously waited his turn in the queue. When he finally got into a cab, the driver talked non-stop for twenty-five minutes about how evening traffic bollocksed the roads. Ordinarily,

Niles found the London chit chat charming, but today, he cut off the driver's banter.

Niles tried calling Jude's cell phone. The line rang and rang until it hit voicemail. He started to leave a message when he reconsidered talking about his whereabouts and closed his phone.

Finally, the cab steered to the curb, stopping in front of the Notting Grill. A large party of urban professionals entered the restaurant. Niles paid the driver and dashed toward the crowded establishment, eager to see Edward and Charlene. A burgundy Peugeot recklessly pulled up, blocking his path to the Grill. Niles scanned the driver's face. He recognized him. The man behind the wheel of the Peugeot was his stalker from the train. Niles froze, horrified.

The man looked Niles squarely in the eyes, holding a gun. "Get in, Tully!" The man jabbed the barrel at Niles.

Adrenalin kicking in, Niles wheeled around and darted after his departing black taxi, waving and shouting like a mad person. The taxi stopped. Niles brusquely clambered into the backseat and slammed the door closed. "Just drive! Hurry. That Peugeot driver behind us is a psychopath who wants to get me."

The black cab pulled away sharply with the Peugeot trailing. Niles sat motionless inside, gripping his arm that sent shooting pain through him from his jerky movements. Stories about abduction cases played in his mind. The abductor's primary goal was to get his victim to a second location. That's where the victim was usually killed. Niles turned frequently to see if the Peugeot was following. It was close behind, copying every turn to their route. A cold chill went down his spine. He imagined he'd become rich amusement for his captor.

Niles was too flushed with mortal fear to digest the disappointment of his failed rendezvous. There was no way he'd be seeing Edward or even his reserved hotel room at Claridges on this London trip. His heart beat furiously, sizing up his options. He needed to shake this guy and go underground until things calmed down.

"I've got two hundred quid in my wallet. If you get us out of here alive, it's all yours!" Niles shouted to the cabbie.

"This beauty may not be greased lightning, but put the knowledge to the test and we'll see who comes out on top."

The knowledge was a pre-requisite for all qualified black cab drivers who had to demonstrate their intimate familiarity with every side street, mews and back alley in London. This set a London cabbie apart from any other cab driver in the world.

Suddenly the diesel engine revved to its max. Niles was flung from one side of the cab to the other. As his cab ducked through the brightly lit west London streets, the driver finally lost the Peugeot and Niles's tenacious hunter. Drained of mental energy, Niles dropped his head against his seat back and breathed the dank London air. Gradually his pulse slowed to normal as a plan came to mind. He would not to take his scheduled flight home to San Francisco tomorrow; instead, he'd steer clear of public places and disappear altogether.

Thirty-Seven

Thursday, November 3
Stanford, CA

At 1:30 in the afternoon the hallways at Stanford bioengineering had never been quieter. Wagner had more than enough work to catch up on when he played a voicemail that Charlene had left. "Niles never showed up. I waited for ninety minutes at the restaurant and left messages for him, but no word."

That didn't sound good at all. He hoped that Niles had simply encountered a random travel complication. Wagner contacted Nathalie.

"I'm probably jumping to conclusions, but Niles never met up with his son. He's punctual and was really looking forward to seeing him."

"What can I do?" Nathalie said softly.

"Can you monitor his 10 a.m. flight tomorrow from London Heathrow, use your agent pull with Virgin Atlantic to find out if he boards?"

She agreed.

Wagner hung up, not certain about what to do next. He had to stay focused on the task at hand: he desperately needed a DNA repository to corroborate Kate's cancer diagnosis. At least Knowlan was hard at work. In a few hours, he'd be back to piecing together a Grid-based database of mammograms. However while Knowlan had run sample images and indexed them electronically, they lacked real data. Wagner downed a protein drink and paced.

* * *

The clock tower at the sunny Cal Berkeley campus chimed two down the road from where Roger Knowlan worked. Even with a corduroy coat on, he felt cold inside this network operating center that Wagner called the steel igloo. Knowlan had just finished powering up a Grid backup server for Stanford at Berkeley. He couldn't have done it if Wagner hadn't pre-configured it for offsite redundancy. But with Hideo gone, Wagner tied up with the FBI and Niles abroad, Knowlan had to fill the gap. He was relieved to get the job done, and move on to analyzing Kate's genes at Stanford.

A wild mix of emotions ran through Knowlan, crouched with his laptop PC between aisles of seven-foot-tall server racks. Everything had been peaks and valleys. He was convinced that Hideo's death was caused by someone wanting to slow the arrival of deeply discounted medicine. Added to that, Hideo's absence doubled the workload at Stanford.

But to Knowlan's surprise, he actually enjoyed tinkering inside the 15x30 foot network operating center. He felt safe here at the SETI@home Department—Wagner's and Niles's old office. The six-floor citadel had tinted windows and enough concrete to serve as a government bomb shelter. It looked like a remnant from World War II and it was. Situated among trees, the University of California's Mathematics Institute loomed on a hilltop over Berkeley's main campus and most of San Francisco Bay.

Knowlan relished the legacy of these buildings that made up the Ernest Orlando Lawrence National Laboratory. The lab had hosted breakthroughs in uranium research. It provided a home for what the Department of Energy called Big Science—big machines, budgets, staffs, laboratories and bombs. The human genome had become the latest focus of Big Science.

Surrounded by buzzing computer machinery, he tested the last bank of server racks.

It ran perfectly. In the event of network failure, Stanford now had a backup computer server to call on for their Grid data.

Still, Knowlan could not stop thinking about the possibility of curing Kate's advanced breast cancer. The opportunity to prove the

Grid's capabilities boggled his mind. He closed his notebook PC and headed out, intent on getting a soft drink from the downstairs cafeteria when the door creaked over the steady whirring of the fans.

"Mr. Roger Knowlan?" A girlish voice made him jump.

"Yes, how can I help you?" Knowlan opened the door fully for her to come in. He sized up the young woman from her carefully styled hair to her pointy-toe boots.

She nervously twirled a pen in her long fingers. "Someone who I spoke with in the bioengineering department at Stanford mentioned you might be working here today. Quite a meat locker you have."

"And you represent?"

She crossed her arms for warmth. "I'm with a new scientific journal, *BioMed Review*. It's an L.A. publication. I'm visiting here for a couple days, just arrived this morning."

She offered her hand as if to demonstrate that she came in peace. "Maureen Kenner." They shook hands.

"On deadline for a story?" he asked.

"How did you know?" She removed a tube of lip gloss from her purse and slowly rubbed the stick across her lower lip, then put it away. She gave him a pearly grin, adjusting her purse that held a pad with a pen secured in its spirals. She had an hourglass figure even in wool gabardine trousers and a simple sweater. "I realize I'm interrupting," she said with a pouty expression. "But I wonder if I could impose on you for just a few minutes of your time?"

She inched closer, a cultivated maneuver that appeared to be a well-worn ploy for information. At the very least she needed his help. He saw restlessness in her eyes and tension in her curled fingers. She appeared perplexed by her job. He sympathized with her. Knowlan checked his watch. "I'll chat for a minute but I won't do a formal interview."

She adjusted the heavy bag over her shoulder. The bag's weight forced her to thrust one hip, revealing a vulnerable schoolgirl beneath that diligent and determined exterior. While dressing this morning, she probably hadn't anticipated spending time in an igloo. "I was heading to the cafeteria for a late lunch," he said. "You can join me. It's warmer there." He gestured for them to proceed down the hallway.

"Good, I haven't eaten yet either."

He guided her out of the NOC and down the staircase to the building cafeteria. Along the way, Knowlan explained how SETI@home became the Grid that inspired grids.

She smiled warmly at him while they walked.

A moment later they slid turkey sandwiches from a cafeteria counter onto trays.

They found a free table and sat in white pod-shaped plastic chairs. She swiveled. "You gotta love these. Anyway, glad I found you. I wandered into the wrong building at first . . . aerosol something."

"That's the Berkeley Lab's Indoor Environment Department where they do Aerosol Testing. One of my partners used to swap computer equipment with them—sort of a recycling co-op he started. Equipment swapping makes the University system go round."

"Makes sense," she said.

"The aerosol lab tests chemicals like anthrax that become weapons when airborne."

"Leave it to me to stumble into the hazardous chemical area," she said with a shrug.

"Those doors are always locked unlike the building entrance here. How did you hear about me again?"

"I've read articles that cite your work in genomics. You have been the expert on the top of my list to interview. The focal point of my feature article is about what your team does. I'm sure many topics will be too confidential to cover."

"That's absolutely right."

Swigging his lemonade, he watched her dig out a digital recorder from her bag. "I can't allow you to record us."

She returned her recorder to her bag. "No problem." She took a huge bite of her sandwich. "Maybe you could start by telling me what's so different about this Grid." "Briefly, it sorts our DNA on a molecular level. You might say it's an information service that's poised to save lives."

"How?" she asked, twirling a strand of her hair.

"With strategic partners, millions more people will be downloading the Grid program onto their desktop so their PCs becomes working parts of the project."

"What partnerships?"

She reminded him of how long it had been since he had been with a woman and how lab work dictated his schedule. "CERN, for one. We have another in the works."

"Let me get this straight," she said with seriousness. "The public can support Grid computing by downloading software?"

"Yes, that's how they can donate PC power. The Grid sends jobs out for PCs to process. Every little completed work unit is sent back to the Grid." He leaned in slightly to smell her perfume, then slouched back.

"So, why aren't doctors using grid technology already?"

Knowlan interlocked his fingers, adjusting in his pod chair. "Some are wary of us for reasons of confidentiality; others think the Grid represents Big Brother. Truthfully, the jury is out on whether or not the Grid should be free or not. It would be a steal as a pay-as-you go online system too."

"I see. Clearly, your innovative thinking is exactly what medicine needs. Do you feel the drug industry is behind?" She touched the corner of her mouth.

"Absolutely. The whole system is dangerously outdated. So many die from mistakes—hundreds of hospitals don't even bar code their inventory. The nation's tied to an antiquated business model, based on blockbuster drugs, when the world needs personalized attention."

"I think I get it."

"One quarter of all U.S. senior citizens forgo their prescribed medicine because pills cost too much."

"Really," she said, tapping her chin. "Last question—doesn't the Grid rely on Big Pharma for the manufacturing of drugs and won't that keep them fat and happy?"

"Only partially. Big Pharma makes its money on patented products, not manufacturing. Specialty businesses are already doing independent manufacturing— mainly pharmacies. I'm not talking about your average pharmacy that dispenses prescriptions for commercially available drugs. These pharmacies only produce custom-made drugs in a special facility with highly-trained pharmacists. It's called compounding and any doctor can prescribe compounded drugs." He paused. "Unfortunately, I have to get back to Stanford."

"Of course. Just set me straight on one more thing."

"Okay, make it quick."

"Isn't all this patient information on Stanford's Grid vulnerable to hacking?"

"Technically, yes. There's no such thing as being totally immune to corruption, especially to DDoS attacks, or flooding web pages with hits from various computers. DDos attacks have even terrorized government websites. Fortunately, our soon-to-be partner can fend off cyber attacks handily with teams of programmers. Our Grid volunteers need to know that. That's all I can say."

"Is it true, the rumor about Stanford joining Google?"

Knowlan shook his head and scooted his chair, ready to leave. "By the way, don't misquote me."

"I thought we agreed this wasn't an interview?"

"Just in case our talk finds its way into becoming a story. Stanford could always use good PR. Good luck Maureen."

Strawberry-blonde hair fell over her eye and she tucked it behind her ear. "Thank you." She hurriedly straightened her oversized purse. A designer wallet of some kind poked out from her purse pocket. Two monogrammed letters, HS, showed on the top corner of the leather.

Knowlan thought it odd that those letters weren't MK. The feeling bugged him. He had to get more information. "Hey, my apologies if I came off as cagey. Can I walk you to your car?"

"I actually need to run . . . have to get off this hill and find the freeway going south."

With directions in hand, she got up and slung her enormous bag over her slender shoulder.

The reporter departed as abruptly as she appeared.

He was left mulling over exactly who had just paid him the inquisitive visit.

Thirty-Eight

Thursday, November 3
Stanford, CA

Wagner hated the lull of activity at the Stanford lab when he was accustomed to having the old team working alongside him. Putting that aside, he needed a large set of cancer records—one with patients' reactions to drugs. Without it, the Grid was unequipped to isolate the drug combination to treat Kate's exact tumor type. Johnston & Quib had the largest breast cancer database. There had to be some way to access it. Alas, this presented another dark maze to maneuver. He certainly wasn't going to come by that goldmine of information by asking J&Q for it, especially since Stanford had cut their ties.

An embarrassing chapter from Wagner's past suddenly came back to him with new relevance. Back in his teenage hacker days, he'd learned that the quickest way into a data center didn't involve breaking in, but social pretexting—masquerading as someone trustworthy to trick a legitimate user into giving up a password to the network. An idea struck. He could exploit a person's natural tendency to help a co-worker or friend. Users were the weak link in security. Companies spent fortunes on firewalls and intrusion detection, but if someone could persuade an employee to give up a password, then all of that security meant nothing.

Wagner called his old pal from university days at Berkeley, hoping Alfonso could be his connection. Good thing he was the spontaneous type. Alfonso, known as "Mr. Upbeat," was second in command of

Information Technology for Johnston & Quib. He gladly agreed to break from work and meet for a beer—a stroke of luck for Wagner. Perhaps this bode well for his plan. Wagner unlocked his desk drawer and grabbed what he needed. With his pocket hard drive in hand, he went to his car.

* * *

Alfonso stood in the entrance to the Pyramid Brewing Company waiting for Wagner. Lofty and rustic, the brew pub could pass for a comfortable ski lodge. Studying black-and-white photographs on the wall with the amazement of an adult who's never seen a history book, Alfonso was reading aloud the captions beneath old images of Berkeley.

"Have you lost your way?" Wagner hollered.

They caught up quickly, rehashing old times at a round picnic-styled table. The high ceilings and lack of soft furnishings had them talking loudly over the brew pub racket.

"I hear you're lighting the world on fire with that work of yours at Stanford. Ever consider teaming up with a search engine company to deliver your Grid to the world?"

"As a matter of fact, that happens to be something we're looking into." A glint of curiosity played in Alfonso's face.

Wagner glossed over things enough to satisfy Alfonso, minus the heinous incidents and mention of Google.

"Yeah, yeah. It's under NDA—I'll respect your non-disclosure," Alfonso said. "I won't ask anymore. I just think your algorithm success is monumental."

"It's nice to have one groupie in this upside down world."

"With the right bandwidth, nothing should keep your project from going to Pluto."

Wagner had to push Alfonso along, enlist help for the Grid's repository. Alfonso did love to show off and Kate's cancer wasn't waiting for anyone. Wagner bought a round of beer before his phone rang twice. He saw it was an international call. Wagner told Alfonso he'd be right back, he stepped away and picked up.

"Jude, it's Charlene—" Her voice, frantic. Wagner held his mobile tightly to his ear. "Are you okay?"

"I still haven't heard from him. This is so unlike Niles not to even call. I shouldn't get so undone."

"No," Wagner insisted. "We should be very concerned. Where were you meeting him? I'll call the local police station."

"Notting Hill. I'm sorry, Jude. I'm beside myself."

He strained to make out every word of her bewildered voice over the din of the beer hall. Finally, he said, "Okay. I'll call you back if I get anything."

"Thank you," Charlene's voice went to a whisper, then her end dropped off.

Wagner silently fought his emotions. Alfonso shot him a curious look from their table.

Wagner walked outside, preparing what he would say if he actually reached the Notting Hill Police Station in London. It was a long shot, but he recalled the restaurant name where they were going. Niles had only been missing a few hours. Using his cell phone, Wagner succeeded in looking up the international number to the station. He punched in the numbers and was connected more easily than expected, directly to an officer's desk. He was transferred to another constable before Wagner succinctly explained his missing person. The officer hesitated.

"I'm not next of kin," Wagner said, "but I'm calling on behalf of his partner."

"No missing person report yet," the officer said. "Wait. I do see that a call came in about a man brandishing a gun that night around 8:00 p.m. outside the Notting Grill restaurant.

Blood drained from Wagner's face.

The constable added, "Notting Hill may be gentrified, but violent crime always festers in neighboring housing estates. Still, guns don't come easily to anyone in England and they're almost nonexistent in such high profile districts."

"Did anyone get a description of the man?"

"All we have is that the bugger drove a burgundy Peugeot, erratically, but the caller didn't give us the license plate. There's no other information."

Wagner thanked the constable, left his phone number in case anything more turned up and clicked off. He felt as if an invisible octopus with deadly tentacles was strangling everyone around him. Maybe Nathalie would know who could assist them from the office. He needed to find out what had happened to Niles and how it connected to this well-coordinated plot. Wagner pictured Hackman coming at him with that awkward walk and double-chin. There had to be a way to find out if Hackman was associated.

Wagner returned to the table hefting two steins of frothy beer.

Alfonso took his and swigged a gulp off the top. "Are you all right?"

"Yes," Wagner said, probably unconvincingly. He opted not to involve Alfonso with all these twisted events—it was easier for now. Niles's disappearance made Wagner more determined to help Kate. He thought about how many gigabytes of data he could store on the ample pocket hard drive he had in his glove compartment. It should be more than enough capacity to store an average cancer database. Wagner's mental wheels turned.

"I'm really not myself right now but—"

"We can do this another time."

"It's an annoying problem I'd like to knock out."

"Go ahead."

"We're having issues at Stanford. Our data center is running really hot. I've gotta find a workaround."

"Sorry, Jude but I'm sure you're now off the list for access privileges. What is this really about?"

Wagner put both hands on the table. "The truth is my sister has advanced breast cancer and I'm shit out of luck because we don't have the data. My insane idea or attempt was to transfer files to my pocket drive while you toured me around your data center."

Alfonso swilled his beer and licked his lip. "That is insane."

"If you do this for me, I'll give you my latest antivirus security when it's done."

"You do know my hot buttons." Alfonso thought for a moment. "Your sister is really bad off?"

"She's stage three."

Alfonso let out a puff of air.

"If I agreed to take you round, would you swear under oath that you leave me out if this stunt blows up?"

"You have my word." Wagner tried not to look too anxious. With so many former colleagues disappearing, he had to get what he could as quickly as possible.

"You cannot and will not repeat this to a soul and you will remember me in your will."

"Okay, yes," Wagner said.

Alfonso took a long, reflective pull from his stein and set it down. "Here's how we have to work this—there are absolutely no guarantees this cockamamie scheme is going to fly. If I signal you, then walk out with me immediately. We can only do this when Luke Rubowski is out."

"Your director?"

"Right. He takes long late lunches. Still, we will have to act quickly. We go with your first story in case things go off the rails. You begged me to show you around our facility and cooling system—I'm offering you alternatives for a solution."

"Okay."

"If you don't lower temperatures ASAP, something will blow. We'll be talking about cooling configurations and my personal tour for you is a goodwill gesture. You'll be lucky if I can leave you on your own for more than five minutes."

"You're a saint for trying."

"I hope you're satisfied because you won’t get an offer like this again. Rubowski will flip if he sees me escorting you. So, stay in character. And when you sign-in, don't use your real name. The receptionist usually doesn't ask to see personal guests' IDs. This is really a life or death situation, right?"

"Trust me," Wagner said. "I never would have put you out like this if it wasn't."

Thirty-Nine

Thursday, November 3
Berkeley, CA

Wagner's head pounded as he pressed the accelerator pedal, overtaking cars. He thought over the punishment he'd face for a corporate information theft. At least a few years in prison. Weighing consequences didn't simplify matters or change his plan.

A scent of jasmine wafted through his open car window while traveling the busy surface streets of south Berkeley. The sweet fragrance oddly reminded him of funeral flowers and how Hideo Onagi would never be coming home. God forbid his buddy Niles was lying on a coroner's gurney somewhere.

He passed more cars. Alfonso followed through the stop and go intersections. He'd tell Alfonso the whole story but the matter was too layered to get into it with him. Palms sweating, Wagner pulled his Mazda into the J&Q parking lot. Kate's custom therapy depended on Knowlan's ability to get the Insilico molecular modeling program working and that depended on Wagner obtaining the Johnston & Quib database.

He eased into a visitor spot at Johnston & Quib's private parking lot. Alfonso drove into a space beside him. Wagner transferred the pocket hard drive from his glove box into his front pocket. He'd been toting the special storage device from Stanford to the FBI and home.

Time to think like a hacker. He was working with the FBI to apprehend cyber hackers, yet today he would become one—another twist, and it was more ironic that his algorithm never would have happened if he hadn't tested his wits against governmental security systems at age sixteen. The delinquent teenage hacker of his past had to pull a final trick.

He and Alfonso cut across the parking lot to the main entrance. Inside the lobby, a Hispanic receptionist in her mid twenties applied heavy face powder, using a compact mirror to admire the results.

Wagner swallowed, his throat dry.

The receptionist looked Wagner over, checking for his badge.

Alfonso spoke up, showing his laminated clearance ID. "Rubowski approved him as a guest."

"Okay. Sign in, please," she said, waving sharp red nails at Wagner. "No cameras."

Wagner wrote his made up name and the date. Down the hall they walked. Once they turned the corner, Alfonso whispered, "Watch out for hot-blooded Latinas, they're scorpions."

"Tell that to my French-Canadian friend."

Alfonso chortled. "Now to the factory. We're strung like pianos today, behind deadline. The computer server you're looking for is labeled 'Big C,' by the way."

With a dramatic flourish, Alfonso opened the metal door to the computer lab. They entered a wide, open-plan room with clusters of cubicles. Creative engineers in T-shirts, spikey hair cuts and edgy glasses sat before computer screens. Seeing the familiar tribe oddly calmed Wagner's nerves. The room smelled of fresh popcorn—giving the place a homey touch. A row of brightly lit vending machines lined the back wall.

"They don't want the worker bees to leave," Alfonso said. "I put out fires while the higher-ups divine ideas to make IT more results-driven. They take us for dolts. But whatever rolls downhill, these guys are my family. In an emergency, I'd match the wits of mine against the whole exec team upstairs."

"I'm sure upstairs isn't wanting for sunshine and exercise either."

"Don't remind me." Alfonso led the way past cubicles.

At the end of the aisle sat two tables, large as barn doors. The lab benches were festooned in computer parts. The young denim-and-tee-shirt-clad computer techs didn't break focus from their diagnostic and repair work.

Alfonso guided Wagner past an empty corner office to the Data Center. He swiped his electronic passcard at the dark glass door. The two of them entered the windowless room. Its server cooling fans buzzed. Wagner saw aisles of black racks, a far more impressive data center than even the FBI's in San Francisco—an encouraging start.

They proceeded past a main monitor with a keyboard console and down one aisle of mounted computer servers, a dozen to a rack.

"The data center is all redesigned," Alfonso boasted. "Of course, our HVAC is set at sixty-one degrees with a humidity range of forty to fifty-five percent. The secret is to cool the return space air below the dew point."

Wagner followed attentively.

"Any specific questions just shoot. Moving right along . . . the website runs on these."

Alfonso pointed to a gun-metal rack that looked no different from the others. "Our databases are mounted on the far wall."

Alfonso moved to the recess of the room, pulled a chair in front of the keyboard console and sat. He logged in to the network and quickly showed Wagner how they had configured their cancer database, pointing.

Wagner felt a charge of excitement. He checked to see that he still had his jump drive in his pocket. "Impressive." He turned to look at the raised floors of the server racks. "Do you have paper and a pen I could borrow to take notes?"

Alfonso gave a knowing grin. "I've gone paperless. It will take me a few minutes to round up a paper and pen for you. Wait here." Alfonso walked off.

After the door closed behind him, Wagner sat down in front of the same computer console. Alfonso left the screen up that listed the computer servers. The second in the list was labeled BIG C. Wagner clicked on it. At first he didn't recognize the file system layout. He navigated around. Several keystrokes later, he had a basic mental picture of things. But where were the actual breast cancer data files? Randomly he opened directories. No luck. He rushed up a level and quickly scanned file folders names for the right subsection. At last, he came upon one folder labeled B_CANCER. He clicked that open, then another folder labeled MARKERS.

What he saw stopped his breath. Countless files named BREAST_CANCER_TRANSCRIPTIONS, followed by a number. Each held hundreds of breast cancer patient transcriptions—a priceless trove of cancer data and distinguishing markers for analyzing disease.

Wagner pulled his pocket hard drive from his front pocket, inserted it into the server's USB port and transferred the files.

Lastly, he copied the network routing information to the drive as a navigation reminder, and then logged out. Hopefully, Knowlan would get what he needed from this. Wagner removed his pocket drive from the USB and shoved it back into his pocket.

Wagner opened the door to meet his pal. Alfonso was coming his way to hand him a pad and pen. Wagner asked a final question relating to the air conditioning system. Alfonso answered, cordially leading Wagner out the building complex. "Thanks, Alfonso, for your help and impromptu acting."

"I do what I can. I built my career on maintaining appearances, so I suppose this all came pretty naturally."

Forty

Thursday, November 3
Oakland/San Francisco Bay Bridge, CA

Behind the wheel of his Mazda again, Wagner anxiously hoped the cancer data he'd copied was sufficient. He cruised in the FasTrak lane to the Bay Bridge toll plaza. He touched his car stereo button and pushed in an opera CD, Maria Callas's *Tosca*, one of his Mom's favorites.

His thoughts shot frenetically in every direction to the music while the wind noticeably swayed the Mazda from side to side. He actually had J&Q's breast cancer database in his pocket. He flipped down his visor, blocking the blinding sun that set over the western sky. The Bay Bridge advisory sign read HIGH WINDS ON BRIDGE. Beyond the side rails, the bay appeared dishwater gray with white caps. He pressed on, weaving to avoid a van that was nudging into his lane. Even before rush hour traffic was heavy. The wind forced him to focus on the road when *wham!* His car jolted forward, whipping his upper body. Something had slammed into his bumper.

His Mazda shot to the right. He cranked left to avoid crashing into the side of a Lexus. In his rearview mirror, he saw it—a pickup truck had come from nowhere.

Wagner punched his accelerator, pulling ahead—six, nine, twelve car lengths.

The pickup truck was barreling up behind him like a rocket-propelled grenade from hell. Wagner changed from the second to the third lane. He checked his mirror. The Ram truck changed lanes behind him. Wagner's stomach dropped. Had he been busted by Johnston & Quib Security? *Impossible.* J&Q couldn't have given chase so quickly and they would've just called the cops.

Battling the unpredictable sways of the wind, they stormed across the Bay Bridge. Wagner raced through the Treasure Island tunnel, then neared downtown. The San Francisco Ferry Building and the tops of large buildings grew. He pinned the accelerator to the floor of his Mazda MX6. The speedometer climbed to 89. Threading five lanes of cars, his vehicle wobbled from the gale.

The Dodge Ram truck behind him blasted too, cutting left then right. Wagner glimpsed the face behind a scarf and wrap-around dark sunglasses under a wool cap. The person was unrecognizable. No way to tell if it was the same stocky man who broke into his apartment. The driver grimaced, holding a gun in one hand. The bull bar on its front bumper moved closer. Wagner tried to read the license plate when he saw the chrome plate frame said Avis Rental Cars.

Maneuvering past slower cars, Wagner came to the Fremont Street exit. He downshifted. The orange RPM needle sprang, his engine whined. He curved sharply down the off-ramp.

The trailing truck swerved right to make the exit late. Wheels shrieked. The truck slew into the curve and continued.

Wagner fed through the Financial District and a labyrinth of city blocks. Gliding through the first light, he studied his rearview mirror. The truck followed two cars behind. He found a hole in the flow of traffic then pulled away from the pack, leaving the truck behind. He couldn't drive to his apartment. The secluded Filbert Street hilltop offered no escape. Wagner hooked left toward Chinatown, then wrenched the steering wheel to the right, onto narrow Grant Street. But he misjudged and under steered.

The Mazda bumped hard over the curb and flew onto the sidewalk. His trajectory put him head on with three kids crossing the road. He pulled the wheel and narrowly missed them.

Pedestrians thronged the streets. He'd entered Chinatown, the densest district. Illegal aliens, sweatshops and gangs found refuge in its chaos. Vendors' merchandise hung on low-slung shop awnings.

Wagner knew the neighborhood better than the average round-eye, having often walked downhill from his apartment to get acupuncture for neck strain. He parked in a red zone. Pulse racing, he yanked the e-brake, sprang from his car and ran north on Grant Avenue. The pickup sat in traffic. Orange and red plastic lanterns danced across the battered street, as if the neighborhood were permanently set for a Chinese New Year's celebration.

He breezed past a gilded pagoda. Ducks hung in the windows of a dim sum restaurant. He caught the aroma of steamed pork dumplings. Checking over his shoulder for the Ram truck, he collided into a clothing rack outside a crowded market. Red and yellow Chinese robes sailed off hangers.

"Slow down," a young woman shouted from a painted balcony.

Hearing a honk, he turned. The Ram truck was trailing on the sidewalk a block away, getting around traffic. His feet couldn't keep up with his adrenaline. He narrowly avoided running into a clump of bricks stacked in front of a store. Some Chinese believed that they promoted good *feng shui*. Luckily they didn't send him airborne.

He looked back over his shoulder again down the dusky street. A van obscured his line of site. He crossed a pearl business, then an open storefront displaying fish that emitted a pungent smell. Squid, shrimp, halibut and catfish sat on trays of ice. He slipped on a fillet of something and fell backward onto it. Its essence ground into his denim. Picking himself up, he barreled on, wearing half of the putrid catch on his thigh.

Wagner neared his acupuncture office, but saw a closed sign outside. He remembered the office had an adjoining business. That business had a poster-sized cardboard sign taped to the door showing a hand with a stylized eye in its palm. He darted into the dark room, which emanated red light. He slipped behind a purple velvet curtain that acted as a doorway to the small room. Cardboard letters spelling *Tarot Reader* were push-pinned into the wall above a round table with a beaded tablecloth. Incense had burned to ash on the table. He could hear a TV in a back room. An irate woman wearing an apron and holding a Louisville slugger poked her head around a screen.

"We are closed," she shouted.

Wagner apologized, but the lady kept shouting. He ducked through a side door and into the acupuncture business. He'd visited Dr. Wong's office so regularly that she sent him Christmas gifts of Alaskan salmon.

The boxy space reeked of incense, root and ginger. The lights were out, but a streetlight outside shone through the window beside the shelves. Dr. Wong came in lugging shopping bags. Wearing her usual medical coat with large pockets, she flipped on the overheads. A quizzical look turned to amusement when she saw Wagner.

Catching his breath, Wagner whipped out his pocket drive. "Someone is after me. Please leave!"

Dr. Wong dropped her bags on the floor. "Don't worry."

"No, go!" Wagner begged, sliding his drive on one of the top shelves.

The doctor hit the wall switch, dousing the lights and obscuring her face. "You'll be safe."

In the faint light from the window, Wagner pointed at the desk as a place for the doctor to take cover. Instead, she slipped into a closet area, partitioned by a long silk shawl.

Through the window, Wagner saw the Ram truck pull to the curb in front of the store. It blocked traffic. Car horns beeped. For a weapon, Wagner emptied a thick glass container of dried herbs. He angled his body behind the window. He watched the pursuer jump from his car holding a handgun. Wagner now made out a ruddy-complexioned person with lifeless features. But he wasn't the intruder Wagner wrestled with on Columbus Avenue. Wagner stepped behind the open door to the tarot shop.

Footsteps stomped into the tarot shop.

The gray-haired Tarot woman screeched from next door. "Who you looking for?"

Wagner heard the attacker's heavy breathing. The footsteps continued, advancing closer.

On the balls of his feet, Wagner held a weighty jar. He prepared to pivot around the open door and let his attacker have it. Tension filled the air.

The attacker moved to the threshold. The Taro woman shrieked again.

The attacker looked back. Dr. Wong sprung from behind her shawl. With fists full of long needles, the doctor swung her arms high. In one arching motion, she jammed the needles into the back of the attacker's neck.

The pursuer moaned in agony. He clawed at the needles, staggered into the office until he dropped to the vinyl floor. Long Chinese needles jutted from his lower neck.

Wagner set the jar down. Finally, he got a closer look at this guy who had the thick-boned build of a corn-fed Midwesterner. This person vaguely reminded Wagner of his neighborhood butcher who rarely spoke or showed expression. The only notable thing on her was an empty pancake holster strapped to her ankle. Wagner yanked the sunglasses and hat from the attacker's head, revealing short brown hair. Then it struck him. This florid face belonged to a woman, dressed like a man in heavy dark jeans and high lace up boots—possibly Danner Military boots but he couldn't tell. She appeared to be breathing. The assailant was coming to. She muttered something just barely intelligible. "My partner is close behind."

Wagner stepped in front of Dr. Wong, and moved toward the woman's limp hand to grab her gun when she sat up. With a groggy motion, she pointed her pistol. Wagner stumbled backward, found his balance and snatched his pocket drive from the high shelf. The doctor was already on her office phone reporting a robbery in progress.

Wagner shouted, "Run."

The attacker pulled needles from her neck.

Seeing the woman upright, the doctor dropped the receiver. She swung open her office door. She and Wagner ran outside the little office to Grant Street.

Without pausing, Wagner weaved through the crowd until he made it to his car.

A parking ticket was tucked under his wiper blade. Eager to get the drive uploaded to the Grid, he ignored it, got in, placed the hard drive on the floor of the passenger seat and sped toward Russian Hill still reeking of raw fish. Too keyed up now to think straight, he forced himself to breath slowly. He did still have the cancer files on a drive in his pocket . . . his palm-sized gadget that contained hope for Kate’s future. But he wouldn’t discount the possibility of another blinding surprise. At this rate, anything could come charging from behind.

Wagner texted Nathalie: "A brunette woman with a gun just came after me."

She instructed him to drive to the bureau right away to provide a description.

He texted her again, "No time for that. Gotta go."

"Call me soon. Be careful."

He could almost picture the look of concern on her otherwise mild-mannered face. He set his phone down to concentrate on the streets of San Francisco, intent on getting this data to Roger Knowlan without more delay or another maniacal incident.

Forty-One

Thursday, November 3
Stanford University, CA

Kate Wagner massaged her temples in a circular motion with her fingertips, seated once again in the lab chair. Her illness might have been the source of her fatigue. But she banished the thought, chalking it up to nervous excitement. She'd made Knowlan promise her that she could return the following evening to follow up on the processing of things and here she was.

"I expect your brother to contact us soon about the database. I gather he didn't go into any of that with you."

"That's right."

"He's rustling up a Berkeley pal named Alfonso," Knowlan said. "A well-connected friend, whatever that means."

"What results do you have so far?"

"We have the breast cancer segment of your genome sequenced. We are all set for stage two."

Returning to his workstation, Knowlan launched the Grid application. "The Grid will analyze your sequenced genome and the white cells from your tissue sample by delivering your computer job to at least 90,000 processors. First we'll explore which breast cancer medicine matches your gene type." He tapped his foot, and slid a small pack of chewing gum from his tight jeans pocket. After taking a piece, he put the pack away, forgetting to offer her one.

"So," she said, "we check my protein folds against those that are known to be cancerous in a database and identify a targeted drug therapy based on genomic matching?"

Knowlan's eyes brightened as if his fellow scientific academic had hit a hole in one. "Yes, so tell everyone you know to volunteer their computers to do the crunching. All they have to do is download the small program which contacts the server to get work units. None of this works without tons of electronic records to sharp–shoot disease."

"But where do those online patient records come from?" she asked.

"Great question. Obtaining sufficient medical data has always been our problem. Even researchers have struggled with statistical analysis because information was stored in silos—it blocked access to any broad comparison so vital information couldn't be cross-referenced. Pharma companies had the upper hand just by virtue of the vast amounts of data they collect during clinical research. But that's ending. Now computers systems are communicating: from research scientists to hospitals and we have access to consolidated, anonymous data. Very soon search engines will pool what we need to create a great dataset."

He checked his watch. "Anyway, in addition to accelerating the Grid with his algorithm, Jude has proposed something more."

"What next?" she said.

"Those who donate their idle processor and their anonymous, secured genome to the data pool will be awarded special Grid access privileges for analysis of their own health."

Kate sat up. "Like a resource trade?"

"Precisely, profoundly enhancing our dataset."

Kate rubbed her chin. She felt guilty for not giving Jude more credit. If she was going to have faith in anything, she should have it in her twin.

Knowlan slid the keyboard toward him and pecked.

Enthralled, Kate watched the large screen animate with dancing, 3-D DNA objects. But this wasn't just a screen saver. This was real. What she was looking at was her own DNA—with linked, multicolored, three-dimensional orbs, spiraling and changing colors like cartoon geometric figures in space.

"We can handle a million user requests for diagnosis a day," he said.

Kate was spellbound.

Hitting the space bar, Knowlan cleared the display. A slide show glowed on the projector screen. He snatched up a remote control. "Soon, when we visit our physician and get blood analysis, he will identify what ails us and instantly prescribe a medicine specific to our genetics.'"

"If only we were there today."

"The better the data processing, the better our snip analysis and the closer we come."

Kate was only half convinced as Knowlan talked faster. More than that, she wanted to act. "What now?"

"I'm ready to run the Grid program. I'll be doing it twice: first to diagnosis your tumor type, then we'll rule out drugs your biology will be less responsive to based on the history of similar patients. If there's no existing drug that's a perfect fit, we'll have a drug formulated for your unique needs, genomically."

"Could the whole world be playing catch up to this stuff like I am? I'm never the early adopter of anything."

"Not until today," he said. "You're a leader now, without question. Jude once mentioned that his sister was an old-school skeptic. Fingers crossed, analyzing your genome will take us a step closer to healing you and making you a believer."

"I'm still on pins and needles."

"Jude had better hurry up," Knowlan confessed. "At this point in our development, we can only maintain the entire Grid for short periods of time. We've got a very high number of volunteers donating processing power currently. But their back-end computer support fluctuates and might not be around for us to call on tomorrow."

Forty-Two

Thursday, November 3
San Francisco, CA

A branch from a maple tree scratched at the kitchen window pane outside Jude Wagner's apartment. Winds blustered. It would be nice to have a Glock like Nathalie's. Maybe he could get one outside of San Francisco. Yet that demanded a waiting period. Enough of that. He had to get this pocket drive with the data over to Knowlan. The fastest way to do that would not happen by driving an hour to Stanford, but by uploading it right here. Besides, he didn't want Kate returning to this apartment alone after that sudden Chinatown situation.

Wagner called Knowlan. No answer. Typical. The man hated interruptions to his work. Wagner left a voicemail relaying that he'd acquired the cancer files and would save them to a server folder labeled BREASTCANCER.

Wagner booted up his notebook computer. Before starting the process of uploading the breast cancer files to the Grid server, he copied the data to his hard drive. He navigated through the Grid and started the upload. His Internet connection was just fast enough for this. Hopefully, very soon Knowlan would be running his comparisons of Kate's tissue against patient records to get reactions to drug treatments.

Famished, Wagner microwaved a frozen burrito. Looking at his rail-station-style clock hanging on the wall, he saw 8:09 p.m. The data should be halfway uploaded.

He demolished the hot burrito sitting in front of his computer, making sure there weren't any connection hiccups. Gradually, the investigation seemed to be coming to a head, especially with what Nathalie had explained about DeltaCorp's role in all this. He called his enigma-of-an-FBI-agent again to relay more about his incident in Chinatown. "It's me."

"So, you are positive this person was not the unsub—the unidentified subject—who chased you on Columbus Avenue?"

"Right."

"And she was after you?" she asked.

"Me and probably my Grid security token."

"Do you still carry one?" she asked abruptly.

"Yes. As a precaution, I keep one off campus while Roger Knowlan carries his at Stanford. Did you find that photo roster of DeltaCorp employees?"

"No such thing exists, I'm sorry to say."

"Shit."

"By the way, that profile we started on our shooter wasn't right."

"What do you mean?" he said.

"I'm reevaluating everything. I think I was absolutely right about this perp having a base locally. Every recent incident, including yours today, occurred in the Bay Area, from Woodside to Stanford to San Francisco."

"Right."

"But these religious quotes," she said, "they are more consistent with a crime of passion than an assassin for hire. I simply mean there could be an emotional element. We cannot just consider professional hitmen, although our primary focus needs to be on religious conservatives within DeltaCorp in the Bay Area."

"That's another baby step."

"I wish I had more. I have limited access to info on DeltaCorp. I've asked for a list of DeltaCorp names, but I am not getting help during this professional review." She wished him a goodnight and hung up.

Wagner's mind wandered to when Nathalie lay in his arms. It felt good—more than that even, it felt right. *Am I in love with her?*

She'd become his artificial limb—a vital appendage which he had mixed feelings about. A dependable presence that wasn't entirely real .

. . once this thing wound down, they'd surely part company, or would they? Crazier things could happened. He'd closed off sentimentality to everything but family and the past. Though maybe Nathalie somehow affected his avoidance of commitment.

At his desk he checked on the file upload status. The job was done. *Good.* A big gust came from out front. He jumped, then kicked himself for not moving Kate to a hotel, where she'd be safer. He remembered he'd left a notebook in the car trunk that held notes on the Grid work he was doing the day his papers were stolen. Setting down his fork, he threw on his suede jacket and zipped it.

After locking up, he headed out into the dark to retrieve his notebook. With another workday ending, several cars circled the hilltop for parking. Standing behind his Mazda, he unlocked his trunk. He picked up the spiral notebook, only to have the threat letter fall out. He snatched it and was putting it into his pocket when a hand from behind him grabbed his arm. Acting on self-defense reflex, Wagner gripped the wrist. He pivoted, ducked and whipped the guy's arm behind the man in a hammerlock, heaving him against the Mazda.

"Hey, it's Agent Speer."

Aghast, Wagner dropped the man's arm.

"What are you doing?" The rangy agent with the baggy gray suit did a slow turn, adjusting his shoulder holster. "We tried your mobile and I knocked on your door."

"I could've broken your nose with your sneaking up on me."

"Lucky you didn't," Speer squawked. "Hackman wants you right away."

"Why on earth now?" Wagner suspected this had to do with the church incident at Woodside.

"I'll tell you what I know once you get in the car."

"No. What's this about?" Wagner demanded.

"He's got business to go over and it must be important or he wouldn't have me chasing you down." The supervisory agent removed his car keys from his front pocket and dangled them in Wagner's face. "I'm not expecting trouble, but if you're going to drag your feet—"

Wagner shot him a dirty look.

Gripping Wagner’s left bicep, Speer marched him to his brown Crown Victoria. At least it wasn’t a Chevrolet Blazer or Dodge Ram truck.

Speer opened the door. "Don’t sit on the hat." He watched Wagner get in.

"What else did Hackman say?"

Speer turned over the engine and hit the gas, thrusting Wagner’s head into the vinyl headrest.

Speer looked in his rearview mirror. "Swiss authorities have contacted us about a death that’s linked to your project at Stanford—no one’s accusing you of being the perpetrator but if it were up to me, I’d interrogate your whole team."

Wagner leaned forward. "What else do you know about this threat?"

"Enough for you to be concerned."

Wagner remained silent, thinking about Hackman. Obviously Speer’s intention was to intimidate him. Feds used intimidation as indiscriminately as beat cops did.

Speer looked into the mirror again. "Jude, that’s the patron saint of lost causes, isn’t it? Seems to me you’re your own lost cause."

"Is that your best shot?" Wagner said. "You should be ashamed of the carbon footprint you're leaving on the earth."

"And why is that?"

"The very fact that you're breathing is wasting space."

"Real clever—meanwhile everything's boomeranging on you, Wagner. I heard from Geneva that no one was closer to Niles Tully, Hideo Onagi and Jűrgen Hansen than you. And you've been sneaking around that Pharmaceutical company Johnston & Quib, probably working on an under-the-table deal."

"So you've been following me?"

"You're really in no position to be asking questions. All this puts you right in the thick of things. It's hardly a good spot to be in." Evidently, Speer had convinced himself that he was on to something.

"You pegged me. I’m the homicidal maniac."

They drove for a while. Speer turned, "I’ve read the hype about your mathematical discovery—it doesn't look like disruptive genius to me."

Wagner started to feel caged. He eyed Speer. "So now I’m a fraud too."

"I'm not the judge, but Hackman's definitely not a fan of wannabe field agents."

Wagner ignored the android. If Hackman had it in for him, he would find out soon enough. In the artificially pine-air freshened sedan, Wagner tried to figure out what the hell was really happening. Still, he didn't like what Speer had said: Wagner looked like a suspect. Who knew how Hackman, the gulag chief, figured things? Wagner stared out his window at the passing buildings, considering everything.

Any more resistance right now might make circumstances worse for him later.

Wagner felt acutely aware of being in the line of fire. Nathalie had warned him to stay out of Hackman's way. *Maintain a distance and follow protocol* were her exact words. The advice was taking hold. He'd possibly poked his nose where he shouldn't have and was about to feel the repercussions.

Forty-Three

Thursday, November 3
San Francisco, CA

After parking in the garage of the federal building, Supervisory Agent Warren Speer escorted Jude Wagner to the elevator and up to the thirteenth floor. The semi-dark hallways were quiet. The regular staff had finished their day. Vacant office cubicles appeared suspended in animation across the familiar floor. Wagner walked rigidly. Milliseconds passed like minutes before the meeting—or grill session, as the case may be. Speer led Wagner around the floor looking for the boss. SAC Hackman was waiting for them in the library, leaning against a bookcase. He put down the leatherbound reference book he'd been leafing through and motioned them to follow him.

They passed the meeting room, which still had stacks of file folders spread across the long table from the ongoing OPR investigation, and then came to the holding room.

The windowless space had an oppressive air—three chairs around a dull metal table.

On the table rested a stack of brown files, a lamp and a plastic bucket. The place was designed for one task and one task only: extracting information. Half the overhead lights flicked on, leaving shadows in the corners. Speer pushed the door closed. It snapped shut like a rat trap.

Speer sat beside Hackman. Wagner took the angular armchair across from them. Avoiding a defensive posture, he kept his arms at his sides. Sheepishness might imply admission of wrongdoing. Surely that would bring harsher punishment.

If the FBI wanted something from you, they'd do what every law enforcement team did—search for your emotional trigger, then question you until you trip yourself up in contradiction. Just like it was done in TV episodes.

Hackman held the unwavering gaze of a prison warden then cleared his throat. "Empty your pockets."

Wagner pulled out his keys, his Stanford cards, computer access key, cell phone and wallet and put them on the table."

"Did Speer tell you why I called you here?"

"Not exactly."

Speer scooted closer to the metal table.

Hackman rubbed his jaw. "I have this feeling you're trouble—like a plum that turned out to be a prune." Hackman's jowly face went blank with seriousness. "The other day I was driving along and I noticed something familiar in my rearview mirror; the bad prune in his red vehicle. I wondered, what interest would Jude Wagner have in our religious service?"

Wagner remained still.

Hackman slid his hands from his paunch to the table. "You've crossed the line, Wagner. You think you've made some clandestine discovery about me. You could paper the walls with the rumors I've heard. And rumors don't go away on their own. You have to deal with them." Hackman's puffed chest heaved as he breathed.

"It's dangerous to invent stories, even if they're just in your head and reckless to act on them. In my office insubordination is a punishable offense. If you were my asset, I'd put you on the bricks for this. So, why did you meet with your erstwhile partner, Johnston & Quib?"

"To get ideas for an improved cooling system. A friend of mine works there. He was my escort. You can look him up and ask him." Jude gave Hackman Alfonso's name and phone number.

"Frisk him." Hackman said.

Wagner reluctantly stood.

Speer ran his hands over Wagner, top to bottom, then went through his pockets and pulled out a one page printout and a plastic baggie that contained the threat letter left to Niles.

"Look at this." Speer proudly handed both items to Hackman.

Hackman looked over the print out from the lab. "What's this all about?"

"It's just work," Wagner said, returning to his seat across from them.

Hackman set the printout down and picked up the note sealed in plastic. "And this?"

Wagner considered his answer while Hackman read the note through its plastic sheath.

He looked at both sides of the page. Holding the letter to the light, he examined the white space Wagner had circled. Hackman quickly ascertained the watermark and read it aloud, "United Bishops Association."

Hackman fixed his gaze on Wagner, waving the plastic sheath. "Why didn't you tell us about this?"

"Frankly, I didn't know what to make of it."

Hackman leaned toward Wagner, palming the tabletop. "You believe I had Jűrgen Hansen killed, don't you? Maybe you think I arranged to have your friend Hideo Onagi attacked in Tokyo too."

Wagner shoved his hand through his hair. He also wanted to know who had come after him but he remained quiet on that.

Hackman said, "Follow me."

Speer plopped Wagner's things into the plastic bucket. Hackman plied both arms to get out of his chair and they went.

In Hackman's office, he took his high-back chair and gestured for Wagner to sit and he did. Speer put the bucket on Hackman's desk and leaned against the door, resting a foot against it. He looked like someone eager to supervise an execution. Speer was tall and had the posture of a flagpole. But after their tussle outside his apartment, Wagner felt he could take him.

Hackman's fedora perched on the end of one oar that hung on the wall behind the boss.

"Listen," Hackman said, glaring. "I want to make something clear. I'm a member of a family-based organization, a devout group of long-established Catholics. We're founding a new chapter—there's no self-flagellating albinos or Roseline leading to Mary Magdalene, okay?"

Wagner remained silent.

"This marks the end of your shadowing me."

Hackman moved to a drawer. The big man pulled out a leaflet and pushed it at Wagner. "Hope you find this edifying."

Wagner glanced over the trifold sheet that explained conventions of a local branch of Catholics.

Sedevacantivists practiced ritualized traditions in Latin that others might find strange and anachronistic ...

He read on. The leaflet gave a plausible rationale for Hackman's old world religious denomination. In an instant, Wagner's hunch about Sedevacantivists felt all wrong. He'd gone down a dead-end alley to investigate these homicides and could feel his face flush from embarrassment.

Speer sighed with indifference.

"There's something else." Hackman shifted his weight forward and reached across his desk to grab a manila case file, labeled 174A-INT-56125. INT. "I'm going to tell you what's been going on while you've been on your religious witch hunt. This is an international case file, hence the letters 'INT'. Inside is an investigative chronology, listing dates and times, accounting for agents' phone calls, movements and media inquiries. As you know, it all started with two homicides. The begging question has been, what's the larger plan?"

Wagner wondered if anything in that file might narrow the suspect list to DeltaCorp. But how would he raise his suspicions of an internal conspiracy?

Hackman held up one of the pages for Wagner see. It had the headline: "POSSIBLE LINK BETWEEN INTERNET TERRORIST CHATTER AND HIDEO ONAGI AND JŰRGEN HANSEN HOMICIDES."

Reading those names in print hit Wagner like bullets. Hideo and Jűrgen had been reduced to numbered case files: crime scenes with routine photographs and autopsies that needed investigating—files that surely would be relegated to a stack labeled solved or cold case, then go to archives.

Hackman recited how Jűrgen died and how Onagi's double-dog attack looked deliberate, based on Onagi's daughter's report. "I'll spare you the photos. These aren't blitz-style attacks. Sure, some might argue that the dog-mauling is, but I wouldn't. These are methodically planned MOs, organized killings, not to mention your friend's sailboat mishap."

Sounding irritated, Hackman added, "What we've been lacking is behavioral evidence. Anyway, also in this file is a report on the crimes according to our Threat Analysis Group. The scope of this goes beyond what Noiret may have confided with you."

Had Nathalie kept a secret about Internet chatter?

Hackman continued, "Speer should've pressed you harder for details at the marina when you had your sailboat incident. I don't care what kind of shape you were in, you must suspect something."

"Suspect what?" Wagner asked.

Speer took his spidery hands out of his pleated trouser pockets.

"Give me the latest developments at Stanford," Hackman said.

Wagner clasped his hands together. "Stanford signed a deal with Google and CERN.

It extends the reach and power of the Grid."

Hackman nodded. "Morris already brought it to our attention. So Stanford will have new power to fight disease."

"That's right."

"Is there any one group or individual who would want to stop the Grid?"

"It's not that neat."

"Trust is a two way street. Who is your biggest rival?"

"Probably Johnston & Quib, the Pharma company."

"Really? Because Stanford's got the new game in town that poses a competitive threat?"

"To cancer drugs, yes."

"If we weren't so jammed up at Stanford, I'd like to hear more."

Speer folded his arms. "Something else new has come up from Agent Morris's group.

They detected something in the IRC chat room babble, involving hostiles plotting to terrorize Stanford, and not just virtually, but physically."

Wagner wondered if Speer was serious until Hackman interrupted to clarify, "While you were running all over town, our assets picked up on a planned strike to the Stanford campus—in the vicinity of an electrical substation. We've spent the last twenty-four hours substantiating it—sounds legit. I've green lighted Agent Noiret. Stanford's campus police are evacuating the campus. Stanford fire department is on standby."

Nothing made sense to Wagner. None of the computer analysts Wagner was working with, who were looking for Internet threats to Stanford on the IRC Channels, raised any flags. Wagner had to ask what he'd bottled up: "What's your connection to DeltaCorp? It's too convenient that the pistol that killed my friend Jurgen came from this very office and that you had no prior knowledge of the handgun going missing." Hackman and Speer exchanged glances.

The boss pointed his finger at Wagner. "We're keeping you out of sight."

Speer couldn't keep quiet. "For your information, what started as a case for the Watch Group of the Bureau of Intelligence and Research was escalated here."

"And that means?" Wagner asked.

Hackman stared at Wagner. "That means Special Agent Nathalie Noiret is going to Stanford as my lead . . . without you. The helicopter team is on the roof. They need to clear the Stanford campus of any threat. Noiret should be boarding now."

"What does she know about our lab? I should be onboard," Wagner exclaimed.

"We talked about that idea, but no." Hackman stood up and tugged at his belt. "We're doing this surgically. You may have facilitated a chain reaction by kicking the Grid up a notch, but you can't contain this. This is bigger than you."

"Obviously, that campus is a city," Wagner said.

"Yup, with 678 major buildings. We'll use you here to guide the team by video monitor and blueprints of the University. One of the flight crew onboard has a camera-mounted helmet."

"But no one has a better idea how to anticipate an attack on the Grid than me."

Hackman’s eyes narrowed. "Forget it. You’re a marked man—one of the last Grid project heads standing. I hope you know where Niles Tully is. I’ve been informed he’s missing."

"I don’t. And Noiret needs my help down there—"

Hackman stopped walking and put his hands on his chair back. "I'm not pulling a civilian into a high security-level field operation."

"Whatever happens," Speer scoffed, "Noiret doesn’t need you."

"Enough," Hackman told Speer, then turned back to Wagner. "I’ll be supervising Noiret myself on this end with our CT—counter terrorism—supervisor. Take your things. By the way, Speer will continue to keep an eye on you."

Wagner picked up everything from the bucket, stood, opened Hackman’s door and proceeded down the hall to his alcove desk area. He didn't trust this helicopter operation and how he was being detained. Wagner's stomach-churning nerves weren't going to let him rest.

Forty-Four

Thursday, November 3
San Francisco, CA

Wagner walked from Hackman's office toward Nathalie's alcove area, feeling Speer's eyes boring into the back of his head. The supervisory agent followed close behind. "Let's hope this'll be a false alarm, Wagner. Then you can go home, put a log on the fire and rent *Pulp Fiction*."

Wagner stopped walking. "If you say so." He grinned sarcastically.

"Exactly. That shouldn't be too hard."

"Push me, Speer, and tomorrow you'll mysteriously find every web search you've done outside this office on Hackman's desk."

Speer casually elbowed him as he walked by.

Wagner gripped Speer's wrist and boxed him into a bookcase.

Speer tried to tear free, seething.

Wagner fixed a stare on Speer's face. "Keep out of my face or I'll flatten your larynx with one punch."

"Speer." The shout came from Hackman, still in his office.

Wagner dropped the agent's hands.

Speer took a swipe. His jab only got air. The agent hesitated, preparing to do something, then he turned to the hallway grumbling obscenities.

Wagner dropped into his temporary desk. He didn't sweat the altercation. If Speer snitched to Hackman, it would only show that the agent was manhandled by the civilian he was assigned to cover. Speer's ego would prevent that.

Wagner turned his attention to the terrorist chatter. He texted Knowlan to warn him about the threat on the Stanford campus. A text came back: "Got your messages. Am in the middle of working with Kate. We'll leave ASAP."

Wagner fired back, "No. Leave now."

Knowlan couldn't be trusted to evacuate anytime soon. When immersed in his work, he even ignored the occasional fire alarm drill that went off on the Stanford campus.

Wagner left a voicemail message for Kate on her crappy cell phone service, warning her to get out too. Hackman could arrest him if he ignored his orders to stay put, but Wagner couldn't sit idle. His gut tightened again. Kate and Knowlan were in harm's way. He had to get on that helicopter and protect the Grid for Kate's sake. He'd seen where the exit door was to the stairs—they had to lead to the roof.

That was all well and good, but how would he elude Speer, who would enjoy his new post as bodyguard? Speer would be all too eager to limit Wagner's freedom of movement.

Wagner got up and looked. Speer was out of sight. Wagner speed-walked down the hall, pulled the heavy latch of the exit door and stepped into the passage that led to the roof. The narrow double-backing staircase flickered under fluorescent light tubes, smelling of mildew. Wagner could barely make out the landing as the fluorescent tube above the first runner had blown.

He bolted up the concrete steps to echoes of his own footfalls. But something didn't sound right. He didn't hear the self-closing door snap shut behind him. Wagner froze in the darkness to hush his own movement. He listened. With his back to a cinderblock wall, he looked down toward pulsing light.

Wagner heard a fleeting noise of a shoe scuffing the floor. The concrete staircase obstructed his view of the door. Wagner eyed the rooftop door, marked by a green exit sign. He needed to round the corner and run up two flights of stairs, a greater distance than he'd expected. Wagner continued up the staircase.

He heard another shoe scuffle. A hand clawed Wagner's back. His nerves shot, and he fell on the dusty steps. A concrete corner met his jawbone, snapping his mouth closed. The crack rattled Wagner's skull with throbbing pain. He must've chipped a molar with this stomach-churning taste of bony calcium. He saw it was Speer. The supervisory agent dragged Wagner by one leg down steps.

Digging in his toes, Wagner finally found traction on the concrete.

Speer stood over him, short-winded.

Wagner hooked the back of Speer's right knee and brought him down. They wrestled on the sharp-angled steps. Wagner maneuvered behind Speer, and flung an arm under his shoulder, trying for a headlock.

Speer hammered an elbow into Wagner's ribcage.

Wagner took it, gasping. But he held on to Speer.

Wagner tightened his head and arm lock on Speer. Speer thrust his leg backward to kick Wagner, but missed. Wagner closed the wrestling hold on Speer's neck and shoulder, constricting his breathing.

Speer grunted and squirmed. After several slow seconds Speer's body turned heavy. It dropped, slack in Wagner's wiry arms like a marionette with its strings cut.

Wagner eased him down to the landing of the steps. Seeing that Speer was still breathing, Wagner caught his own breath. Those bruised ribs of his panged again. Words from a wrestling instructor came to him. *No matter how much I train you—in a real match, every move is improvisation, unrehearsed.*

Climbing up to the building roof, Wagner knocked open the door and saw the helicopter idling in floodlights that ringed the rooftop. He lowered his head in the wind of whirling overhead rotor blades. Pounding air flattened his shirt against his chest. He was taken aback when he got a better look at what was running on the helipad: no standard-sized bird, it was a MH-60 PaveHawk Helicopter.

Wagner had seen pictures of Black Hawk helicopters on TV. They were used to conduct day or night operations in hostile environments. This one had additional radar and dual weapons pylons attached to both sides of the fuselage. Instead of FBI markings, it appeared to have civilian markings and civilian numbers.

Through the open aluminum door, he saw two pilots in front of two crew chiefs.

Behind the crew chiefs Nathalie sat with an empty seat beside her. At the rear were three S.W.A.T. operatives with helmets who held M4 rifles. Everyone, even Agent Noiret, wore full-weather garb.

Heads turned as Wagner climbed inside.

"One more for the maneuver. Hackman's orders," Wagner exclaimed.

One of the crew members took Wagner by the arm. "Who are you?"

Nathalie shouted, "He's with me. He's from Stanford." She then slammed the sliding cargo door, then realigned her headset. Jet fuel odor dissipated.

He took the empty seat. Nathalie's eyes shone as large disks. To his surprise, only she questioned him further.

"My god, what are you doing here?" she mouthed over the *chet-chet* of the engine and blades. Her hands clutched the edge of her seat.

"Hackman told me about the coded bomb threat on Stanford's Grid team."

"They picked it up over the Internet," she said. "I couldn't talk about it."

Even under the dim red overhead light, he fixed on her gentle features: the straight slope of her nose and her air-brushed skin. She could not have appeared more out of place.

Wagner buckled a waist harness as the turbine noise increased. The rotors went from *fwop-fwop* to a high-pitched whir as the aircraft lifted vertically from the helipad.

Wagner mouthed to Nathalie, "Thanks."

Nathalie reached under her seat and pulled out a lightweight headset. She handed it to Wagner and pointed out where he could plug the jack into this seat. After he plugged and donned the headset, she discreetly showed him that she was dialed to channel 33.

He dialed in 33, hoping there were enough channels for them to talk privately as the other crew members probably had communication built into their helmets.

"There is no way Hackman approved this." Her voice transmitted loud and clear in his ears.

"Okay, you're right. I'll be in a lot of trouble for this."

"And you are a target also," she said over the gyrating whine of the engine.

"Moving target," Wagner said.

She gestured for him to pull on his harness. "Without hazardous duty pay."

"Nathalie, someone's gotta break my losing streak—might as well be me. I need your help with something else."

She gave him a speculative glance.

"I want to make sure my sister is okay. She's on the campus."

"At Stanford?" Nathalie put her hand on his arm. "You should've been alerted about this terrorist threat earlier—maybe we could have done more—" She stopped at the sound of the landing gear retracting. The helicopter tilted, angling its nose into forward flight.

She pointed at the side of Wagner's chin. "What happened?"

He touched what felt like a swollen gash. "I slipped." He gazed out his helicopter window. The dense urban high-rises gave way to a view of the freeway and South San Francisco hills. At first he saw the matchbook-like homes of Daly City, then the familiar Crystal Springs reservoir to the southwest. Fingers of fog spread over the hills. The helicopter cabin darkened.

Wagner closed his eyes to concentrate energy on saving Kate. She was his primary cause now, superseding everything else.

"You think your sister is really at your lab, no?" Nathalie asked.

"Yes I do, there with Roger Knowlan." Wagner gave every crew member a cursory once over. He noticed disturbing discrepancies. At least two members of the helo team had equipment belts which looked more like that of hired militia than FBI.

He knew he was paranoid about someone turning him in, but their high lace-up black boots resembled the type worn by the woman who chased him into his acupuncturist's office.

Forty-Five

Thursday, November 3
San Francisco, CA

The pilot pulled back on the cyclic stick. The aircraft surged and climbed. Jude Wagner and Special Agent Nathalie Noiret gripped the stretched mesh on their seats as the G-force increased. The fwap of the rotors changed in pitch. The mechanical hum wound louder.

Wagner's adrenaline still rushed. Speer would be coming around in the stairwell. Could he handle the embarrassment? The moment Hackman heard of that, he'd turn this helicopter around.

Wagner looked over the cabin, then leaned over to Nathalie. "What's their role?"

"They're DeltaCorp," Nathalie said stiffly.

Wagner kept his surprise to himself.

She said, "Like I told you, they are hired to support special field ops. It will be a coordinated effort when we land—for whatever happens on the ground." She rolled her eyes so that only Wagner could see.

Questions about DeltaCorp's culpability darted in his mind.

The helo hit a pocket of turbulence. Wagner, Nathalie and the crew chief took a grab handle for stability.

"What are they doing here?" Wagner asked.

Nathalie adjusted in her seat. "I only just learned about this operation."

Wagner listened intently over the aircraft noise.

She shoved a fist into her jacket. "It's not good. I do not trust Hackman. What I do know is that campus police already identified a male who snapped photographs of the power substations."

The helo dipped. Someone shouted, "Air pocket."

Wagner imagined how the attackers might have targeted Knowlan, aware that he worked late on campus. Wagner covered his lips with his hand. "When we touchdown, I'll check the lab and look for them. The bomb threat could be a diversion by someone who wants to kill him."

"I will keep the DeltaCorp team occupied," she said. "After thirty minutes, I will leave them to find you."

"Alright," Wagner said.

Nathalie's radio crackled. After speaking on it, she pulled her headset lead from it and handed the radio to Wagner. "It's our SAC on the line for you."

Wagner breathed deep, disconnected his audio lead from the seat and plugged it into the radio.

"Running rogue, Wagner?" Hackman barked. "I could have you arrested. I'd turn that bird around if I had time to waste."

Wagner pushed to talk. "But you don't, Sir."

"We've verified the authenticity of the coded threat. Hostiles are planning some strike on the Stanford data center. Remember, Agent Noiret is in charge. You stay out of play, Wagner and I'll deal with you when this is over. Give me Noiret."

Nathalie took the radio.

SAC Hackman shouted so loud that even Wagner made out a few of his words. "We're evacuating the Department of Medicine."

"Yes, Sir." she said.

Chirp.

Nathalie mumbled, "*Il y a une couille dans le potage*."

"What's that?" Wagner asked.

"Everything is going wrong—literally it means there's a testicle in the soup."

Wagner showed no reaction.

Nathalie relayed Hackman's message: *University security sent images of a man studying the campus electrical substations—now referencing the photograph against the NCIC.* Hackman ordered that

Noiret set up an attack defense. He reminded her that she had every resource in abundance, except for time.

Nathalie gave Wagner a spare radio from an equipment bag. "You'll need this on the ground."

Holding the radio, Wagner peered through the acrylic oval window. The helicopter approached a labyrinth of terracotta roofs and neat paths that led to plazas and grassy spaces. Under amber lights, the clusters of buildings resembled a Spanish architect's model. Wagner marveled over how orderly the Stanford campus looked from above. Even one of the power substations was camouflaged by pine trees beside the football field.

The aircraft descended until it was about four stories above the Stanford football field. The transmission whir became louder. There was very little light below to gauge ground distance. Then the ground rushed up. The helo struck the earth with a deafening jolt.

Everyone inside whipsawed. The force of impact tested the landing gear's resilience. The engine made a high-pitched whir until the pilot struggled to flip a switch and shut it down. Gradually the crew groaned to life. The DeltaCorp pilot cussed, testing his neck.

"Nathalie, are you okay?" Wagner shouted.

Moving her head from side-to-side, she checked her condition. "I'm not hurt." She grabbed two helmets from a duffel bag and handed one to Wagner. "These are for night vision." She pointed at the goggles which came attached to the helmets, flipped up over the visor.

"Okay."

They pulled on their helmets. A Delta man slung open the helo door. Nathalie and Wagner stepped from the aircraft with the op team following.

With a squad of six soldiers, Nathalie was the only one Wagner could trust. Some natural light was needed for the night vision goggles to work. Thankfully, there was a half moon shining. The clock tower chimed 9:00 p.m. into the autumn air. Wagner wanted to watch Nathalie's back. She called the team together, "Alpha and Bravo units."

One Bravo ops member reported that the video camera in his helmet broke under impact from the rough landing.

Wagner joined Alpha and Bravo in a huddle around her. She unfolded a campus map from her jacket pocket; they examined it under flashlight. He looked over her shoulder as she opened her phone and saw a message—one of the electrical power stations was overloading. She pointed to a crease in the paper, coordinating where this was occurring. Next, she indicated where two additional electrical power stations were located.

Nathalie radioed: "We had a hard landing. No major injuries but one with a neck strain." She lowered her radio and looked at the field ops. "There are three substations. The Fire Department is on standby. We will divide into two teams of three. Survey and contain the substations."

She got the nods she needed. Everyone flipped down his goggles.

As Wagner lowered goggles over his eyes, his surroundings flared a fuzzy blue until his eyes adjusted.

Hackman's voice came on. "There'll be hell to pay if that 'copter is damaged. Report back soon."

Nathalie turned down the volume on her radio. She made eye contact with the team. Like a marine sergeant, she belted her order to go. Wagner stopped worrying about her.

Alpha and Bravo fanned out: one advanced toward the electrical power stations situated a few hundred yards south, to an area Wagner knew as Manzanita Field, and the other went toward the Data Center. Wagner attached the earpiece that came with his radio. Silently, he shot off in the direction of the Data Center, located in the medical building. He moved slowly at first as the depth perception in the goggles had thrown him. He was glad to have them. Without the goggles, he surely would've construed the row of young maple trees with wood supports up ahead as a waiting ambush.

Forty-Six

Thursday, November 3
Stanford University, CA

Several yards behind Wagner, a twig snapped in the dark. Night vision revealed nothing more than trees rustling in a breeze between quad buildings. Jude turned the squelch on his radio to maximum. This side of campus never felt so confined. He wanted eyes in the back of his head—anything to help his tunnel vision. He scanned round. None of the green images were moving.

He crept around the Department of Medicine complex, coming right to the stucco wall of the Data Center Building. Now inside the building, he stepped towards the Data Center's closed metal door. With the light on, he flipped up his goggles and looked through the window. What he saw sucked the wind out of him—a masked man sat at the computer terminal, a few feet from the exit door in the back. A substantial knife rested on the table in front of him. Kate and Roger Knowlan sat in opposite corners of the floor, rigidly hunched with their hands tied in front of them, constrained at their wrists. Their legs were drawn up to their chests and tied at their ankles. Kate's tear-filled face was swollen, red.

The attacker typed frantically at the Grid terminal desk. He looked over six-feet tall, had a wiry build and a bullet-shaped head under a black ski mask. He wore brown jeans and a snug-fitting parka. Wagner quietly stepped back from the door and radioed for Nathalie. "I'm on the south side of the lab, inside the Medical Building, standing right outside the Data Center. I found him."

"Don't move. I am on my way."

He imagined how Nathalie would plan her shot on the attacker who sat in the same line of sight as Kate, in the far corner of the room. If the round strayed, it could hit her.

Through a hallway window, Wagner saw an explosion—*Kaboom.* A yellow-white nova filled the cobalt sky with a brilliant flash.

The deafening blast thundered from outside. Data center walls rattled from the shockwave. Wagner's feet vibrated on the shaking floor. Kate shrieked inside the closed room. The hallway lights went dark. Wagner's stomach leapt into his chest.

Special Agent Nathalie Noiret and the other DeltaCorp ops dropped to the ground. They were thirty yards from reaching the Data Center when the substation blew up. Smoke mushroomed into the air from a fire on campus, wafting a sulphuric odor. Under moonlight, a cloud of grey billowed. It swirled above their heads, above buildings, creating a war-zone aura on the college campus.

The sky changed from deep blue to a murky charcoal.

One field op adjusted his goggles. Smoke partially blocked the moon, but there was still light.

Nathalie covered her mouth. The smell of debris permeated the air. Fire alarms blared in stereo from multiple buildings on campus. A tall eucalyptus tree had caught fire and was blazing. She ordered both Alpha and Bravo teams to form a perimeter around the Data Center. Carrying her field radio in one hand, her Glock in the other, she crouched and moved to the west wing. Her Bravo team followed, though they had no clear path ahead.

Smoke interfered with her vision. The power station blast had extinguished the lights on this side of the campus. They couldn't use flashlights for fear that it would broadcast their presence. A fire truck siren wailed in the distance. Her ears rang. They relied on moonlight filtered through smoke to find their way.

* * *

Wagner took a ragged breath and let it out. Red and blue lights beamed on the building wall. Sirens sang. Campus police probably moved about in the background. He dialed down the squelch on his field radio.

Suddenly his radio wouldn't quit chirping with talk. He lowered the volume and heard Nathalie's voice: "We just witnessed an electrical substation explosion on the north side of campus."

Hackman: "What? The police and fire department should be onsite. There could be more detonations. Are you confident with being incident commander?"

"10-4. We are on the move and hear emergency vehicles."

"I'll have locals check to see that the other substation isn't rigged to go. What are your knowns?" Hackman asked.

"We have one suspect at the data center with a knife, over. I will need help with the media outlets that will be on their way."

"Roger that. I'll keep them at bay. Stanford police will establish a perimeter around the bioengineering department and a command post site by the substation. The fire department—"

"They are here."

Perchip. Hackman was gone.

* * *

Not a sound came from the inky black data center. Wagner pulled on his light sensitive gear and peered into the laboratory window. From behind his goggles, the cavernous void showed green. The intruder sat on his haunches beside the computer bench holding the knife on Kate's head.

Wagner's entire body stiffened. The blast must've caught him by surprise—making him defensive. Wagner concentrated to remain calm—to overcome his sensation of strangulation. Excruciating seconds passed before a door latch clicked behind him. A faint silhouette with a gun raised advanced down the Data Center hallway. The stature and gait were familiar. He heard, "Jude."

Recognizing Nathalie, Wagner's shoulders dropped in relief. He pointed at the room.

She lightly moved to his side to look in when another fire engine blared in the distance. The data center lights popped on. It was the back-up generator, kicking in late for some reason. The generator buzzed, background noise to the klaxon. The computer utility room glowed under a menacing backup power light . . . a portion of the University hung by a life support system.

They peered through the smudged glass. Only Kate and Knowlan were visible. Had the attacker moved out of view? There was an exit door. He must've escaped through the back. Wagner exhaled.

Nathalie radioed for back up. "Suspect with a knife is fleeing by the north side of the data center. Both teams, hurry."

She swung the door open and ran through the data center and out the back exit.

Wagner rushed to Kate. He worked to untie her, asking if she was okay.

She cleared her throat and opened her mouth but no words came out. The pulse in her neck beat rapidly. At last she said, "I guess so."

Wagner untied Knowlan in the opposite corner.

"It's going to be a while before we're really okay," Knowlan said. His button-down shirt was untucked and sweat stained. He drew deep breaths, wiping his eyes with his fingers. "Amazed you got here."

Wagner put his arms around Kate, hugging her trembling body. "Relax."

She gasped.

Wagner checked the redness of her wrists. No bleeding. He helped her sit on one of the three rolling chairs. Wagner was tempted to send her to his apartment, but a bigger part of him wanted to keep an eye on her and other potential gunmen. He kept her nearby.

"That evil bastard," Knowlan said.

Wagner turned to Knowlan. "Listen, what did he do?"

"He forced my thumb on the token and worked at the terminal. For all I know, he could've created backdoor access to the Grid. He pulled a flash drive from his pocket and snapped it into the main server terminal. He could have been infecting the Grid with something."

Knowlan's eyes were ringed with red from rubbing. He pointed at two jewel cases containing DVDs which obviously contained Kate's prepared genome data. "I keyed in all of her information for upload to the Grid this morning, long before he showed up. It should've been fully processed before this happened. But I haven't had time to check what the Grid churned out."

Wagner shook his head. "I'm going to hope those results are done and look good."

"We can't trust anything until we do a full diagnostic test of the server," Knowlan said.

"It was awful." Kate shook out her legs to improve her circulation. "I thought we were going to die."

Wagner's phone vibrated on his belt. He unlatched it and checked the display.

GRID AUTO WARNING: DATA CHECKSUMS BELOW THRESHOLD

Wagner nudged past Knowlan. "There's been some damage to the Grid that we need to repair." He wheeled the chair up to the Grid console and typed commands on the Grid server keyboard. The status screen glowed with red warning messages. His mobile device flashed error messages. He ripped the device off his hip and removed the battery.

Nathalie came back inside the room with a desultory posture.

"You didn't get him?" Wagner said.

"No. With his head start and the campus lights out, it appears he is gone."

"So, we won't know if he was with DeltaCorp."

She shook her head. "I couldn't even tell you if he was wearing Danner boots. I'm having the teams go through the fragments to see if there are signs of an IED—improvised explosive device." Nathalie answered her radio for a quick communication exchange.

"What was that about?" Wagner asked.

Nathalie glanced at her watch. "Hackman will be coordinating with local police to try to chase him down."

"Good luck to them," Wagner said.

Nathalie stared at her smart phone screen intently. "*Mon Dieu*, we have a name."

"Who?"

"Liborio Russo," Nathalie said. "It's the name they pulled from that photograph Stanford security had taken. An agent is running this through the FBI database. It's all we have." She continued to look at her screen. "Hmm."

"What?" Wagner asked.

"A social security came up, but there is nothing on Russo's profession. Nothing on where he lives either. If it's the same suspect, he does have a criminal record for computer hacking into a government department."

"Really." Wagner said. "I wonder, could he be the one in charge of everything?"

"It is possible."

"You just gave me an idea," Wagner said. He pulled a cocktail napkin from his wallet with the phone number that the woman left for him at the Hyde Out Bar. "Do a reverse look-up of this."

"Okay." Looking at the napkin, Nathalie keyed in the phone number to the analyst at her office. She worked her phone for a minute longer. "That number goes to a Heather Styles. Lives in Berkeley, California. They are working on her social."

Nathalie's phone vibrated. "Hold on." She read her screen.

"What do you have?" Wagner leaned closer.

"This Heather Styles—her employer is Johnston & Quib."

"What, really?" Realization crashed into Wagner's consciousness. "That has to be why she pumped me for information at the Hyde Out. It was to help J&Q."

Knowlan shook his head with torment. "What did she look like?"

Wagner cracked his knuckles. "Like a strawberry blonde bombshell. Quite a seduction artist."

"I don't believe this," Knowlan said. "Mid twenties?"

"Yeah, that's her."

"She played me too," Knowlan added. "Introduced herself as Maureen to me. She interviewed me as a journalist for a Los Angeles science journal, claiming she lived there. Then I saw different initials, engraved on her wallet. I knew she had screwed with me, but I didn't have a real name. We were perfect patsies." Knowlan rolled his eyes. "Now what?"

Nathalie put her phone away. "They're cross-referencing. It'll take a while."

The campus alarms finally shut off. Kate looked away, tuning out. "We've gotta keep moving here," Wagner insisted.

Nathalie tucked her phone away. "You are right about that. An investigation is like a shark—once it stops, it dies."

"Let's get swimming," Wagner said.

His radio beeped. Hackman's voice came on. "Wagner, you're going to speed me to an early death. That said, I'm going to allow you to help Agent Noiret because you're there with inside knowledge. But the second you misstep, you're outta there and I'll have you arrested for interfering with an investigation."

"At the moment, the threat of discipline is the last thing I care about. My sister, who is here, is depending on this Grid for her life."

"Is that a fact?"

"Yes, Sir."

"You have more going on than I knew. Keep me informed." The airwaves went quiet.

Wagner set his radio down. "I just realized something. The Grid came into the public eye before anyone anticipated it would."

"Yes, and?" Nathalie rubbed her eyes.

"And Hackman opposes biotechnology . . . which obviously framed him in our minds."

Nathalie didn't look convinced.

Wagner scratched his head. "I wouldn't say Hackman, specifically, was framed. I feel like someone set up the religious right."

Nathalie asked. "So the religious right was just a scapegoat."

"Why not? We ran with it. Hackman just happened to fall into that profile."

"So what if it's not Hackman?" she said slowly. "Assume I accept your hypothesis. What then?"

"We track down this Heather Styles."

Finally, another text came back on Nathalie's phone which she read aloud. "The only history we show on Ms. Styles, by the way, is that she keeps a horrific credit score."

"Great," Wagner said. "So, we know she's dangerous with a credit card."

"Calm down." Nathalie looked up from her phone. "I will talk to her. If I can find her."

Wagner pulled a folded page from his hip pocket. He'd transferred the printout he took from Onagi's lab from one set of pants to the next, thinking he'd eventually make sense of it. He reexamined the page.

"What are you doing?" she asked.

Wagner typed at the terminal, comparing what he saw on the screen with the printout from the lab. "Several keystrokes we printed from the lab break in match procedures the attacker just performed here. This whole thing could've been an effort to gain access to the Grid and control its power to the electrical substation."

"How likely is that?" Nathalie asked.

"I don't know, but access is everything. With that, you can control the power and also release a virus onto the secured network. My bet is that the explosion was a screw up."

"An unintended consequence?" she said.

"It looks that way. This attacker didn't want to draw a world of attention to himself. Maybe he was monkeying around with the electrical source."

Knowlan said, "I would believe anything at this point."

Nathalie turned to Wagner. "They must've been following Knowlan. And you think this perp did it to interrupt the Grid, possibly even cut off its power?"

"Like I said, I think that the latter attempt was botched," Wagner added. Kate vacantly rubbed her wrists while Nathalie listened.

Wagner explained his theory that those who were trying to stop the Grid were handling it in a haphazard fashion. The thief who broke into his place had no clear idea about where the security token might be and settled for whatever he could get. "That must be what they were after when they killed Hideo. That, and to slow the Grid project by eliminating him. Killing Jűrgen also hampered the project."

"But why didn't they try to kill you?" Nathalie asked.

"They just tried in Chinatown and possibly on Niles's boat. It's hard to say who that boat explosion was intended for. It's Niles's boat after all not mine." Wagner touched his sore jawbone. "Also, these assailants could be starting with those Stanford Grid team members who are not working directly with the FBI."

Nathalie adjusted the vólume on her radio. "I could believe that. Still, breaking into this center while it is occupied is daring, you-know."

"I agree," Wagner said. "Apparently they wanted Knowlan to be here to get hold of his access key. His car is parked right there. It wouldn't be hard to observe who drove it. Very soon the Grid will be secure with Google. It was now or never."

Knowlan shouted, "Stop talking about me like I'm not here. Let's get to work on restoring our network."

Forty-Seven

Saturday, November 5
Stanford University, CA

Power generators lit the smoke-filled night through the small hours of the morning. Wagner and Knowlan had worked through the evening running diagnostic testing on the Grid. Chunks of data processing code had been disrupted. They would not even venture to pull Kate's drug prescription results until they saw that the Grid was functioning properly. It was eight-thirty a.m. when a squad car pulled up outside the building. A local police detective took his own pictures of the scorched earth in daylight and asked Agent Nathalie Noiret probing but routine questions to review last night's explosion. Kate rested in the corner of the room in a sleeping bag which Wagner had rounded up from a firefighter.

Physically drained, Wagner stood from his flimsy chair at the Grid console. Pain had flared up in his lower back from the *Tipsea* explosion. They had concluded that the man with the knife had used Knowlan's access token to implant a malware program.

To be on the safe side, Wagner and Roger Knowlan rolled back the servers to reverse whatever sabotage the attacker could have caused. But they could only revert things in three hour increments, to right after the attacker arrived. If they went back further in time it would overstep the point in the day when Kate's results were completed.

The backup generators were holding, but neon lights flickered. Wagner stared at the Grid display, holding his side. He tapped away at the keyboard. Nathalie came back into the lab, waving a fistful of foil-wrapped health bars. "All of the fire trucks but one are gone."

She distributed the bars and opened one for herself when she stopped. "By the way, Jude, I just found out that the Virgin Atlantic agent confirmed that Niles Tully didn't take his scheduled flight from London this morning."

"Holy shit," Wagner said.

"We are trying to track him down," she told him. "An analyst is looking into his whereabouts using credit card payments and the airlines will notify us if he boards any future flights."

Wagner didn't have time to speculate. He pulled out his cell and tried reaching Niles again, but didn't get an answer. "Anything else?"

"I spoke with Morris at the office. He says he's doing even more work on your antivirus protection. And the DeltaCorp team has left. I also spoke with Hackman again."

"And?" Wagner said.

"The backup team is here and can escort us out safely."

"Okay," Wagner said without thinking, still fixated on repairing the Grid. He turned to Kate, on the far side of the room. "Would you like for me to take you to a hospital?"

"If we're making progress and we are safe, I'd rather not leave," Kate said.

Wagner looked out the window at the cordoned off substation area. A news helicopter circled and four Stanford police officers were talking just outside the building. "For now, I think we're safe." He motioned for Nathalie to come close.

She did and he whispered, "I want Kate to rest but I think it's better if we stick together to solve these problems."

Nathalie nodded when her radio chirped again. After having placed a number of calls to the bureau, she turned down the volume.

Kate stood up as if she couldn't listen any more. She went to the window and rested her arms on the sill ledge, watching the officers on patrol and the last fire truck leave.

Knowlan crunched tortilla chips he'd retrieved from the main lab after a dark adventure through the building.

Nathalie thumb clicked the buttons on her phone. "I'm going to call human resources again at Johnston & Quib."

"Why?" Wagner asked.

"Because Heather Styles listed a dependent on her W-2 form."

"And."

"They informed me that she has a child."

Wagner could see a plan hatching behind those almond eyes, a knowing glint. "What are you thinking?"

"About added negotiation power," Nathalie said. "Before there's another strike."

"Something tells me never to have a falling out with you."

"*Avec ma bite et mon couteau.*"

"What?"

"An old expression. You'll be safe around me if you don't act stupid. It means, 'Don't confuse your cock with a knife.'"

Wagner shook his head.

Nathalie left the building, giving Wagner the space he needed to patch the Grid server together. Unfortunately, the explosion had forced dust into the room which compromised the computer server integrity as much as anything else had.

* * *

Working another Saturday, Mark Ferguson hastily leafed through phone messages at his J&Q office in Emeryville, checking to see if testing results had come in on his Huntington's disease drug. No luck. He tossed the sheets aside.

A folder filled with papers on the Stanford Grid Project sat on his desk. He cursed the day that he'd roped Ramsey and Pinsky in to invest in the Stanford Grid. What on earth had he done?

Too much change, too fast.

Ferguson was sick of the accusations of overpaid CEOs in America. Tobacco makers, real estate mortgage brokers, auto makers, and Pharma chiefs had all become subjects for public scrutiny. Ferguson's rise to power from a Pennsylvania steel-working family was the stuff found in fables. Ferguson's desk phone rang. He picked it up to find it was his lawyer-turned stock broker, Julian Stark.

"Bad news. You had a drastic sell off of J&Q stock end of day Friday."

"And I thought things couldn't get worse."

"Someone sold two million shares this morning, and I'm afraid that someone is your daughter." It was automatically disclosed in the stock report.

Ferguson felt shunned, as if he'd been punched in the gut—why wouldn't his daughter confide in him before doing such a thing?

"I warned against any sudden sell off," Stark said. "You need gradual retreat. Plus this looks like insider trading."

"Tell me all about it," Ferguson said.

"The stock price is in rapid retreat. Once the public gets the full meaning of free access to the Grid, J&Q stock will really hemorrhage. I'm surprised the story hasn't run already on CNBC."

For a fleeting moment, Ferguson considered dumping his stock too, but he shuddered at the thought of being remembered as the talented Mr. Ferguson who fell like Kenneth Lay or Bernie Madoff. "How do we stop this bloodbath? What do you advise?"

"I could buy call options in your name. This small bullish bet might camouflage your daughter's sell off. In the unlikely event J&Q goes up, these calls will be a hedge."

"Fine, buy two hundred k or as much as you see fit." Ferguson quickly hung up the phone. While it took an army of foot soldiers to build Ferguson's J&Q realm, just one slip up might precipitate its crash. How could his own daughter do this?

Ramsey barged into his office again. "Ferguson, my eyes are failing, but you look like an old man, slumped there." Ramsey stood in front of the desk, glaring down at Ferguson in his chair.

Not a gray hair moved on the CEO. Ferguson would rather suffer in isolation than reveal self-pity to a Wall Street whore like Ramsey.

"You realize," Ramsey said, "Stanford's Grid is going to be our demise. I'm taking emergency precautions."

"What do you mean?"

"Advanced technology can seize up, right?" Ramsey said. "If we're lucky, the Grid might conveniently freeze."

Ferguson sat, too burned out to concentrate.

Ramsey walked up to a row of black walnut-framed photographs on the wall. One of them pictured Ferguson holding a Golden Gloves trophy. Another caught him at a beach house. The last photo showed him on a luxury yacht, standing at the helm like a marine surveyor, gazing into the distance.

"If only you could navigate J&Q like you can that yacht of yours," Ramsey said.

If Ferguson was granted one wish right now, he'd transfer his terminal illness to Ramsey and enjoy watching it chip away at him one week at a time. Ferguson grabbed his keys off his desk. He needed distance from this office and anyone connected with it.

Forty-Eight

Saturday, November 5
Emeryville, CA

Nathalie rode a noiseless, mirrored elevator to floor fifteen at Johnston & Quib pharmaceuticals. She took directions from the downstairs security desk clerk to where the CEO's executive assistant worked. The clerk assured Nathalie that Heather Styles was in this office on this tranquil morning. Nathalie anticipated it should not be too difficult to locate the woman in this office building on a Saturday at nine thirty a.m.

A young woman in her late twenties, with strawberry-blonde hair and low-cut sweater, leaned against the office printer, watching paper automatically collate and staple. Nathalie showed her badge. "Are you Heather Styles?"

"Yes." Heather snatched a piece of paper from the printer tray and closed the top of the copier.

"Special Agent Noiret. I'd like to speak with you."

Heather turned pale beneath her makeup. "What is this about, please?"

"We need your help with an inquiry."

"Do I have a choice?" Heather whispered.

Nathalie shook her head. "I think that-uh, we should walk outside. Is there a corner where we can speak about a private matter."

Heather led Nathalie to the lobby, then through a glass door to an interior building courtyard. They sat on a wrought iron table with cushioned chairs in a downstairs garden that served as a break area.

After Nathalie flipped open her leather-bound notepad, Heather looked around nervously. "What do you want with me?" Heather's voice strained.

"We believe you might have knowledge, knowledge about efforts to stop the Stanford Grid project. Who do you report to here?"

"Are you going to read me my Miranda rights?"

"If I charge you with something, I will."

Heather anxiously twirled her hair. "Mark Ferguson," she said abruptly, "The CEO here. I'm his executive assistant."

"Consider this an opportunity to clear your record."

"Record? You said I'm not being charged."

"Not now, but you could be charged later. I know that you posed as a reporter with Grid Program Director, Gary Knowlan, and tried your charms with Jude Wagner of Stanford."

"Believe me, I'm not who you're looking for."

"This is a serious matter. Lives are at risk. There has been a terrorist attack on the Stanford University campus."

"An attack?" Heather was becoming jumpy.

"Yes, an electrical substation exploded. If you cooperate, a judge should look favorably upon you."

Heather's lower lip trembled. "Hold on. How on earth does that relate to me?"

"You're under suspicion for conspiring in a felony," Nathalie said. "I suggest you cooperate. Whether it is fact, fiction or amnesia, you appear as an accomplice. If that's proven, you will serve prison time and be separated from your child."

Heather Styles lunged across the table at Nathalie, trying to grab her. But Nathalie caught Heather's arms by her wrists.

Heather let out a cry. Her carefully curled hair tossed out of place. Tears rolled down Heather's cheeks. "I know nothing about that campus attack, okay. All I did was make a deposit or two in a Cayman Islands bank account. Nothing criminal."

"Why and who for?"

"For Olivier Ramsey, our investment partner from Pinsky in New York. He didn't exactly explain his requests. I just take orders."

"Did you act as a gofer on this attack?"

"Me? No!" Heather gritted her teeth.

"How much did you transfer and to whom?"

"A hundred and twenty-five thousand . . . twice. I only set up an account and wired money for Mr. Ramsey." Heather was speaking fast. "He only mentioned the payee's name to me once. It sounded Italian to me."

"Does the name *Liborio Russo* sound familiar?"

"Yes, yes. That was the payee's name."

"Good. And you assist this Mr. Ramsey how?"

"He's in town every sixty days. I help him, act as his admin when he visits. He's a financial principal. Mr. Ferguson's gotta jump whenever Olivier Ramsey's investment firm says so. Ramsey's a tyrant. Really he's mad. Those two have been arguing for days. They were friendly once. I don't see how. And Mr. Ferguson's been acting very strange, even paranoid. He's not well at all. Company morale is bad. I know people who are going to quit."

"But why did Ramsey send this money?"

Heather looked at her watch. "How would I know?"

"You can do better."

Heather looked away, thinking. "I did hear about a computer contractor payment."

"A payment?" Nathalie said. "What did he hire that computer contractor to do?"

"All I heard is that the contractor required the account be setup right away."

"How can we find this contractor?"

Heather nervously pulled a tuft of hair behind her ear. "Ask Olivier Ramsey. I think he called the contractor Cezar once. I think Cezar and Liberio Russo are connected. Maybe they are one and the same."

Nathalie gave Heather a serious look. "Ramsey will undoubtedly shut me down. I need you to find out what this Cezar is doing."

Heather shook her head.

"The system will look favorably on you if you help us. No one has called Child Protective Services yet. Keep it that way, no."

"How do you even know about my child?"

"Ms. Styles, think," Nathalie said. "All we want is information on Cezar."

"How am I supposed to do that?"

Nathalie tapped her cell phone with her finger nail. "I'll be calling nightly after eight p.m. on your cell phone for updates. What is your number?"

A block away from the J&Q building in Emeryville, Nathalie rang Wagner's cell. "I got quite a report from Heather Styles."

"Really?"

"She helped Olivier Ramsey wire a quarter million dollars to a Cayman Islands account for a computer job."

"Whoa." Wagner processed this. "So it seems Ramsey paid to have the Grid hacked."

"Yes," Nathalie said, "though, I still have unsolved homicides and loose ends, from those quotes to an FBI handgun used in Geneva."

"My gut feeling is this was all intended to frame the FBI," he said. "Sedevacantists are not behind this. Hackman doesn't have motive."

"You think Ramsey did it all?"

Wagner sighed. "I don't know. Ferguson has his in with DeltaCorp. I never trusted J&Q, even when they sponsored the Stanford Grid. For now, we have to recover good data and gauge the scale of the attack."

"That is the challenge," she said.

"This hacker is probably roaming around with a notebook computer. At some point, I think the virus writer will update Ramsey. So, the next move should be to get access to Ramsey's machine."

"I don't know how that would happen. And what then?" Nathalie said.

"There could be an email from the hacker to Ramsey. I wonder if Morris or someone in your office could get into Ramsey's email account?"

"That would require a warrant. It would be easier to make a case for tapping his voice calls. We may or may not see email through his phone account, though, and it would take, you-know, a day or two."

Wagner added, "There has to be a quicker way. No one can walk in snow without leaving a footprint."

"I'm glad one of us is an optimist."

* * *

Cez@r slurped the last of his venti café latte. He'd accepted the exploded substation as a learning mistake. Never engage someone you don't know. The important thing was that he had access to the Stanford Grid. He chucked his coffee cup before walking into the San Francisco's public library on Sacramento Street where he took the only available computer station by the window. Doing his work on library computers was preferable, so the feds couldn't locate his home. Cez@r opened his laptop to check status. His bots were spreading across the Internet to the Grid server at Stanford Grid. He had several thousand infected computers, available for his bidding. He typed, directing those new bots to hit the Stanford Grid.

Two hours later, and just to be safe, he switched libraries—moving to one on Mission Street. He wasn't going to have anyone track his location based on the library's IP address. The feds weren't going to dupe him that easily.

Cez@r continued coding his next attack from the Mission Street library until it closed at nine p.m. Before leaving his computer station, he saw an opportunity he couldn't pass up. A bleary-eyed college girl at a computer beside him set down her cell phone on the table.

Cez@r put his backpack on the computer table and packed his notebook into it. With a subtle movement, he slid the girl's blue Nokia inside his pack. He was out of the library and in his compact Toyota before she could miss her phone.

Then, two miles down the road, Cez@r parked on a side street lined with boxy 1960s-style apartment buildings where he finished his work for the day. Using one of the many cables he carried, he connected his laptop computer to the girl's cell phone. Online again, he quickly surfed under an anonymous Internet Protocol. He snapped in his jump drive, called up a file, clicked to the Stanford network and signed into the Stanford Grid server.

If Stanford thought that his corrupting their data locally was their only worry, they were in for a terrible surprise. Putting a bot into general circulation so other users would be infected would be round two. The news of a compromised Grid would flood the 'Net like a Tsunami warning, prompting volunteers to stop donating their processing power, shutting down the entire Grid.

He estimated that his bot strike would reach its full magnitude in several hours, just after midnight. He pecked away at his keyboard, sitting in his car for nearly two more hours when the girl's phone battery died. After driving to an even quieter street lined with juniper, he wiped his fingerprints from the Nokia with a wet nap. He disassembled the Nokia into two pieces and slipped it into a storm drain before driving back downtown.

His final stop for the day was the XYZ bar at the W Hotel. He caught his breath as he stepped up the wide staircase and swaggered into the trendy bar. He found a chair and table in the back corner of the semi-darkened room. There he ordered a tall mojito and mused over his day's deeds.

Forty-Nine

Saturday, November 5
Piedmont, CA

Afternoon rain pattered on Mark Ferguson's bedroom window, watering the roses behind his grand Piedmont estate. The CEO sat up in bed, frustrated and unable to focus. Why wasn't Lori answering her cell phone? He wondered if after years of sending his daughter to therapy for her quixotic tendencies and mood swings whether it did an ounce of good? He hung up the receiver on his bedside table. Beside the phone sat a silver tray with a prescription bottle, a cut-glass tumbler, soda siphon and bottle of Johnny Walker Black Label. He sat up, shot soda water into his glass and petted his dog, Zeus. He carried his filled glass to the bathroom and shaved his four o'clock shadow while watching his mini-wall-mounted TV covering the week's financial report.

Just as Julian Stark had said, Johnston & Quib stock had dropped from 92 to 69 by end of day Friday. Although some investors seemed to have bought J&Q stock to hedge bets with traditional medicine, a greater number had sold on reports that one of J&Q's drug champions caused side-effects. How could J&Q's former partner turn arch rival?

An energetic, male news anchor covered a follow up news report: "In other news, last night's fire and explosion on the Stanford campus has now been attributed to a blown electrical substation transformer. Experts believe this was a failed attempt by computer hackers to control power to the controversial Stanford Grid Project. This elevates the terrorist threat level, not only to Stanford, but to the electrical power grid overall."

Ferguson could only imagine Ramsey was involved. Ferguson weighed what it would mean if the explosion put the Grid Project on hold. He wasn't sure how to judge it and drained his water in one shot.

His thoughts turned to how cunning the Stanford team was. If they got their hands on good cancer data, Kate Wagner would become their cancer test case success story—a testimonial to their Grid therapy. It would be cited by every scientific journal. Jesus, that would prove the efficacy of genomic medicine and pave the way for the demise of big-ticket drugs.

Meanwhile J&Q stockholders were getting hammered and so were his holdings. "No," he exclaimed aloud. His voice bounced off the walls of his aqua-tiled bathroom. He stopped himself just short of slamming his tumbler on the tile floor and shattering it into a thousand shards. Ferguson trudged back to his bedside table. He pulled a business card from his wallet with Kate Wagner's cell phone number. The not-for-profit Grid program might have stopped for now, but who knew when Stanford's network might be running again? Who knew when they would get the necessary breast cancer data? Who knew when Kate would become a Grid success story, leaving him and his company to die?

He punched Kate's number. "Kate, it's Mark Ferguson."

"Oh, hello." She sounded surprised to hear from him.

"You should drop into our office for a visit to review our new drug offerings."

"Um, well, Stanford is where I'm focused now."

"Let me help you, please." He cleared his hoarse throat. Sounding desperate, even to himself, he changed his demeanor. "Why not be my special guest at our Emeryville office? Meet our onsite medical specialist. He'll make a drug sample available to your treating physician. It's our latest and greatest offering."

"I appreciate the offer. Maybe in two weeks."

"I'll call you Monday morning?" he said.

"Fine."

He hung up, torn over what to do next.

Nothing would make him accept the bitter truth that he was dying and that the company he created—his life's work—was ailing too.

His dog, Zeus, barked beside his feet.

Even Zeus thinks I'm a goner.

Ferguson's phone rang. He answered on the first ring.

"Mark, it's Olivier. Are you at home?"

Not Ramsey. "Yes. What—what could you want from me now?"

"I want to talk to you eye ball to eye ball about Jude Wagner and the Stanford Grid. I'm gonna pay you a home visit. Don't go anywhere." Ramsey hung up.

Ferguson couldn't bear to see Ramsey. Debating if he'd stick around, the CEO saw a Jeep motor up the drive on his Foyer security monitor. The security camera captured a fish-eye view of his driveway in the rain. He recognized the uninvited visitor, but had no clue what motivated her to stop by.

The door to Heather Style's Jeep Cherokee opened. She stepped out of her vehicle.

Sliding open an umbrella, the attractive woman straightened her hair and put away the unnecessary sunglasses that were perched on her head. She leaned back inside the Jeep to the passenger seat and picked up a manila folder, swollen with paper and closed the door. Heather approached the house looking at the ground as if she was preparing a somber speech.

The doorbell chimed its lyrical melody.

What could possibly be the purpose of this house call? She had let herself in through the driveway gate using the clicker he'd given her. Heather kept the spare remote gate opener since she house-sat the property whenever Ferguson traveled and his daughter was away. More than just Ferguson's EA, Heather was the CEO's personal life assistant too.

The voice could be heard through the door. "Mr. Ferguson—hello—it's Heather."

Ferguson tucked in his shirt. "Hold on a minute."

"I have something urgent," she said.

He opened the door wearing his topsider sailing shoes. "Yes, what do you have?"

Heather pulled papers from the file, shielding them from the rain at her back. "Please don’t shoot the messenger."

Ferguson grabbed the papers and the file folder and held the pages up close. "What is it?" he asked.

"It’s about the phase-two clinical trials for your experimental Huntington’s disease drug," she said.

"Okay, and the results are?" He sniffed.

"I'm sorry. It's very bad news. The trials proved to cause liver failure in apes."

Ferguson’s stomach jumped sending a nervous heat to his face. He feared this might be the case—what he had long hoped might save him, failed. There was no traditional cure for Huntington’s disease. An awful truth circled back to him. A blinding fog broke. The Grid was his only hope for survival. If he wasn't so consume with his illness, he would have considered this sooner. If the Grid worked it could diagnose him precisely and isolate a custom drug treatment. "Okay, thank you for making the trip. You're welcome to come in." Ferguson suppressed how shattered he felt. He honestly wanted to be alone to be mad at the world.

"I should be going. But, Sir, I need to know."

"What, Heather?"

"Was Olivier Ramsey behind that explosion at Stanford? The FBI questioned me."

"The FBI?"

"Yes," she blurted.

"To be honest, I don’t know. Olivier is an egotist on a good day and narcissistic psycho on all the rest—we know that much. Even if I had more to disclose, though, I wouldn't drag you into this pileup."

Heather lowered her head, appearing unsure about everything.

He hated this lingering. "Cancel my appointments for Monday, okay. Tell everyone on my calendar I'm away."

She started for her Jeep before he'd even said goodbye.

Ferguson closed his door. He made the snap decision to escape on his yacht. He hastily packed up a duffel bag with food from his fridge. He rummaged through a cabinet in the garage for his wind resistant sailing clothes, and gathered an arm load of other sailing gear. Without putting away his fishing net and toolbox in the kitchen, he jumped in his car, clicked open the gate and took off from his estate to avoid Olivier Ramsey.

Ramsey parked his rental car in front of the pink adobe wall surrounding the Ferguson property. The rain let up while he pushed the intercom button. No one answered to open the gate. He cursed Ferguson, fearing there'd be no way to detain Jude Wagner from stopping the virus. All that greeted him was the barking of some loud dog.

Ramsey took out his phone and called a certain well informed EA from J&Q. "Mr. Ferguson's office."

"Heather, it's Olivier Ramsey—"

"Mr. Ferguson isn't in—and I need to speak with you, Sir."

"Not now. Where is he?" The hound bayed in the background.

"Maybe he doesn't want to see you."

"Heather, damn it. This is urgent. I didn't fly out from New York to waste my time. Your company's fortune is at stake."

"Okay, okay. He's at his place."

"Try again. That's where I am now and I doubt he's ignoring all my buzzing at his gate. If anyone could guess his whereabouts it would be you."

"Hmm . . ."

"What are you thinking?"

"He's been going to his yacht, to get away. But it's raining today."

"Was raining. It just stopped here."

She gave him the address to Ferguson's yacht club.

Ramsey hung up. He needed to direct all of his mental energy to stopping the medical revolution or at least Stanford's version of it. Olivier Ramsey started the ignition to his car when a new call came in with no caller ID. Immediately Ramsey answered.

"Guess who."

"I don't play guessing games."

"It's your *wunderkind*, miracle worker calling."

For the first time, the business man was hearing his hacker's voice. "Cez@r."

"You guessed me right—" the boyish voice answered.

"Have you lost your mind with that explosion on the Stanford campus?" Ramsey said.

"The smoke and fire wasn't by design. But I did gain access, and I'm orchestrating things worthy of an encore. By the way, this Stanford Grid team of yours is horrifically accident prone. I read the news, boss. You should've said you were roping me into a campaign of murder—"

"No, no! I'm not having people killed. I have no idea who's—"

"Easy, dude. These clumsy assholes will get caught, that's for sure. And when the feds march 'em to the slammer, they'll probably be hanging my work on them too. I look at that as convenient cover."

"Fine," Ramsey said. "Where do things stand?"

"I'm making finishing touches on the bot virus. Stanford probably still thinks they're data is okay, but it's not. That's step one."

"What do you mean step one?"

"No one action is sufficient here. Next, I'm going to corrupt the broader Grid and cause lasting failure using a botnet. My army of robots will flood the Grid with bad results. There are no guarantees in life, but I think the second strike will please you, so I'm pulling both switches."

"And when will this broader event happen?"

"Around midnight tonight is the target. It's auspicious, right. The Grid team should be worn out by then." Cez@r hung up.

Ramsey scrutinized the situation. This virus strike wasn't watertight if Jude Wagner, Stanford's algorithm man, was out there monitoring things, free to detect the attack and shoot it down. It would be foolish to underestimate his capabilities. Ramsey wanted to keep Jude Wagner tied up and away from the Grid for several hours. But how the hell would Ramsey accomplish such a thing?

Fifty

Saturday, November 5
Stanford University Data Center

Shafts of sunlight beamed through hazy air outside the data center at two p.m. Jude Wagner was more intent than ever to retrieve Kate's drug results. At least the electricity had come back up, eliminating the grating noise of the power generator. Kate dozed off in a chair a few feet away leaving Wagner and Knowlan to work at the Grid terminal. The stench of smoldering eucalyptus trees turned Wagner's empty stomach, but he couldn't bear to take a break, not until he saw Kate's customized prescription. The stakes were high with this online system; the margin for error, incomprehensibly small.

Roger Knowlan sent a query to the Grid to generate Kate's data.

CPU lights flickered on the screen. A green progress bar lengthened. Wagner kept his eyes glued to the monitor with wary optimism. He and Knowlan waited, watching the Grid's display monitor. Wagner's radio crackled, broadcasting updates on the aftermath of the explosion. He shut it off right away. They stared in anticipation, eyeing the progress bar until it stopped. Knowlan nimbly navigated to another screen for the result.

Wagner and Knowlan looked over Kate's results in the screen field beside PRESCRIBED COMPOUNDS. Nothing about the report appeared accurate. Her blood type on the screen showed B+ instead of the correct O+. Her age was listed as 48 instead of 31. Even the processing date read incorrect.

"This is all wrong." Knowlan said softly so as not to disturb Kate.

Wagner shook his head in disbelief.

Knowlan assured him that the system had enough time to run Kate's job, comparing her sequenced DNA to that of tens of thousands of other breast cancer tissues to isolate her tumor type, but the targeted treatment results which came back were all askew. They could never trust this gibberish.

A horrible realization dawned on Wagner. "That's what the hacker was doing with that flash drive. He was loading a program to alter data and he must have succeeded."

"That's not the worst of it." Knowlan swiveled his chair closer to the computer terminal and pointed at the computer display where it read RESULTS FINALIZED. "The system is still working and operational, which means other results are also in the process of being corrupted. All of our existing diabetes patient records could be compromised too."

Kate moaned with bloodless lips and circles under her eyes. "Jude, I feel lightheaded."

"Have some water," Wagner said trying to maintain composure; when by now he'd hoped he would be hollering *success,* sweeping Kate up with a great hug.

Knowlan's studious face never looked more drained of energy. "I don't know what else to do."

A crick lodged in Wagner's neck. He swapped seats with Knowlan, putting himself in command. Wagner tugged the keyboard closer and typed "TOP" to monitor the Grid's performance. He changed screens and saw that externally the world system was still grinding away. The Grid was done feeding Kate's data into a massive simulation computer that screened molecules that could be synthesized to custom-make her unique cure. Wagner looked at Roger Knowlan. "We don't have any other data backup points to go to."

"I know," Knowlan groaned. Knowlan knew better than Wagner that Kate's work had to be done. It just wasn't accessible at Stanford in un-tampered form.

Wagner rechecked the server logs. Kate stood up from the desk, rubbing her neck.

Squinting through hundreds of lines of code, Wagner's breath caught. He spotted the foreign program that had been added to

Stanford's Grid server. Wagner pointed to the screen. "That confirms it. The checksum is wrong."

What Wagner feared most had happened. The Stanford attacker, Liborio Russo, had used Knowlan's access permissions to implant a malicious program in the Grid.

Wagner typed more while everyone else looked on.

Knowlan's mouth gaped. "What now?" he asked.

Wagner just shook his head, downplaying the problem so as not to alarm Kate.

"So," she said with apprehension, finishing her cup of water. "Are we stuck?"

"Temporarily," Wagner said.

Kate brewed ginseng tea she found in the cabinet to keep everyone going.

Wagner lowered his voice for only Knowlan to hear. "Precious minutes are wasting."

Indeed, they should have been retrieving accurate personalized medicine results by now, but the information that was compiled was scrambled. For the next several minutes, Wagner and Knowlan thought about the problem.

Kate handed out cups of tea, then returned where she was sitting.

Finally, Wagner pushed the keyboard aside and reeled back in his chair. "I checked the backup server again. Kate's results have been overwritten with bad data." The virus had caused damage that Wagner couldn't fix. Kate's results would have to be completely recomputed. Desperate, Wagner wanted to slam the expensive scientific machine into the wall. Their shot at diagnosing her cancer seemed to be slipping away. They could not rerun Kate's information and expect to get clean results based on what Grid diagnostics showed.

Wagner walked out into the sooty air to think. A light breeze carried away smoldering smoke from the early morning fire. Computers could always be tweaked, given enough time, he thought. Believing that a solution existed was half the battle of finding it. Tormented by the breakdown, he trod around the building. The anxiety he felt about Kate's chances now would only be a twinge of pain compared to what he would face if he lost her. He searched the corners of his mind for ideas.

After several minutes, he remembered something obvious that Knowlan had done.

With a purposeful gait, he returned to the room where Knowlan sat slouched, looking deflated.

Wagner put his hand on Knowlan's shoulder. "I might have something. The attacker's malware may be eating us alive at this location, but not everywhere. Not yet."

"We have the Berkeley backup," Knowlan said. "I was so fixated on everything here that I forgot. We could possibly pull her data from there."

"How often does that backup run?" Wagner said.

"Only once a day. The next backup will run at four-thirty p.m. Let's just hope that mirroring is working."

If they could access yesterday's backup at SETI before that data was corrupted also, then they could get Kate's results. But it was only a matter of time before today's backup would overwrite yesterday's and corrupt Kate's results at Berkeley too.

Wagner checked his watch. "We have to hurry. It's after two p.m. We have to get to SETI before the next backup. You do still have the key to that office, don't you?"

Roger checked his jeans pocket. "I have it."

Kate jerked to attention. Wagner could see a shift in their mood—a remnant of hope in her eyes.

Wagner didn't wait for agreement. He grabbed Kate's DVDs and prodded Knowlan to get moving. Together, they walked with Kate out the building and into Knowlan's Jaguar.

Knowlan briefed Kate. "SETI@home and Stanford agreed to act as an offsite backup for each other in the event of an earthquake or some other unforeseeable event. As you heard, that intruder corrupted your data on our server here, so we're doing a work around to access your prescribed treatment at Berkeley before it gets corrupted there too."

From the front seat of the Jag, Kate turned to look back at Wagner. "Like an emergency backup power generator?"

"Sort of," Wagner said.

Knowlan accelerated the Jag along Page Mill Road to the freeway.

"I'm confident we'll get your prescription result," Wagner said. "The question is if the Grid virus will spread to those other 90,000 volunteer computers."

Fifty-One

Saturday, November 5
Between Stanford and Berkeley, CA

Rain dotted the windshield as Roger Knowlan drove Wagner and his twin sister up from Stanford toward the San Mateo Bridge. The radio weatherman reported that hurricane Linda in the South Pacific had triggered the thunderstorms. High above the freeway sign, a cloudy sky darkened to slate. The endless tide of gray took on a life of its own, threatening to smother the bay area.

Windshield wipers whopped over glass.

Kate kneaded her leg muscles and stomped her feet.

"What?" Wagner asked.

"My feet are numb."

Wagner reached over to place a comforting hand on her shoulder. "I think we should get you to the hospital to rest."

"No, Jude. I am dead tired, but I'm not changing course now. Please, have Roger just drive us to Berkeley so we can do this together."

Wagner looked out the back window. He noticed a white SUV trailing behind them from Page Mill Road and again miles later on the freeway. Only now, through the rain, could he verify that it was a Range Rover. "Come on, Roger, faster." Wagner started to explain that he thought they were being followed, but chose not to worry Kate anymore.

"Faster, in this weather?" Kate asked. "If it rains any harder animals will start pairing up."

"Someone is following?" Knowlan blurted.

Wagner checked behind him again "I don't know for sure." The white Range Rover had disappeared from view. He called Nathalie. "I think we're being tailed by a white, late model Range Rover. We're heading from Stanford to the Space Science Laboratory at the University of California at Berkeley." Wagner described Knowlan's Jaguar also.

"Do you have a license plate for this Rover?"

"No and there may not be one."

"I'll get you a police backup. What are you doing?"

"Getting data." Wagner clicked off.

"There's still no sign of it." Knowlan said, checking his rearview mirror.

"Yeah. It's gone for now. But I have a feeling we're going to meet up with that Range Rover again before this day is over."

They soon traveled around the back of the Cal Berkeley football stadium, driving through deep puddles. Mud spattered. It trickled from the hillside across the street, limiting their speed to twenty miles per hour. The road climbed past Botanical Gardens and side roads with fences marked FEDERAL GOVERNMENT, NO TRESPASSING. The Berkeley hills were famous for what Wagner called "Uber-government projects," from primate laboratory testing to national defense research. They drove by a long wooden staircase that ran up the hill and a sign that said SPACE SCIENCE LABORATORY. Atop the hill sat three hulking concrete slab structures and a parking lot.

Knowlan parked the car in the mini-parking lot at the foot of Wagner's old place of work and study. There was no police backup in sight yet. Thunder boomed from the leaden sky as they climbed out of the car. The three of them trucked through the rain. Wagner and Knowlan supported Kate. Arm-in-arm, she uneasily jogged between them. She looked up at the Mathematics building. "Wait, I'm lightheaded." After a few deep breaths, they continued, quietly focused on the objective.

Inside the building and up the whitewashed stairwell, they trudged to Wagner's former desk area. Long tables and desktop computers flanked the narrow room. Wagner seated his sister into one of the basic office chairs. "Tell me if you need anything."

Without speaking, Knowlan booted up the desktop computer by the window and signed into Stanford's backup server. He successfully located the directory backup of Kate's data.

Wagner paced anxiously while Knowlan typed, checking her data. "This will take several minutes to verify," Knowlan said.

Wagner thought about that SUV following them. "Let's just keep working and stay calm," Wagner told Knowlan.

Wagner left the office and proceeded down the corridor. He peered out the window at the parking lot below. To his dismay, he spotted the Range Rover parking. He sensed that whoever this person was, he or she was on their way to search them out. Jude darted back down the wide, white staircase. He wanted to find this pursuer and lure him away from the office, away from Kate and Knowlan if possible. He dashed out the side exit of the SETI@home building and into billowing sheets of rain. Then he scrambled to the parked SUV at the top of the rustic wooden stairs, built into the hillside. Reflexively, he looked over his shoulder for the driver . . . nowhere in sight.

Sweating in wet clothes, he saw for sure that the Range Rover had no license plates. The engine still ticked with heat. He peered through the windshield trying to see a Vehicle Identification Number on a metal plate on the dashboard. This one was covered in duct tape.

The SUV's doors were locked. He banged the window several times with his cell phone. Finally, the safety glass spider-cracked. He rapped on the broken window three more times before he could break a hole. He reached inside, tore the duct tape off the metal plate, and called his office. He read the VIN off to the special agent who answered the phone and reported the car as suspicious. Next, he tried to disable the car by cramming muddy rocks into the exhaust pipe.

Wagner's pulse raced again. He wiped his hands on his pants, then placed two more calls. He left an urgent message for Nathalie to check the VIN number of the Range Rover. A minute passed before Wagner hustled back upstairs to the SETI@home office.

From the desk Knowlan stared at Wagner's drenched shirt and pants."What the hell happened?"

"I'll explain later."

Knowlan would not stop asking questions. "Did you see someone?"

Wagner shook his head, more anxious than ever. "Forget it for now. Where is she?"

"The ladies room," Knowlan said.

Wagner leaned over Roger's shoulder, dripping wet. He examined the monitor. "How are things?"

"We're connected to the backup server."

Wagner moved closer, both hovering over the monitor display. "I assure you that the medial profile for Kate is all correct here." Knowlan clicked to another screen and pointed. "These are her data results."

"Okay."

Knowlan analyzed the screen for two to three minutes.

"Well," Wagner asked. "What do you think?"

"The backup perfectly mirrored all the results from four-thirty p.m. yesterday—just as scheduled, and a few hours before our intruder corrupted everything at Stanford. It all looks clean."

"Good, good."

Knowlan silently moved his finger across the screen, double-checking the final output which the Grid had generated for Kate. "It's all here, Jude."

"You mean you've got the prescription?" Wagner said rapidly.

"Yes, yes I do. The Grid did it."

"Fantastic." Wagner shouted.

Knowlan anxiously saved Kate's prescription results to a flash drive he brought with him from the data center.

Wagner slapped his shoulder, celebrating their feat. "You're masterful. But let me check the Grid resources so I know we're out of the woods."

Knowlan stood to let Wagner sit at the console.

Wagner navigated to the Grid server node at Stanford, entered his access credentials then analyzed the server logs again to the wider Grid at work. He changed screens to read the antivirus software summary. A red flag on the screen appeared: NEW INFECTION, URGENT PRIORITY. GRID INSTRUCTION AGENTS CORRUPTED.

Wagner cursed.

"What, what does this mean?" Knowlan said.

"The Grid seems to be getting hit with a new attack and this type only grows."

"How exactly?"

Wagner sighed with a note of despair. "Right now the hacker is only tying up Stanford's resources by having his bots send bad data to our local Grid server. But if this continues, he could poison the entire system, slowing down all our donor computers."

"Infecting the entire world Grid network?"

"Yes, we'd better figure out a remedy fast. We could be dealing with hundreds, if not thousands, of other computer zombie bots uploading infected instructions." Wagner looked up. "It's like he's got his own Typhoid Mary, cooking away, spreading her fever."

Knowlan put his hands on his head. "How could this be happening?"

Wagner wanted to heave the hacker who did this into a fire pit and strike a match, even though he'd been one himself years ago. This could destroy public confidence and ruin the whole initiative. Errors coming into the Grid forced it to reconcile the result against a thousand other computers. The simple act of fact-checking could force the Grid to go round and round. If new errors came in, the Grid would send those to even more computers for validating until everything locked up.

Knowlan's stoic stare registered nothing but blank incredulity.

Wagner heard light noises come from outside the office. A shuffling of feet maybe that sent a nervous tingle up his neck and into his scalp. Somewhere down the hallway a door opened and closed. He figured it could be a janitor, but it prompted him to looked around. "I'll check this."

A scream came from down the hall. "Jude."

It was Kate's voice, unmistakably panicked.

Wagner and Roger froze.

The restrooms were at the far side of the building. Wagner ran, his steps echoing in the deserted hallway. He turned the corner and pulled open the door of the ladies room. "Kate?"

No answer. Knowlan arrived, puffing from the effort.

Wagner grabbed his arm and turned him. "You take the left hall." He indicated the long expanse of floor leading deeper into the complex. "I'll go right. Check every exit. Got your phone?"

Two minutes later, Wagner ran back into the office and snatched Roger's keys off the computer desk. He passed Roger in the hall again as he ran out of the building. "I'm going to need to drive. Do you want to come with me or wait? Campus police are coming."

"I'll wait for the campus cops."

When Wagner got downstairs and outside the building, he found the white Range Rover he'd just broken into was gone.

Fifty-Two

Saturday, November 5
Piedmont, CA

Scud pulled her white Ranger Rover up to the gate and clicked it open with her remote. After parking, she dragged Kate to the mansion, making sure that her wool sack stayed secure. Scud rummaged for her house keys.

In the foyer the dog barked. Scud quickly tapped off the alarm and shouted, "Shut up, Zeus!"

She bolted the door behind her, removed her dark sunglasses and tucked them in her cargo pants pocket.

Kate screamed and thrashed her arms to free herself.

Scud slapped Kate across the side of her bagged head. The blow knocked Kate down to the wood floor. At her captor's feet, Kate managed to remove the sack. She looked up, surprised to be staring directly at her female abductor. Broad chested, she had shoulder length, bottle-blonde hair and bad make-up caked on a distinctly unfeminine face. "You're deranged," Kate said. "Have you come after me to get to my brother?"

Scud froze for a moment in her high lace-up boots. With arms twice the size of Kate's, Scud yanked Kate's forearm, chafing her skin.

"Ow! Let go of me."

Moving like a man, the woman in the military get-up hauled Kate from the marbled foyer, then dragged her down the hallway to the guest bedroom. She contemplated how she could kill them once Jude Wagner got here.

Kate kicked, losing a shoe along the way to the guest bedroom. The bedroom, like the mansion overall, had lavish décor: ornate toile wallpaper, a king-sized bed and a Persian rug. A huge TV was built into the wall.

After unplugging two bedside table lights, Scud tied Kate’s hands and feet with extension cords. Scud also bound Kate's hands to the French-country bed post using a belt. Seeing that Kate was secured, Scud reconsidered her plan to lure Wagner here, using his sister. He could overpower the situation. She needed to go where she could box Wagner in and finish him off, with his sister, once and for all. It would be better to get rid of the Wagners at sea where their bodies wouldn't leave a trace. Yes, she'd take Kate to the yacht to draw him there, away from the estate. Once she got the boat out in the bay, Wagner would be stuck. *What can he possibly do on the yacht, swim to shore? That's too perfect.*

She hunted through drawers for the spare keys to the yacht.

Kate couldn’t undo her hands, but she wriggled her feet free from the belt that fastened her to the bedpost. She moved off the bed to the bedroom window. Peering from the shutter, she looked outside the rain-smudged window to size up her escape. A thorny rosebush covered half the wall on the other side. She’d never make it out this way, not in her weakened condition.

She explored the room for anything that would give her a clue about where or why she was taken. She opened the bedside drawer. With tied hands, she shuffled through papers until she happened upon a business card. What she read on that card made her knees lock: Mark Ferguson, Chief Executive Officer, Johnston & Quib Pharmaceuticals. What? Was Mark Ferguson, the man she'd had lunch with, behind her abduction, her being taken to this mansion?

She heard nothing but the beating of her own heart, then footsteps. She flung open the bedroom window and rolled under the bed. Hiding in the cramped, dark space, she hoped when her captor returned the woman would believe that she’d escaped out the window. Moments passed, adding pressure to Kate's panic stricken state.

Scud crouched on all fours, staring directly at Kate under the bed. "Hey."

Kate shot back, pulling away.

Scud grabbed Kate's left wrist. "Got you, bitch."

Kate gasped with despair.

"Go ahead, test my resolve and scream." Scud removed a buck knife from her pocket and opened the blade. Handle and all, it was six inches long.

Kate shook her head. Her cheek still shone red from the blow earlier. She touched her pocket to feel for her cell phone.

"I took your phone, remember." Scud bound Kate's wrists again, tighter this time.

She packed a few things and located her duffel bag. Scud duct-taped Kate's mouth, bound her feet with extension cords and forced her body into the canvas zipper bag. But the huge sack of potatoes duffel holding Kate wouldn't zip closed.

Scud had to pull the woman from the duffel, unbind her feet and prod her straight out the front door, into the rain and into the SUV for another joy ride. In a matter of minutes, they would be free of the car anyway. At that point, no one would be around them but a few deserted boats. Scud started the ignition and motored down the long driveway, bound for open water and a floating, private holding area.

Fifty-Three

Saturday, November 5
Berkeley, CA

Forcing himself to take deep breaths, Wagner sat in Knowlan's plush car seat, parked at the SETI building, secluded high in the Berkeley hills. He inserted the key, and pushed the ignition button. The Jaguar purred to life. He didn't even know where to start to find Kate. From an empty parking lot with a wide view of the Bay Area, he sat. His own sister was a WAT—a person who'd vanished *Without a Trace*. Though in this case, he had one lead: that VIN number from the white Range Rover.

As if on cue, Wagner's mobile phone rang. Nathalie's name appeared on the mini-LED. He answered the phone before putting the car into gear.

"Nathalie. Kate's gone, she's been taken."

"Jude, no."

"I'm gonna break Ramsey's neck . . . if it's him."

"I cannot confirm that it is. That VIN you gave me is registered to a trust."

"No name?"

"That's right. And since trusts aren't recorded, there is no easy way to look up the beneficiary. I checked DMV records to see where the car registration is being mailed— another dead end street. It's going to a P.O. Box in Piedmont, California."

"Try checking that VIN against a vehicle history report."

"Okay."

Wagner heard her typing.

"I show the car was once used as a rental with Premium Auto." Wagner hung on the phone while Nathalie used another line to call the Premium rental agency. Reading the VIN, she asked the representative to look up who the car was sold to. The rental agency only showed the name of the trust but it did show an address where a transfer of ownership was sent: 246 Sea View Avenue, Piedmont, CA.

Nathalie hung up the second line and pulled up the home owner to that address. "Jude, for that property—the owner's name is Mark Ferguson."

"Mark Ferguson," he exclaimed.

"Do you know him?"

"If it's the same person I'm thinking of, yes. I have to drive there now." He keyed the address into his GPS.

"There is a lot of information in the database about Mark Ferguson at Sea View Avenue. Oh, he is CEO to Johnston & Quib."

"That's the one!"

"Divorced, but has a daughter—by the name of Lori. She has the same mailing address."

Wagner could hear Nathalie at her keyboard. "Jude, if you have to go inside, don't break anything."

Wagner knew where she was going with that. If he forced entry and it was found out, any evidence he uncovered against Ferguson would be dismissed for trespassing and illegal entry.

"How long would it take for you to get here with a warrant?"

"I think that-uh, the magistrate will require a few hours to approve probable cause."

"That's no good."

"Jude:"

"I can't debate this with you, Nat. I can't wait around. Kate could be inside."

"As a law enforcement agent, I warned you about this."

"Don't worry," he said. "This will all be on me."

Nathalie let out a big sigh. Wagner heard more typing, then a pause. "With him being a CEO, there is a lot of background info. I show he not only serves on DeltaCorp's board, but he does attend some of their corporate functions. You might say he has a private army for a friend."

"Ferguson's got the means. That makes him a possible suspect."

"In theory," she said. "I will see if I can find his cell phone number so we can triangulate his location."

"Ring me back if you get anything at all," he said. Click. Wagner checked his rearview mirror. No one was behind him. He easily found the property using the Jag's GPS. He came to the driveway and stopped at the gated entrance to Ferguson's estate when the rain abated. Frustrated to find an eight-foot wall surrounding the property, he started to scope out the perimeter. About thirty feet to the left of the driveway, he spotted oak trees outside the wall with large branches.

He walked over to the oak trees. The branches wound in all directions, some right up against the wall. He drove his car to the end of the driveway and right over the low shrubbery beneath the trees. Trying not to slip, Wagner climbed on the hood. He then jumped and grabbed the lowest limb of the oak nearest to him, and hoisted himself on top of it. Balancing on that limb, he grabbed a higher branch. Finding his grip, he moved hand over hand over the wall. Finally, he dropped to the other side. He opened the gate from the inside with a button on the wall and drove his car inside.

The property was a lot to absorb. The main house had pink walls and a steep gray shingled roof, and it was flanked by a turret, capped with a round top and spire. Wrought iron lamps hung from vaulted doorways. The property appeared to have time traveled from the days of horse and carriage.

Wagner tried the handle to Ferguson's front door and rang the bell. No answer. He knocked loudly and waited. The noise roused a barking dog—a large one, given the racket. He stood back and rushed the door, colliding into it with his shoulder—thud. The door didn't open. He winced under the pain of a new bruise.

The barking was nonstop. The loyal sentry stood directly behind the door. Wagner wondered if Ferguson was going to swing open the door with a gun pointed at Kate's head.

Wagner vaulted a side fence that partitioned a pool area surrounded by large and small potted plants on one side of the house. He dropped on the pool side, laid in flagstone. He spotted a sliding glass kitchen door. Standing on the entrance mat, he looked inside—the room was empty, but he noticed open cabinets and drawers. Ice trays and empty beverage containers cluttered the marble island. He was surprised to see a large fishing net, a tackle box and items for sailing strewn across the counter.

Wagner tried this door—locked.

He picked up one of the medium-sized potted plants and heaved it through the sliding door. Glass shattered. A house alarm bell pealed. Wagner folded the thin entrance mat and used it as a giant set of tongs to remove the remaining shards. He hunched through the still partially jagged window and crawled inside.

He pulled out his phone and called Nathalie back. "Are you inside the house?" she asked.

Wagner shouted over the alarm. "Yes. Can you call the police and tell them to disregard the alarm? Can you lie and tell them an agent is investigating the property?" She let out a long sigh.

"Can you, please?"

"I'll try, okay. That is all."

Even over the alarm, Wagner heard the dog's growl from a nearby room.

"Jude, I found something. Ferguson's own daughter works for DeltaCorp."

"What, she does?"

"Yes, I'm positive."

Wagner dragged his hand through his hair. "Everything's piecing together. I wonder if Ferguson used his daughter somehow to do his dirty work to stop the Grid and kill Jűrgen, Onagi and possibly Niles."

"I suppose it is possible," Nathalie said. "She had access to trained gunmen, killer canines and non-commercial plane flights . . . whatever a private military company has."

"And probably Ferguson's money." After a second, he said, "Ferguson could be using Kate as some bargaining chip, though, I wouldn't know why. Kate did tell me he's dying from Huntington's disease."

"Ooh."

"Wait, that's it," he said. Wagner heard Nathalie stop typing.

"What?"

"Kate told Ferguson that she's going to be the Grid's first test patient. He could fear she might be our first success story."

"This is all hard to digest. No luck with tracking him by his mobile. He has some type of encrypted phone—I would like to see if his car has crossed any bridges via FasTrak but that will take a little time, you-know."

The sound of a growling dog came closer.

"Gotta go." Just as he was closing the phone, a Rottweiler turned the corner into the kitchen and bound on to him, knocking him to the marble floor under the fishing net.

Wagner's phone dropped. The black and brown animal had the muzzle of a bear. It flashed its fangs. As Wagner tried to push the dog away, it gnashed into his shoulder. Blood dripped and smeared into his shirt. He and the animal rolled over broken glass to the edge of the island. The dog got hold of Wagner's belt. The Rottweiler's large, clenched mouth held him by leather. The tug-of-war prevented Wagner from breaking free. The belt ripped and the dog lunged again—its teeth now held on to Wagner's leg.

He grimaced under the dog's bite, kicking the animal's chest and face, but its grip held firm. Bursts of pain shot up and down Wagner's leg. He ripped free part of his already torn shirt. Frantically, he used the fabric to smother the dog's muzzle, nose and closed jaws, forcing it to open its locked jaws for air.

As the dog unclasped its bite, Wagner freed his leg. He kicked the animal in the mouth again. With one arm, he reached above for the net. He snagged it. It slung down over the animal, from tail to head. The dog fought and gnawed. But the net tethered it.

Rolling to his side, Wagner grabbed two ends of the net. He pulled the net's ends around the dog's body and tightened them to hold the beast. Next, he grabbed his phone. At last, he pushed himself to his feet. His leg and shoulder throbbed with stabbing pain from dog bites.

As the alarm continued to sound, he trod through the kitchen, leaving the barking Rottweiler behind.

In the foyer on the floor, Wagner saw Kate's K-Swiss tennis shoe—the only shoe she wore with her sore joints. His gut wrenched. At least he was getting closer.

He moved to a bedroom in the back. With a bath towel, he staunched blood dripping from his shoulder. He searched through drawers for possible gauze and tape. There were none. But he did find a gun. The Glock was in the back of the drawer beside the bed. He took it with him.

Finally, that maddening dinging of the alarm stopped, but the dog was still barking.

He returned to the hallway where envelopes of mail sat on an antique table with flowers. He saw a FasTrak beside the mail. Ferguson had obviously taken the precaution of leaving the electronic bridge pass behind, realizing it would transmit his travels if he took a bridge. Wagner flipped through the stack of mail on the table. On the bottom of the pile, beneath a sailing magazine called *Latitude 38*, rested a property management bill. Wagner opened it. The property management company had billed Ferguson for cleaning, utilities and maintenance of an address in Aptos. Wagner knew Aptos to be a popular and exclusive beach community. A message reported that the ice maker in the house had broken and the company had ordered a new one.

In the hallway again, he looked at the sparkling floor and saw faint dirt of a shoe print. He crouched to look closer. The track resembled that of a topsider shoe like the one he owned. Wagner went to the master bedroom. A tangled comforter and pillows lay on the floor. He searched the room but turned up nothing, ending in the walk-in closet. Below hanging suits and dress shirts sat boxes of shoes—many of which appeared unworn. Rifling around, he found one box that was empty. He whiffed the cardboard bottom and got a familiar acrid odor. Niles's jacket smelled of it the last time they sailed—some type of teak oil. The type used to treat boat decks.

With a whiff of creosote, Wagner moved back to the kitchen. Walking clear of the dog, he stepped into the garage. No car. He concluded that Ferguson had packed up to go to his Aptos house or go sailing. An open plastic toolbox sat on the garage floor. The top drawer contained a boat wrench, tape measure, nautical maps, fishing line and hooks. It was time to go. But instead of facing that berserk dog again in the kitchen, Wagner opened the garage door and left that way. The calamity of everything played over and over in his mind while driving. He hit speed dial again. "Nathalie?"

"Jude, are you okay?"

His face was hot with adrenalin. "Listen, I think Ferguson took Kate to his beach house or maybe to a boat."

"What is it you want me to do?" she said.

"Check if he has a boat slip registered in the Bay Area."

Wagner heard her at her keyboard again.

"You're right. He has a slip. It's at the Oakland Yacht Club."

Wagner figured he'd gone to his yacht—not his beach house or anyplace where Wagner could easily surround him with FBI agents. "That's where I'm headed."

"The address is 1101 Pacific Marina. It happens to be in Alameda, okay."

"Got it."

Wagner held the steering wheel tight, winding his way to the freeway. He wondered what had led Ferguson to this point. What if the man had no intention of releasing Kate? Would he remove her to preempt Kate's Grid trial from becoming a success that would sink his business?

It appeared that Ferguson had nothing else to lose. It was something Wagner had to take into account—he'd be negotiating with someone who probably had little promise to live and every impulse to act irrationally.

Fifty-Four

Saturday, November 5
Alameda, CA

The night's heavy rain turned to a sporadic mist. Still, more heavy clouds resembling great blimps rolled toward the yacht club harbor. Seagulls swooped through the salt air. Shoulders slumped, CEO Mark Ferguson checked the barometer on the deck of his glittering white sailboat, tethered at the marina. His view of the Grid had shifted: what was once a thorn in his side now stood as his one promise and only rescue. He had to reevaluate, especially after learning of his death sentence from Heather. He still could not bear to see Ramsey, but he had to get answers out of him. He needed to know if the Stanford explosion crashed the Grid permanently. Could it be repaired? Ramsey might know. Ferguson pulled his phone from his windbreaker pocket and swallowed his pride.

"Olivier. It's Mark."

"Thanks for standing me up at your house," Ramsey said.

"Forget that. I was wrong to let you corrupt Stanford's Grid. You need to call off your dogs."

"Not on your life."

"Damn you. I don't even want to know if you were behind that explosion at Stanford. But you need to tell whatever virus writer you found to stop everything."

"Even if I wanted to I couldn't."

"Why?"

"Our man has a virus in place that is going to take care of this Grid. He's going to let it rip tonight around midnight. He's the dramatic sort."

Ferguson persisted. "Tell your hacker you'll pay him double to quit."

"You can't reverse what's already in motion. This comet is speeding along. Those Stanford Grid scientists are getting what they deserve."

"Such prophetic words. But what if your life was on the line one day? You might need to the Grid, to apply its innovation. You've got to see that—clear as day!"

Ferguson thought quickly. "Jude Wagner can stop your virus. I'm going to inform him."

"Have you gone hopelessly insane?" Ramsey said. "You can't do that. Wagner wants to protect the Grid Project, sure, but he's not going to listen to you."

The sound of wind fluttering and the pinging noise of the halyard striking the boom played around Ferguson. "Wagner's probably the only one who knows the Grid well enough to stop this virus."

"If you breathe a word about this to Wagner," Ramsey said, "he could go to the feds and then I'm done for. If that happens, we're both doing time."

"What?"

"You heard me. If I go down, the cops will hear you plotted this with me for the good of medicine. P.S. Better to be a villain than a victim . . . and I will find you." Ramsey clicked off.

Ferguson felt stuck. God willing, Wagner could block the virus, but how was he going to get word to him? Ferguson didn't even have the man's phone number. The CEO settled for Kate.

Ferguson spent the next fifteen minutes agonizing over what to do. He was just leaving an urgent message for Kate when he spotted the strangest sight—Olivier Ramsey. Ferguson couldn't believe his eyes. That madman Ramsey had found him and was striding this way. How'd he manage that so quickly?

"I thought I might catch you here." Ramsey climbed aboard the yacht deck and braced himself against the chrome railing. "We need a plan. I won't let you blow this and I can't trust you. Together, we're going to locate Wagner and do what we can to detain him. He's the one who accelerated this goddamned Grid project."

"I'll agree to no such thing." Their verbal fireworks escalated, echoing across the fiberglass hull and deserted marina. The debate became so heated that it covered all signs of someone else nearing the yacht. Finally, Ferguson noticed the new arrivals. He raised his hand for Ramsey to shut up.

Kate Wagner was being led down the dock by a platinum-haired woman who resembled his daughter. In an instant, it occurred to Ferguson that the blonde hair was a wig. His daughter moved onto the gangplank with unusually heavy make-up and an intense stare. Ferguson was at a loss for words. Lori, disguised almost beyond recognition as a blonde, looked as surprised as her father felt.

"Who the hell is this?" Ramsey asked. Ferguson shook his head in disbelief.

Lori, with a travel bag on her shoulder, roughly prodded Kate to walk in lockstep, down the wobbly gangplank. Kate seemed to be a hostage. As they came aboard, Ferguson saw Kate Wagner's face burning with rage.

"What's this all about?" Ferguson exclaimed.

Lori hesitated. "Looks like I'm interrupting a meeting." Still taken aback, she added. "Now all three of you can follow my lead. We're coming on board."

Olivier Ramsey touched his thick glasses to focus.

Ferguson's daughter had one hand firmly gripping Kate Wagner, pulling her by the arm forcibly.

"Lori?" Ferguson said more forcefully.

His daughter ignored him. Her other hand was tucked in her pocket. *Could she be carrying her gun?* He didn't believe she'd go that far. Ferguson knew he looked aghast.

She was agitated, unstable, not the loving daughter he knew. "Wh-wh-what in God's name do you think you're doing?"

Lori stood proud and determined, the ultimate house cat carrying a mouse. "You'll understand soon enough."

Ferguson's gaze fixed on Lori's arrogant expression, unable to cope with the stranger his daughter had become.

Lori guided Kate down the steps into the cabin below. He could just barely see that his daughter was tying Kate's feet using cords Lori had carried in a travel bag.

Ferguson remained on deck with Ramsey, shocked by how out of control his daughter was, just as the fortunes of J&Q were.

She returned above deck, leaving Kate below. Lori held her gun in the open now.

Ferguson gritted his teeth.

Amazement drew over Ramsey face before he glanced over his shoulder to see if anyone was watching. As far as the eye could see, the marina with all of its sails, motorboats and yachts, was empty.

Over the years, Ferguson had turned a blind eye to his daughter's emotional swings and anger with the world when life didn't go her way. He should've kept up more closely with her. "Lori, stop. Give me your gun," Ferguson said flatly, extending his open hand to her.

She shook her head, pursing her lips.

Ferguson rolled up his dress shirt sleeves. "I'll take it if I have to. I don't know what you're doing with Kate Wagner, but that Grid could save my life and hers."

"What?" Ramsey said.

Lori shook her head. "I don't believe it. Stop trying to protect Stanford, Daddy."

"What the hell are you doing with Kate here like this?" Ferguson demanded.

"I'm keeping the goddamn company afloat." Lori tucked her pistol into a shoulder holster inside her jumpsuit.

"Damn it, Lori. Listen to me—"

"You're forgetting who has the gun," Ramsey said.

Lori glared at her father. "Can't you see what I've done for J&Q?"

Ferguson stared, speechless while his daughter went on. "So much that you should really be grateful. And proud."

"Just, just stand aside Lori and leave," the CEO said. "I'm in charge of this yacht. Now go."

"You're not in charge. Not today, Daddy."

Ferguson shot a pleading look at his daughter. "I need Stanford's help."

Ramsey still had a curious expression.

Lori shouted, "Quit talking about your dying."

Ferguson gasped. "But you can't be caught here with a gun and this slug."

"One thing I'm planning on is not getting caught," she said, lowering her voice.

Ferguson’s sea legs went shaky. No one’s eyes were more familiar than Lori’s. Yet they’d changed. They were empty and unreachable. Her face betrayed nothing but soullessness. Ferguson’s daughter had always longed for his praise, though he never expected it might lead to this. "Why in God’s name do you have Kate Wagner?"

"The feds could arrive eventually, but I'm counting on getting Wagner getting here first . . . that is, if I can pry his phone number out of his sister to let him know where she is."

Olivier Ramsey subtly nodded in agreement.

Fifty-Five

Saturday, November 5
Alameda, CA

Pressing the accelerator, Wagner sped Knowlan's Jaguar along Highway 24 to the 12th Street exit in Oakland toward Mark Ferguson's yacht. Ominous clouds teamed in the sky casting a filmy light over the wet roads. Windshield wipers cranked intermittently. He veered left onto 5th. Wheels skipped across the pavement. Still dripping wet in his T- shirt and bleeding, he followed highway signs to Alameda. He came to the east side of Alameda Island, on the estuary and shut off the engine outside the two-story shingled clubhouse. In the lot he saw the white Range Rover with the broken window parked. His hands clenched involuntarily. With the sun setting, it wasn't going to be light for long. He scrambled down to the scuffed marina dock, passing a sign commemorating Jack London's boat slip.

Where was Ferguson's yacht? Wagner could've had Ferguson apprehended, but he asked Nathalie to stay clear. He didn't want to chance it. A fed coming to the scene might misread the CEO and make matters worse.

The familiar stench of barnacles accosted his senses. Wagner scoured the marina until he heard voices. From that same direction, he identified the flashy boat—a blue-water mega yacht, with all her on board lights on. At around sixty feet long, almost three times the length of the *Tipsea*, she had aerodynamic lines with tinted Mylar windows.

Spruce Goose adorned the stern in script, a tribute to Howard Hughes's aircraft.

Wagner kept his distance behind another yacht. He wanted to know where Kate was on board relative to Ferguson and what weapons he'd be dealing with—if any. He assessed the situation visually. There was very little movement and he couldn't make out Kate. Wagner did see that Mark Ferguson wasn't alone, but was accompanied by a thin man in business attire.

Ferguson sat, fidgeting, while the businessman ranted at him. Wagner couldn't tell if either one of them was armed. The businessman's back was turned to Wagner. He reckoned that his sister was held or bound below deck. Finally, he saw a platinum-haired woman in her mid thirties wearing a jump suit emerge from the cabin steps, unobtrusively holding a gun. Wagner's palms went clammy. As she came up to the deck her automatic pistol came into plain view.

Dressed in combat garb with boots, her outfit appeared to be DeltaCorp issue—the realization unsettled Wagner even more. She would've fit right in with the field ops he crash landed with at Stanford. The blonde woman was lecturing Ferguson. Could it be Ferguson's daughter? Wait, this was the woman who came after him in Chinatown.

Wagner had to let go of his idea of a surprise maneuver to rescue Kate. Just too risky with four people on board and Kate so frail. Wagner waited and watched until the woman disappeared below again. He steadily walked toward Ferguson's yacht.

With his weapon drawn, he pointed it at the CEO. "Is Kate on board?" Wagner shouted, preparing to climb aboard the broad deck with the Glock he took from Ferguson's house.

Ferguson put his hands high. The other man spun around.

In a shock of realization, Wagner recognized him. It was Olivier Ramsey—the financial tycoon who'd invested in J&Q. He was pictured in several articles. Though Ramsey in the flesh differed from his photos. His jaw set hard—nothing hinted at his being stable or predictable.

"Is this, Wagner?" The man's eyes aimlessly roved Wagner's face.

"That's right," Jude said, thinking Ramsey was probably less surprised to see him than he was Ramsey.

Lori Ferguson bolted up the cabin steps again. Her pistol leveled on Wagner's head. "I didn't expect you here so soon," Lori said with haughty superiority. "I wanted you to sweat this out a little before calling the number your sister gave us."

"Kate." Wagner shouted into the air without hesitation.

"Jude." Kate's muffled cry came from the cabin.

Ramsey said, "That's right. She's here."

Wagner's chest moved into his throat. "If you hurt her, I'll gut you. What do you want?"

"Spare your vitriol, asshole," Lori spat. "You're going to sail with us."

"Lori," Ramsey said with a hoarse voice. "I want you to know I'm behind you."

Wagner still held his gun on Lori. "I'll call it quits if you let her go."

Lori scoffed. "What, and let the cops take me down? Did you come with anyone, FBI backup?" She held her gun on Wagner.

Wagner shook his head calmly and deliberately. "I wanted to handle you myself."

"That's wise for your sister's sake," she said.

Ramsey's lips barely moved when he spoke to Wagner, "In case you haven't had the pleasure of meeting this woman, she's more than prepared to stunt your motor skills."

Lori added, "It's bottom of the ninth inning for you, Wagner. You're benched, while a star batter is swinging for the fence." The woman's broad shoulders and square jaw bore a striking resemblance to Mark Ferguson's. "Toss the gun on the deck," Lori told Wagner.

"What, so you can finish us both?"

Lori stood, grimly determined. "Test me you arrogant bastard and the next sound you'll hear will be your sister's scream ringing in your ears—seconds before she dies."

Everyone's eyes went wide but Lori's.

Lori leered sharply at Wagner. "Your sister is depending on you. You're in no position to bargain."

Wagner didn't flinch. "Show her to me."

The woman marched down the steps to the cabin. The noise of a tussle and a whimper carried to the deck. Lori returned with a fistful of Kate's hair in one hand, scissors in the other. She opened her hand and let the shock of hair fly in the wind. "I can scalp her down there for you if it would give you more proof."

Wagner saw that Kate's captor's movements were quick and practiced. Reason and rationality departed. His heart pounded with rage. He laid down his pistol on the edge of the boat deck and slid it toward Ramsey's feet. The Glock banged against his shiny slip-on shoe. Ramsey snatched Wagner's gun and stuffed it in his waistband.

Wagner was keenly aware of how much control he'd relinquished—in a second he had handed over his fire power. "So, why my sister?"

"Without Kate-the-bait, the mackerel wouldn't be here," Lori said.

Ramsey dared to interrupt. "It seems everything is connected—this position we're in. You gotta rescue your sister. I need to recoup my investment and they want to save J&Q."

"Let's make things easier and walk off this deck," Wagner said.

"Not on your life," Ramsey said.

"Forget that," Lori added. "You're not driving off with Kate while our millions blow away like her hair."

A fury boiled behind the business tycoon's smirk.

Lori added, "Sit beside my Dad before you feel the blunt end of that gun on the back of your head."

Wagner took the bench beside Ferguson who was biting his lip. *Ferguson wasn't behind this. Maybe Ramsey wanted to kill them too. Whether that was true or not, Wagner had more than one person to get past.*

Lori dutifully pulled in the boat bumpers, then walked up to Ramsey. With a snap of her wrist, she grabbed his gun from his waistband and threw it in the tumbling water, kissing it goodbye.

"Hey!" Ramsey shouted.

"It's suicide to have two firearms on this boat," she said. Ramsey swore.

"You saw how easily I took that," she told him. "It's a lesson. Keep your hands on this one and don't let go." She handed Ramsey her Colt. "It's all we've got. I'm going below now to turn on the radio. We have to monitor local news." She stepped down into the cabin again.

The investment banker lowered the gun on Wagner. "You need to relax, enjoy our scenic cruise."

Lori marched up the cabin steps with radio news playing on the deck speakers. She looked at Wagner. "When I first had the idea of going after you directly it didn't occur to me that I could draw you in, as a spider does."

"She is resourceful," Ramsey said.

"Yeah, a real visionary," Wagner hazarded, staring at the piece that was pointed at his head.

Ramsey looked down the gun barrel at Wagner. "Goad me, kid—go ahead. It'll just keep you away from your precious Grid longer."

Wagner felt he'd pressed his luck. Resisting wasn't going to get Kate off the yacht. The way things were going at the moment that choice might just shorten both their lives.

Fifty-Six

Saturday, November 5
Alameda, CA

Wagner chose to obey Lori Ferguson's orders—at least until he could find a break in her warpath tirade. She issued her next command to her father, "Get up here and man the wheel."

The CEO dully made his way to the helm.

Lori told her father to crank up the yacht.

Ramsey kept the Colt trained on Wagner who remained seated while the CEO pushed the key in the yacht ignition switch and cranked the diesel motor of the Oyster yacht. The starters whined. The yacht engine obeyed kicking up a husky sound. On the dock, Lori untied the yacht from its mooring. She hopped back on board.

Clutching the throttle, Ferguson nudged the boat into motion.

Moving systematically, Lori went to a control panel beside the yacht wheel. She flipped toggle switches activating automatic levers. A small electric motor sounded. Sails trimmed without a single crank on a winch. The *Spruce Goose* steered out the marina boat harbor under a dusky sky. As they headed into the estuary the tide grew stronger. A blustering mist marked the start of another storm. Shallow swells lapped against the boat side. The main sail ruffled in the wind.

Ferguson appeared more dislocated than his yacht, steering it into the swaying bay. He was a captain without control of his crew or his fate. The engine chugged loudly, gliding them along.

Suddenly Ferguson shouted to Wagner. "A worldwide virus is scheduled to go off and disrupt your Grid at midnight tonight."

"Ferguson!" Ramsey rasped. "Another word and I'll heave you overboard myself."

Wagner saw how Ramsey's emotions were overtaking him, making him volatile. Midnight was less than seven hours away. Wagner had to believe what Ferguson said. Wagner never wanted to kill anyone in hatred until now. His eyes trained on Ramsey. With any sudden movement, Wagner would jump him. But how could he do that and not endanger Kate? "It's me you want, right? If you keep me here, then I can't defend the virus attack. Why not release Kate?"

Ramsey comfortably hefted the Glock in his hands now. "Nobody gets off this yacht."

"Then tell me this," Wagner asked Ramsey. "Have you been the man behind the curtain all along? The great puppeteer?"

"You give me too much credit."

"Who is the real Olivier Ramsey?" Ferguson shouted.

Lori cleared her throat. "This isn't about him. Come on, Daddy. Who did you really imagine took care of those Stanford Grid people? You think this Wall Street dinosaur did it or some assassin just happened to share your interests? That would be a little too much good fortune, even for you."

Ferguson visibly bristled at the words. Ramsey remained mute, neutrally observing.

Ferguson stood perfectly stationary despite the slight sway of the boat. His gaze fixed on his daughter's resentful face. "You're not going to tell me you killed Jűrgen Hansen and Hideo Onagi?"

"And nearly Niles Tully. Thankfully he's never seen my face." Wagner's breath caught.

"Why?" Ferguson's voice cracked, appalled by his daughter's callousness as she cavalierly admitted to multiple murders. He could scarcely utter an intelligible word.

"Holy shit. Wake up, Dad. For us, obviously." She'd dragged out the word *obviously*. "In for a penny, in for a pound, right?"

Ferguson's face paled.

Olivier Ramsey appeared equally stunned by Lori's admissions. Finally, the banker broke the silence. "She acted to block a threat—did what she thought was right."

Ferguson shook his head as if he was trying to shake off reality. With downcast eyes, the CEO looked strangely subdued—too devastated to square off in the face-off. The wind picked up just as Wagner saw something that seemed to go undetected by Ramsey and Lori. Ferguson was moving his fingers, almost imperceptibly at the wheel. Imitating the flow of the tide, he clenched and unclenched his fists. Then it hit Wagner. This could be a signal to coordinate a break. Wagner tested his theory, copying the gesture, ever so subtly. Ferguson looked at Wagner. He nodded ever so discreetly.

Clouds grew darker overhead. A tanker ship passed, leaving a strong swell in its wake under a half moon.

A gagged voice was heard from below. "Jude?"

Wagner leaned across the deck to a point where he could view down below. The dining area was lavishly furnished. A pair of white sofas stood out but no Kate. She had to be tied up down there somewhere, in one of the cabins.

"I think you should check that she's secure," Ramsey said, then he shouted at Wagner, "I'd like to see you bound too."

Lori lumbered below.

Ramsey pointed the pistol directly at Wagner's head. "Remember, no quick moves."

Wind gusted in bursts. Ferguson steadied the course toward rough bay swells while Ramsey ordered Wagner to put his hands behind his back. A fine wave of water curled and splashed across the deck.

Wagner said, "You think I'm just going to sit here while the Grid comes apart?"

"If you care about your sister, yes," Ramsey said.

Wagner read Ramsey's bloodshot eyes. There was no bluff. The Wall Street man appeared desperate, willing to go along with a mad woman, even if it linked him to Lori's homicides.

A large wake silently surged toward the yacht. At the helm, Ferguson gave no warning of it. He recklessly steered parallel to the encroaching tide.

Lori barged up to the deck with a nylon line from below.

"Is she tied up?" Ramsey said.

"And gagged too," she said. "Trust me."

Wagner opened and closed his fists in rapid succession, eyeing the wake.

Ferguson nodded from the wheel. Lori grabbed Wagner's fists to tie them.

But the great swell tipped the yacht at an angle, upsetting everyone's balance. Ramsey stutter-stepped to gain footing. All on deck became like mice on a see-saw, scrabbling.

Wagner ducked low and knocked Lori backward.

Ferguson locked the wheel in position. He lunged at Ramsey who was taking aim at Wagner. The CEO and Ramsey fell to the teak wood. Ferguson unleashed a flurry of punches to Ramsey's midsection. Ramsey went flat on the deck and didn't move. The pistol scooted along the deck when Ferguson ran back to the helm.

Wagner got hold of Lori when she snapped open a serrated buck knife from her pocket. Wagner fought to control her knife hand. She whipped the knife tip at Wagner's face.

He head-bobbed, avoiding her.

Her second swipe connected, though, lacerating his side. Wagner grimaced at the searing pain. The slash carved over his bruised ribs. Pain filtered from the cut through every capillary of his brain. He grabbed the woman's forearm. Her buck knife dropped, banging onto the deck. Blood trickled down his side.

They jumped for the knife. Together, Wagner and the woman landed flat on the deck.

Ferguson shouted, "Stop!"

Jude's raw side twanged again as the bloody blade slid across the deck away from their reach.

The boat swayed. The knife then slid sideways through an open window into the cabin where it disappeared and clanked.

Wagner took the pain and stood up. He pawed at his blood-drenched side. As he looked up, Lori rushed to the gun and came at him with the Colt automatic in her hand. She wedged him against the yacht railing. Wagner forced Lori's gun hand high. The gun jerked upward. They wrestled to control the weapon until it slipped from her grip.

The gun splashed in the bay then sank under the yacht's wake. In agony, he shoved her to one side and focused on getting down below to Kate. Ramsey still lay unconscious.

Lori limped his way.

His adrenaline surged again. He charged her at full speed. His old standing takedown move came back. Grabbing her wrist and holding it tight, he darted behind her and slung his other arm around her waist. He let all his weight drop, pulling her down.

The woman's knees buckled.

Together they fell with him controlling her midsection. Prone on the deck, they skirmished. He went for his head and arm move when the boat heeled leeward in the wind. The wind tossed the boom across the boat. The yacht tilted sideways. It was a wild jibe. Ferguson tried to regain control of the wheel. All but Ferguson skidded from port to starboard. Across the teak deck, they banged knees and arms. Wagner's side throbbed. Still, he kept his eyes on Lori who fell beside the bench seats.

A stronger gust filled the main sail above them. The boat's speed picked up.

They scuttled to their feet. Wagner held his side, wincing. "Why'd you kill them?"

No answer.

The yacht heeled farther on her keel. Pots and pans clanked in the hull. The deck slanted like a rock face.

Ferguson worked the helm.

Lori grimaced.

Spray from oncoming swells washed over them. Waves sent more water over the yacht's side. Lori crawled toward the cabin opening.

Wagner charged her. The yacht pitched sharply. At once they were wrestling on their sides on the rail again. She managed to get on top of him and forced his head over the rail. Her weight and gravity held him over the swells. The water level rose—it submerged Wagner's head. He was weakened from lost sleep, dog bites and a slashed side.

He struggled to come up for air. His head tilted above the water line. He coughed salt water from his lungs, still gripping her hands. His core strength was sapping away.

She shoved harder at Wagner's chin.

White hot rods of fire flared from his wound. His heart beat furiously. He struggled to disassociate his mind from his pain. As seconds passed, he slipped further from his surroundings. In a solitary darkness, his consciousness faded to a void.

The boat rocked back letting Wagner come up for air. He gagged and gasped—air filled his lungs. The wind shifted. Lori slid away.

She leveraged her leg against a bench to regain balance.

Abruptly, the boom cranked around in a fast sweeping motion. Wagner, standing, ducked as it crossed overhead. Sails flapped then ballooned. The boat turned twenty degrees into the wind.

Talking to herself inaudibly, Ferguson's daughter flipped up the seat of a long bench and dug around in the compartment underneath. From his angle, Wagner couldn't see what she was after. When the seat slammed shut, she turned around, aiming a three-foot steel speargun at Wagner's chest.

He breathed raggedly, getting a sharp ache from his bleeding side. The sail arched full of wind. He reached for the automated mainsheet cleat.

As she stood up to take aim, Wagner pushed the button on the cleat, releasing the line. The huge sail whipped away from the yacht. The yacht rocked violently.

In one motion, the sail shot back across the yacht deck, flinging the boom. Wagner ducked. Like a bat to a ball, the boom slammed squarely into Lori's head. The thud was sickening.

"Lori!" Ferguson yelled. Her body tumbled onto the blood-stained deck with the speargun. It set off the sling that was intended for Wagner. The sling lodged in the main sail, ripping a hole in the sheer fabric that swung above Wagner's head.

Ferguson leapt from the wheel to his daughter. "Lori! Answer me!" The man sounded inconsolable. "What have you done?" Ferguson asked Wagner. The CEO checked his daughter's motionless body on the deck.

Wagner grabbed the wheel.

Looking over his shoulder, Wagner saw Ferguson lay his daughter out flat and put his head to her chest. He announced that she had a pulse.

Wagner locked the wheel in place and clacked downstairs to the cabin. Down below, he untied Kate's cords with trembling hands—her eyes, red. He hugged her, found a beach towel in the bathroom and wrapped it around his midsection. He and Kate came above. Kate couldn't take her eyes off Ferguson's daughter's limp body and Ferguson himself, crouched beside her as a broken man. He pulled the blonde wig off his daughter's head, exposing matted, shortly cropped brown hair.

Wagner turned Ramsey, in his deflated state, on his stomach and bound his limp hands with the rope that was used on Kate.

"What about her?" Kate asked.

"She's no longer a threat."

Kate blinked rapidly then covered her mouth as if that prevented her from crying uncontrollably.

Wagner wanted to heave Lori overboard into the rolling swells, let her disappear into the deep, watery abyss and never let anyone set eyes on her image again. But that wasn't an option. The situation was bad enough without arousing her father's accusations of murder.

"You look weak," Wagner said to Kate.

She checked her chafed wrists, then up at him. "But I guess I'm okay." What she spotted next caused her alarm. "You're bleeding . . . badly."

Wagner looked at his wounded side again. The cut was deeper than superficial, but not gravely serious. "Can you take the helm here? Ferguson isn't going to be of much use to us right now."

Ferguson, head in hands, was kneeling over his unconscious daughter.

Kate took hold of the wheel while Wagner searched under the deck seats for a first aid kit. He found a kit below and taped a big gauze onto his side using adhesive. Back on deck, he pulled in the main sail and cleated it. But the tear in the sail had enlarged, preventing the boat from holding wind.

Kate set her sights on the water ahead. Still kicking up white caps, the wind died some.

Wagner told her the key should be in the ignition." Maybe you can get us going again. The sail is really ripped."

"Right." Kate fumbled around and started the yacht motor.

The luxury boat began to move. Inside a seat bench, Ferguson found a sail cover. He draped it over his daughter's battered body in an effort to keep her warm. He weighted the ends of the cover with seat cushions for the sail home.

Wagner re-checked his ribs. For everyone's benefit, he had to get the *Spruce Goose* to shore as soon as possible. He went below, shut off the stereo and used the yacht radio to call in the on board incident. He requested an ambulance come to the Oakland Yacht Club to check out four people. He also requested a police unit. He then put in a call to Nathalie. She started speaking immediately. "I'm almost at the yacht club, where are you?"

"I'm on Ferguson's sailboat, bringing her in. You should know that Ferguson's daughter is on board but she's knocked out."

"How?"

"You'll get the story soon, after I turn her over to you with Olivier Ramsey. They were our suspects, not Ferguson."

"Really?"

"Yes, but this doesn't solve everything." He put the hand mic to the radio down.

He couldn't sit still. Kate obviously wasn't experienced enough to guide the yacht for long. He came up beside her, nursing his side. "I'll take it from here."

She silently moved away from the wheel. Kate adjusted herself in her deck seat behind Wagner.

Clutching his ribs with one hand, he pulled back the chrome throttle handle, giving a burst of power to the engine. They let off a husky grumble. "You're still bleeding. How serious is it?" She asked.

Wagner looked around the helm at Kate. "I need stitches, but we've still got much bigger problems." Jude's expression said*, the bigger problem is your condition.*

Kate pulled the ends of her hair and looked at them. "That woman was a sociopath. You know that, right?" Kate nervously touched the bald spots on her head and mumbled the name "Lori Ferguson."

"We've gotta try to forget about her and Olivier Ramsey." He said, trying to change the subject. While motoring back as quickly as possible, he periodically checked on Kate. She focused her sights on a distant point over the water. Then she glanced up as if to thank the sky that they were heading to shore.

He steadily steered the *Spruce Goose* toward the Alameda marina to resume the sprint against time.

"Kate, let me ask you an odd question. Do you know the term dead reckoning?"

"No."

"It's a gut calculation. It means finding where you are using your memory of where you traveled."

"Oh yeah, I know it," she said. "That's how the Polynesian people would find their way home on the open sea—by feeling the currents."

"That's it. They had a native sense for direction. On some level, I think that reckoning ability is wired into all of us."

Kate looked at him. "Of course it is. The knack we have for finding our path back home is deeply ingrained in the human brain—it's a fundamental part of our survival instinct. What made you bring up dead reckoning?"

"I don't know exactly. I was just thinking about instinctual problem solving and what I can do to keep the Stanford Grid ticking."

Fifty-Seven

Saturday, November 5
Alameda, CA

The *Spruce Goose* glided up to the harbor's neon-lit dock finger. Wagner could see Nathalie, arms crossed tightly, waiting on the dock under a bright lamp. Steering at the helm, Wagner told Kate how to sling the yacht's dock lines. Nathalie looped the stern line over the piling at the end of the boat slip. With the yacht secured, she opened the yacht gate and climbed aboard. "You're bleeding?" she said to Wagner.

"An ambulance is on its way," he said.

Wearily, Wagner gave Kate a hand helping her step off the boat.

A police car arrived. Wagner told the officers if it wasn't for Ferguson he'd be a dead man. Wagner directed the officers to where Mark Ferguson was in the cabin of his yacht.

Nathalie waved over the arriving paramedics. While an EMT checked out Wagner's rib injury, two other paramedics started carrying Lori, then Ramsey off the boat, restrained on stretchers. Kate sat on a bench and watched the officers manage the situation.

As the EMTs lifted Ramsey's stretcher off the yacht, he came to and shouted, "Wagner, I'm coming for you."

Wagner watched without moving. A dull pain still drummed at his blood-crusted lower ribs. He sandwiched a towel from the boat firmly between his ribs and arm to staunch the bleeding. Kate's cancer was now his most pressing issue along with the crippled state of the Stanford Grid Project.

The paramedics speedily moved the stretchers to the waiting ambulances.

With bangs falling in her eyes, Nathalie moved to Wagner's side while the paramedics saw to him. One paramedic prepared to stitch the skin over his ribs. "I need to get to the Grid before our entire program goes under," he told her.

"Ferguson says a virus will hit around midnight tonight."

Nathalie covered her mouth, then pointed over Wagner's shoulder to where Knowlan was being dropped off at the marina by a Berkeley police cruiser.

Nathalie touched Wagner's shoulder. "I made a late discovery. Lori Ferguson has training in K-9 security, judo, chemical explosives and sniper assaults."

"That explains a few things." Wagner grimaced while the paramedic pulled a thread through his side. They turned as Knowlan strode up with circles under his eyes. With mussed hair and coffee-stained necktie, Knowlan bore relief on his face. Wagner handed Knowlan his keys.

"Yeah, I'll take those," Knowlan said. "I have something good to tell you. I contacted McGruff." McGruff was a compounding drug company. "I sent over her prescription results. McGruff's preparing a rush order and will deliver the medicine to your place by Federal Express."

"That's very positive," Wagner said. "But—" Wagner let out a sigh of exhaustion.

Knowlan said, "What?"

Wagner recapped Ramsey's virus plan. "We have to stop that corrupted agent from being downloaded across the Grid. The hacker is going to widely release it tonight or try."

Knowlan cursed.

Wagner signed a medical release for the paramedics, waiving their responsibility to take him into the hospital for an exam. Wagner and Nathalie walked Kate to Nathalie's Crown Vic while the paramedics carried Lori Ferguson off the yacht on a stretcher.

Nathalie told Wagner, "I will need to drop you and Kate off at your apartment and then come back later. I have to stop into the office."

"You need to deal with Hackman," Wagner guessed.

She nodded apprehensively. "I must fill him in. But forget about him, you-know. All I care about is that you get in front of your computer. We don't want you to be too late."

Fifty-Eight

Saturday, November 5
San Francisco, CA

In his rigid Aeron desk chair at the Russian Hill apartment, Jude Wagner swallowed long sips of coffee. The deadline was only three hours away. Nathalie slid a chair beside him. He adjusted a rolled up beach towel, a make-shift lumbar support, to prevent anything from jabbing at his fresh stitches. He clacked away at his laptop.

Nathalie gently rested a hand on the back of his neck. "How are your ribs and Kate?"

"Better now that I'm loaded with pain killers. Kate's still tense. Sleep will do her good. And tomorrow or Monday her drugs should arrive. Let's hope for the best."

"You still look awful," she said.

"Thanks. I'm in a foxhole here."

"A fox hole?"

“Never mind."

"Can I make you an icepack, or get you something?"

He indicated not right now.

Nathalie watched him work, coding as rapidly as possible. "Are you cutting off access by firewalling the Internet Protocol?" She was asking if he was isolating the hacker who'd maliciously accessed the Grid. "You know our analysts can track his hacking and find him by his IP address?"

"Nice idea." Wagner's tone remained flat. "But identifying the hacker's IP address only tells us where he's located based on that one IP. A guy of this caliber is always on the move, spoofing IPs."

"Where are we with this virus attack then?"

"I'm managing a bigger threat than I first thought. The infected bots are sending erroneous information to the Grid's server. The information on the Stanford Grid has been corrupted. All the results that are filtering in are incongruous."

"So the Grid is not only useless but misleading?"

He dragged his hand through his hair. "That's exactly the problem."

"But why did the hacker not shutdown SETI too?"

"For one, he didn't know about it, and it's not easy to access an offsite backup server.

But even so, it would be just a matter of time before the good data that was backing up to Berkeley would've been overwritten with corrupted data from Stanford. The entire Grid network is at risk now."

Wagner didn't need to explain to Nathalie that a bot was a zombie computer agent—a discreet program operating undetected on a computer system. Hackers used bots to take control of other remote systems. Combined, these bots reached out to more bots forming a botnet which could be ordered around like an electronic army.

Nathalie gripped her thighs with her hands. "What have you done so far?"

"Morris helped me modify the machine learning code with a special tag. I've already tailored the program to disregard the information returned from those bots. Based on what Ferguson said, I have until midnight before the timed virus goes off." Wagner checked his watch. "That's two hours and fifty minutes."

Nathalie looked up from her smart phone, temporarily ignoring a call from Hackman. "Is it dumb to ask why you are not just walling out all incoming instructions to your computer servers?"

"That's not a solution. It would only temporarily shut down the Grid, allowing a different attack. He may catch on, but I want him to believe he's got us so I can shut him down."

She put her arm on the back of his chair. "How do we do that?"

"I'm using a classic jiu-jitsu—martial arts strategy."

With a confused look, Nathalie took off her bolero jacket.

"Turn you enemy's strength against him," Wagner said.

"Pardon?"

"In the martial arts, that's how you handle a bigger rival in a fight. Look at 9-11. How did nineteen Muslim extremists, armed with nothing but box cutters, take down the twin towers? They didn't fly their own jets over here; they forced our planes—full of fuel—into our towers in the sky and into our own Pentagon. They used our strength against us."

"And your idea is?"

"We turn the hacker's hack against him."

"Go on."

"The Grid is passing computer instructions to and from volunteer computers to a central server. The hacker is using bots to mimic those instructions and jam up the Grid with bad information. Morris came up with a way of tagging batches of computer instructions with an identifier that will only go to the hacker's computer bots, not our volunteers'. Fortunately, I've managed to trace where the hacker's bots have originated in cyber space. Once my tagged instructions hit his computers, he'll corrupt them and send them back to the Grid for processing—but now the Grid will recognize those instructions as the hacker's and filter them because they are tagged. In a few hours, the Grid should be free of all the corrupted data, moving it beyond this loop of trying to reconcile garbage data. In fact, now that I've tagged his bots, I'm going to send them right back to the hacker to tie them up in a vicious circle. It's called reflecting."

Nathalie quietly laughed and undid her sling back shoes. "Too clever. You and agent Morris make good team partners."

"I suppose so," Wagner said, looking at a notepad with a diagram he'd mocked up for how he would tag this hacker's bots.

Wagner changed screens and showed her how the machine-learning program he installed on the Stanford Grid could detect the tag and the unauthorized botnet.

"Impressive," she said.

He shrugged. "All I can say is that this virus attack is either going to destroy the Grid or make it stronger."

Nathalie looked over his shoulder, watching him work.

He recycled code he'd already written, checked it and then had Nathalie recheck every line. At eleven-forty-seven p.m., Wagner said, "I hope this works." He ran an error-checking routine to verify that everything would run according to plan.

Nathalie said, "Jude, it's eleven-fifty-one."

"Okay, I know. I'm just doing a final check of my code."

She placed her hand on his wrist. "I wish we could properly test this. Before you execute it, you-know."

"I'm looking at this as a live test." She rolled her eyes.

At exactly eleven fifty-seven p.m., he distributed his newly enhanced Grid instructions across Stanford's Grid network.

A burst of red appeared in the bot monitor dial on Wagner's computer display. His pulse thumped. Traffic had spiked. At first, a few bots were getting through, then suddenly, thousands. "It's not working!"

* * *

Before midnight, Cez@r was busy lining up his botnet for cyber warfare. Thousands of little computer programs were armed with bad information to go to the Grid and disrupt its efforts everywhere.

* * *

Hairs bristled on Wagner's neck as he proofread his work. He forced himself to slow down, checking every line of the new code. There! He found a syntax error deep in his program routine. Cursing quietly under his breath, he fixed the code and uploaded his corrected work. He watched the screen for what seemed like an agonizingly long time, waiting for his counter attack to take effect. Slowly, the redlined computer traffic gauges started to recede. It worked.

The program he'd created successfully contained the attack. Wagner's display monitor showed thousands of tagged bots circling back to their sender.

Nathalie dozed beside him in his chair. He nudged her. "It's done."

"What? What time is it?"

"It's 12:20. The Grid is free and clear of the hacker's dirty bomb. There are no signs that any virus has penetrated the network—even though some of the bots got through initially."

She gave him a groggy smile and pulled him close by the back of his neck. They kissed. "Congratulations. You should monitor this for a few hours at least."

"Of course." He held her close. Some pressure on Wagner's brain lifted. He couldn't believe the ripple effect that interpreting the human genome had had. Like global warming or skyrocketing oil prices, it disrupted everything—including Wagner's work with the FBI and his foreseeable future with Nathalie Noiret.

A strange noise interrupted their exuberance. A light metal clap tinged from Wagner's apartment front door. "That sounded like my mail flap," Wagner said with a curious tone.

A new piece of paper lay on the hardwood floor at his front door which was just slid through his mail slot. Wagner anxiously read the sheet with Nathalie looking over his shoulder.

> JW,
> In case you wondered, I'm alive and am obviously back home— with no help from my assassin. I asked Charlene not to contact you. If only I had disappeared sooner. That would have saved her and Edward the anguish. Either way, I'm taking no chances with mobile phones, email or even hanging around at yours. I'll explain soon, then we can raise a glass with Alfonso.
> NT

Wagner flung open his door to see if he could spot Niles. "Hey you wily goat. Where are you?" He didn't see anyone and there was no answer. Wagner returned inside. With a grin, he shut his door.

Nathalie stretched and hugged him, holding on to him loosely around his neck. She whispered. "Your luck has finally turned round."

"Yeah, the great pendulum of life is finally on my side, which means we deserve a glass of red wine."

* * *

At 1:10 a.m. in his parent's garage, Cez@r twisted uncomfortably in his chair. His lower back had gone numb from sitting for so many hours at his laptop. His fingers flew across the keyboard. He bounced from screen to screen, trying to interpret the status of his precious botnet attack. *What, no!* The bots were failing to penetrate the Grid servers. His digital robots were walled out from the Stanford Grid . . . frozen in processing deadlock. This was supposed to be foolproof. Invincible. The entire plan for his Internet army had gone belly up.

Instant messages already flashed on his computer display. They were streaming from his darknet buddies who were watching the infection show remotely around the world from their private computer screens—front row seats to the global bot fiasco. The first messages that pinged onto Cez@r's screen read: "How much did you bank from this?" The second said: "Cez@r, the great botmaster who couldn't hack hacking." Cez@r felt his face warm with rage. His ego was shattered.

He attempted clever retorts to the humiliating messages as a bright halo of light beamed into his parent's garage, shining around him on the wall at his desk. Finally, he stopped typing. Some large vehicle idled outside the closed garage door. He raised his head from his computer screen. The next three words shouted at him would bring his Internet fun on the electronic superhighway to a grinding halt:

"FBI. Open up."

* * *

At one thirty in the morning, Nathalie set down her wine glass, and pulled on her sling back shoes to leave Wagner's apartment. Before she could get on her bolero jacket, Jude squeezed her hand and gently led her to his bay window in his living room, carrying his wine glass. They gazed out the window at white and amber city lights. He took a sip of the silky cabernet and held it before swallowing. Pinpricks of light glimmered in the grainy night air. The dots pulsed in the atmosphere like Kentucky fireflies until they disappeared into enveloping fog. He realized that before Nathalie came along, he didn't allow anyone past his guarded exterior. "It's almost two in the morning," he said, "and I'm still wired. I would offer you my bedroom if sleeping beauty wasn't there."

She looked over at his narrow living room sofa where a pillow and blanket sat for his makeshift bed. "I need a decent night of rest anyway. I hope that this new course of treatment will set your sister on a fast road to recovery."

"Thankfully, her drugs should arrive by Monday." He pulled her by her waist, then met her small, open mouth with his lips. Her hair brushed his face. The smell of her conditioner filled him.

Nathalie took the jacket she'd draped over her arm and carelessly flung it on his sofa. He undid the third button on her top when her phone vibrated on his coffee table. Begrudgingly, he stopped himself from kissing her neck.

She wiped a smudge of her dark lipstick from his lower lip and checked her voicemail message. Her expression turned serious. "Hackman wants both of us in his office first thing Monday morning, at 7:30 a.m., to answer questions. I'm sure we have a number of violations to account for. You may not work for him, but he can still file charges against you and make your life uncomfortable."

He shrugged. "You say that like I'll be accused of assault or something. I didn't commit a crime."

"You did have a long struggle with Ferguson's daughter."

Wagner glanced away, taking another sip of wine. "Let's pretend you didn't get that voicemail message, huh?"

She gazed at him. "I am just saying this review with Hackman can go very badly for us."

Wagner took a gulp of his wine then set the glass down. "We'll see. New subject: when would you be relocating to LA?"

"My transfer may not happen for a long time. Hackman says it is terribly slow to finalize, you-know."

"We need to make a decision about us," he said.

Nathalie straightened her blouse . . . a sure sign she was growing anxious about where this was going. "I know. I tried to keep my distance. But I can't ignore how I feel."

Wagner tapped the top of his glass. He thought about how ambitious Nathalie was and how her work focus might prevent them from having a regular relationship. "I want to give this a try, I mean us."

She looked at him again, slowly releasing her hand from his grip. Then she tugged the hair on the back of his head, pulling him in for a kiss.

That simple gesture suggested they would not lose steam and go their separate ways anytime soon; albeit he also had the distinct sense that this beguiling Special Agent from San Francisco would sooner go to battle with a man than be tamed.

Epilogue

Monday, November 7
San Francisco, CA

With trepidation, Wagner and Nathalie took the high back leather chairs opposite Hackman, bracing for some harsh criticism. The FBI SAC was feeding paper into the shredder behind his desk. *Gezzzziiippp, gezzzziiippp.*

The grating noise had a visceral effect on Wagner.

Hackman stopped with the paper. "This firestorm with Stanford could have gone a lot worse. Lucky for you, you're still here. I just spoke with the hospital. That financier, Olivier Ramsey, has been moved from their care to the county jail. Lori Ferguson is comatose. The DeltaCorp team nicknamed her Scud, by the way."

"One missile down." Wagner said, still wondering what Hackman wanted from them.

Hackman scratched on the label of an unopened orange juice container on his desk. "Her father is in the same ICU. He attempted an overdose."

Wagner sighed with regret.

"He is suffering from Huntington's disease. Now for you, Wagner." Hackman switched gears abruptly. "I will need a statement about your breaking and entering Mark Ferguson's house."

"Sir, with my sister missing, I had to do whatever—"

"Save it Wagner. Noiret explained. There's a greater concern."

Wagner knew he had a curious expression. He tried to suppress it.

"I have a police report of bruises all over Lori Ferguson. Her condition in the hospital arouses suspicion."

Wagner's stomach dropped. "You say that like I'm being accused of assault. I'm innocent."

"No one's innocent. The best you can be is not guilty." He looked at Wagner's reaction, apparently testing him. He chuckled. "I'm toying with you." He was getting the last laugh at Wagner's expense. "There's no question you were acting in self-defense. The police are dismissing charges. You had defensive wounds. It's enough to put you in the clear."

Wagner relaxed his grip on the mahogany arms of Hackman's leather-backed chair.

"Noiret," Hackman said, "you, on the other hand, should have called for backup when Wagner went for that yacht. You're getting a written warning. Fortunately, the scene was volatile. Bringing backup might have made matters worse. Ferguson could have acted unpredictably with feds arriving and two weapons on board. Huntington's disease has disorienting effects. Though, if anything like this occurs again, it's the bricks. That's two weeks administrative leave without pay, in case you're curious Wagner and knowing you, you are."

"Understood," Nathalie said softly.

"What else?" Wagner said.

Hackman opened his orange juice container and gulped down a third of it. "Ramsey was deemed stable enough to be questioned. A confession came out that he tried to slow the Stanford Grid to protect good medical practices."

Wagner asked, "Does that mean he was or was not involved with the murders?"

"Was not, according to Ramsey's words." Hackman leaned back in his chair. "He only admitted to having someone hack into the Grid. He's still a hazard. He said the hacker's online moniker was Cez@r. His real name is Liborio Russo."

"Okay," Wagner said.

"That hacker's keystrokes are all over this," Nathalie said.

"While Ramsey says that Lori and this Cez@r were the ring leaders, Heather Styles accuses Olivier Ramsey of everything. You know that routine," Hackman said.

"What can I do?" she asked.

"We made the arrest of Russo early this morning," Hackman said.

"Really?" Wagner said, surprised.

"We traced the calls made to Olivier Ramsey to a disposable phone. That make of phone was only sold at the Radio Shack on Lombard. We mapped the time of purchase with the security video and his driver's license photo, taking us to his address."

"I'm happy to hear that," Nathalie said.

"Also," Hackman added, "we found a file of DeltaCorp applicants under Lori's mattress, in her bedroom. The applicants were rejects with criminal records. Interpol worked on a cell phone picture that Niles Tully snapped of his stalker. They identified him as a bounty hunter in the file of DeltaCorp applicants. One soldier of fortune evidently hired another."

"You mean Lori hired the reject?" Nathalie said.

"Right," Hackman added. "You couldn't make this stuff up. DeltaCorp admitted to me that Lori Ferguson had too much latitude because she was the daughter of a board member—Ferguson. Anyway, I misjudged you, Wagner. You have a prying nature, but you have talents we could use. If you want an agent job in electronic surveillance, I have an opening reserved for you."

Wagner sat up. The Grid *would* survive without him to support it . . . now that the Google security was in place. "I'll consider it, Sir."

Nathalie looked at him with surprise.

Hackman dismissed them. Wagner and Nathalie took the opportunity to break away from the building for a quiet cup of coffee at a nearby diner with orange Formica tables and an open grill-kitchen. They took a table for two in the back of the tiny shop, so they could talk without being overheard in case someone from the office strolled in.

She finished her first sip. "I need a holiday from the thirteenth floor."

He blew on his coffee. "Ramsey lost touch with reality just like Ferguson's daughter. Maybe Huntington's disease is contagious."

Nathalie smiled, "Or genetic, which would explain Lori's actions."

"Right, blame it on genetics," he said.

"I wish we had identified her sooner. But she was a professional. *C'est la vie*."

"I wonder if she wanted to impress her father," Wagner said.

"Some children will do any crazy thing to win parents' admiration, no?"

Wagner sipped. "Nothing says I love you like a killing spree. Hackman must regret hiring DeltaCorp to handle the San Francisco office re-org."

"DeltaCorp definitely had too much security access to our field office."

He grinned. "There will be hell to pay for how they allowed Lori Ferguson to go off the reservation."

"Hackman probably still has explaining to do, you-know, about how Lori Ferguson obtained an FBI-registered handgun."

Wagner could tell by the glint in Nathalie's eye that she found the idea of SAC Alexander Hackman being hauled over the coals as amusing as he did. For the first time in days, they chuckled aloud.

She added, "I did receive an email saying the OPR will allow Hackman to finish working his final year. It delays his monastic seclusion, no. Can you believe he offered you, of all people, an agent role?"

"He must have DeltaCorp resources to backfill."

"Yes, but you are not, uh, entertaining his offer?"

"I am. They need me."

Nathalie's eyebrows raised. "That means we cannot continue, I mean together."

Wagner pensively wiped his mouth.

A wistful expression came over her. "We can't be together if we are both agents. It is not permitted. The bureau keeps a watchful eye." She looked frustrated. "I guess I thought this whole experience would make you want something permanent, maybe even come to LA and be a computer consultant." Her eyes fixed on his. She leaned back an inch from the table but it felt like a mile.

He put his hands together on the bright Formica table top. "I just don't see why my working for the bureau has to stand in our way. It is where we met."

Her tongue slowly traced her bottom teeth. "Relationships are so difficult. I struggled to not feel things for you and now we will have to watch our every move so we don't get discovered."

"If we can keep the Stanford Grid from going offline, I believe we can overcome any boundary Hackman might put between us."

A little grin broke across her face. "This means we might officially become partners and not just romantically."

"Yes, I know."

Nathalie gave him an intense glare. "If that is the case, you cannot forget who is senior in our relationship."

"Or else?"

She reached out and grabbed his fingers firmly. "Or else you will suffer at the hand of a vengeful fed who is skilled at taking control and skilled at carrying out her methods of physical punishment and torture."

"I'll take that."

If you enjoyed this book, please write a brief review of it on Amazon. It would be much appreciated. Please watch for the next installment of Jude Wagner's journey. Meanwhile, readers of *Gridlock* might enjoy any book by the talented thriller author, Barry Eisler.

Actual Timeline of the Genome

Four Billion Years Ago	The precursor of DNA is thought to be created by the aggregation of simple molecules in the primordial swamp that existed at that time.
1850's	Gregor Mendel, "the father of modern genetics" establishes the principles of genetic inheritance by studying pea plants.
1900	Thomas Hunt Morgan, American geneticist discovers the basics of dominant and recessive traits and links on a chromosome. Awarded the Nobel Prize.
1950	Barbara McClintock, the world's most distinguished cytogeneticist, determines that chromosomes exchange information by "jumping genes."
1953	James Watson and Francis Crick ascertain the structure of DNA.
April 2003	The Human Genome Project, a full map of our genetic code, is completed for $2.7 billion in thirteen years.
December 2005	The Cancer Genome Atlas—a three-year, $100 million pilot project to explore the genetic connection to cancer—launches.
May 2007	James Watson's whole genome is sequenced at a cost of less than $1 million dollars.
September 2007	Craig Venter publishes the results of his own sequenced genome.
October 2009	IBM announces plans to bring the cost of DNA sequencing to as low as $100 a person, making a personal genome cheaper than a ticket to a Broadway play.

End Note

The MiSeq DNA Sequencer from Illumina is a real machine which Universities currently use. How the machine operates in *Gridlock* is true to life. Scanning technicians rely on it to analyze human tissue samples for targeted genomic sequencing.

Around the non-fictional world scientists are also using dozens of grids to fight cancer. The grid described at Stanford University really exists. It's called folding@home. This computer network does function as a distributed system, drawing processing power from hundreds of thousands of donors' idle computers. CERN's grid in *Gridlock* is also real; although, the author is not aware if Stanford University has any physical connection to it. Also, Stanford's folding@home grid group is strictly a research department. To the author's knowledge, the department is not currently treating breast cancer patients. Lastly, Mcguff Compounding Pharmacy actually produces individualized drugs.

9182416R00200

Made in the USA
San Bernardino, CA
06 March 2014